Basket Case

Carl Hiaasen

Basket Case

Thorndike Press • **Chivers Press**
Waterville, Maine USA **Bath, England**

This Large Print edition is published by Thorndike Press, USA and by Chivers Press, England.

Published in 2002 in the U.S. by arrangement with Alfred A. Knopf Inc.

Published in 2002 in the U.K. by arrangement with Pan Macmillan.

U.S. Hardcover 0-7838-9771-5 (Core Series)
U.S. Softcover 0-7838-9770-7
U.K. Hardcover 0-7540-1785-0 (Windsor Large Print)
U.K. Softcover 0-7540-9177-5 (Paragon Large Print)

The text of this Large Print edition is unabridged.
Other aspects of the book may vary from the original edition.

Set in 16 pt. Plantin by Minnie B. Raven.

Printed in the United States on permanent paper.

British Library Cataloguing-in-Publication Data available

Library of Congress Cataloging-in-Publication Data

Hiaasen, Carl.
    Basket case / Carl Hiaasen.
        p.   cm.
    ISBN 0-7838-9771-5 (lg. print : hc : alk. paper)
    ISBN 0-7838-9770-7 (lg. print : sc : alk. paper)
    1. Obituaries — Authorship — Fiction.   2. Journalists — Fiction.   3. Florida — Fiction.   4. Large type books.
I. Title.
PS3558.I217 B37 2002b
813´.54—dc21   2001059676

For my sisters,
Judy and Barb

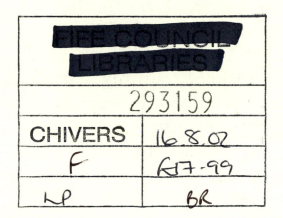

Acknowledgments

For their advice, expertise and patience, I am most grateful to Kevin Kliesch, Michael Krumper of Artemis Records, the incomparable Warren Zevon, Dr. Charles Wetli of the Suffolk County Medical Examiner's Office, Dr. Joseph Davis of the Miami-Dade Medical Examiner's Office, Jimmy Buffett, Dave Feder, Steve Whalen, Roger McGuinn and the appallingly prolific John Camp. I especially want to thank my wife, Fenia, for inspiring the band.

However, the frozen-lizard episode is based loosely on the tragic true-life demise of a voracious Savannah monitor named Claw, who now sleeps with the Dove bars.

1

Regarding the death of James Bradley Stomarti: what first catches my attention is his age.

Thirty-nine. That's seven years younger than I am.

I'm drawn to the young and old, but who isn't? The most avidly read obituaries are of those who died too soon and those who lasted beyond expectations.

What everybody wants to know is: Why them? What was their secret? Or their fatal mistake? Could the same happen to me?

I like to know, myself.

Something else about James Bradley Stomarti: that name. I'm sure I've heard it before.

But there's no clue in the fax from the funeral home. Private service is Tuesday. Ashes to be scattered in the Atlantic. In lieu of flowers the family requests donations be made to the Cousteau Society. That's classy.

I scan the list of "survived-bys" and note a wife, sister, uncle, mother; no kids, which is somewhat unusual for a 39-year-old straight guy, which I assume (from his marital status) James Bradley Stomarti to be.

Tapping a key on my desktop, I am instantly wired into our morgue, although I'm the only one in the newsroom who still calls it that. "Resource Retrieval Center" is what the memos say, but morgue is more fitting. It's here they keep all dead stories dating back to 1975, which in a newspaper's memory is about as fresh as dinosaur dung.

I type in the name of the deceased. Bingo!

I am careful not to chuckle or even smile, as I don't wish to alert my ever-watchful editor. Our newspaper publishes only one feature obituary each day; other deaths are capsulized in brief paragraphs or ignored altogether. For years the paper ran two daily full-length obits, but recently the Death page lost space to the Weather page, which had lost space to the Celebrity Eye page, which had lost space to Horoscopes. The shrunken news hole leaves room for only a single story, so I am now cagey about committing to a subject. My editor is not the flexible sort. Once I tell her whom I'm writing about, there's no turning back, even if someone far more interesting expires later in the news cycle.

Another good reason for not appearing too excited is that I don't want anyone to suspect that the death of James Bradley Stomarti might be an actual *news* story; otherwise my editor will snatch it away and give it to one of our star feature writers, the way a cat presents a freshly killed rat on the doorstep. This piracy of newsworthy assignments is the paper's way of reminding me that I'm still at the top of the shit list, that I will be there until pigs can fly, and that my byline will never again sully the front page.

So I say nothing. I sit at my desk and scroll through the computer files that inform me in colorful bits and pieces about the life of James Bradley Stomarti, better known to the world as Jimmy Stoma.

That's right. *The* Jimmy Stoma.

As in Jimmy and the Slut Puppies.

Stashed somewhere in my apartment is one of their early albums, *Reptiles and Amphibians of North America*. Jimmy sang lead and sometimes played rhythm guitar. He also fooled around with the harmonica. I remember really liking one of the band's singles, "Basket Case," off an album called *Floating Hospice*. That one I lost to a departing girlfriend. Jimmy was no Don Henley, but the ladies found him very easy on the eyes. The guy could carry a tune, too.

Stoma also got arrested on a regular basis, and was unfailingly booked under his given name. That's how I got the computer to hit on "James Bradley Stomarti."

From the morgue:

December 13, 1984: With Steven Tyler, John Entwistle and Joan Jett in attendance, Jimmy Stoma marries a chorine turned pro-

11

fessional wrestler in Las Vegas. He is arrested later that evening for urinating on Engelbert Humperdinck's stretch limousine.

February 14, 1986: Mrs. Stoma files for divorce, alleging her husband is addicted to alcohol, cocaine and aberrant sex. The Slut Puppies open a three-night stint at Madison Square Garden, and from the stage Jimmy introduces his new girlfriend, a performance artist who goes by the name of Mademoiselle Squirt.

May 14, 1986: Stoma is arrested for indecent exposure during a Charlotte, North Carolina, concert in which he takes an encore wearing nothing but a Day-Glo condom and a rubber Halloween mask in the likeness of the Rev. Pat Robertson.

January 19, 1987: With the Slut Puppies' fourth album, *A Painful Burning Sensation*, poised to go triple platinum, Jimmy Stoma announces he is canceling the band's long-awaited tour. Insiders say the singer is self-conscious about his weight, which has inflated to 247 pounds since he gave up cocaine. Stoma insists he's simply taking a break from live performing to work on "serious studio projects."

November 5, 1987: Jimmy Stoma is arrested in Scottsdale, Arizona, after punching a *People* magazine photographer who had tailed him to the gates of the Gila Springs Ranch, an exclusive spa specializing in holistic crash-dietary programs.

November 11, 1987: For the second time in a week, Stoma is busted, this time for shoplifting a bundt cake and two chocolate eclairs from a downtown Phoenix bakery.

February 25, 1989: Stoma and an unidentified woman are injured when his waterbike crashes into the SS *Norway* in the Port of Miami. The collision causes no damage to the cruise ship, but surgeons say it might be months before Stoma can play the guitar again.

September 25, 1991: Stoma's first solo album, *Stomatose*, is panned by both *Spin* and *Rolling Stone*. After debuting at number 22 on the *Billboard* pop charts, it plummets within two weeks to number 97 before —

"Jack?"

This would be my editor, the impossible Emma.

"What'd you do to your hair?" I say.

"Nothing."

"You most certainly did."

"Jack, I need a story line for the budget."

"It looks good shorter," I say. Emma hates it when I pretend to flirt. "Your hair, I mean."

Emma reddens but manages a dismissive scowl. "I trimmed the bangs. What've you got for me?"

"Nothing yet," I lie.

Emma is edging closer, trying to sneak a

glance at the screen of my desktop. She suspects I am dialing up porn off the Internet, which would be a fireable offense. Emma has never fired anyone but would dearly love to break her cherry on me. She is not the first junior editor to feel that way.

Emma is young and owns a grinding ambition to ascend the newspaper's management ladder. She hopes for an office with a window, a position of genuine authority and stock options.

Poor kid. I've tried to steer her to a profession more geared toward her talents — retail footwear, for example — but she will not listen.

Craning her pale neck, Emma says, "Rabbi Levine died last night at East County."

"Rabbi Klein died Monday," I remind her. "Only one dead clergyman per week, Emma. It's in my contract."

"Then get me something better, Jack."

"I'm working on it."

"Who is James Stomarti?" she asks, peeking at my computer screen. With her intense jade-green eyes, Emma has the bearing of an exotic falcon.

I say, "You don't know? He was a musician."

"Local guy?"

"He had a place on Silver Beach," I say, "and one in the Bahamas."

"Never heard of him," Emma says.

"You're too young."

Emma looks skeptical, not flattered. "I think more people will care about Rabbi Levine."

"Then bump him to Metro," I suggest brightly.

Emma, of course, isn't keen on that idea. She and the Metropolitan editor don't get along.

"It's Sunday," I remind her. "Nothing else is happening in the free world. Metro can give the rabbi a fine send-off."

Emma says, "This musician — how old was he?"

"Thirty-nine."

"Yeah?"

Now I've got her chummed up.

Emma says coolly, "So, how'd he die?"

"I don't know."

"Probably drugs," she muses, "or suicide. And you know the rule on suicides, Jack."

Newspapers customarily do not report a private death as a suicide, on the theory it might plant the idea in the minds of other depressed people, who would immediately rush out and do themselves in. These days no paper can afford to lose subscribers.

There is, however, a long-standing journalistic exception to the no-suicide rule.

"He's famous, Emma. The rule goes out the window."

"He's not famous. I never heard of him."

15

Again she is forcing me to insult her. "Ever heard of Sylvia Plath?" I ask.

"Of course."

"Do you know *why* you've heard of her, Emma? Because she stuck her head in an oven. That's what she's famous for."

"Jack, you're not funny."

"Otherwise she's just another brilliant, obscure, unappreciated poet," I say. "Fame enhances death, but death also enhances fame. That's a fact."

Emma's fine-boned lower jaw is working back and forth. She's itching to tell me to go screw myself but that would constitute a serious violation of management policy, a dark entry in an otherwise promising personnel file. I feel for her, I really do.

"Emma, let me do some checking on Stomarti."

"In the meantime," she says sharply, "I'll be holding twelve inches for Rabbi Levine."

A death notice isn't the same as an obituary. A death notice is a classified advertisement written and paid for by the family of the deceased, and sent to newspapers by the funeral home as part of its full-service package. Death notices usually are printed in a small type known as agate, but they can be as long-winded and florid as the family desires. Newspapers are always happy to sell the space.

The death notice of Jimmy Stoma was remarkable for its brevity, and for what was omitted:

STOMARTI, James Bradley, 39, passed away Thursday in the Berry Islands. A resident of Silver Beach since 1993, Jim was a successful businessman who was active in his church and neighborhood civic groups. He loved golf, sailing and diving, and raised thousands of dollars to help restore damaged coral reefs in the Florida Keys and the Bahamas. A cherished friend, devoted brother and beloved husband, he will be deeply missed by his wife, Cynthia Jane, and his sister Janet Stomarti Thrush of Beckerville. A private family mass will be held Tuesday morning at St. Stephen's Church, followed by a brief shipboard ceremony near the Ripley Lighthouse, where Jim wished to have his mortal remains committed. In lieu of flowers, the family asks that contributions be made to the Cousteau Society, in Jim's memory.

Odd. No trace of his life as a Slut Puppy, the six million records sold, the MTV video awards, the Grammy. Music wasn't even listed among his hobbies.

Maybe Jimmy Stoma had wanted it that way; maybe he had worked so hard to put the wild years behind him that he'd wanted nothing, not even his own death, to revive the past.

Sorry, pal, I'll try to be gentle.

There is no James or J. Stomarti in the county phone book, but a Janet Thrush is listed in Beckerville. A woman picks up on the third ring. I tell her who I am and what I'm writing.

"Sorry," she says, "it's a bad time."

"You're Jimmy's sister?"

"That's right. Look, can you call back in a couple days?"

Here comes the dicey part when I've got to explain — very delicately — that when it comes to obituaries, it's now or never. Wait forty-eight hours and nobody at the paper will give a rat's ass about your dead brother.

Nothing personal. It's the nature of news.

"The story's running tomorrow," I tell his sister. "I really hate to bother you. And you're right, there's lots of stuff I could use from our clippings. . . ."

I let this ghastly prospect sink in. Nobody deserves an obituary constructed exclusively from old newspaper stories.

"I'd prefer chatting with those who knew him best," I say. "His death is going to be a shock for lots of people all over the country. Your brother had so many fans. . . ."

"Fans?" Janet Thrush is testing me.

18

"Yeah. I was one of them."

On the other end: an unreadable silence.

"Jimmy Stoma," I press on. "Of Jimmy and the Slut Puppies. It *is* the same James Stomarti, right?"

His sister says, quietly, "That was a long time ago."

"People will remember. Trust me."

"Well, that's good. I guess." She sounds unsure.

I say, "There wasn't much information in the death notice."

"I wouldn't know. I didn't see it."

"About his music, I mean."

"You talk to Cleo?"

"Who's that?" I ask.

"His wife."

"Oh. The funeral home gave the name as Cynthia."

"She goes by Cleo," says Jimmy's sister. "Cleo Rio. The one and only."

When I say I've never heard of her, Jimmy's sister chuckles. A television murmurs in the background. *Meet the Press*, it sounds like.

"Well, pretend you know who Cleo is," she advises, "and I guarantee she'll give you an interview."

Obviously Sis and the widow have some issues. "What about you?" I ask.

"Lord, don't mention my name."

"That's not what I meant," I say. "I was

hoping you would talk to me. Just a few quick questions? I'm sorry, but I'm on a tight deadline —"

"After you get hold of Cleo," Jimmy's sister says, "call me back."

"Do you have her phone number?"

"Sure." She gives it to me, then says: "I've got an address, too. You ought to go out to the condo."

"Good idea," I say, but I hadn't planned to leave the newsroom. I can do five phoners in the time it takes to drive to Silver Beach and back.

Jimmy's sister says, "You want to get this story right, you gotta go meet Cleo." She pauses. "Hey, I'm not tryin' to tell you how to do your job."

"I appreciate the help, but just tell me one thing. How'd your brother die? Was he sick?"

She knows exactly what I mean. "Jimmy's been straight for nine years," she says.

"Then what happened?"

"It was an accident, I guess."

"What kind of accident?"

"Go ask Cleo," says Jimmy's sister, and hangs up.

I'm on my way out the door when Emma cuts me off. She's almost a whole foot shorter than I am; sneaky, too. I seldom see her coming.

She says, "Did you know Rabbi Levine

took up hang gliding at age seventy? That's good stuff, Jack."

"Did he die in his hang glider, Emma? Crash into the synagogue, by chance?"

"No," she concedes. "Stroke."

I shrug. "Nice try, but I'm off to visit the widow Stomarti."

Emma doesn't budge. "I like the rabbi better."

Hell. Now she's forcing me to show my cards. I glance quickly around the newsroom and notice, with some relief, that none of the young superstars are working today. That's one good thing about a Sunday shift, the newsroom is like a tomb. Emma wants to take away my story, she'll have to write the damn thing herself.

And Emma, bless her sorority-sister soul, has never been a reporter. Judging by the strenuous syntax of her memos, she likely would have difficulty composing a thank-you note.

So, here goes.

"James Stomarti was Jimmy Stoma," I say.

Emma's brow crinkles. She senses that she ought to know the name. Rather than admitting she doesn't, she waits me out.

"Of Jimmy and the Slut Puppies," I prompt.

"No kidding."

"Remember that song, 'Basket Case'?"

"Sure." Emma turns slightly, her raptor

eyes scanning the rows of cubicles. The plan, I know, is to hand off Stoma to another reporter and dispatch me to do the dead rabbi.

But Emma's coming up empty. The only warm body on the city desk is Griffin, the weekend cop guy. Griffin is sixty years old, nasty and untouchable. Emma has no authority over the police reporters. Griffin looks up from his desktop and stares right through her, as if she were smoke.

With a trace of a frown, Emma turns back to me. "Suicide, right?"

"Nope. Accident."

Grudgingly, Emma moves out of my way. "Twelve inches," she says curtly. "That's all we've got, Jack."

"For a dead rock star," I say drily, "a Grammy Award–winning musician who dies tragically at age thirty-nine? Honey, I promise you the *New York Times* will give it more than twelve inches."

Emma says, "Not on the Death page, they won't."

I smile. "That's right. Not there."

Emma's expression darkens. "Ungh-ugh, Jack. I'm not pushing this for Page One. No way!"

Jesus, what a hoot. The *Times* won't put Jimmy Stoma out front — he'll be lucky to end up as the lead obit. But Emma's in a sweat, rattled at the possibility of me breaking out of the dungeon. No doubt she

22

perceives that as a career-threatening crisis, for part of her mission as a junior editor is to see that I remain crushed, without hope of redemption. The next best thing to canning me would be to make me quit in disgust, which of course I'll never do.

This is too much fun.

I say to Emma: "You might mention Stoma in the budget meeting, just in case."

"Twelve inches, Jack," she reiterates sternly.

"Because my guess is, there's at least one Slut Puppies fan on the masthead." I'm referring to Abkazion, the new managing editor, who is my age and works weekends.

"Fifteen inches, max," amends Emma.

I wave goodbye with my spiral notebook, and stride toward the elevator. "We'll talk when I get back from visiting Mrs. Stomarti."

"What kind of accident?" Emma calls after me. "How did he die? Jack?"

2

My all-time favorite obituary headline is:

**Sir Seewoosagur Ramgoolam
Of Mauritius Dies at Age 85.**

This did not appear in a Dr. Seuss book, but in the *New York Times*. Maybe three dozen readers in all Manhattan had ever heard of Sir Seewoosagur Ramgoolam, but that's what made the matter-of-fact tone of the headline so splendid — the dry implication that even non-Mauritians *ought* to have known who he was.

Obituary headlines often contain helpful (though sometimes unnecessary) identifiers — **Joe DiMaggio, Former Baseball Star, Dead at 84** — yet no clue was provided as to the occupation or achievements of the departed Ramgoolam patriarch. Perhaps the headline writer was hamstrung by a lack of space, due to the phenomenal length of the deceased's name, though I prefer to believe the succinctness was intentional.

Sir Seewoosagur is gone. Enough said.

I won't be writing the headline on Jimmy Stoma's obituary because, contrary to what readers think, reporters don't come up with the headlines for their stories. Copy editors do.

One time the copy editor on the Death page called in sick, and Emma herself was left with that duty. It was September 11, 1998, and here's what she put above one of my obituaries:

Keith Murtagh, Inventor of French Toast, Dies at 96 After Brief Illness

The man's name was Kenneth Murtaugh, he had invented a toaster oven, and he was sixty-nine when he crashed his Coupe de Ville into a palm tree along Perdido Boulevard. That he died was the only fact Emma managed to get right.

The one who got the angry letters from the dead man's family was me, because it was my name on the story beneath the fucked-up headline. Weeks later, Emma sent me a memo of apology, in which she again misspelled Murtaugh's name. God, if only it had been out of spite and not incompetence. . . .

Driving across Pelican Causeway, I'm imagining the headline possibilities for Jimmy Stoma.

James Stomarti, Former Pop Star, Dies in Accident at 39

Or, slightly better:

Rock Musician Known as Jimmy Stoma Dies in the Bahamas

That's if the story remains on the obit page, where headlines are customarily subdued and colorless. All bets are off if the duty editor bumps Stoma to Metro or Page One, in which case I would give my right testicle to see a "Slut Puppy" reference in 40-point type, such as:

Rocker Jimmy Stoma, Ex–Slut Puppy, Perishes at Age 39 in Bahamas Accident

Now there's a headline to sell papers. You've got the irresistible ingredients of glamour (rock music), notoriety (the famously naughty Slut Puppies), youth (age thirty-nine), tragedy ("perish," an exquisite verb, implying a rich life cut short), all set against an exotic tropical backdrop. . . .

Ugly but true: Death is what pays my bills.

At one time I was a serious reporter doing what passed for serious journalism. Now I write exclusively about the unliving — I go to bed each night thinking about the ones I've laid to rest in tomorrow's paper, and I wake up every morning wondering who will be next. My curiosity is strictly and professionally morbid. Shamelessly I plot to resurrect my newspaper career by yoking my byline to some famous stiff. My days are spent dodging dead Rabbi Levines in the hope that someone more widely known will pass away before the first-edition deadline.

Certainly this is no life to be esteemed. Yet I like to think I bring uncommon style and perspective to the obituary page, which is traditionally a training ground for interns and fresh-out-of-college rookies. Emma, of course, would prefer that her modest stable feature an obit writer who was younger and less experienced than herself; someone she could guide, counsel and occasionally intimidate.

But she's stuck with me, and I make her as jittery as a gerbil in a cobra pit. Emma keeps a stash of Valiums in her top drawer — the pills are disguised in a Bayer aspirin bottle, to avoid discovery by any of her ambitious rival editors. They would unhesitatingly use the information to cast doubt on Emma's fitness for newspaper management.

Poor girl. She has a decent soul, I'm certain, and an untested heart that doesn't deserve to be wrung like an old dishrag. Yet that's what is bound to happen if Emma stays in this miserable profession. I'm determined to save her; she is one of two pressing personal projects.

The first being, to save myself.

Before heading to Silver Beach, I make two

quick stops. The first is a record store, where I purchase the only unremaindered copy of *Floating Hospice*. Next, with Jimmy Stoma belting from the dashboard of my Mustang — "My baby is a basket case, a bipolar mama in leather and lace!" — I drive to a drugstore that employs a worldly young woman named Carla Candilla.

Carla is the daughter of my favorite ex-girlfriend. She works the drugstore's photo counter. She waves when she spots me standing in line — we are on closer terms than her mother and I.

Carla smiles. "Black Jack!" Her nickname for me, inspired by my occupation.

I lean across the counter for a fatherly hug. "Once again I'm in need of instruction," I say.

"Fire away, old-timer."

"Cleo Rio. There wasn't much in the morgue."

"She's new on the scene," Carla concedes. "Is this research, or personal?"

"That's right, darling, we're a hot item, me and Cleo. Tonight we're going to a rave and later we're getting a suite at Morgan's. Tell *that* to your mom. Please, Carla, I'll pay you."

When Carla laughs she looks just like Anne, her mother. And Anne laughing is one of my all-time happiest recollections.

Carla asks if Cleo Rio is dead.

"No, it's her husband," I say.

"Oh, that's right. She got married," Carla nods. "It was in *Ocean Drive*."

Carla keeps track of all local and visiting celebs. At seventeen she is a wily veteran of the club scene and a regular pilgrim to South Beach, where she keeps current on music, movies, dietary trends and fashion. Carla is a key source; my only reliable link to modern youth culture.

"So what has Cleo done to make herself semi-famous? What exactly is she?" I ask.

"More specific please. You mean her sexuality? Nationality? Personality?"

"Carla," I say, "in about twenty minutes I've gotta sit down with this woman and drag three decent quotes out of her. This will require first-class bullshitting."

"She's a singer."

"That helps. What kind of singer?"

"Angry," Carla says, "wounded but not hardened."

"Alanis clone?"

Carla shakes her head. "Cleo's definitely going for a more precious effect. You know the type — the suddenly fuckable former fashion model."

Carla is not trying to shock me. She's talked this way since she was twelve.

"Tell me some of her hits," I say.

"Hit singular, Jack."

"So everything you're giving me is based on one song?"

"Plus the video," Carla says.

"Certainly."

"Directed by Oliver Stone."

"Who else."

"Supposedly she flashes some pubes. That's how she got her name in *Spin*," Carla reports. "Personally, I don't think it was even Cleo on the video. I think they used a double."

"For pubic hair?"

"Show business, Jack. Hul-lo?" Carla, who has come under the suspicious gaze of the store manager, now pretends to arrange some color slides on the light table for my inspection.

"What was the name of Cleo Rio's one and only song?" I ask.

" 'Me,' " says Carla. "That's all. Just 'Me.' "

"And it charted?"

"Only because of the pube hype."

"Gotcha. Thanks, darling."

"Where's the big interview?"

"Her place."

"I expect a complete debriefing."

"Of course. Hey, you ever hear of Jimmy and the Slut Puppies?"

Carla arches an auburn eyebrow. "They new?" She's afraid she's missed something.

"Nope. Old as the hills."

30

"Sorry, Jack."

Before leaving the drugstore, I can't stop myself from asking: "So how's your mom?"

"Good," says Carla.

"Really?"

"Really good."

"Shit," I say.

Carla laughs fondly. The fact that I still miss Anne buoys her opinion of me.

"Tell her I said hi."

"You're quite the dreamer, Jack."

Jimmy Stoma's condo is on the nineteenth floor of an eyesore skyscraper at the southernmost tip of Silver Beach. Twenty minutes she keeps me waiting in the lobby, Jimmy's widow, but truthfully I'm surprised she agreed to see me at all. From the briefness of the death notice, it would seem that the family doesn't want much attention.

The door of 19-G is opened by a squat, bald, neckless man with two small platinum hoops in each earlobe. Straight from Bouncers-R-Us, this guy, down to the bomber jacket and the understated armpit bulge. Wordlessly he leads me through the hazily lit condo to the living room, where Mrs. Stomarti is standing before a wraparound bay window.

I have indeed seen her face before, on the cover of a couple tabloid-style celebrity magazines to which I subscribe for professional reasons. (I clip and file some of the juicier profile pieces in case the celebrity subject someday expires within our circulation area.)

"I'm Cleo," says Mrs. Stomarti. "Jimmy's wife."

She is maybe twenty-two years old; twenty-three, tops. Medium tall, thin but not skinny, and alarmingly tan. The hair is bleached snow white and cut in a mock pageboy. The lips are done cherry red and the cheekbones are heavily shadowed, like a pair of matching bruises. She's wearing a beige sleeveless shell and tight white slacks. Her toenails, also white, remind me of paint chips.

No wonder she quit calling herself Cynthia.

"I'm Jack Tagger," I say. "It's a pleasure to meet you. I only wish the circumstances were different." Implying I am aware of her blossoming fame, and would otherwise be delighted to interview her for the Arts & Music page.

We sit down; the widow on the end of a long cream-colored sofa, and me on a deacon's bench. Wasting no time, I tell Cleo Rio how much I liked her hit single, "Me."

She brightens. "You catch the video?"

"Who didn't!"

"What'd you think — too much?"

"Did Jimmy like it?"

"Loved it," Cleo says.

"I vote with Jimmy." I uncap a felt-tip pen and open the notebook on my lap.

"You're the first one to call," Mrs. Stomarti says.

"I was a fan."

A faint smile. "Next'll be the trades, I suppose."

"I'm sorry," I say. "I know you're trying to keep it low-key."

"That's what Jimmy wanted."

"I promise not to take much of your time."

The bald guy brings Cleo what looks like a screwdriver in a tall frosty glass. He doesn't so much as glance in my direction, which is fine with me.

"Want somethin'?" Cleo asks.

I should mention her eyes, which are rimmed pink from either crying or lack of sleep. She's wearing ice-blue contact lenses.

"A Coke? Beer?" asks Jimmy's wife.

"No, thanks."

To get the ball rolling, I start with the easy ones. How did you two first meet? *A VH1 party.* How long were you married? *Not quite a year.* Where was the ceremony? *Sag Harbor. On a friend's boat.* Oh? Who was that? *I forget the name. Some sax player Jimmy knew. A session guy.*

Here I pause longer than necessary to write down her answer. The interval is meant to give Mrs. Stomarti a moment to prepare. I still dread this part of the job, intruding so bluntly upon the grieving. Yet I've found that many people don't mind talking to a total stranger about their lost loved one. Maybe it's easier than commiserating with family members, who know all there is to know about the deceased, good and bad. A visit from an obituary writer, however, presents a golden opportunity to start from scratch and remake a person as you wish to have them remembered. An obituary is the ultimate last word.

I drop my voice from casual to somber. "Mrs. Stomarti, tell me about the Bahamas trip."

She sets her drink on a teak coffee table. "Jimmy loved it over there. We had a place down in Exuma."

Glancing down, I notice the toes on both her feet are curling and uncurling. Either it's some type of yoga routine, or Cleo Rio is nervous. I ask if they were on vacation when it happened.

She chuckles. "Jimmy was *always* on vacation when we went to the islands. He loved to dive — he was, like, obsessed. He used to say that being underwater was better than any dope he'd ever tried. 'The deeper I go, the higher I get,' is what he said."

Writing down every word, I'm thinking about how easily Mrs. Stomarti has settled into the past tense when speaking of Jimmy. Often a new widow will talk about her deceased husband as though he were still alive.

For example: *He's always on vacation when*

we go to the islands. Or: *He loves to dive.* And so on.

But Cleo hasn't slipped once. No subconscious denial here; Jimmy Stoma's dead.

"Can you tell me what happened," I ask, "the day he died?"

She purses her lips and reaches for the drink. I wait. She slurps an ice cube out of the glass and says, "It was an accident."

I say nothing.

"He was diving on an airplane wreck. Fifty, sixty feet deep." Mrs. Stomarti is sucking the ice from cheek to cheek.

"Where?" I ask.

"Near Chub Cay. There's plane wrecks all over the islands," she adds, "from the bad old days."

"What kind of a plane?"

Cleo shrugs. "A DC-something. I don't remember," she says. "Anyway, I was up on the boat when it happened." Now she's crunching the ice in her teeth.

"You don't dive?"

"Not that day. I was working on my tan."

I nod and glance down meaningfully at my notebook. Scribble a couple words. Look up and nod again. The worst thing a reporter can do in a delicate interview is seem impatient. Cleo takes another slug of her drink. Then she rolls her shoulders and stiffens, like she's working out a kink in her spine.

"Jimmy went down same as always," she

says, "but he didn't come up."

"Was he alone?" I ask.

"No, he never dove alone."

I'm thinking: Again with the past tense.

"Jay was down there, too," Jimmy's wife says, "only he was diving the tail section. Jimmy was up in the nose of the plane. See, it's in two pieces on the bottom."

"Jay Burns? From the Slut Puppies?"

She nods. "He and Jimmy were, like, best friends. He swum up off the wreck and starts climbing into the boat when all of a sudden he's like, 'Isn't Jimmy up yet?' And I'm like, 'No, he's still down.' See, I was reading a magazine. I wasn't watching the time."

Cleo lifts the empty glass and turns her head toward the kitchen doorway. In a flash, the neckless bouncer guy hustles forward with a fresh screwdriver. A bodyguard who knows how to mix a drink — every pop star should have at least one.

The widow takes a sip and continues:

"So Jay grabs a fresh tank and jumps back in the water and . . . no Jimmy. He wasn't anywhere on the wreck." Cleo rocks back on the sofa cushion. She's no longer looking at me; she's staring out the bay window that faces the Atlantic. Her eyes are locked on something far away and invisible to mine.

She says, "Jimmy was everything to me, you know? My husband, my best friend, my lover, my manager —"

I'm writing like crazy. Trying to slow Cleo down, I say, "Have you got a phone number for Jay?"

"He's still in the islands. He's bringing Jimmy's boat across tomorrow."

"It's nice they stayed so close after the band broke up."

"Jay was the only one," Cleo says, "the only one in the music business Jimmy would even talk to. Until he met me."

She pauses while I catch up on my notes. Obviously she's done interviews before.

"Anyway," she goes on, "we called for help. They found him about three hours later, like, half a mile away. He was already gone. His tank was empty."

I ask Mrs. Stomarti if an autopsy was performed in the Bahamas.

"Yeah, they said he drowned. I guess he just got wore out trying to find the boat. The currents get pretty strong out there, and all those years of smoking weed, Jimmy didn't exactly have the lungs of a teenager."

"But he'd been straight for some time, right?" I make the question sound casual.

Cleo says, "Totally."

I don't write that down because I don't want her to think I'm too interested in Jimmy's wild days.

"So what do you think happened," I ask, "on that last dive?"

"I think . . ." Jimmy's wife pauses to

37

snatch a pack of Marlboros off the teak table. "I think my darling husband swam off and got lost —"

Now I'm jotting again.

"— simple as that," says Cleo Rio, lighting up. "Knowing Jimmy, he saw something way cool down there and went swimming off after it — a hammerhead or a big moray eel, who knows what — and got all turned around. It's easy to do." She gives a rueful smile. "When he went diving, he was like a little kid. Totally preoccupied."

"How were the seas?"

"Flat when we got there. But we'd had some wind the night before and Jay said visibility on the bottom was shitty."

"And this happened when?"

"Thursday afternoon. A police boat took Jimmy's body to Nassau and we didn't get him back until yesterday."

The way she's dragging on the cigarette, I can tell she's tired of talking.

"You've been very generous with your time," I say. "I'm almost finished."

"It's okay."

"You said Jimmy liked to keep a low profile. Is that why the death notice didn't mention the Slut Puppies, or even his Grammy?"

"Right."

"But he wrote some good songs. People will remember."

"Tell me about it. I was his *numero uno*

fan." Cleo stubs out the butt. "But Jimmy always said it was another lifetime, and he was lucky to get out alive. He didn't want any reminders."

"Not even the music?"

"*Especially* the music," she says. "One of his songs came on the car radio, he'd turn it off right away. Didn't get mad or nothin', just changed the channel." Cleo sweeps a hand through the air. "Dig, in this whole place there's not one of his records. Not one! That's how he wanted it."

Out of the corner of my eye I see the neckless man, leaning against a wall; waiting, I assume, to escort me out.

I say to Jimmy's wife: "He was good."

"No, he was awesome."

Shamelessly I jot this down, too, knowing it's a word that Cleo uses probably fifty times a day to describe everything from bubble bath to frozen yogurt.

She says, "That's why I was so stoked about him producing my CD."

"Jimmy was producing? That must've been a blast, working together in the studio."

"For sure. We're almost finished," she says.

Finally, the present tense. Unless the "we" doesn't include her husband.

"You have a title? I'd like to mention it in the story."

Cleo Rio perks up, scooting to the edge of the sofa. "*Shipwrecked Heart.* But we've still

39

got some mixing left, so it won't be out for a while."

I write it down: *Shipwrecked Heart.* Slightly mawkish, but it gives me a semi-ironic kicker for the story. Even Emma might get it.

Standing up, I flip the notebook shut and cap my pen. "Thank you," I tell Jimmy's widow. "I know this was difficult."

We shake hands. Hers is damp, the knuckles showing pink and raw.

"When will this be in the paper?" she asks me.

"Tomorrow."

"Will there be a picture of Jimmy?"

"Most likely," I say.

The bald guy has materialized at my side.

"Well, I hope they pick a good one," says Mrs. Stomarti.

"Don't worry. I'll talk to the photo editor." Like he'd give me the time of day.

No sooner has the door to 19-G closed behind me than I think of a dozen other questions I should have asked. But that's what always happens, and the truth is, I've got more than enough material for the obit. Plus I still need to talk with Jimmy's sister, Janet, and make some calls to the Bahamas.

I scan my notes as I'm waiting for the elevator, which is taking forever. Finally there's a double beep and the door opens, and I nearly walk smack into some tall guy who's on his way out. I don't see his face because he's carrying an armful of grocery bags from a gourmet deli. We both grunt apologetically and manage to sidestep each other. As he turns the corner, leaving me alone in the elevator to gag on his cologne, I see quite a lush mane of copper-red hair shimmering down past his shoulder blades.

The elevator door doesn't close immediately, which annoys me because I'm on deadline. Every pissant delay will annoy me until the Jimmy Stoma obit is finished.

Repeatedly I punch the elevator button. Nothing happens. From down the hall, I hear the guy knocking on a door to one of the apartments. I hear the door open. I hear the voice of Cleo Rio, and though I can't make out her words, the tone is clearly friendly and familiar.

Leading me to the brilliant conclusion that the shimmery-haired man who got out of the elevator was not a grocery-delivery guy, but an acquaintance of the bereaved.

And, as the elevator door finally closes in my face, I wonder: Why would anyone wear so much cologne to visit a widow?

3

Where is Janet Thrush?

I keep calling; no answer. I leave two messages on her machine.

Meanwhile, Emma hovers. She thinks I ought to be writing Jimmy Stoma's obituary by now, but she knows better than to nag. Emma dislikes being reminded that I haven't missed a deadline since she was in Huggies.

Come on, Janet, answer the damn phone.

From Jimmy's sister I need two things. One is a nice warm quote about her brother — I hate to hang the entire obit on Cleo Rio. Second, I want to bounce Cleo's version of Jimmy's life off of Janet to make sure I'm not being steered off course. Wives have been known to lie extravagantly about dead husbands.

Janet Thrush could tell me if her brother had been producing *Shipwrecked Heart* for Cleo, and if the CD was nearly finished. Even if Jimmy's widow is exaggerating for self-promotional purposes, at least the title ought to hold up. That's all I need for my last sentence, which we call the kicker.

While waiting for Janet, I try the Bahamian police. Talk about a long shot. Headquarters in Nassau refers me to Freeport. Freeport refers me to Chub Cay, which refers me back to Freeport. Sunday, it seems, isn't the best day to track down a coroner in the islands.

Finally I hook up with a person who identifies herself as Corporal Smith. She's aware that an American has "very unfortunately" passed away while on a diving trip to the Berry Islands, but she has no further information at hand. She politely instructs me to call Nassau tomorrow and ask for Sergeant Weems.

It's futile to plead my case but I give it a try. And, as expected, Corporal Smith wants to know why I can't wait one more day to write the obit. It's a logical question. Jimmy Stoma certainly isn't going anywhere.

"It's news," I explain valiantly to the corporal. "I'm in a competitive situation."

"No one else from the press has called."

"But they will."

"Then they'll be advised to phone back tomorrow," she says, "just like you."

I hang up. Emma is behind me, her presence a clammy vapor.

"How's it going?"

"Peachy," I say.

"When can I see something?"

"When it's done."

She slides away like a fog.

Desperate for a second quote, I look up the home phone number of our music critic.

43

His name is Tim Buckminster, although he recently began using the initials T.O. in his byline, because he liked the rhythm of it: T. O. Buckminster! He even sent an all-points e-mail instructing everyone at the newspaper to refer to him henceforth as "T.O.," please, and never Tim.

I cannot bring myself to do this. Tim Buckminster is only twenty-five years old, which is too young to be reinventing oneself. So I call him Timmy, as does his mother. Unfortunately, he turns out to be utterly unfamiliar with the music of the Slut Puppies, or of Jimmy Stoma as a solo artist.

"But you've heard of him, right?" I ask.

"Sure. Didn't he marry Cleo Rio?"

Next I try a rock-writer pal in San Francisco. He is kind enough to cobble together an instant quote about the *Reptiles and Amphibians of North America* CD, which (he speculates) had an influence on current bands such as the Red Hot Chili Peppers and Foo Fighters.

Good enough.

I glance at the clock on the wall. Maybe Janet Thrush will call before deadline, which is ninety-four minutes away. On my desk I spread my meager notes and the morgue clippings, and begin to write:

James Stomarti, the hard-living singer-songwriter who founded the popular rock group Jimmy and the Slut Puppies, has died in an apparent skin-diving accident in the Bahamas. He was 39.

Known to millions of youthful fans as Jimmy Stoma, Stomarti disappeared on the afternoon of August 6 while exploring the sunken wreckage of a smuggler's airplane near Chub Cay, according to his wife, the singer Cleo Rio.

Ms. Rio said her husband went diving in 50 to 60 feet of water with a former band-mate, keyboardist Jay Burns, while she waited aboard the boat. Burns came up after an hour, she said, but there was no sign of Stomarti.

His body was found later by Bahamian police, in calm seas a half mile away, Ms. Rio said.

"I think my darling husband swam off and got lost," she said Sunday, still dazed by the tragedy. "When he went diving he was like a little kid. Totally preoccupied."

Ms. Rio said it appeared Stomarti had gotten lost underwater, and succumbed to fatigue. She said an autopsy determined that her husband had drowned.

Bahamian Police Cpl. Cilla Smith acknowledged that an American died last Thursday on a dive in the Berry Islands, but declined to confirm that it was Stomarti or provide details of the coroner's findings.

Stomarti's body was returned to the

United States on Saturday. A private service will be held Tuesday afternoon at St. Stephen's Church in Silver Beach. Afterwards the singer's ashes will be scattered in the Atlantic Ocean, according to his wishes, Ms. Rio said.

It is a quiet final chapter to a life that had, until recent years, been tumultuous and troubled.

Jimmy and the Slut Puppies barged onto the rock scene in 1983 with the raunchy hit single, "Mouthful of Muscle." Over the next seven years the band sold more than six million albums, according to *Billboard* magazine.

As front man Jimmy Stoma, Stomarti played rhythm guitar, harmonica and sang lead vocals. He also wrote the group's best-known singles, including "Basket Case" and "Trouser Troll," the latter of which appeared on the Slut Puppies' last album, the Grammy Award–winning *A Painful Burning Sensation.*

"Jimmy and the Slut Puppies was a high-octane act," rock biographer Gavin Cisco said, "and the spark came from Jimmy Stoma. He was a screamer, for sure, but he was also a sly and solid songwriter."

Cisco cited the "obvious" influence of one Slut Puppies album, *Reptiles and Amphibians of North America*, on the Red Hot Chili Peppers and other current rock bands.

Born in Chicago, James Bradley Stomarti grew up listening to hard-driving, mainstream rock-and-roll. He had a fondness for zippy, double-edged lyrics, and among his early idols were Todd Rundgren and Jackson Browne.

Stomarti was sixteen when he put together his first basement band, Jungle Rot. Several years later he and his best friend, Jay Burns, formed the Slut Puppies and went on the road.

"Mainly to get girls," Stomarti joked in a 1986 *Rolling Stone* interview, "and it worked like a charm."

Stomarti always performed bare-chested in trademark black overalls and combat boots. He was known for his elaborate tattoos, lewd comic asides and indefatigable stage energy.

Offstage, he exuberantly sustained the Jimmy Stoma persona, sometimes with embarrassing results. Stomarti had numerous brushes with the law, including one memorable arrest for indecent exposure during a concert in North Carolina. In that incident, Stomarti strode onstage wearing only a prophylactic, and a mask likeness of the Rev. Pat Robertson, the Christian broadcast personality.

Another time, the singer and an unidentified woman companion were injured when he crashed his high-powered waterbike into the stern of the luxury liner SS *Norway* while it was berthed in the Port of Miami. Later Stomarti admitted he'd gotten "seriously lit" before the accident, in which he fractured nine out of ten knuckles.

Indeed, his years of greatest fame and success were marred by heavy substance abuse, leading to the breakup of numerous romances and one marriage.

Stomarti eventually dissolved the Slut Puppies, and in 1991 released his first and only solo album, *Stomatose*, to mixed reviews and disappointing sales. He soon dropped out of the Los Angeles music scene and moved to Florida.

His wife said Stomarti gave up drugs and alcohol, and became an avid outdoorsman, fitness enthusiast and environmentalist. He bought a second home in the Bahamas, where he indulged his passions for boating and scuba diving.

Last year, while attending a VH1 party for guitarist Eddie Van Halen, Stomarti met Ms. Rio, the former Cynthia Jane Zigler. Three weeks later they were married in Reno, Nevada.

"Jimmy was everything to me, you know?" Ms. Rio said. "My husband, my best friend, my lover, my manager."

At the time of his death, Stomarti was producing an album for his new wife. The title: *Shipwrecked Heart*.

I re-read the piece and decide it's not terrible, for a forty-five-minute writing job. Maudlin as it is, the kicker works.

Jimmy Stoma's obit is 810 words, or about twenty-four column inches of type. The fastidious Emma will be plenty steamed. She told me fifteen inches, max. Anything longer won't fit into the layout of the Death page, meaning the story must be trimmed or moved to another section of the paper.

Emma would rather French-kiss an iguana than try to cut nine inches from one of my obits, because she knows I'll be breathing down her collar, giving her hell about every measly comma she has the gall to delete.

Even when allowed to toil unmolested, Emma's editing cannot be described as seamless. In the fever pitch of battle, she tends to quaver; even her punctuation (normally a strong suit) becomes shaky. Trimming an inch or two from one of my stories is merely excruciating. Cutting nine inches would be indescribable torture, and Emma knows it.

Which leaves the other option: Move the Jimmy Stoma obit to a section front. That would shift the editing duty into the hands of one of Emma's competitors. More unpalatably, it might result in a prominent display of my byline — an event as rare and mystical as a solar eclipse.

Poor kid. What choices!

Before pressing the Send button to ship

her the Jimmy Stoma obit, I go through it once more, tidying up.

I delete the "likeness" after "mask."

I wince at the Chili Peppers reference, suspecting that the Slut Puppies had no influence whatsoever on that particular band.

I cringe at the "marred by heavy substance abuse" line, but I can't come up with anything that isn't equally clichéd.

I insert the phrase "highly publicized" in front of "romances." . . .

Tinkering is a way of stalling, and I'm stalling in the hope that Janet Thrush might still phone with a quote or two about her brother. Except for a few paragraphs of background from old clippings, the obituary is pretty much all Cleo Rio. Single-sourcing always makes me uneasy, and I'm stuck with Cleo's word on lots of material facts, including the cause of Jimmy Stoma's death.

I keep thinking of the shimmery-haired guy with the deli bags who got out of the elevator. Hell, there could be a dozen innocent explanations. Maybe he was Cleo's big brother, or some diving buddy of Jimmy's. That bull-semen cologne, though, was definitely too heavy for the occasion.

My eyes fall skeptically on the phrase "still dazed by the tragedy," which I've used to describe Jimmy's widow. I should probably take it out, but I won't. It paints a gentler scene than if I'd written she was "knocking back screwdrivers and staring blankly out a window," which was the sad truth.

One more detail jumps out of the obituary to give me a twinge of acid reflux: the bit about how Jimmy and Cleo Rio first met at a VH1 party. That's what Cleo told me.

Yet she also told me her husband had broken completely from his past, and wanted nothing more to do with the music world until he'd met her. So why was he attending a Van Halen bash?

One of many things I'll probably never know.

I check the clock. I punch the Send key, then e-mail Emma to tell her Jimmy Stoma's on the way. I head downstairs to grab a soda. Upon my return I see Emma has responded with an electronic message of her own: "We need to talk as soon as I'm out of the news meeting!"

She probably hasn't even read the obit — all she did was scope out the length, then freak. Minutes later I see her crossing the newsroom and I pounce like a wolverine.

"Metro took it," she says, acting as if she couldn't care less.

"Yeah? For out front?"

Emma says nothing. She knows where the Jimmy Stoma obit is being played, but she won't give me the satisfaction.

"Talk to Metro," she says, now pretending to edit a story by young Evan Richards, our college intern. Upon my approach Evan warily has drifted away from Emma's desk; he has witnessed too many of our dustups.

"What about you?" I say to Emma. "You got enough to fill the page?"

"I'll find something on the wires."

She won't look directly at me; her slender hands appear bolted to the keypad of her computer, her nose poised six inches from the screen. The worst part is, the screen is blank. I can see its bright blue reflection in Emma's reading glasses.

Unaccountably, I am overtaken by pity.

"Rabbi Levine won't be on the wire services, Emma. You want me to make a few calls?"

Her eyes flicker. I notice the ivory tip of a tooth, pinching a corner of her lip. "No, Jack. There isn't time."

Back at my desk, I dial three phone numbers: the rabbi's wife, the rabbi's brother and the synagogue. I bat out twelve inches in twenty minutes flat, shipping it to Emma with the following note:

"You were right. The hang-gliding stuff makes the whole piece."

On the way out of the newsroom, I hear her call my name. Walking back to her desk, I see the rabbi's obituary up on her computer screen. It's easy to guess what's coming.

"Jack, I like the brother's quote better than the wife's."

"Then move it up," I say, agreeably. Emma needs this one more than I do. "See you tomorrow."

Out of the blue she says, "Nice kicker on Jimmy Stoma." Not exactly oozing sincerity, but at least she's making eye contact.

"Thanks. Was it Abkazion who bumped it to Metro?"

Emma nods. "Just like you said. Our new boss is a Slut Puppies fan."

"Naw," I say, "a true fan would have put it on Page One."

Emma almost smiles.

Dinner is a lightning stop at a burger joint. Then I go home, open a beer and ransack the apartment in search of my copy of *Reptiles and Amphibians of North America*. Finally I unearth it from a loose pile of Dylan and Pink Floyd CDs. At the touch of a button, Jimmy Stoma is alive and well, shaking the rafters of my living room. I flop on the couch. Maybe he's no Roger Waters, but James Bradley Stomarti is not without talent.

Correction: *Was.*

I close my eyes and listen.

One night I fell through a hole in my soul,
And you followed me down, followed
    me down.
I fell till the blackness broke low into dawn
And you followed me down till
    you drowned. . . .

Smiling, I drain the beer. Irony abounds! Poor Jimmy.

Again I close my eyes.

When I awake, it's daybreak. The phone is ringing and with chagrin I realize I've forgotten to turn off the call-forwarding from my newsroom number. It can only be a reader on the other end of the line, and no possible good can come from speaking to a reader at such an ungodly hour. Yet the interruption of sleep has made me so bilious that I lunge for the receiver as if it were a cocked revolver.

"Yeah, what?" I say gruffly, to put the caller on the defensive.

"Is this Mr. Tagger?" Woman's voice.

"Yeah."

"This is Janet. Janet Thrush. I read what all you wrote about my brother in the paper."

Idiotically, I find myself anticipating a compliment. Instead I hear a scornful snort.

"Holy shit," says Jimmy Stoma's sister, "did you get scammed, or what!"

4

When I went to work for this newspaper I was forty years old, the same age as Jack London when he died. I'm now forty-six. Elvis Presley died at forty-six. So did President Kennedy. George Orwell, too.

It's an occupational hazard for obituary writers — memorizing the ages at which famous people have expired, and compulsively employing such trivia to track the arc of one's own life. I can't seem to stop myself.

Not being a rotund pillhead with clogged valves, I am statistically unlikely to expire on the toilet, as Elvis did. As for succumbing to a political assassination, I'm too obscure to attract a competent sniper. Nonetheless, my forty-sixth birthday brought a torrent of irrational anxieties that have not abated in eleven months. If death could snatch such heavy hitters as Elvis and JFK, a nobody like me is easy pickings.

Implicit in the dread of early demise is a lugubrious awareness of underachievement. At my age, Elvis was the King; Kennedy, the leader of the free world. Me, I'm sitting in a donut shop in Beckerville reading a newspaper story about a dead musician, a story I apparently have botched. Nice display, though: front of the Metro section, above the fold. The text is accompanied by a recent Reuters photo of the deceased, looking tanned and happy at a benefit barbecue for Reef Relief. Even the headline isn't terrible: **Ex-Rocker Dies in Bahamas Diving Mishap.** (James Bradley Stomarti, by the way, passed away at the same age as Dennis Wilson and John Kennedy Jr.)

Janet Thrush — who else could it be? — takes the stool next to me and says, "First off, nobody calls me Jan."

"Deal."

"It's Janet. My ex once called me Jan and I stuck a cocktail fork in his femoral artery."

I am careful to display no curiosity about the marriage.

"So, *Janet,* exactly how did Cleo Rio scam me?"

"She lied about her new record — 'Water-logged Heart' or whatever. Jimmy's not producing it."

Janet has freckles on her nose and unruly ash-blond hair and green bulb earrings the size of Yule ornaments. She's wearing Way-farers and a pastel tube top over tight jeans, and looks at least five years younger than her brother.

"How do you know he wasn't producing it?" I ask.

"A, because Jimmy would've told me. B,

56

because he was too busy working on his own record."

"Hold on." I reach for my pen and notebook.

"Fact, I didn't even know Cleo *had* a CD in the works. My brother never said a word about it."

"When's the last time you spoke?"

"Day he died." Janet blows on her coffee, steaming up the sunglasses.

"He called you from the Bahamas?"

She nods. "I can't ever call *him*. Not with her around. Cleo goes jiggy."

In contrast to Jimmy's widow, Janet speaks of her late brother in the present tense, which enhances her credibility. I write down what she says, even though there's little chance of using it in another story. Obituaries tend to be one-shot deals.

Besides, it's her word against Cleo's.

"She didn't even mention his new record?" Janet sounds incredulous.

"Not a word."

"What a tramp." Her voice cracks. The coffee cup is suspended halfway to her lips.

"She told me Jimmy was finished with the music business until he met her," I say.

"And you believed that?"

"Why wouldn't I? He hasn't had an album out since *Stomatose*. Besides, you never called me back yesterday. The story would have been different if you had."

This is low on my part, pinning a factual omission on a grieving relative. Janet, however, seems unoffended.

"FYI," she says, "my brother's been working on that album for four years. Maybe five."

I feel vaguely sick to my stomach. Some reporter in the music trades probably knows about the unfinished Jimmy Stoma CD, and it'll be the lead of his story. It would've been the lead of *mine*, too, if only Jimmy's widow had thought to tell me about it.

"You don't look so good, Mr. Tagger. You get a bad cruller?"

"Call me Jack. Why doesn't Cleo like you?"

"Because I know what she is." Janet smiles tightly. "Now you know, too."

In the parking lot, I walk Jimmy's sister to her car, an old black Miata that looks about as perky as a rat turd. By way of explanation, she says, "I clobbered an ambulance." Then she adds: "Not on purpose, don't worry."

I tell her I've got one more question; a heavy one. "You think your brother's really dead?"

Janet gives me a long look. "Glad you asked," she says. "Let's go for a ride."

The mortuary is only a few blocks off the interstate. It looks like every suburban funeral home in America; pillars, inlaid brick, and a tidy hedge.

I hate these places. Writing about death is as close as I want to get, but given a choice, I'll take a chainsaw-murder scene over a funeral visitation any day.

"This is where I was," says Janet, "when you tried to call yesterday."

We must climb out of the little convertible because the crumpled doors will not open.

"So you already saw the body?" I ask.

"Yup."

"Then I'll take your word that Jimmy's dead."

When Janet removes her sunglasses, I see she's been crying. "That's what they teach you in newspaper school?" she says. "To believe every damn fool thing you're told? What if I'm lying?"

"You're not." Me, the wise old pro.

I follow her inside. Some guy who smells like rotten gardenias and looks like a used-furniture salesman sidles into the foyer, then recoils at the sight of Janet, with whom he obviously has interacted before.

"You cooked my big brother yet?"

"Pardon me?" The man wears a dyspeptic grimace.

"The cremation, Ellis. Remember?"

"In an hour or so."

"Good," says Janet. "I want to see him one more time."

The funeral director, Ellis, glances at me

59

warily. I know that look; he thinks I'm a cop. Possibly this is because my necktie could be an artifact from Jack Webb's estate.

Ellis says, "Is there something wrong?"

Without missing a beat, Janet says, "This is the drummer in Jimmy's first band. He flew all the way from Hawaii."

Ellis is relieved. We follow him down a hallway to a door marked Staff Only. It is not, thank God, the crematorium.

Four wooden caskets sit side by side, each on its own padded gurney. In Florida, every corpse gets embalmed and every corpse gets a coffin, even for cremation. It's a law that exists for no other reason than to pad the profits of funeral-home proprietors. Janet points to a blond walnut casket with an orange tag twist-tied to one of the handles. "Burn ticket," she explains.

Ellis dutifully opens the top half of the bisected lid . . . and there's Jimmy Stoma.

All things considered, he looks pretty darn spiffy. Better, in fact, than he did on some of his album covers. He's so lean and fit, you wouldn't guess he once outweighed Meat Loaf.

James Bradley Stomarti lies before us in splendid attire: a coal-black Armani jacket over a white silk shirt buttoned to the throat. A fine diamond stud glistens in one earlobe. His cropped brown hair, flecked with silver, shines with mousse.

Every dead rock musician should look so good.

As his sister steps closer, I'm thinking it's fortunate that Jimmy Stoma's body was recovered right away. Ellis, the funeral guy, undoubtedly has the same thought: One more day of floating in shark-infested waters under that hot Bahamian sun, and you're talking closed casket.

Tightly closed.

"You did an awesome job," I tell Ellis, because that's what Jimmy's geeky drummer friend would have said.

"Thank you," Ellis says. Then, for Janet's benefit: "He was a very handsome fellow."

"Yeah, he was. Jack?" She beckons with a finger.

I ask Ellis to give us some privacy, and with practiced aplomb he backs out of the room. He will return later, I know, to make sure we didn't spoil his Christmas by beating him to Jimmy's earring.

"Diamonds won't burn, you know," I whisper to Janet.

"That's Cleo's problem. She's in charge of wardrobe," says Janet, making me like her even more.

"Well, it does look good. *He* looks good."

"Yeah," she says.

We're standing together at the side of the coffin. Now that I've seen with my own eyes that Jimmy Stoma is deceased, the heebie-jeebies are setting in. I'm fighting the urge to bolt from the premises. The body reeks of designer cologne; the same cologne worn by Deli Boy in the elevator. Cleo's favorite, I'm sure. Poor Jimmy will probably explode when they slide him into the flames.

Janet says, "What do you know about autopsies, Jack?"

"Come on. Let's go."

"You ever seen one?"

"Yeah," I say. A few, actually.

"They yank out everything, right?" Janet says. "I saw a special on the Discovery Channel — they cut out all the organs and weigh 'em. Even the brain."

Now she's leaning over the coffin, her face inches from that of her dead brother. I am gulping deep breaths, endeavoring not to keel over.

"Amazing," she's saying, "the way they put him back together. You can't hardly tell, can you? Jack?"

"No, you can't."

"Well, maybe they do autopsies different in the islands."

"Maybe so," I say.

"Hmmmm." Janet, peering intently.

In about three minutes I've sucked all the oxygen out of the room. Time to go. I prefer not to asphyxiate on a dead man's perfume.

"Let's get this over with," I say.

"What?"

"You know."

Janet steps away from the casket. "Okay. Do it."

My hands shake as I fumble with the buttons, starting at the neck. Inanely, I try to open Jimmy Stoma's silk shirt without wrinkling it — like it matters for the crematorium.

Finally the shirt is undone. The singer's chest looks tan, the fine hair bleached golden by long days in the tropics. Undimmed by death is the most prominent of Jimmy's tattoos, a florid sternum-to-navel depiction of a nude blonde rapturously encoiled by a phallus-headed anaconda.

But that's not what grabs my eye.

"Strange," I mutter.

The singer's sister touches my sleeve.

"Jack," she whispers, "where are the autopsy stitches?"

An excellent question.

5

I wouldn't be working at the *Union-Register* if it weren't for a pig-eyed, greasy-necked oaf named Orrin Van Gelder.

He was an elected commissioner of Gadsden County, Florida, where his specialty was diverting multimillion-dollar government contracts to favored cronies in exchange for cash kickbacks.

Fortunately for me, Van Gelder was an exceptionally dull-witted crook. At the time of his most carefree and imprudent bid-rigging, I was covering Gadsden County for a small local newspaper. I'd like to say it was my own intrepid investigating that ensnared the corrupt commissioner — that's what my editor proclaimed in the letter nominating me for a big journalism award.

The truth, however, is that I nailed Orrin Van Gelder simply by picking up a ringing telephone. A voice at the other end said:

"Some prick politician is trying to shake me down for a hundred large."

The voice belonged to Walter Dubb, whose occupation was selling buses outfitted for the handicapped. Gadsden County was seeking to purchase fifteen such vehicles; a worthy expenditure, all had agreed. Four competing companies began preparing bids.

Shortly thereafter, Walter Dubb, who sold more handicapped-customized buses than anybody in the South, was approached by Mrs. Orrin Van Gelder for a private lunch invitation. In thirty years of selling transit fleets to municipal governments, Dubb had been shaken down by a multitude of public officials, but Orrin Van Gelder was the first to use his wife as a bagperson.

"Here's the deal, Walt," Pamela Van Gelder informed him over crabcakes at a local catfish joint. "Even if you're not the lowest bidder, Orrin will see to it the county buys your buses, and *only* your buses. His fee is five percent."

"Fee?"

Mrs. Van Gelder smiled. "Call it what you like."

"I call it a corncobbing," said Walter Dubb.

The commissioner's wife didn't flinch. "My husband's a reasonable man. He'll settle for a flat hundred grand, plus one of those fancy Dodge minivans with the electric lift."

"Like hell."

"For Orrin's mother," Pamela Van Gelder explained.

"She's in a wheelchair?" Walter Dubb, experiencing a pang of sympathy.

"No, she's a whale. Can't hoist her fat ass

up and down the steps."

The bus contract was worth $3 million and change, so Dubb had some thinking to do. Dubb didn't object to reasonable briberies but he was disgusted by Van Gelder's greedy gall. So, one Saturday morning, Walter called up the city desk to nark out the commissioner. A preoccupied editor cut him off mid-sentence and transferred him to my line. (The only reason I answered is because I thought it was my then-girlfriend calling to explain why she hadn't yet returned from Vancouver, where she was shooting a panty-hose commercial. She never did come home.)

After hearing Walter Dubb's story, I made a couple of calls. The following Wednesday night, Commissioner Gelder and his co-conspiring spouse sat down for dinner with Walter Dubb and a man named George Pannini, whom Dubb had introduced convincingly as the vice president of his bus-customizing division. In fact, Mr. Pannini was employed by the Federal Bureau of Investigation, and was wearing both a sidearm and a microphone.

I was sitting at another table with a photographer, who was discreetly shooting pictures over my left shoulder. Orrin Van Gelder, who had the appetite of a tapeworm, had ordered a T-bone steak, stone crabs, a dozen oysters, a tureen of potato soup and a whole fried onion the size of a softball. His gluttony would be fully documented in my story the next day, along with his crime. The decibel level in the restaurant made eavesdropping difficult, but the gaps in conversation would be filled in, colorfully, by a broadcast-quality FBI tape recording.

The bust went down in the men's room, where Agent Pannini had lured Van Gelder with the promise of a $25,000 down payment on the kickback. It was at a urinal, with one hand on the cash and the other hand on his pecker, that the commissioner was arrested for bribery.

It was a glorious scandal, and my byline stayed on the front page for a solid week, a personal record that stands to this day. Even better, the heavy news coverage flushed from the muck three other vendors who'd been hustled by the commissioner. Each of the aggrieved businessmen consented to an interview, including the fellow who'd sold $1.7 million worth of self-cleaning toilets to the county airport. Van Gelder had insisted that in addition to his customary cash kickback, he wanted a deluxe model self-cleaning commode installed in his private master bathroom. The fixture later malfunctioned while the commissioner himself was enthroned upon it, an errant geyser of bleach scalding both buttocks and his scrotum.

The story, needless to say, was golden. Orrin Van Gelder wound up copping a plea and doing nineteen months at Talladega. I wound up winning that journalism award and being wooed away to a bigger place and a igger newspaper, where I did some pretty decent work until the shitstorm struck.

And here I am.

Janet drops me off at the donut shop.

I offer to make some phone calls and find out about her brother's so-called autopsy. She's not listening.

"Damn, I almost forgot," she says, and starts to drive away.

"Hey, where you going?"

She hits the brakes. "Back to the funeral place. I've got something that belongs with Jimmy. Something special he gave me."

"Can I ask what?"

She reaches behind the seat and pulls out a white paper shopping bag. She opens it to display a rare gem — a genuine long-playing 33 rpm album. The jacket is faded, and one corner appears to have been gnawed by a puppy. I'm smiling because I recognize the record. *The Soft Parade.*

"1969," I say.

"Jimmy loved the Doors. This one was his favorite — he gave it to me for my birthday." Janet studies the band's photograph on the cover and asks, "How old was Morrison when he died?"

You bet I know the answer. "Twenty-seven."

"Jimmy told me where it happened, but I forgot."

"In a bathtub."

Janet busts out with a laugh. "No, I meant where, like what city."

Now we're both laughing. "Paris," I say.

Janet gathers herself. "I remember now. My brother went to see the grave. Listen, I better get rolling before they light the bonfire, or whatever."

"You're putting the album in the coffin?"

"Yeah." Sheepishly she slips it back into the bag. "I mean, I've got to do *something*. Cleo won't ever know."

"Janet, don't you think you should tell somebody about what we saw. Maybe it's not too late to —"

"I don't know." She shrugs drearily. "I don't know anything except Jimmy's gone." And off she goes, peeling rubber.

Moments later I'm in a phone booth talking to my friend Pete, a forensic pathologist at the county Medical Examiner's Office. When I tell him about James Bradley Stomarti's lack of autopsy stitches, he gives a sour chuckle.

"Whenever there's a death in a foreign country, it's dicey. The protocol drives you nuts — plus everybody wants to be so damn polite about the cutting."

"What do I do?"

"Try to stop the cremation," he suggests.

"You could get a court order, but for that you'll need immediate family."

"How about a sister?"

"Perfect. But she's gotta call the State Attorney's Office and get them to find a judge. Then the judge needs to send a deputy out to the funeral parlor right away, because once your boy goes into the oven —"

"Adios."

"That's right, Jack. Case closed."

Next I try Rick Tarkington, a state prosecutor who once helped me on a story about a mob murder in exchange for tickets to a Springsteen concert. Being a rock fan, he'll probably remember Jimmy and the Slut Puppies.

Unfortunately, Rick's surly and unhelpful secretary says he's in depositions and cannot be interrupted.

"It's an emergency," I plead. "Can't you give him a message?"

"Not today, sir. I'm leaving early for a doctor's 'pointment."

"Oh? Something serious, I hope."

Janet Thrush is my only chance. The battered Miata is still parked in the lot when I return to the funeral home. After a quick search I find her among the mourners at an open-casket viewing in one of the lavender-scented chapels. According to the remembrance cards being distributed at the door, the deceased is Eugene Marvin Brandt, who was born in 1918.

Janet is quite a standout in her tube top, poised beside a spray of gladiolus and tulips. She's chatting with a spry-looking elderly woman dressed in widow black.

"Gertie, this is Jack," Janet says. "Jack, this is Mrs. Gertie Brandt. Gene's wife."

Gene?

"Nice of you to come." Gertie shakes my hand. She is dry-eyed and composed, leading me to conclude that her husband had been ill for some time, and that his death might have been a blessing. Either that or he was a miserable jerk and she's glad to be rid of him.

Gertie asks, "How do you know my Gene?"

"Professionally," I say. "It was years ago, but he made quite an impression."

Gertie smiles fondly. "He always does." She gestures toward the coffin. "Did you see him? They did a wonderful job."

"He looks real peaceful," Janet chimes in. "And handsome, too," she adds with a wink.

Gertie beams. "Go on, Jack. Have a look."

So, like a moron, I'm standing here admiring a dead stranger. It would appear that Eugene Marvin Brandt is heading for the pearly gates in his favorite golf ensemble, including spikes. Janet appears at my side and squeezes my arm.

"You're a good sport," she whispers.

71

"And you are one twisted sister."

"I didn't want to be alone."

"So you crash a viewing?"

"Everyone's been so nice," she says. "What a sweet-looking man, no?"

With her chin Janet points at the eternally recumbent Mr. Brandt. "Guess what he did for a living!"

"We need to talk."

"Catheters. He sold them."

"That would have been my second guess."

"And other medical supplies," Janet adds.

This room, too, is rapidly emptying of oxygen. I take an audible gulp and clutch the rim of the coffin.

"Cancer," says Janet Thrush. "Case you were wondering."

"Can we go now?"

"Cancer of the prostrate."

"Prostate." My voice is raspy and ancient. I'm wondering if it's medically possible to choke to death on the scent of stale flowers.

Janet says, "Once I had a noodle cut out of my armpit."

"A nodule, you mean."

"Whatever. Main thing, it was benign. But still it freaked me out — somethin' growing in my armpit!"

Her words are spiraling down a long gray tunnel. Any second now, I'll be fainting. No joke, I'm going to pitch face-forward into the casket of a dead catheter salesman wearing golf spikes.

"Jack, you don't look so hot."

Firmly Janet steers me out the door, into the fresh air. We sit on the grass under a black olive tree near a small stagnant pond. Slowly I lie back and squeeze my eyelids shut. Two stiffs in one day, Sweet Jesus!

A breeze springs up and I proceed to drift off for an hour, maybe longer. The next thing I know, a cold soda can is being pressed into my right hand. I raise up and take a sip and my eyes tear up from the carbonation. Janet is next to me, sitting cross-legged. Folded in her lap is the white paper shopping bag, now empty.

"You did it," I say, pointing at the bag.

"What?"

"*The Soft Parade*. Somewhere Jimmy is smiling, I'm sure."

Touching two fingertips to my forehead, Janet says, "Jeez, you're in a cold sweat."

"I'm a wimp," I admit. "The sight of poor old Gene did me in. Gene, all decked out for the eternal dogleg."

"Drink the Coke. You'll feel better."

And soon I do. Taking her by the hand, I lead her back toward the funeral home. "Listen, I checked it out. As Jimmy's sister you can stop the cremation. We'll get a court order," I tell her. "You're a blood relative. You can demand a proper autopsy."

"No, Jack —" Janet, pulling free as we enter the front door.

"Meanwhile we've got to put the fear of Almighty God into young Ellis. Scare him into thinking you're going to sue his ass off if he goes ahead with it today —"

"No," Janet says again. She looks sad and exhausted, holding the empty shopping bag to her breasts. "Jack, it's too late."

"What are you talking about?"

"When you fell asleep, I went inside. Back to that room," she says. "He's gone. It's too late."

"Goddammit."

"I know."

I sag against a planter featuring a lovely plastic rhododendron.

"But what about the album? I thought you put it in with —"

"Too late. So I threw it in the pond — it was a stupid idea, anyway," Janet says. "I mean, the record's vinyl. All it's gonna do is melt all over his damn bones."

I'm thinking Jimmy wouldn't mind.

"Come on," she says, sniffling. "Let's get outta here."

"In a minute."

I see oily-fingered Ellis alone in his cubicle, intently tapping on a portable calculator. Janet hangs back while I peer in the doorway.

Ellis quickly turns his head sideways while simultaneously swiveling his chair toward the

74

wall. "Can I help you?" he squeaks over his shoulder.

"Nice earring, dickhead. But it looked better on Mr. Stomarti."

Ellis claps one hand over his right ear in a futile effort to conceal the stolen diamond.

"I don't know what you're talking about!" he yelps. "Doesn't anybody ever knock anymore!"

6

Emma is off on Mondays, but this can't wait.

The phone rings busy for an hour so I do the unthinkable and drive to her apartment, a duplex on the west side. I know how to get there because I gave her a ride on the day her car got stolen from the newspaper's parking lot. The car was a silver two-door Acura, a gift from her father. The cretin who drove off with it later tried to rob the drive-through window of a bank. He was shot by a guard and died bleeding copiously on Emma's gray leather upholstery. The car was impounded as evidence.

So I agreed to give Emma a lift, which was risky. I feared she might be so upset that she would require consoling, which I couldn't offer. To show sympathy would have thrown slack into a relationship that had to remain as taut as a garrote. If I was to save Emma from the newspaper life, I couldn't become someone in whom she confided, or even (God forbid) a casual friend.

As it turned out, the drive proved uneventful. Emma was remarkably philosophical about the dead robber in her Acura; at no time did she appear in need of a hug or even a pat on the hand. She said she'd spoken to her father and he'd offered to buy her another car once the insurance money came through. She'd told him thanks just the same, but she was a grownup and it was time she paid for her own wheels. Good for you, I said mildly. Then, dropping her off at the duplex, I heard myself asking if she needed a ride to work the following morning. What possessed me, I cannot say. Luckily, Emma already had lined up a rental.

Her apartment is a block off the main highway, but it takes two passes to find the right side street. In the driveway sits Emma's new car, a champagne-colored Camry with the paper license tag still taped in the rear window. Parked on the swale by the road is a familiar black Jeep Cherokee. It belongs to Juan Rodriguez, a sportswriter at the paper. He also happens to be my best friend.

Juan recently began dating Emma, an unnerving development. There was a time when Juan and I could go have a couple beers and bitch self-righteously about the newspaper. Not now. Whatever I might say about the deplorable state of journalism would come off as a rap against Emma, and I don't want to offend Juan. However, his interest in Emma is vexing — for two years he listened to me rail about her, and still he asked her out.

She's different in all ways from the other three women that Juan dates — one is a professional figure skater, one is an orthopedic surgeon and one is a halftime dancer for the Miami Heat basketball team. Contrary to appearances, Juan is in serious pursuit of a lifetime partner. Maybe Emma's the one, but a selfish part of me hopes not. It would suck dead toads to have my best friend romantically involved with my editor.

The question of the moment: Have Juan and Emma started a sexual relationship? If so, there's a strong possibility that I'm about to interrupt an act of copulation, which is hardly ever a good idea. In Emma's windows the blinds are open, but no movement is visible except for a bony calico cat, grooming itself on a sill. Apprehensively I check my wristwatch — at four-thirty in the afternoon, it's more likely that Juan and Emma are screwing than watching *Oprah*.

But what the hell. This is more important. While James Bradley Stomarti might be ashes, serious work lies ahead. The whole true story of his life and death remains untold, and Emma must be made aware of our duty to set things straight. I walk up and ring the bell. No reply. The duplex has a corroded, wall-mounted air conditioner that sounds like a bulldozer at the bottom of a canal. I try knocking, first with knuckles and then with the heel of my hand. Even the cat refuses to react.

"Shit," I say to myself.

Halfway to the car, I hear the apartment door opening — it's Emma, and to my relief she appears neither disheveled nor recently aroused. She's wearing old jeans, a short white T-shirt and her reading glasses. Her freshly trimmed bangs are parted, and the rest of her hair is pulled back with a navy blue elastic band.

"Jack?"

"Is it a bad time?"

Briskly she descends the steps. "I *thought* I heard knocking —"

"I tried to call but it kept ringing busy."

"Sorry. I was on the computer," Emma says. I think I believe her.

"What's up?" she asks.

"The Stomarti obit."

Emma looks surprised. Even when riven with errors, obituaries rarely cause headaches for editors. Legally, it is impossible to libel a dead person.

Hurriedly I tell Emma about Janet Thrush's phone call and the visit to the funeral home and the absence of autopsy stitches in Jimmy Stoma's corpse. Emma listens with an annoying trace of restlessness. At any moment I expect my buddy Juan to come sauntering out the door, zipping up his pants.

When I'm done with my pitch, Emma purses her lips and says, "You think we should run a correction?"

79

Christ, she's serious. I bite back the impulse to ridicule. Instead I lower my eyes and find myself gazing at Emma's bare feet, which I've never seen before. Her toenails are painted in alternating colors of cherry red and tangerine, which seems drastically out of character.

"Jack?"

"There's nothing to correct," I explain evenly. "The story wasn't wrong; it just wasn't all there."

"What do you think happened to the guy?"

"I think I'd like to see a coroner's report from the Bahamas."

"How would we handle that?" Emma is beginning to fidget. She glances over her shoulder but still hasn't acknowledged Juan's presence inside the apartment.

"We would handle that," I say, "by me flying to Nassau and interviewing the doctor who examined Jimmy Stoma's body."

Emma looks exasperated, as if I'm the one who is confused. Turns out I am.

She says, "No, what I meant was — Jack, you can't do it. You've got to finish Old Man Polk right away. They say he's fading fast. . . ."

"What?"

MacArthur Polk once owned the *Union-Register*. If the clippings are accurate, he has been dying off and on for seventeen years. I am the latest reporter assigned to pre-write an obituary.

"Emma, are you serious?" My disgust is genuine; the incredulity, feigned.

She removes a green silk scarf from her back pocket and nervously begins twisting it like an eel around one of her slender wrists.

"Listen, Jack, if you really think there's something there —"

"I do. I *know* there's something there."

"Okay, then, tomorrow you get all your notes together and we'll go see Rhineman. Maybe he's got somebody he can pull free to make some phone calls."

Rhineman is the Metro editor, the hard-news guy. My stomach knots up.

"Emma, *I* can make the calls. I'm perfectly capable of working the phones."

Stiffly she edges back toward the apartment. "Jack," she says, "we don't do foul play. We don't do murder investigations. We do obituaries."

"Please. A couple days is all I'm asking."

I can't believe I actually said *please*.

The retreat continues, Emma shaking her head. "I'm sorry — let's talk at the office, okay? First thing in the morning." She reaches the door and disappears as lithely as a ferret down a hole.

I sit in her driveway for several minutes, letting the rage burn out. Eventually, the urge to grab a tire iron and mess up her new champagne-colored Camry passes. Why am I surprised by what happened here? What the hell was I thinking?

Driving home, I turn up the bass for the Slut Puppies. I find myself entertaining a ribald image of Juan Rodriguez trussed with silk scarves to the bedposts while being straddled boisterously by Emma.

Emma, with her goddamn two-tone jellybean toenails.

I live alone in a decent fourth-floor apartment not far from the beach. Three different women have lived here with me, Anne being the most recent and by far the most patient. A snapshot of her in a yellow tank suit remains attached by a magnet to the refrigerator door. Inside the refrigerator is half a bucket of chicken wings, a six-pack of beer and a triangular slab of molding cheddar. Tonight the beer is all that interests me, and I'm on my third when somebody knocks.

"Yo, Obituary Boy? You home?"

When Juan opens the door, I salute from the couch. He grabs a beer for himself and sits down in one of the matching faded armchairs. "The Marlins are playing," he says.

"That's a matter of opinion."

"Where's the TV?" Juan motions to the vacant space in the center of the wall unit. "Don't tell me you launched it off the balcony again."

That sometimes happens when I try to watch music videos. "It's pathetic," I say to my friend. "I'm not proud of myself."

"Who was it this time?"

"One of those 'boy bands.' I don't re-member which." I roll the cool sweaty bottle across my forehead.

Juan looks a little uptight.

"You're how old now — thirty-four?" I ask.

"Not tonight, Jack."

"You should be on top of the world, man. You've already hung in there longer than Keith Moon or John Belushi." I can't help myself.

Juan says, "Why do you do this?"

I put a Stones record on the stereo because you can't go wrong with the Stones. Juan knows most of the songs, even the early stuff — he has fully acculturated himself since arriving in the 1981 exodus from the port of Mariel, Cuba. He was sixteen at the time, four years older than the sister who accompanied him on an old Key West lobster boat. They were with a group of thirty-seven refugees, among whom were a handful of vicious criminals that Castro yanked out of prison and shipped to Miami as a practical joke.

Everyone at the paper knows Juan came over on the boatlift. What they don't know is what happened forty miles at sea in the black of night — Juan told me the story after too many martinis. One of the convicts decided to have some fun with Juan's sister and one of the others offered to stand watch, and neither of them paid enough attention to the girl's skinny brother, who somehow got his hands on a five-inch screwdriver. Many hours later, when the lobster boat docked at Key West, the immigration officer counted only thirty-five passengers, including Juan and his sister in a ripped dress. The others said nothing about what had taken place on the voyage.

Juan takes a slug of beer and says to me: "Good piece today."

"Come on, man."

"What?"

"It's a goddamn obit."

"Hey, it was interesting. I remember hearing the Slut Puppies on the radio," he says. " 'Trouser Troll' was kinda catchy."

"I thought so, too." I'm eager to tell Juan about the Jimmy Stoma mystery, but I'm wondering if he already knows. If he does, it means he and Emma are tighter than I thought.

"Did she tell you?" I ask.

"Who? Oh — Emma?"

"No, Madeleine fucking Albright." I set my empty bottle on the floor. "Look, I hope I didn't interrupt anything this afternoon. Normally, I'd never —"

"You didn't." Juan grins. "I was helping with her computer. She got a new browser."

"I'll bet she did."

"Honest. That's all."

"Then why didn't you pop out and say hi?"

Juan says, "She asked me not to."

That's just like Emma, worrying that Juan's presence as my friend and her potential sex partner would somehow undermine her primacy in the editor-reporter relationship.

"Hell," I say, "I thought she had you lashed to the bed."

"I wish." Juan, smiling again. Sometimes he's too charming for his own good.

"Did she tell you or not?"

"Why you stopped by? Sure, she told me."

"And did she tell you what she said?"

Juan nods sympathetically. "It really blows."

"That's why I'm drinking."

"Three beers is not drinking, Jack." He has counted the bottles on the floor. "Three beers is sulking."

"What should I do about Emma?" I rise out of a slouch. "Wait — why the hell'm I asking *you?*"

"Because I'm wise beyond my years?"

"Do me a favor," I say. "If you're screwing her, please don't tell me. Just change the subject and I'll get the message."

"Deal," says Juan with a decisive nod. "Hey, there's a rumor Marino's coming out of retirement!"

"Very smooth, asshole."

"Jack, I'm not sleeping with Emma."

"Excellent," I say, "then you're free to advise me. This woman intends to dump Jimmy Stoma on the Metro desk. *My* story, Juan, and this cold-blooded wench wants to give it away!"

"And I thought the Sports desk was a pit."

I hear myself asking, "What can you possibly see in her?"

Juan hesitates. I know he's at no loss for words because he is a fine writer, much better than I am, even in his second language.

"Emma's different than the others, Jack."

"So is a two-headed scorpion."

"You want, I'll talk to her."

"No!"

"Just trying to help."

"You don't understand," I say. "There's a complicated dynamic between Emma and me."

Juan's right foot is tapping to the music; Jagger, singing of street-fighting men.

"It's my story," I grumble, "and she won't let me do it."

"I'm sorry, man." Juan knows what happened to me, the whole odious business. He knows where I stand at the newspaper. He calls me "Obituary Boy" to keep things light, but he truly feels lousy about the situation. It can't be helped. He's a star and I'm a lump of jackal shit.

"Quit," he says earnestly.

"That's the best you can do?"

Juan has been advising me to resign ever since my demotion to the Death page. "That's exactly what Emma wants — didn't she tell you? It's what they *all* want. So I'm not quitting, Juan, until the day they beg me to stay."

He's not up for one of my legendary rants. I can't imagine why. "Tell me about Jimmy Stoma," he says.

So I tell him everything I know.

"Okay," he says after a moment's thought, "let's say there was no autopsy. What does that really prove? It's the Bahamas, Jack. I'm guessing they know a drowned scuba diver when they see one."

"But what if —"

"Anyway, who'd want to kill a has-been rock star?" Juan asks, not cruelly.

"Maybe nobody," I admit, "but I won't know for sure unless Emma cuts me free for a few days."

Juan sits forward and rubs his chin. I trust his judgment. He would have made a terrific news reporter if he didn't love baseball so much.

"I've got something to show you," he says, bouncing to his feet, "but I left it in the car."

He's out the door and back in two minutes. He hands me a printout of the Jimmy Stoma obituary that will run in tomorrow's *New York Times*. The header says: **James Stomarti, 39, Rambunctious Rock Performer.**

Although the story isn't half as long as mine, I refuse to read it. The *Times* has the most elegant obituary writing in the world, and I'm in no mood to be humbled.

"Look at the damn story," Juan insists.

"Later."

"Yours was better."

"Yeah, right."

"Pitiful," Juan says. "You're a child."

I peek at the first paragraph:

James Bradley Stomarti, once the hell-raising front man for the 1980s rock group Jimmy and the Slut Puppies, died last week on a laid-back boating excursion in the Bahamas.

I mutter to Juan, "The lede's not bad."

"Check out what Pop-Singer Wifey has to say. Check out the premonition," he says, pointing.

"What premonition?"

Six paragraphs into the obit, there it is:

Mr. Stomarti's wife, the singer Cleo Rio, said she had been apprehensive about her husband's plan to explore the sunken plane wreck, even though he was an experienced diver.

"I had a wicked bad vibe about that dive," Ms. Rio said. "I begged Jimmy not to go. He'd been down sick with food poisoning from some bad fish chowder. He was in so much pain he could hardly put his tank on. God, I wish I could've stopped him."

I can't believe what I'm reading.

Juan says, "I'm guessing the lovely Ms. Rio didn't tell you the same story. You wouldn't have passed up a chance to work the phrase 'bad fish chowder' into an obituary."

"Or even 'wicked bad vibe,' " I say, indignantly waving the pages. "The girl never said anything about this. She said she was lounging around the boat, reading a magazine and working on her tan. Didn't sound the least bit worried about her old man diving a plane wreck."

"Something's screwy," Juan agrees.

"Any brilliant ideas?"

"You've already made up your mind, no?"

My eyes are drawn again to the *Times* obit. I am relieved to see that the reporter had no more luck than I did in locating the Bahamian coroner. Also missing: any mention of Cleo Rio's *Shipwrecked Heart* project. Boy, will she be pissed.

"Jack, what are you going to do?" Juan presses.

"The story, of course. It's mine and I'm writing it."

"How? Emma won't back down. . . ."

He's right. She won't back down, she'll

crumble. That's the plan. Juan looks worried, but I can't say whether it's for me or for her. Maybe both.

"What're you going to do?" he asks again.

"Well, tomorrow I plan to call in sick," I say.

"Ugh-oh."

"So I can attend a funeral."

"I fucking knew it."

"You're smiling again, you dog."

"Yeah," Juan says. "I guess I am."

7

Sure, it would be a kick to write for one of those big serious dailies in Miami, St. Petersburg, or even (in my dreams) Washington or New York. But that's not in the cards. This is my fifth newspaper job and surely the last. I am increasingly unfit for the trade.

The *Union-Register* was founded in 1931 by MacArthur Polk's father, who upon retirement passed it to his only son, who kept it both solvent and respectable until three years ago, when he unexpectedly sold out to the Maggad-Feist Publishing Group for $47 million in cash, stock and options. It was the foulest day in the newspaper's history.

Maggad-Feist is a publicly traded company that owns twenty-seven dailies around the country. The chairman and CEO, young Race Maggad III, believes newspapers can prosper handsomely without practicing distinguished journalism, as distinguished journalism tends to cost money. Race Maggad III believes the easiest way to boost a newspaper's profits is to cut back on the actual gathering of news. For obvious reasons, he was not a beloved figure at any of the twenty-six other papers owned by Maggad-

Feist. He would not be beloved at ours, either, although only one reporter would dare stand up and say so to his face — at a shareholders' meeting, no less, with a stringer for the *Wall Street Journal* in the audience. The remarks were brief but shockingly coarse, causing young polo-playing Race Maggad III to lose his composure in front of five hundred edgy investors. For his effrontery the reporter could not be fired (or so the paper's attorneys advised). He could, however, be removed from the prestigious investigations team and exiled to the obituary beat, with the expectation he would resign in bitter humiliation.

He did not.

Consequently, he's now saddled with the task of memorializing the very sonofabitch who brought this plague upon the house. MacArthur Polk is rumored to be dying again.

I keep a file of obituaries of prominent persons who are still alive. When one of them dies, the "canned" obit is topped with a few new paragraphs and rushed into print. Usually I update a pre-written obituary when the subject is reported as "ailing," the standard newspaper euphemism for "at death's door."

MacArthur Polk has been ailing since 1983, which is one reason I haven't bothered doing a canned obit. The old bastard isn't really dying; he just enjoys the fuss made over him at hospitals. For about the eleventh time he has been admitted to the ICU at Charity, so Emma is jumpy. Although Polk no longer owns the *Union-Register*, he is a community icon and, more significantly, a major shareholder of Maggad-Feist. When his obituary finally appears, it will be read intently by persons high up the management ladder, persons who might hold sway over Emma's future. Consequently, she feels she has a stake in the old man's send-off. She wants it to be sparkling and moving and unforgettable. She wants a masterpiece, and she wants me to write it.

So I've deliberately shown no interest whatsoever. My own stake in MacArthur Polk's death is *nada*. I could sit down with a stack of clippings and in an hour knock off an obit that was humorous, colorful, poignant — a gem in every way. And it would be filed in the computer until the day the old man finally croaked, when it would be electronically shipped to another reporter for freshening. The story would appear under his or her byline on the front page. At the very end, in parenthesized italics, I might or might not be given credit for "contributing" to the research.

That's how it goes around here. The moment Page One becomes a possibility, it's not my story anymore. Nonetheless, I always make sure to type out my byline in boldface letters:

By Jack Tagger
Staff Writer

To delete my name from the top of the story, Emma must first highlight it with the Define key. I like to think it's a chore that afflicts her with a twinge of guilt, but who knows. She has her orders. She's heard about me and Race Maggad III; everyone in the building has.

The fact that I haven't resigned must chafe Emma, except on those rare days when she needs a first-rate obituary writer, as she does for MacArthur Polk. One measly fact error, one misspelling, one careless turn of a phrase could jeopardize Emma's career, or so she believes. Old Man Polk is like a god, she once said to me. He *was* this newspaper.

Which he greedily sold to Wall Street heathens, I pointed out, causing Emma to cringe and put a finger to her lips.

Every morning she asks how the old man's obit is coming along, and every morning I tell her I haven't started writing it yet, which drives her batty. Today I'm still in bed when the phone rings.

"Jack, it's Emma."

"Morning, sunshine."

"Mr. Polk took a turn for the worse," she says.

"Me, too. What a coincidence."

"I'm not kidding."

"Neither am I. Some sorta stomach virus," I say. "I won't be coming in today."

Long pause — Emma, grappling with mixed feelings. As much as she would revel in a peaceful Jack-free morning, she needs me there. "Did you call a doctor?" she inquires.

"Soon as I get my head out of the commode. I promise."

The unsavory image provokes another pause at Emma's end.

"Talk to you later," I say.

"Jack, wait."

Here I moan like a terminal dysentery victim.

"They put Old Man Polk on a machine over at Charity," says Emma. "They say his heart and lungs are failing."

"What kind of machine?"

"I don't know. For heaven's sakes."

"Emma, how old is he now? Ninety-five, ninety-six?" I picture her seething because she thinks I don't even know the old geezer's age.

Tersely she says: "Eighty-eight."

The same as Orville Redenbacher when he died!

"And how old is the new Mrs. Polk?" I

ask. "Thirty-six, if I recall."

"What are you saying?"

"I'm saying the old man isn't going to die at Charity with a tube up his cock. He's gonna die at home in the sack, with a grin on his face and a jellybean jar full of Viagras on the nightstand. Trust me."

Emma's tone turns cold. "You don't sound very sick to me, Jack."

"Oh, it's quite a nasty bug. I'll spare you the grisly details."

"You'll be back in the office tomorrow?"

"Don't count on it," I say. "Gotta run!"

St. Stephen's is the trendiest church on the beach. I arrive early and sit in a pew near the door. In the front row I spy a snow-white noggin that belongs to either Cleo Rio or Johnny Winter in drag. Propped on a velvet-cloaked table in the center of the stage are a red Stratocaster and a small brass urn.

I count five TV crews, including one from VH1, hanging around near the confessionals. It's an eclectic, funky flow of mourners — sunburned dock rats and dive captains; pallid, body-pierced clubbers too young to be Slut Puppies fans; chunky, gray-streaked rockers from primeval bands like Styx and Supertramp; anonymous, half-stoned studio musicians with bad tattoo jobs and black jeans; and a sprinkling of pretty, unattached women in dark glasses, who I assume to be admirers and ex-lovers of the late Jimmy Stoma. One person I don't see is Janet Thrush — maybe Cleo told her not to come, or maybe Janet felt she'd be uncomfortable. Another person not in attendance is the tall, shimmery-haired guy from the elevator at Cleo and Jimmy's condo. It makes me curious; if he were a family friend, wouldn't he attend the funeral?

The church is nearly full when the notables begin arriving — the Van Halen brothers, the wild percussionist Ray Cooper, Joan Jett, Courtney Love, Teena Marie, Ziggy Marley, Michael Penn and an auburn-haired beauty who was either a Bangle or a Go-Go, I'm not sure which. It's a colorful group and the TV guys are hopping around like meth-crazed marmosets.

The last to enter St. Stephen's are the surviving ex–Slut Puppies: bass players Danny Gitt and Tito Negraponte, followed by Jimmy's keyboardist and diving buddy Jay Burns, who in midlife has come to project an unsettling resemblance to Newt Gingrich with a ponytail. Missing from the gathering is the band's notoriously moody lead guitarist, Peter P. Proust, who three years ago was fatally stabbed in a bizarre confrontation with a sidewalk Santa Claus on Lexington Avenue in Manhattan. As for a drummer, the Slut Puppies went through a dozen and, according to the trades, not one departed on amiable terms.

Jay Burns and the two bass players walk stiffly up the aisle and file into the pew where Cleo Rio waits. Scanning the crowd, it occurs to me that this doesn't look or smell like the funeral of a man who turned his back on the record business. The church is packed with musicians and ripe with reefer.

As the priest instructs us to rise, two more women slip in the back door. They sit near me — one is black and one is Latin, both in their early twenties. Pals of Cleo, I'm guessing. The black woman notices the notebook in my hand and reacts with a shaded smile. "I'm with the newspaper," I whisper. She nods, and passes the information to her friend, who is mouthing along to the Lord's Prayer. Afterwards, the priest, an earnest Father Riordan, begins reflecting upon the short but full life of James Bradley Stomarti. It is painfully obvious to the whole assembly that Father Riordan never met the deceased, but he's giving it the old college try.

I lean over to the two women and ask, not too smoothly, "Were you friends, or just fans?"

"Both," the Latin girl says, flaring an eyebrow.

"Can I get your names?"

Maria Bonilla and Ajax, no last name.

"We're singers," Ajax says.

"Backup singers," Maria adds. "We worked with Jimmy."

I'm skeptical, since neither one could have been older than fourteen when his last CD came out.

"No kidding? On which album?"

The women glance glumly at each other, Ajax saying: "The one nobody's ever gonna hear."

At the podium, a former A&R man from MCA is telling a humorous anecdote about Jimmy blasting a mixing board with an Uzi during the recording of *A Painful Burning Sensation*. Normally I'd be taking down every word, but today the notebook is a prop.

To the backup singers I say, "Yeah, I heard he was working on some great new stuff."

"Not from us you didn't," sniffs Maria.

Again the door opens, and into the church strolls T. O. "Timmy" Buckminster, our so-called music critic. I shrink into the pew and lower my head, hoping not to be seen. Obviously the smarmy little shitweasel is here to cover the funeral — or, more accurately, the widow. He couldn't care less about Jimmy Stoma.

Buckminster boldly advances to the front of the church and squeezes into the second row, behind Cleo Rio and the former Slut Puppies. Danny Gitt rises and threads his way to the podium, where he makes a weak joke about why the band needed two bass players instead of one — something about alternating time-shares at a rehab clinic. The line draws a polite chuckle. Danny Gitt goes on to tell a few stories about Jimmy Stoma's wacky sense of humor, his unsung generosity, his passion for performing live onstage. I jot down a couple of quotes in order to maintain credibility with Ajax and Maria, who shoot me a look every so often. I'm waiting for a lull so I can quiz them about Jimmy's last project — undoubtedly the secret, unfinished album his sister mentioned. . . .

A murmur rolls like a soft breaker through the crowd, and I look up to see Cleo Rio, dagger-straight in front of the altar. She's wearing a diaphanous, ankle-length black dress and a Madonna-style headset microphone. The bald, bomber-jacketed goon I saw at the apartment hops the rail and hands her an acoustic guitar. Cleo waits while the TV crews jostle into place.

"Lord Jesus," Ajax says to Maria.

And Jimmy's widow begins to strum and sing:

Who do you have at the end of the day,
Who do you touch in the deep of the night?
Me, you've got me.
Who do you reach for when the clouds
    go gray,
Who do you hold when no end's in sight?
Me, you need me.

Cleo's voice is weak and watery, but she affects a hard raspy edge on the last beat of each line. As best as I can tell, she's playing only three chords — an A minor, a barred F and a G — and struggling mightily. On the refrain the chords are identical but the sequence is reversed, Cleo now half-snarling:

Me, me, what about me?
You got yours but what about me?
Look in the mirror, what do I see?
Pretty little number, used to be me.

I hear Maria saying: "You believe this unholy shit?"

It is astoundingly tacky — Jimmy Stoma's widow has turned his funeral into a promotional gig. The guys from her record label must be turning cartwheels.

"Bitch," Ajax mutters.

"Whore," Maria says.

Cleo's style is grating — thank God she's only got the one hit. When she finally warbles the last note of "Me," a jittery silence grips the church. Eventually Tito Negraponte starts to clap, followed tentatively by the other ex–Slut Puppies. Pretty soon the place fills with applause that I interpret as unanimous relief that Cleo's solo is over.

Except she's still holding the guitar.

She clears her throat and sips from a glass of water ferried to her honey-skinned hand by the neckless bouncer. She says, "Here's a number —"

"Lord help us," groans Ajax, under her breath.

"Here's a number," Cleo says, "that me and Jimmy wrote just a few months ago. It's the title cut on my new CD and, well, I'm just bummed because it turned out so awesome and he's not around to hear me do it."

"Lucky him," says Maria to her friend. "Let's roll."

Ajax shakes her head. "Hang on a minute, girl."

I consider bolting for some fresh air myself, but I'm perversely curious about "Shipwrecked Heart." The widow Stomarti commences to sing:

You took me like a storm, tossed me out
  of reach,
Left me like the tide, lost and broken
  on a beach.
Shipwrecked heart, my shipwrecked
  heart. . . .

The tune is pretty and pleasing to the ear, and I could probably learn to like it once I heard the whole song, but apparently that won't happen today. Cleo Rio is singing the same verse over and over, meaning she's either forgotten the rest of the lyrics or the lyrics don't exist — that is, the song isn't finished.

Ajax pokes me in the ribs. "You gettin' all this down? Ain't it unfuckinbelievable?"

"Maybe she's just nervous," I say.

"Ha!"

Afterwards, waiting to pay condolences to Jimmy's widow, I'm standing in the line between Ziggy Marley and the guitarist Mike Campbell, one of the original Heartbreakers. I believe Ziggy has taken notice of the notebook sticking out of my back pocket — in any event, nobody's chatting much.

Shaking the pudgy hand of Jay Burns, I introduce myself and say I'd like to get together for a profile of Jimmy that I'm writing. He grunts agreeably, which is a surprise. Then I notice he's completely ripped, eyelids at half-staff and a tendril of drool hanging from his lower lip. Tomorrow he won't remember agreeing to an interview; he'll be lucky to remember his name.

When I finally work my way up the line to Cleo, I notice that she's switched to black contact lenses in honor of the somber occasion. She greets me as if we've never met.

"Jack Tagger," I prompt helpfully, "from the *Union-Register.*"

"Oh. Right."

I embrace her and say, "We really need to talk again."

Cleo pulls free.

"Oh, not now," I add solicitously. "Not today."

"I'm leavin' for L.A., like, tomorrow," Cleo says. "Talk about what?"

"Bad chowder. Bad autopsies." I smile. "Just a few questions. Won't take long."

Cleo looks like she's got a hockey puck lodged in her gullet. "You . . . no, g-g-get the fuck outta here," she stammers.

"You're upset. I'm sorry —"

Cleo turns to flag down the bald guy in the bomber jacket. "Jerry? Jerry, I wa-wa-want this g-g-guy outta here —"

But already I'm moving for the door. There seems no point in asking if I can tag along on the boat ride for the scattering of James Stomarti's mortal remains.

Outside in the parking lot, I catch up with Ajax and Maria as they're getting into a rented Saturn convertible. They inform me that they're legally not allowed to talk about the recent studio sessions with Jimmy Stoma.

Maria says, "We signed a, whatcha call it, a confidentiality agreement. I'd like to help you, man, but I don't wanna get blackballed. I need the work."

Ajax says, "Same here. I got a little girl at home."

"Then forget the sessions. Tell me about Jimmy. What was he like?" St. Stephen's is emptying fast. The limo drivers forsake the shade of an ancient banyan tree and, stubbing out their cigarettes, hustle back to their cars.

"Jimmy was real cool. A nice guy," Ajax says.

"And Cleo?"

Maria laughs acidly. "No comment, *chico*."

"Ditto for me," Ajax says, disgustedly. "Why you even gotta ask? You saw the bitch with your own eyes. She's in it for capital M-E."

"Think he loved her?"

Ajax howls and starts up the car. Maria waves me around to her side. "You're gettin' a little carried away," she tells me, not unkindly. "We're backup singers. You unnerstand?"

I watch them drive off. Then I go find my Mustang, toss the notebook on the front seat, crank up the air conditioner. I feel whipped, as I always do after a funeral service. But through the windshield I notice a scene that makes me grin — the widow Stomarti, clutching the brass urn on the steps of the church while being interviewed by Timmy Buckminster.

I roll down all the windows and crank up the Slut Puppies full blast and roll out of the parking lot nice and easy.

Rock on, Jimmy Stoma.

8

Janet Thrush opens the door and says, "Oh. You."

"I come in?"

"Look, lemme explain."

"Not necessary."

"About this getup," she says sheepishly. "I wanna explain."

Janet is decked out in a Halloween-quality police costume: shiny black boots, dark blue slacks with a gray martial stripe down the sides, a starched white shirt with a cheap tin badge on the breast, and a holster with a toy pistol. Hooked over the top button of her shirt is a pair of plastic reflector sunglasses with neon-blue lenses. In her back pocket is a ticket pad. All that's missing is a set of handcuffs.

"Sorry," I say. "Didn't know you had company."

"I don't have company. Not exactly."

She waves me in and signals me to keep my voice low. The small living room is lit as brightly as a TV studio, which evidently it is. She directs me to a corner and whispers, "I'll just be a sec."

Janet slips on the sunglasses and runs a

hand through her hair. Then she steps into the lights and, cocking one hip, squares to face a video camera no larger than a pencil sharpener. The camera is centered on a coffee table next to a personal computer. Lines of words appear in staggered bursts on the screen, but I'm not close enough to read them.

Janet bends over the keyboard and punches out a message to her cybervisitor. Straightening, she announces, "Larry, you're still under arrest, so don't try anything funny. Call me back in twenty."

Once more she taps the keyboard and the screen goes black. Then she steps around the aluminum tripod racks on which the hot photo lights are mounted and jerks the plug from the wall. She swipes the shades off her face and tosses them on the coffee table.

"Wanna Bud?" she asks me.

"Sure."

"Or something stronger?"

"Whatever you're drinking is fine."

We move to the kitchen, where the temperature is at least fifteen degrees cooler. Janet hands me her last beer and pops opens a cola for herself.

"See, it's Meter Maid–Cam," she says. "You know about this stuff? You on the Net? How it happened, I was sorta between jobs and this girlfriend a mine, about my age, tells me I can make real good money just by . . .

well, she strips, you know, all the way down to her birthday suit. Myself, I stop with my undies. Anyhow, my girlfriend helped set it all up, got me my own Web site and 900 number and so forth. Her deal is Convent-Cam, she and three other girls dress up as Dominican nuns. You mighta read about 'em in *Salon*." Janet tilts the Coke for a long drink.

"The meter maid theme is good," I say supportively.

Janet nods. "It was my idea. Because most guys got a thing for lady cops. Don't you?"

"I try not to sleep with authority figures."

"I bet you could." Janet's tone is clinical, not suggestive. "Anyhow, you probably think it's pretty sleazy, the whole setup."

"I think it's none of my business."

"Four bucks a minute, Jack, that's what these gomers pay me to give 'em a 'parking ticket.' "

"In your bra and panties."

"Yeah, but still . . ."

"It's good money," I agree.

"This guy Larry" — Janet, cutting her eyes toward the living room — "he likes me to write him up for double-parking his timber rig in front of a massage parlor. That's his secret fantasy, I guess. He's calling all the way from Fairbanks, Alaska. Now, ask me do I care if he's whacking off in Fairbanks, Alaska, while he's staring at me in my underpanties on his PC? Not really, Jack. For four bucks a minute he can tie his cock in a knot and clobber a moose with it, far as I'm concerned."

"Don't give him any ideas."

Janet laughs. "I try not to think about what's going on at the other end, but half these guys, they do a play-by-play. I guess they learn to type with one hand or somethin'. Hey, you're not drinkin' that beer."

"I went to your brother's funeral today," I say.

"Oh." Janet adjusts the toy holster and sits down on a stool at the counter. "I couldn't pull myself together. I got dressed up all in black and gassed the car but I couldn't make the damn thing drive to the church."

"I understand, believe me. You want a review?"

"Just tell me Cleo didn't sing."

"I'm afraid she did."

Janet groans and slaps her hands to her cheeks.

"Not that 'Me' song!"

"It's probably best you weren't there."

"Jimmy woulda puked. Don't tell me any more, 'kay?" Janet looks up at the wall clock.

I say, "The reason I stopped by —"

This is the ball game. Without Jimmy's sister I'm done. I'll never get the newspaper to go after the story.

"— it's about the autopsy," I say. "Are you going to pursue it? Do you want to?"

"How? I don't have enough to take to the cops." Janet shakes her head. "Anyways, I wouldn't know where to start."

"I do."

Her smile is grateful but sad. "You know, I haven't slept a night since he died. I can't believe it happened the way they said it did. Fact, I can't believe a word that greedy no-talent twat says."

"Think she murdered him?"

"Well, somethin's not right," Janet says quietly. "I honestly don't know. You're the reporter, what do *you* think?"

"Did your brother have any money?"

"Any money left, you mean. Sure he did. Even in the bad old days Jimmy was pretty sharp — whatever he blew on dope, he'd make sure to send the same amount to Smith Barney. For a junkie my brother was very disciplined. That's how come he could afford a place in the islands."

"Speaking of which, you wanna go?"

"Right." Janet, with a sarcastic sniff.

In the living room, the computer clicks to life and beeps out a greeting.

"Shit," she mutters. "My lonely lumberjack."

"The Bahamas. You and me," I say. "We'll talk to the cops who investigated Jimmy's drowning."

"You serious?"

Behind her, the PC keeps beeping entreatingly.

"Jack, I can't afford a trip to the islands."

"Neither can I," I say lightly, "but young Race Maggad easily can."

"Who's that?" Janet asks.

"Please go with me. It won't cost you a dime. The newspaper will pay for everything." I'm not trying to sound important so much as convince myself that I can pull this off. For obvious reasons, the obituary beat doesn't come with an expense account.

"How about it?" I ask Janet Thrush.

"Damn, you *are* serious."

After the fifth beep, she rises to attend to her caller.

"Please," I say. "If I go alone, they'll just blow me off. They've never even heard of my newspaper in Nassau. But you're his sister, they've got to talk to you."

"Doesn't mean they gotta tell the truth."

"Sometimes you can learn more from a lie. Think about it, and call me later."

"Might be late. After Larry I've got Doctor Dennis logging on from Ann Arbor and then there's Postal Paul from Salt Lake. My very first Mormon."

"I'll be up," I say.

As I'm backing the car out of the driveway, the camera lights flare on in Janet Thrush's living room. The drapes are lined so there's nothing to see but a hot white glow around the margins of the windows. From inside the house, though, I hear the beat of some jazzy music, accompaniment to the dance of the modern meter maid.

My mother knows when my father died but she won't tell.

"What does it matter? Gone is gone," my mother says.

I'd like to know when my father died in order to avoid dying at the same age, which is my deepest fear. My mother disapproves of this obsession and therefore refuses to provide useful clues about Jack Tagger Sr., who stomped out the door when I was only three and never returned.

"How did he die?" I've asked her many times.

"Not of a heredity disease, I can assure you," she usually says. "So stop this ridiculous fretting."

My mother kept only one photograph in which my father appears. He is tall and sandy-haired and bare-chested and, to my eye, radiantly healthy. In the picture he has a tanned arm slung around my mother's shoulders. They are squinting into the afternoon sunlight — this was on a beach in Clearwater, where my parents lived at the time. I am in the photograph, too, sleeping soundly in a stroller to my father's right.

Once I asked my mother what my father did for a living, and she replied, "Not much. That was the problem." In the photo I would guess his age to be between twenty-five and thirty years old. That means if he were alive today he'd be at least sixty-eight and possibly as old as seventy-three. But he's not alive — on this point my mother wouldn't lie.

After Jack Sr. skipped out, our lives moved briskly along. My mother worked long hours as a legal secretary but she always made time for me, and a social life. Although she seriously dated several men, she didn't remarry until after I'd finished high school. I went off to college, fell into the newspaper business and never thought much about my father until many years later, when I got demoted to the obituary beat at the *Union-Register*. It was then I started worrying unhealthily about mortality; my own, in particular. So I phoned my mother in Naples (where she and my stepfather retired for the golfing opportunities) and asked if my father was still alive.

"No," she said evenly.

"When did he die?"

"Why do you want to know?"

"Just curious," I told her.

"I'm not sure when it was exactly, Jack."

"Mom, please. Think."

"It's not important. Gone is gone."

"How did it happen? Was it something congenital?"

"For heaven's sake, don't you think I'd tell you if it was," my mother said. "Now let's drop the subject, please. It happened a long time ago."

"But, Mom —"

"Jack!"

A long time ago. That clinched it. When my mother says "a long time ago," she means at least twenty years — which by my calculations would have made my father no older than fifty-three when he died, and possibly as young as . . . well, that's the gut-gnawing, ball-clenching question.

Was he thirty-five? Forty? Forty-six?

One time I came out and asked my mother: "Was he older or younger than I am when he died?"

"Don't be morbid," she scolded.

"Come on, Mom. Older or younger than me?"

Younger is what I wanted to hear her say, because that meant I was out of the woods. I'd skated through the year of doom.

"What difference does it make, Jack? When God calls us, we go. Obviously your father got the call."

"He was in his forties, wasn't he? He was exactly my age and you're afraid to tell me!"

"This job isn't good for you, Jack. Maybe you should try something lighter, like a dining-out column?"

Not knowing the specifics of my father's

death keeps me up some nights. Whenever I speak to my mother I find myself prying a little more, which explains why she doesn't call so often.

"Just tell me," I asked her recently, "was it natural causes?"

"Of course," she replied soothingly. "Death is always natural."

It was a monologue I'd heard before.

"If a man falls off a twenty-story building," my mother said, "it's only natural he should die. Same thing if he lies down on the railroad tracks in front of a speeding train. Or a bolt of lightning strikes him on the thirteenth fairway —"

"Okay, I get your point."

"The heart seizes up, the lungs puddle, the brain shuts down. End of story."

"Sheer poetry, Mom. May I borrow that for your eulogy?"

Tonight, waiting for Janet Thrush to call, I impulsively decide to try again. My mother picks up on the first ring.

"Oh hi!" she says. "I thought you might be Dave."

Dave is my stepfather. He enjoys the occasional late poker game.

"There's something I've been wanting to ask," I say.

"Oh, not again."

"Look, you don't have to tell me what happened or when, or whether it was a car accident or a heart attack or a brain embolism —"

"Jack, I'm very worried about you."

"— all I want to know," I say to my mother, "is *how* you knew about it. I mean, the man had been gone all those years. Did you two stay in touch?"

"We did not!"

"Didn't he ever call or write?"

"Not once," my mother declares. "Nor did I expect him to."

"Then how'd you find out he died? From his family? The cops? Who called you?"

"You're getting on a plane tomorrow, aren't you?" my mother says.

"What if I am."

"You always get weird like this before you go on a trip."

"That's not true." I'm faking and my mother knows it.

She says, "If it makes you feel better, your father didn't die in an airplane crash. Where are they sending you, anyway?"

"The Bahamas."

"Poor baby," says my mother. "I wish somebody'd send *me* to the Bahamas."

"I'm going to look at an autopsy report. Wanna come?"

"Yuk."

"It's a seaplane. We land in Nassau harbor."

"Airplane, seaplane, don't sweat it. That isn't how your father bought the farm."

"Don't I have a right to know?"

My mother laughs. "Maybe we should go on Sally Jessy, you and me. See who the audience cheers for."

"Did I tell you I get a complete physical every month? Head to toe."

"That's a little extreme, Jack. Every month?"

"And I mean a *complete* physical."

"See, this is why Anne left you," my mother says. "This kind of craziness."

As if I need reminding.

"Who was it back then — Stephen Crane?"

I grunt in the negative. "Scott Fitzgerald."

"Right!" my mother exclaims.

At the time they put me on obits I was forty-four, the same age as Fitzgerald when he died. I couldn't get it out of my head, couldn't sleep, couldn't stop talking about it — and I wasn't even a *Gatsby* fan.

At first Anne tried to help but eventually she decided it was no use. Then she left. On my forty-fifth birthday I instantly snapped out of it, but Anne stayed away. She said if it wasn't Fitzgerald it would be some other dead famous person, somebody new each year. Often I feel like calling her up and telling her how much better I'm doing at age forty-six, considering the heavy Elvis and JFK portents.

"Anne was no Zelda," I hear my mother saying. "Anne was a grownup. I liked her.

Her daughter was a wild one but Anne I liked."

"Me too, Mom."

"It's this godawful job of yours — writing about deceased persons every day. Who wouldn't start to unravel?"

"I'm doing much better. Really I am."

"Then why these phone calls, Jack?"

"Sorry."

"You could switch over to the Sports page. Write about the PGA. Or even the LPGA — maybe you'll meet a nice girl on the tour!"

"All I'm asking," I say calmly to my mother, "is how you knew when my father died. It just seems peculiar, since you say you hadn't seen or heard from the guy all those years. . . . How did you find out about it, Mom?"

My mother delivers one of her trademark sighs. "You really want to know?"

"I do."

"I'm warning you. There's an element of irony."

"Fire away. I'm sitting down."

"I read it in a newspaper, Jack," she says to me. "Your father's obituary."

9

The belly of the seaplane is hot. It smells of fuel, grease and sweat. We're fanning ourselves with rolled-up magazines, but I'm not as jumpy about flying as I usually am.

I like the concept of an aircraft that floats. It makes a world of sense.

Janet Thrush says, "I've never been on one a these contraptions."

I can barely hear her over the racket of the propellers. She's sitting across the aisle, wearing a yellow sleeveless pullover, cutoff jeans, sandals and a floppy canvas hat. She looks perhaps a bit too ready for the islands.

Through the window I see the indigo rip of the Gulf Stream behind us. The waters ahead are turning clear and brilliant, a silky dapple of gemstone blues. Janet leans closer. "I love it here. I used to visit Jimmy all the time till he hooked up with Cleo."

"She keeping the place in Exuma?" I practically shout.

"Who knows." Janet shrugs. She slips into the same cheap shades that she wore last night as Rita the Meter Maid. "Hey, Jack," she says, "did my brother leave a will?"

"You're asking *me?*"

"Hey, you're the one writin' the story."

The plane splashes down gaily and skims the wake of a cruise liner in Nassau harbor. We clear Customs without incident and I hail a cab. Police headquarters is downtown, across the big toll bridge. I've phoned ahead to make sure Sergeant Weems is on duty today, but that doesn't mean he'll hang around to welcome us to the commonwealth. I warn Janet that we might be in for a wait but she seems determined and calm. The only sign of jitters is the prodigious wad of chewing gum she's been chomping.

"It's either that or Camels," she says.

Incredibly, Police Sergeant Cartwright Weems is at his desk when we arrive. He is young and upright and courteous. His desk is exceptionally tidy. I introduce myself first, and then Janet as "the sister of the deceased."

Weems says he's sorry about her brother's death. Janet says, "Jack, tell him why we're here."

"Certainly. It's about the autopsy."

Weems folds his arms, giving the appearance of polite interest.

"Actually," I say, "we have reason to think there *wasn't* an autopsy."

"Why do you say that?" the sergeant asks.

"Because there were no stitches in the body."

"Ah." Weems sits forward and turns open

the file folder on his desk. Inside is the official police report about the drowning of James Bradley Stomarti.

"When you say autopsy," Weems says, scanning the file papers, "of course you're thinking of how things are done in the States. Forensically speaking." He smiles, then looks up at us. "Here in the Bahamas we don't have the resources or the manpower to conduct what you might call a textbook post-mortem on every accident victim. Unfortunately."

His accent is more British than that of most Bahamians, and I'm guessing he was educated in London.

"May I ask — do you use pathologists?"

"Whenever possible, Mr. Tagger," Weems says. "But as you know, we have seven hundred islands in the commonwealth, spread over a very large area. Sometimes we're able to get a trained pathologist on scene in a timely fashion, and other times we're not."

He turns to Janet and drops his voice. "Because of the hot climate here, we often have problems — and I don't mean to be graphic, Ms. Thrush — but we often have difficulties preserving the remains in tragic cases like this. Air-conditioning is, well, a luxury on some of the out-islands. Supplies of ice are very limited — again, I don't wish to belabor the point but on more than one occasion we've resorted to using fish freezers for body storage."

My notebook remains pocketed because Sergeant Weems would clam up if I started jotting down what he said. Cops are the same everywhere.

"What about my brother?" Janet asks through the bulge of the chewing gum. "Holy shit, don't tell me you stuck him in a fishbox." She has removed the shades and the hat but the cutoffs are difficult to ignore, though Weems is trying. His eyes shoot back to the file on his desk.

"In Mr. Stomarti's case, we were able to retrieve his body fairly quickly and transport it here, to Nassau. But my point," says Weems, "is that we are stretched thin. On the day of your brother's diving accident there was a bad crash in Freeport. A waterbike ran into a conch boat — two tourists were killed. We flew our top pathologist over there immediately."

"So who did the work on my brother?" Janet asks.

"Dr. Sawyer. Winston Sawyer. He is a very capable fellow."

"May we speak with him?" I say.

"Certainly. If he chooses." The sergeant's tone is meant to remind me that foreign journalists have no juice whatsoever in a place like Nassau. Dr. Sawyer is perfectly entitled to tell me to fuck off.

Then Janet pipes up: "Can I get a copy of

the police report?" She remembered, God bless her.

For the first time, Sergeant Weems is unsettled. He twists his butt in the chair, as if he's got an unscratchable itch.

"Well, let me —"

"It's my brother, after all," Janet cuts in. "The people at the embassy said I'm entitled."

Excellent — exactly as we rehearsed. Of course we haven't spoken to a soul at the U.S. Embassy.

"Certainly, certainly." Weems is re-reading the report with renewed urgency, in the event it requires expurgating on the stroll to the copy machine. Rising slowly (and still reading), he says, "I'll be right back, Ms. Thrush. Give me a moment, please."

As soon as he departs, I signal Janet with a congratulatory wink. Upon the young sergeant's return, she accepts the Xeroxed police report and reads through it. Weems and I share the uneasy silence. When Janet finishes, she folds the document and slips it into her handbag. Tearfully she stands and excuses herself. This is no act.

I wait a few moments before saying to Weems: "She's having a tough time accepting this."

"Yes, I can understand."

"You're confident it was an accident?"

He nods with grave assuredness. "We took

statements from both witnesses, Mrs. Stomarti and a Mr. Burns, I believe it was. The details matched up," Weems says. "I'm afraid her brother got disoriented underwater and couldn't make it back to the boat. This sort of thing happens too often, believe me — with experienced divers, as well. You'd be surprised."

"Do you find it odd that Mr. Stomarti didn't ditch his tank and try to swim to the surface?"

Weems leans back in the chair. Stiffly he says, "Not really, Mr. Tagger. Some people wait too long. Others panic. These tragedies seldom reflect a clarity of thought." The sergeant's suddenly chilly monotone signals he is done with me.

Standing, I thank him for his courtesy. "By the way, who interviewed Mrs. Stomarti?"

"I did, sir."

"On the boat?"

"Yes, but later. After they docked at Chub."

"She happen to say anything about a premonition she had that morning? Did she mention begging her husband not to dive on the plane wreck?"

Weems shakes his head skeptically. "No, she didn't. I'm quite sure I would have remembered."

"She said nothing about Mr. Stomarti being sick?"

Weems looks intrigued. "Sick *how?*"

"Food poisoning," I say. "Fish chowder."

Chuckling, Weems rises. "No, sir. Where did you hear that?"

"What's so funny?"

"That's what Mrs. Stomarti was having for dinner while I interviewed her on the boat," he says. "Fish chowder. She even offered me a bowl."

We've got two hours to kill until Dr. Winston Sawyer will see us, so Janet and I order rum drinks and grouper sandwiches at an outdoor joint a block off Bay Street. Somehow we end up talking about death, a subject on which we hold vastly different philosophies. Janet says she believes in reincarnation, which is how she's held herself together after Jimmy's death. In a nutshell, she believes her brother will come back as a dolphin, or possibly a Labrador retriever.

I, on the other hand, believe death is the end of the ride. Death travels on the caboose.

"What about an afterlife?" Janet inquires.

"Don't hold your breath," I say. "On second thought, do."

"You believe in heaven?"

"From all I've read, it sounds pretty tedious. Frankly, your reincarnation program seems more intriguing — except with my luck I'd come back as Shirley MacLaine."

"Don't make fun."

"Or a mullet."

"What's that?" Janet asks.

"A fish whose only purpose in life is to be devoured by bigger, hungrier fishes."

"Jack, you don't understand. The way it got explained to me, whatever happens on earth, your spirit remains safe and whole. Whether you're a fish or a butterfly or whatever."

I gnaw crossly on a pickle. "All right. Say I get reincarnated as a lobster —"

"Let's not talk about this anymore."

"First day of lobster season, some bubble-blower nails me with a speargun. You're saying I won't feel a thing? Even when they drop my tasty red ass into a pot of boiling water, my spirit will feel A-OK? You honestly believe that?"

"Can we get the check please."

Dr. Winston Sawyer is eighty-seven years old, the same age as Jacques-Yves Cousteau when he died. Says Dr. Sawyer: "I've delivered more babies than any other poysin in all da Bahamas."

Janet and I had braced ourselves for such news. The man's waiting room was packed with pregnant women.

"We're here about my brother," Janet says.

"Ah," Dr. Sawyer nods. He continues nodding. "Indeed, indeed."

Janet glances anxiously at me. I am

burning this scene into memory in case I need to write about it later in the newspaper.

"The American who died in the diving accident," I remind Dr. Sawyer. "Last week at Chub Cay?"

"Ah." The doctor smiles warmly. I am impressed by the old man's dentition, which is flawless and luminously white.

I say, "Perhaps we're looking for another Dr. Sawyer."

"I understand your confusion," he says, "but be assured dat I'm fully qualified, fully qualified. The police call me occasionally on such matters, occasionally as I say, due to my long years of experience. . . ."

I ask why there were no stitches on the body of Janet's brother.

"Stitches." The doctor blinks drowsily.

"As are commonly used in autopsy procedures, yes," I say, "to close the chest cavity."

Janet sighs. The color has seeped from her cheeks. She extracts the lump of chewing gum from her jaw and lobs it into a wastebasket.

Dr. Winston Sawyer raises a bony finger the color of polished teak. "You say autopsy, well, I must tell you, sir — and you, madam — dat dere wasn't need for an autopsy. Dat is why you saw no sutures! I was merely ast to attend by the police, who call me on such matters, due to my experience. . . ."

The doctor trails off. The upraised finger

127

curls and uncurls.

"Go on," I say. "You were asked by the police . . ."

Dr. Sawyer's chin snaps up. "Indeed. I was ast to examine the body, which I did, and subsequently certified the death as accidental. Subsequent, as I say, to a postmortem examination."

"But a visual examination only." I take out my notebook and uncap a pen. Blessedly, Dr. Sawyer fails to notice.

"Understand dat I've had occasion to see many drowning victims over dese many years. This was quite routine," he says, directing his words toward Janet, "not that any such tragedy is 'routine,' madam. But in the medical sense, you understand, it was. Drownings are not uncommon here in the Bahamas, not uncommon. Sadly to say."

Numbly Janet asks, "So, how did Jimmy look?"

Dr. Sawyer grunts helplessly. The sage finger is withdrawn.

"I mean," says Janet, "you see any bruises? Any sorta . . . you know, Jack, what's the word?"

"Trauma."

"Yeah. Any trauma?"

"None," the doctor says. "Not a scratch, madam, I give you my woid. Your brother died from drowning. Dere was no need to cut — oh goodness, no need for a complete autopsy procedure."

"You saw nothing at all unusual?" I ask. "You *did* get him out of his wetsuit at least?"

Dr. Sawyer squints in fierce concentration, moving his mottled lips like a cow. Then he explodes in a jolly boom: "Haw! Now I know what this mon be gettin' at! The tattoo. The snake tattoo! Oh goodness, I never see anyting like *dat* before, not in eighty-seven years! Gawd, please!"

The doctor is wheezing, he's laughing so hard. Pretty soon Janet cracks up, too. Then I join in. How could anyone not like the old guy?

"That tattoo, wheeeee, it's like a woik of art," Dr. Sawyer is saying. "Tell you trute, I'm glad I didn't have to mess dat up. Woulda made me plenty sad to do such a ting! Who was the pretty lady with dat snake, if I may ast?"

"Some stripper Jimmy was dating," Janet says, giggling at the memory. "In real life she had a terrible overbite."

"Dat's okay. I hear da same 'bout Mona Lisa."

As the doctor cordially leads us to the door, I tell him I've got one more question.

"Anyting, sir," he says.

"I was wondering if you've had any formal forensic training?"

"Certainly, sir." He tilts his wizened head and peers at me like an ancient turtle. "I

129

woiked as a pathologist right here on New Providence. Nassau Town."

"When was that?"

"Nineteen . . . well, let me tink. Forty-two it was."

"1942?"

"And part of '43. Before I took up da practice of obstetrics." Dr. Sawyer beams. "I've delivered more babies than any other poysin in the commonwealth!"

The seaplane is late. Janet and I wait on a peeling wooden bench in the broken shade of some coconut palms. She lets me skim through the police report — I was hoping for some notation that might trip up Cleo Rio, but there's not much there. The Bahamians kept it simple.

I find myself asking Janet when her father died.

"Nine years ago," she says.

"How old was he?"

"Fifty-two."

"Wow," I say. The same age as Harry Nilsson.

"Too young," Janet adds.

"Does it worry you?"

She eyes me curiously. "No, Jack. It makes me sad. I loved my old man."

"Of course you did. What I meant was, doesn't it make you wonder about your own . . . timetable?"

The question is unforgivably insensitive, which I realize the instant it leaves my lips. This is one aspect of my obsession that aggravates not only my mother but my friends as well.

But Janet's look dissolves into one of understanding. "Oh," she says. "Sure. Dying young and all."

"Not just dying young," I slog on, "but dying at the *exact same age* as a parent or a friend or even a famous person you admire."

"You mean, like, fate? Don't tell me you believe in fate?"

"Not fate. Black irony. That's what I believe in."

Janet whistles. "Ever thought about changing jobs?"

"Can I ask what happened to your father?"

"He was screwing one of his students when her boyfriend showed up. It was, like, her nineteenth birthday. My father jumped out the dormitory window to get away, but six stories is a long way down. Too bad he taught English lit and not physics." Janet smiles ruefully. "That's why I'm not too worried about checking out at fifty-two."

"Gotcha," I say.

"I mean there's fate, Jack, and then there's just plain stupidity."

10

Midnight.

The old days, a newsroom at this hour reeked of coffee and cigarettes and stale pizza. You'd hear the wire machines chittering and the police scanners gabbling and the pasteup guys snorting at dirty jokes.

But like most papers, the *Union-Register* switched to early deadlines to cut costs, so there's hardly a soul around at this late hour. If a plane goes down or the mayor has another coronary, come daybreak we're sucking hind tit to the TV stations.

These days we buy the loyalty of readers with giveaways and grocery coupons, not content. This makes for less clutter, so our newsroom is as spiffy as a downtown Allstate agency, complete with earthtone carpeting. Every editor and reporter has a personal cubicle with padded pressboard walls and a computer station and a file drawer and a phone with a headset. Some days, we might as well be selling term life.

Nobody barks or shouts anymore, they "message" each other from their terminals. The old days, phones in a newsroom never quit ringing even after the final edition was put to bed. Tonight, as most nights, the place is oppressively silent except for torpid electronic bloops from the PCs (most editors favor the tropical aquarium screen-saver option, while the reporters go for intergalactic warfare motifs).

Still, these desolate gaps in the news cycle can be useful. Emma isn't here to circle like a kestrel, and young Evan, the intern, isn't around to dart in and pepper me with questions. Actual fact-gathering is possible. Addictive new technology allows one to sit at a desktop and browse tax rolls, real estate transactions, court files, arrest records, driver's licenses, marriage licenses and divorce decrees, as well as current periodicals, medical journals, trade publications, corporate reports — the bottomless maw of the Internet.

Also accessible are the library banks of other newspapers, large and small; a treasure trove. The only problem is that many papers have come online only within the last decade, and they don't always backfile the morgue stories into computer memory. Consequently, the odds are not so good of locating information about a man who died, say, at least twenty years ago.

But my mother claimed she read it in a newspaper, my father's obituary. And I've nothing better to do than go hunting.

On the keyboard I tap out T-A-G-G-E-R, J-A-C-K.

The joke's on me. Within moments the screen flashes a directory of thirty-six stories, all too familiar. The search engine seems to have locked onto my byline, resulting in an instant and unwanted sampling of my own work. Scrolling through past glories, written before my time on the obit beat, I'm amused to see that several of the Orrin Van Gelder stories popped up, all the way from Gadsden County. Evidently that stands as the pinnacle of my journalism career, at least in electronic dataland. Maybe Jimmy Stoma can change that.

At the moment, though, it's the other Jack Tagger that keeps me plodding through the search directory. But he's nowhere to be found, my father, evidently having died pre-Web. Any record of the event must therefore exist as a yellowed clipping in a musty old folder in some musty old newspaper warehouse. It's likely my mother herself saved a copy, although I doubt she'd admit it. This is some fucked-up game she's playing.

I sign off, lock the desk and head for home. While driving by Carla Candilla's place I see lights in the window and pull a U-turn. I call from a phone booth and she says to come on over, she's all alone and coloring her hair.

"Orange!" I say at the door.

"No, 'Lava,'" Carla says. "Because I'm worth it. Get your ass in here, I'm dripping all over the place."

She's wearing a full-length bathrobe appropriated from the Delano Hotel. I follow her to the kitchen where she toils with her soggy tendrils at the sink. I deliver a compressed but colorful account of my penthouse interview with Cleo Rio, and the celebrity scene at Jimmy Stoma's funeral.

Carla is an avid interrogator.

"What'd she look like?"

"Tan and glassy-eyed."

"The Case of the Suntanned Widow? Was Russell Crowe there?"

"Not that I recall."

"Come on, Black Jack. Rumor has him bonking Cleo."

"I saw no bonking."

"How 'bout Enrique?" Carla demands.

"Enrique who?"

She shrieks from beneath her marinating dome of hair. "How can you be so . . . *out of it?*"

"Cleo's supposedly bonking this Enrique, too?"

"You should've taken me along, Jack. You let me down," Carla teases. "You let me down, you done me wrong."

I feel obliged to inquire about the lava-hued tresses. "For a special event?"

"Saturday night," she says. "Every Saturday night is a special event."

"New boyfriend?"

"Nah," Carla says. "New mood."

She has completed some critical phase of the tinting process. Now we move to the living room where she trowels moss-colored clay on her face. Only eyes, lips and nostrils remain visible.

"So. Black Jack."

"Yeah."

"Think Cleo offed her old man?"

"I honestly can't say. Nobody performed an autopsy and now the body's been cremated so we might never know. Maybe Jimmy drowned just like they said, or maybe he had help. In any case, the widow is making the most of the moment."

Carla says, "I can't fucking believe she sang at the funeral."

"To plug her new CD."

"Skank. What's your story gonna say?"

A damn good question. "Well, I hope it'll say that Jimmy's sister wants a full investigation of the circumstances of his death. I hope it's going to say there are inconsistencies among the witnesses."

"Who are . . . ?" Carla asks through her frogskin cast.

"Cleo, of course, and Jay Burns," I say, "one of the old Slut Puppies. He buddied up with Jimmy for the dive."

"What if he backs up Cleo's story?"

"Then I drink myself silly and crawl back to the cave of dead rabbis."

Carla points to her face. "Can't talk. It's hardening."

The phone rings. She signals for me to pick up.

"Candilla residence," I answer in a British butler accent.

"Who *is* this?"

"Oh hi, Anne." Voice skips. Heart flops. Tongue turns to chalk.

"Jack?"

"Carla's in her mud mask. She can't move her mouth."

On the other end I hear a familiar sigh. Then: "What are you doing over there?"

Twitching like a junkie, I'm tempted to say.

"We're gossiping about fashion, music and models. Carla says I'm 'out of it,' which is surely an understatement. Now I've got a question for you: Why bother your hard-working offspring so late at night?"

A soft laugh. "I just got in, Jack."

"Oh."

"From out of town," she says.

How clever of me to ask. Smoothly I drop the subject.

"Well. You doing okay?"

"I'm good," Anne says. "How about yourself?"

"Better," I lie. "I'm surviving age forty-six just fine. No more obsessing. And this was a heavy year for bad karma — JFK and Elvis."

"And don't forget Oscar Wilde," Anne tosses in.

"Wilde? I thought he was forty-five."

"No, forty-six," she says. "I wouldn't have known except I just saw one of his plays in London. They had a biography in the Playbill. How're things at work?"

I find myself rattled by the Oscar Wilde bulletin, and also by the idea of Anne traveling to England without me.

Meaning with somebody else.

"Jack?"

"Everything's great at the paper," I say. "Big story in the oven — actually that's why I dropped by to see Carla. She knows the cast of characters."

"As long as she's not one of them," Anne says. "I'm glad you're doing well, Jack."

I hear myself blurting: "I'll be doing even better if you have lunch with me tomorrow."

"Can't, Jack. I'm afraid I'm busy." This is followed by a pause, during which I foolishly convince myself that Anne is reconsidering the invitation. But then she says: "Tell Carla I'll give her a shout in the morning."

"Will do."

"Bye," says Anne.

I set the receiver down very gingerly, as if it's made of Baccarat crystal.

"Wanna drink?" The lovely dark eyes staring out of Carla's mud face are brimming with sympathy. Worse, they are Anne's eyes.

"I've got beer," Carla says through fixed lips.

I tell her no thanks. Standing up, I say, "Well. Your mother sounds terrific."

"Surry," Carla mutters, endeavoring not to crack the facial plaster. Either a smile or a frown would do the job. She snatches a notepad from the dining table and scribbles these words: *Least she knows how you feel.*

"And that's good?" I ask.

Carla nods consolingly. Those eyes are killing me. I give her a quick hug and head for the door.

Next morning, Emma calls and commands me to appear in the newsroom.

"But I'm ill! Stricken! Indisposed!"

"You are not. Buckminster spotted you at the funeral."

"Fuckweasel," I remark.

"Pardon me?"

I stage a coughing fit worthy of a pleurisy ward, and hang up.

Forty minutes later comes a stern knock — Emma! This is unpardonable, accosting me at home. I greet her in my sleepwear, a rank Jacksonville Jaguars jersey and a pair of baggy plaid boxers. She is not as horrified as I had hoped.

"You the truant officer?"

"Enough, Jack." Emma charges past me and plants herself on the least stained and faded of the twin armchairs. She is wearing a sharp-looking Oxford blouse, black slacks and a pair of sensible low heels. Her toenails are concealed, but I'll bet the farm she has re-painted them since Monday afternoon; a muted ochre, I'm imagining, something serious to match her mood. Never have I seen her so torqued up.

"Mr. Polk is slipping away. The doctors say it could happen any day," she begins urgently. "Any minute, really."

I stretch out supine on the floor and shut one eye. "I'm onto a possible celebrity murder, Emma. I've got a distraught sister who suspects foul play and I'm the only one who'll help. What am I supposed to do, slam the door in her face? Tell her the paper doesn't care that her only brother got whacked?"

Although I have liberally exaggerated Janet Thrush's state of mind, Emma remains unmoved.

"I told you once, Jack. It's Metro's story if they want it. You did your job; you wrote the obit. You're done." She's glaring at me, really glaring.

"What are you so afraid of?" As if I don't know.

"Don't be such an asshole," she says.

I pop up, wide-eyed and beaming, and jig from foot to foot like a Polynesian coalwalker. What a breakthrough!

"Did you call me an onerous name? Yes, I'm sure of it. You did!"

"We're not in the workplace." Emma, reddening. Then: "Look, I'm sorry. That was unprofessional."

"No, I'm glad. It means we're making progress. Breaking down walls and so forth. You want some fresh orange juice? A decaf?"

Emma says, "Old Man Polk wants to see you, Jack."

I stop prancing and suck a short breath. "What? I thought he was fading fast."

"He wants a deathbed interview, believe it or not. To jazz up his obituary."

"Dear Jesus."

"This was not my idea, I swear."

"A perverse final request."

"I couldn't agree more," Emma says, "but Abkazion already said yes."

"Dipshit," I mutter. "Fellator of mandrills."

"I'm begging, Jack."

"Why me?" I growl, pointlessly.

"Evidently the old man admires your writing."

A side effect of the Halcion, no doubt. I peel off my Jaguars jersey and toss it over a lampshade. Next I tug absently at the waistband of my boxers, Emma eyeing me warily. She is in no mood to deal with a naked employee.

"Don't get cute," she advises.

"Don't flatter yourself." I stalk off to the

shower. Twenty minutes later, I emerge to find Emma still encamped. This, frankly, throws me. She has put on her reading glasses to study an obituary I recently cut out of the *Times*. Wrapped in a towel, I stand there dripping on the floor like some incontinent nuthouse savant.

Emma glances up, waves the clipping. "This is a fantastic headline."

"That's why I saved it."

The single-deck head on the obituary said:

Ronald Lockley, 96, an Intimate of Rabbits

Emma says, "How can you *not* look at that story?"

"Precisely."

"Even if you aren't a fan of rabbits, which I'm not." Then, as if she's reading my mind: "For God's sake, why couldn't I write headlines like this?"

I say, "Here's one: 'MacArthur Polk, 88, Wealthy Malingerer.'"

"Jack, please. I'm begging you."

Swathed in my damp bath linen, I lower myself carefully into the armchair across from Emma. My hair is still sopping and now I feel a droplet of water elongating itself on the lobe of my left ear. I pray Emma won't be distracted.

"Don't you worry. I'll deal with Abkazion,"

I venture brashly.

"It's not just him," Emma grumbles. "Mr. Maggad has taken an interest, as well. He went to see the old man at Charity and believes he's delirious, in addition to terminal."

Exultantly I tell Emma there must be a misunderstanding. Race Maggad III, who despises me, would never recommend me being assigned to a story as important as Old Man Polk's obit.

Emma drums her fingers on her knees. "Abkazion is baffled. I'm baffled. You're baffled. Yet here we are."

I stall, racking my brain. "I get it. Maggad, that conniving yuppie fuck, he's setting me up."

"For what, Jack? Setting you up for what?"

There is a tender note of pity in Emma's question, implying that I've already been so thoroughly shafted by management that there's no place left to fall. My chin drops. Scrutinizing the sparse, south-running trail of hair on my belly, I notice a few shoots of gray.

Emma says, "I'm sorry, Jack. Now go put on some clothes."

I lift my eyes to meet hers and say: "Jimmy Stoma for Old Man Polk."

"No deal." She shakes her head vigorously.

"Emma, do you know how much sick leave I've piled up?"

"Don't threaten me. Don't you dare."

"Tomorrow you will receive a letter from a prominent board-certified health care provider," I say, "attesting to the seriousness of my condition, namely chronic colorectal diverticulosis. By the time my recovery is complete and I am deemed able to resume a full work schedule, Mr. MacArthur Polk will be worm chow, darling. An intimate of maggots, to steal a phrase."

Emma stands up, fuming and spectacular. "You're unbelievable, Jack, getting a doctor to lie for you!"

Murkily I confide to having heavy connections in the gastrointestinal field. "But give me ten days on Jimmy Stoma," I say, "and I'll go see Old Man Polk at once."

"A week. That's all you get," Emma relents. "And we never had this conversation, understand? I was never here."

"Right. And you never ogled my bare alabaster calves. Hey, I'm about to pulp some oranges — stay for juice."

"Rain check," Emma says curtly.

At the door I hear myself thanking her, for what I can't imagine. She pockets the reading glasses in favor of snazzy blue Ray-Bans, new driving shades. "Look," she says. "I really am sorry about that a-hole remark."

"Nonsense. We're bonding, that's all. We're a work in progress."

"Juan says you keep a lizard in your kitchen freezer. Can that possibly be true?"

"An extremely large lizard, yes. Would you care to see?"

"Under no circumstances, Jack," Emma says with a guarded smile. "Though I wouldn't mind hearing your version of the story."

"Maybe someday," I say, "when I'm not feeling so puny."

11

When Anne moved out of my apartment, Carla gave me a baby Savannah monitor lizard. She said I wasn't responsible enough to take proper care of a puppy or a kitten, or even a parrot. Lizards require no companionship, only grubs, water and sunlight. "Even you can manage that," Carla assured me.

I named him "Colonel Tom" because he joined the household on January 21, the anniversary of the death of Colonel Tom Parker, the man who made a king of Elvis Aron Presley. Carla provided a terrarium and a starter bag of mealworms, which Colonel Tom the lizard gobbled down in three days. Quickly he advanced to crickets, palmetto bugs and beyond — hunger incarnate, a perpetual eating machine. Before long he outgrew the terrarium, so I moved him to a fifty-gallon dry tank with a bonsai tree, a water dish and a vermiculite beach.

Lizards are not strung with the high emotions of, say, a cocker spaniel. On a good day Colonel Tom's mood ranged from oblivious to indifferent. Only at mealtimes would he respond approvingly to a human presence, blinking a cold eye while cocking his knobbed saurian head. The rest of the time he skulked inside a toy cave that Carla had found for him.

One evening, after a few beers, I took him out to show Juan, who sensibly armed himself with a mop handle. We watched a baseball game on television, and Colonel Tom lay across my lap for five innings without so much as twitching his tail. "He looks parched," Juan observed. "Fluids, Jack, *ahora!*"

I poured the lukewarm dregs of a Sam Adams into an ashtray and raised it to the monitor's scaly mandibles, and to my wonderment he gingerly extended a tongue as pink and delicate as a Caribbean snail. My lizard, it turned out, had a thing for beer. Inspired, I offered up the remnants of a Key lime pie, which Colonel Tom inhaled savagely. The frothy dollop of meringue clung to his chin like a jaunty white goatee. Juan and I were both drunk enough to be enthralled.

From then on I brought the lizard out on TV nights for beer and dessert. Sometimes Juan would drop by on his way home from work, and a few times he even brought dates to see Colonel Tom in action. The young monitor grew rapidly, soon surpassing three feet in length. The unnatural diet began to soften his prehistoric countenance and bloat his once-chiseled flanks to droopy saddlebags. In retrospect I should have recognized the transformation as plainly unhealthy, though Colonel Tom's disposition had never been rosier. Juan swore the lizard manifested a fan's appreciation of baseball; the fundamentals, if not the finer points. Certainly Colonel Tom was most attentive and bright-eyed when draped across my lap, but I always suspected his spirits were elevated not by the heroics of the Marlins' bullpen so much as the promise of more pastry and distilled hops.

Late one Saturday night, as the Marlins played the Dodgers on the coast, Colonel Tom came down with a brutal case of what I diagnosed as lizard hiccups. Symptoms appeared shortly after he downed a cold Heineken and a slice of rich German strudel that Juan had brought from a renowned bakery in Ybor City.

By my wristwatch I timed Colonel Tom's shuddering burps at eight-second intervals. Discomfort was evident in his lethargic demeanor and blotched, blackening cheeks. Juan had already gone home, so it was left to me to soothe the tremulous reptile. When I tried stroking his corrugated shoulders, Colonel Tom wheeled and snapped percussively. Then, for good measure, he raked a hind claw across my cheek, drawing blood.

"You ungrateful little shit," I muttered, too harshly.

In response the monitor balefully reared

his brick-sized noggin and displayed a well-armored maw, featuring rows of fine needle-sharp teeth. A large opalescent bubble of lizard saliva appeared, then popped moistly on the ensuing hiccup. From the TV set rose a hometown cheer as Gary Sheffield hammered a hanging curve into the left-field bleachers, sinking the Marlins in the bottom of the ninth. Colonel Tom promptly fluttered one eyeball and flopped over dead in my lap.

I didn't move for fifteen minutes, frozen partly by shock and partly by the fact that the lizard's glistening jaws had come to rest two centimeters from the crotch of my boxer shorts. A death-spasm chomp of those fangs would have sent me to the emergency room (where, I knew, no innocent explanation would be accepted for a deceased lizard affixed to one's scrotum).

Once it was evident that the colonel had drawn his final breath, I pondered my options. The balcony offered a clear shot at the Dumpster, but that seemed a cold and indecent goodbye. This was, after all, a gift from Anne's daughter. So I resolved to give the lizard a fitting send-off as soon as arrangements could be made. In the meantime I endeavored to preserve his mortal remains, which, given his bulk, wasn't easy. The only way to fit the beast into the shallow freezer compartment of my refrigerator was to pretzel the long limp corpse into the shape of an ampersand.

To this day there he sleeps, Colonel Tom, frostily coiled beneath my ice cube trays and chocolate Dove bars. Every time I think about burying the poor bastard I get depressed.

Out of guilt I lied to Carla and told her the monitor broke out of the tank and escaped. Only Juan knows the truth, and I'm surprised he spilled it to Emma. I suspect she was pumping him for inside information to use against me in the annual employee evaluation. Even though Juan is my best friend, he'll tell Emma whatever she wants to know if he thinks there's a chance she'll sleep with him. At least that's how *I* always operated in the early stages of a relationship.

Maybe it's better that she knows about the dead lizard in my freezer. Maybe it will upend her set notions about me, and make her wonder what other distasteful secrets I've got.

MacArthur Polk looks like death on a Triscuit.

"He can't speak," the nurse informs me.

"Then what am I doing here?" I ask reasonably.

"I meant, he can't speak normally. Because of the tracheostomy."

The old man points gravely to a surgical

opening in his throat, to which has been attached a plastic valve that resembles a demitasse cup. A clear polymer tube leads from the valve stem to an oxygen contraption beside the bed.

For the interview MacArthur Polk has been moved from the hospital's intensive care ward to a private room. He aims a bloodless finger at the door, signaling the nurse to scram.

"Keep it short and sweet," she whispers to me. "He's not well." She throws up an elbow in time to deflect a plastic bedpan that would have otherwise beaned her on the forehead. "He can be a pill. You'll see," she says.

As soon as we're alone, MacArthur Polk begins fiddling with the throat valve, which enables him to speak by drawing air across the vocal cords.

"Little gizmo goes for fifty-two bucks on the Internet," the old man rasps. "Guess how much the hospital charges — three hundred a pop! Fucking bandits."

The voice lacks for volume but not vitriol. I step closer to listen.

"Sit down, you," Polk snaps. "Where's your damn notebook?"

Obediently I withdraw it from my pocket.

"Open it," he says. "Now put down that I was a fighter. Put down that I was all heart and gristle. I never gave up, no matter what those worthless quacks said." He jabs the air. "Put it down *now!* In your notebook,

Mr. Obituary Writer!"

As I'm scribbling, the old man has second thoughts. "Hold on now. Scratch 'worthless quacks.' My luck, one a those pricks'll slap my estate with a libel suit. See what it's come to? They'd sue a dead man with a hole in his throat, I swear to Christ."

MacArthur Polk is shriveled and fuzzy-headed, with a florid beaked nose, stringy neck and papery, pellucid skin. He looks like one of those newborn condors that zookeepers are always showing off on the Discovery Channel.

After another drag of oxygen, he croaks: "Mr. Race Maggad didn't want you on this story. Why is that, you suppose?"

"I gather he's not a fan."

The old milky eyes sparkle with overmedicated mischief. "I heard you called him some nasty names at a shareholders' meeting. I heard you shook things up, Mr. Tagger."

"Why are we talking about this?"

"Because —" Old Man Polk emits a tubercular wheeze. "Because the reason Maggad didn't want you on this story is the precise reason I insisted on it. What'd you call him exactly? I'm just curious."

"An impostor," I say.

When Polk laughs, his dentures clack. "Him and his father both. What else?"

"I might have mentioned his trust fund.

The fact he never worked an honest day in his life. How he knows more about shoeing polo ponies than putting out a decent newspaper."

The old man rattles a wet sigh. "God, I wish I'd been there. I believe I was in the hospital that day."

"Dying," I say. "That's what Mr. Maggad informed the shareholders."

"Hell, I wasn't 'dying' that time, or any of the others. I was just resting. Screwing with their heads."

"You dying now?"

Polk nods abjectly. "Unfortunately, this one's for real, Mr. Tagger. I wouldn't call you here to waste your time."

I almost believe him, he looks so ghastly. For some reason I think of his wife, age thirty-six, and wonder what in creation the two of them talk about. The old man volunteers that she's holding up like a champ. Considering her future net worth, I don't doubt it for a moment.

"Mr. Race Maggad himself came to the hospital to visit me. Why is that, you suppose?" Polk asks, hacking feebly. "To see how I was getting along? Read me a bedtime story? Or maybe to apologize for ruining my family's newspaper."

Polk will get no argument from me. I hear myself asking: "So why'd you sell out to Maggad-Feist? Them, of all people."

The old man turns away with a snort. "More on that later."

"A lot of us in the newsroom felt . . . betrayed."

Polk's head snaps around. His eyes are hot. "Is that so. Betrayed?"

"It was a good little paper, Mr. Polk, and we were proud of it. Those people are raping its soul."

"You're not the most sensitive fellow, are you? Did I mention I was dying?"

Suddenly he sounds forlorn. Me, I feel like a shitheel.

"I didn't think it was possible to feel any worse," Polk gasps, "until you showed up. Hell, I'd hang myself with this goddamn oxygen tube if I could reach the curtain rod."

"I'm sorry. I honestly am."

"Aw, what the hell — you've got a point. But more on that later. Now, Mr. Obituary Man," the old man says, with renewed spunk, "put down how I turned the *Union-Register* into a first-class outfit. And don't forget to say 'award-winning.' Write that down! I got a list somewhere of all the prizes we won. . . ."

So it goes for an hour. MacArthur Polk's endurance is impressive, as is his enthusiasm for self-aggrandizement. Fortunately he won't be around to read the story, as I have no intention of bogging it down with mawkish deathbed ramblings. Three or four wistful quotes ought to do the job.

Still, he is not an unlikable or tedious interview. He's feisty and coarse and colorfully blunt-spoken, as the dying are entitled to be. For me it's hardly a wasted afternoon, spent in the company of one who has led a full life. Eighty-eight years is something to shoot for.

"I always believed a paper should be the conscience of its community," he is saying for the third time. "News isn't just the filler between advertisements. It's the spine of the business. You write that down?"

"Every word," I assure him.

"Think you got plenty for your article?"

"More than enough."

"Good," Polk growls. "Now all I gotta do is croak and you're good to go."

"Don't hurry on account of me."

"Close that damn notebook, Mr. Tagger. We've got some important matters to discuss, you and I. Off the record."

I can't imagine what.

"Put it away!" the old man tries to bark, though the only sound from his lips is a flatulent sibilance. He paws at the tracheostomy valve and finally grabs for the call button. The same unflappable nurse comes in and calmly clears the valve so that MacArthur Polk can continue speaking.

"Thank you, darling." He squeezes both her hands. She bends down and kisses him sweetly on his blue-veined scalp.

"I love you," says the old man.

"Love you, too," says the nurse.

Now I get it.

"Mr. Tagger, say hello to my wife," Polk says. "Ellen, this is the obituary man from the paper."

"Nice to meet you," says Ellen Polk, shaking my hand. "Did he throw the bedpan again? Mac, are you misbehaving?"

"Sit down, darling," he tells her.

They both see it in my expression. Mrs. Polk says to me: "I'm not what you expected, am I?"

Bingo. I was expecting a shark in designer heels; a predatory blonde with store-bought boobs and probate lawyers in the closet. Ellen Polk is no gold digger; she's a hard-working health care provider.

"We met in the cardiac wing," says Old Man Polk.

"He was a regular," Ellen adds.

"She let me grab her tush," the old man warbles proudly.

"In your dreams, Mac."

"Tell the truth, darling. You wanted me."

"That's right," she says. "I've got a thing for guys on ventilators. That sucking noise really turns me on."

Polk crows. Ellen rises to kiss him goodbye.

"No, stay," he tells her. "This concerns you, too."

Then, to me, the old man says: "Mr. Race

Maggad III came to visit me here, Mr. Tagger. Why is that, you suppose?"

I play along. "He thinks of you as a father figure?"

"No, he detests me."

"Now, Mac —" says Ellen.

"Oh, it's true." When the old man gulps, the valve at his throat gives off a muted peep. "Maggad hates me, Mr. Tagger, but he's kissing ass because I've got something he desperately wants, preferably before I die."

"What would that be?" I ask.

MacArthur Polk looks at his wife, who looks at me. They're both smiling. I suppose I should be smiling, too.

The old man says, "You're gonna enjoy this, Mr. Tagger."

Meeting the lovely Mrs. MacArthur Polk has got me thinking about another young wife, Mrs. James Stomarti, who might not have been so devoted to her husband. After departing Charity Hospital I impulsively decide to go see if Jimmy's widow really left for California, as she told me she would at the funeral.

What little I know about Cleo Rio comes from a back issue of *Spin*, which I tracked down through a friend at a guitar store. The article, which appeared shortly after the "Me" video was released, said the former Cynthia Jane Zigler was born and raised in

157

Hammond, Indiana. At age fifteen she dropped out of school and, joined by two boyfriends, ran off to Stockholm. There she won third place in a talent contest, doing ABBA tunes in a topless rock band. The story said she moved back to the States and occasionally sang backup for Sheryl Crow and Stevie Nicks before being signed by a minor label. Buoyed by the instant success of "Me," Cleo Rio summarily fired her agent, manager, record producer and voice coach. The usual "creative differences" were cited. "It's time I broke some new ground," she told the magazine, at the crusty old age of twenty-three. Her former business manager, who claimed Cleo once tried to run him over with a UPS truck, was quoted as saying, "She's a greedy, ruthless, world-class cunt, but I wish her only the best."

Arriving at Silver Beach, I select a municipal lot in the shadow of the monstrous condo tower where I interviewed Cleo. I luck into a parking spot with a view of the eastern face of the building. Closing one eye, I count upward to the nineteenth floor. Nobody is on the balcony, and the shades are drawn.

I take out a secondhand copy of *Stomatose*, Jimmy's solo CD, which I found at a discount record store. The cover features a photograph of James Bradley Stomarti taken in his Roger Daltrey phase, curly golden tresses spilling to his shoulders. He has been posed in a hospital

158

bed with his eyelids taped and tubes snaking from his ears, nostrils, mouth and even his navel.

Stomatose, comatose. Nobody ever accused a record company of being too subtle.

Surprisingly, the first cut on the album is acoustical. It's called "Derelict Sea," and Jimmy's vocals are stunning; beautiful, really. The next song is "Momma's Marinated Monkfish," a dissonant heavy-metal screech-fest that repeats itself for nearly twelve dirge-like minutes. It's so awful it could be a parody, AC/DC doing a cover of "A Day in the Life." The whole record is similarly un-even and self-indulgent, suggesting an over-abundance of cocaine in the studio. By the sixth track I can't take any more. I switch to FM and doze off serenely to Bonnie Raitt.

It's dusk when passing sirens awaken me; a southbound fire truck, followed by an ambu-lance. I think of MacArthur Polk and wonder if I dreamed the interview; it wouldn't be the first time. Then I notice my notebook lying on the passenger seat. Flipping it open to the first page, I see written in my own hand: *Put down that I was a fighter. . . .*

So it really happened, which means the old loon really asked me to do what I remember him asking me. Which raises the possibility he is clinically insane.

More research is required.

Peering upward, I now see lights in the

apartment of the widow Stomarti. Two figures stand side by side on the scalloped balcony, looking out toward the Atlantic.

From the glove compartment I retrieve a nifty little pair of Leica field glasses, a gift from a woman I once dated. (A life member of the Audubon Society, she had hoped in vain to get me hooked on birding.) Steadying the binoculars, I slowly bring into focus the two figures — Cleo Rio and the coppery-haired, cologne-soaked young stud I'd encountered in her elevator. It would appear they're having cocktails.

Cleo is wearing a hot-pink ball cap and a loopy big-toothed smile, her free hand stroking her companion's phenomenal mane. They turn to face each other, setting their drinks on the concrete parapet. Next comes the predictable kiss and the slow clinch, followed by Mrs. Stomarti's inevitable descent to her knees and the commencement of piston-like bobbing.

Jimmy was everything to me, you know?

Cleo said it. I put it in the newspaper.

I never met James Bradley Stomarti but I find myself pissed off on his departed behalf. I shove the field glasses into the glove box and start my car.

Grubby, tacky, low, slimy, shabby — I know there's a better word for such behavior from a new widow.

Try wrong.

Yeah, that's it.

12

Jimmy Stoma's sportfisherman is docked bayside at the Silver Beach Marina. It's a thirty-five-foot Contender called *Rio Rio*. The name painted on the transom looks new, Jimmy having rechristened the vessel in honor of his child bride.

Led Zeppelin blares from the cabin, where a light is visible. I step aboard and rap on the door. The music shuts off and there's Jay Burns, filling the companionway. He's wearing a black tank top, crusted khaki shorts and skanky flip-flops. He looks drunk and he smells stoned. His pouchy Gingrich cheeks are splotched vermilion and his pupils are shrunk to pixels. The unfortunate ponytail appears not to have been groomed since the funeral.

"Who're you?" Burns blinks like a toad that just crawled out of the bog.

"Jack Tagger from the *Union-Register*. We met at the church, remember?"

"Not really."

Jay Burns is wide and untapered, though not as tall as I am. He would have played middle linebacker in college, before all that lean meat went to lard.

"I'm doing a story about Jimmy. You said we could chat."

"Doubtful," he mumbles. "How the hell'd you find me?"

"Off the police report in Nassau. It listed this marina as your home address."

"Not for long," says Burns.

"It's a helluva nice boat," I say.

"Make an offer, sport. Cleo's selling."

"May I come in?"

"Whatever," he says indolently. Burns is so loaded that our brief chitchat has tired him out.

The cabin is a mess but at least it's air-conditioned. Using an empty Dewar's bottle as a probe, I clear a place for myself among the porn magazines and pizza boxes. Jay Burns sprawls on the floor with sunburned legs extended and his back propped against the door of the refrigerator. He relights a joint, and I'm not at all offended when he doesn't offer me a hit.

Breaking the ice in my usual smooth way, I say: "Hey, I was listening to *Stomatose* on the way over. You played on a few of those cuts, right?"

Burns responds with a constipated sigh: "Jimmy asked me to."

"The notes said you co-wrote 'All Humped Out.' "

"That's right," he says with a sneer, "and I'm saving up the royalties to buy me a

162

Mountain Dew."

I abandon bogus flattery as a strategy. "How old is the boat?"

"Four years. Five, I dunno." Jay Burns is barely glancing my way. The cabin air is severe with pepperoni and reefer.

"Cleo said you brought it across from the Bahamas by yourself."

"No biggie," he says.

"Where'd you learn to run blue water?"

"Hatteras. Where I grew up."

"Ever been through anything like this before?" I ask.

"Anything like what?"

"You know. The diving accident, losing your best friend —"

Trailing blue smoke, Burns levers to his feet and lurches toward the head. "I gotta take a crap," he says, shedding a sandal en route.

I use the interlude to pluck from the galley stovetop the latest issues of *Spin* and *Rolling Stone*, both of which are open to obituaries of Jimmy Stoma. The articles are kindly written and differ little in the details of the drowning. Even Cleo Rio's words are practically the same. "Jimmy died doing what he loved best," she is quoted as saying in *Spin*. And in *Rolling Stone*: "Jimmy died doing what made him happiest."

Interestingly, there's no mention of her "wicked bad vibe" in advance of her husband's fatal dive. Perhaps because I'd braced her at the funeral, the widow Stomarti has omitted the tale of the tainted fish chowder. She has not, however, failed to plug her upcoming *Shipwrecked Heart* in both articles. I would have been flabbergasted if she hadn't. I also expected at least one of the magazines to get wind of Jimmy Stoma's unfinished solo project, yet there's not a word about this — maybe Cleo told them it wasn't true.

When Jay Burns finally emerges, unzipped and shoeless, I ask about Cleo's premonition on the day Jimmy Stoma died. Burns squints blearily. "You lost me on that one, sport."

"She told the *New York Times* she'd begged him not to make the dive. Said he'd gotten food poisoning and was in so much pain he could hardly put his tank on."

As stoned as he is, Burns still senses quicksand. "Cleo would know," he mumbles, "if anybody."

"Jimmy didn't say anything to you before he went in the water?"

"He wasn't no complainer. He coulda had a broken neck for all I know and he wouldn't of said word *uno*. That was Jimmy."

Burns is growing jittery. He spits his doobie and gropes over my head for a pack of Marlboros, stashed beside the CD player. He sucks down half a cigarette before speaking again.

"I'm fuckin' bushed, man."

"Got anything to drink?" I ask.

Burns stares heavily at me.

"Relax, Jay. I'll get it myself." I squeeze past him toward the refrigerator. The cabin is cramped and rank. A cold beer takes the sour burn out of my throat.

Burns says, "These questions, like I tole you, Cleo would be the one to say. She could help you."

"That wreck you guys were diving on — what kind of plane was it? Cleo wasn't sure."

To signal his annoyance, Burns emits a rumbling gastric grunt. "DC-6," he says, cigarette bobbing.

"She said it was a drug plane."

"Twenty years ago, sport. Now it's Disneyland for lobsters." Burns is bracing himself upright on the cabin steps because he doesn't want to sit down again until I'm gone. He figures if he stands there long enough, I'll take the hint.

"Did you see Jimmy swimming around the wreck?"

"The plane's in pieces, man."

"Yes, Cleo told me. You didn't see Jimmy at all?"

Burns says, "We dove off the boat together. He went one way, I went the other."

"How was visibility?"

"Sucko. The wind blew twenty all night long so the bottom got churned to hell." Burns digs a beer from the refrigerator. From his body language it's obvious he's lost his patience, and possibly his temper.

For deterrence I take out my notebook, which Burns regards with a mixture of disgust and apprehension.

"Weird," I remark, as if to myself.

"What?" Burns strains to see what I'm writing.

"A twenty-knot wind all night long in August," I say. "Isn't that pretty unusual for the Bahamas?"

Jay Burns draws on his beer and shrugs.

"Yet it was glassy calm," I say, "the next day when you guys went out."

"That's the islands for ya."

"So the last time you saw Jimmy alive was right after you jumped in the water."

"The tail of the plane is, like, fifty yards from the nose section. Every now and then I could see bubbles but that was it. The bottom was all muddied up, like I tole you."

"Jay, what do you think happened down there?"

"Me?"

The telltale stall. Burns is trying to roust his brain and bear down. He's trying to avoid saying something that might contradict what he told the Bahamian authorities, or what Cleo told me. His fixed, furrowed expression is that of a drunk trying to wobble his way through a roadside sobriety test.

I nudge him along. "Jay, it's hard to understand. Jimmy was an experienced diver —"

"What're you tryin' to say? Anybody can swim off and get lost. It happens," he says. "The cops in Nassau, they said they see it all the time. He coulda used up his tank and had a heart attack on the way to the top. Who knows."

"I suppose. But it just seems weird."

Burns scowls. "You fuckin' people are all alike. Stirring up shit — Jesus, a man's dead. My best friend! Cleo's husband! He's dead and here you're tryin' to make some goddamn mystery out of it, just to sell papers."

I should inform Mr. Burns that the days are long gone when headlines sold significant numbers of newspapers; that the serious money comes from home subscriptions, not rack sales. I should tell him that most of the shrill tabloids have died off, and that the predominant tone of modern American journalism is strenuously tepid and deferential.

But I can't explain any of this to Jay Burns because he's suddenly seized me in a clinch and we're caroming from one side of the cabin to the other, literally rocking the boat. He outweighs me by at least fifty pounds, but luckily — being loaded to the gills — he is neither tireless nor exceptionally nimble. I still remember a few basic wrestling moves from high school and so, in two quick motions, I'm able to twist free and dump Jay Burns on his fat ass. Kicking out with both feet, he manages to nail me in the shins and I topple backward, snapping the door off the head.

Burns struggles to rise, making it all the way to one knee before I jump him. This time I drive an elbow into his nose and he stays down, slobbering blood like a gutshot boar. I sprawl on his chest, plant a knee in his groin and pin both arms over his head.

Lowering my face to his, I say: "Oh, Jay?"

"Huhhggnn."

"You hear me?"

Rage has fled from his eyes. All he wants now is to breathe without choking on viscous fluids.

"How old are you, Jay?"

"Wha-uh?"

"Simple question. How old?"

Burns sniffs to clear bubbles of blood from his nostrils. "Forty," he says thickly.

"That's awful young. Jay, I'm talking to you."

"Yeah, what?"

I point out that Kafka didn't make it to his forty-first birthday. Burns blinks quizzically. "Who's that?"

"Franz Kafka, a very important writer. Died before he got famous."

"What'd he write — songs?"

"No, Jay. Books and stories. He was an existentialist."

"I think you busted my fuckin' nose."

168

"Guess who else checked out on the big four-oh? Edgar Allan Poe."

"Him I heard of," Burns says.

"Raving like a cuckoo bird, he was. No one knows what happened there. When's your birthday?"

"October."

"It pains me, Jay, to think you've had more time on this planet than John Lennon. Does that seem right?"

"Lennon?" Finally Burns looks worried. "He was forty when that asshole shot him?"

"Yep," I say. "Same as you."

"How do you know all this stuff?"

"I wish I didn't, Jay, I swear to God. I wish I could flush it out of my skull. Did you kill Jimmy Stoma?"

"No!" His head lifts off the floor and his red-rimmed eyes go wide.

"Did Cleo do it?"

"No way," Burns says, but with less vehemence. He's giving me a look I've seen many times before. Orrin Van Gelder looked at me the same way during our first interview, when he was trying to figure out precisely how much I knew.

Jay Burns, stoned keyboardist, is wondering the same thing.

"Let me up," he says. Shortly he won't need my permission; he's rallying fast, shaking off the cobwebs.

"What was the name of this boat," I ask,

169

"before Jimmy married Cleo?"

Burns, squirming in my grip, manages a chuckle. "*Floating Hospice*," he says.

"No kidding. That's odd."

"Odd how?" he says irritably. "Lemme up, goddammit."

"Odd that a guy who wanted to forget about the music business would name a boat after one of his albums."

"Man, you don't know what the fuck you're talkin' about. Who said Jimmy was turned off on the business?"

"His wife."

"Oh."

"And she would know, right? You said so yourself."

Before Jay Burns can buck me off, I get up. He allows me to help him to his feet, and reciprocates by retrieving my notebook from the cluttered floor. His ponytail has come undone and his oily pewter hair hangs crimped and lank. I hand him a business card listing my direct number at the *Union-Register*.

"What for?"

"In case you think of anything else you want to say about Jimmy."

"Doubtful," Burns says, though he pockets the card. "Sorry I went postal, man. It's been a shitty week."

"That's okay. I'm sorry about your nose."

"What a fucked-up way to get in *Rolling*

Stone — the 'ex–Slut Puppy' who went on Jimmy Stoma's last scuba dive." Burns spits in the galley sink. "Ten years it's been since they even mentioned my name."

We go outside to the cockpit, stepping into a blessedly fresh breeze. On the dock a snow-white heron uncoils his neck in anticipation of a handout.

Burns says, "That's Steve. Jimmy named him after Tyler on account of his skinny legs."

"Tell me about Jimmy's solo project."

"How'd you — ?" Then, scrambling: "Oh, the 'album.' It wasn't nowhere near finished — years and years he's been screwin' with that damn thing down in Exuma. He built a studio in the beach house but he never puts in more'n a couple hours. Not with all that pretty blue *agua*. Jimmy just about lives on this boat."

I ask Burns how many songs were finished.

"Not a one," he says. "It was just Jimmy by hisself, dickin' around with a Gibson."

"No session guys? No singers?"

"Nope. Just Jimmy, like I tole ya."

I'm always impressed that clods like Jay Burns, whipped and wasted, can somehow summon the energy to lie. It's as if they've got special reserve tanks of bullshit in the basement of their brains.

"Did he have a working title?" I ask.

"About fifty of 'em. It changed every week."

"And in the meantime, he was producing Cleo's new album?"

Burns starts to answer but changes his mind.

"What're you going to do now, Jay?"

"I dunno. She wants a piano on 'Ship-wrecked Heart.' I told her I'd do it."

"That's not what I meant."

"Then you lost me again," he says.

"Get some rest, sport."

As I hop off the *Rio Rio*, the white heron squawks and flies from the dock. I hear Burns call after me: "Wait, man, I gotta ask you somethin'."

I turn around to see him leaning forward intently, knuckles planted on the gunwale. Lowering his voice, he says, "I was just wonderin', Billy Preston — you ever heard a him?"

"Sure. Played with the Beatles."

"One a my all-time heroes, man. Did he, you know . . . make it past forty?"

"Yeah, Billy's still alive and kicking."

"Far out. How 'bout Greg Allman?"

"Hangin' tough," I say, "and he's gotta be pushing fifty-five."

Jay Burns looks vastly relieved. "Thanks," he tells me. "I don't keep up with the news all that much."

13

The next morning I get up early and head for the newsroom, where I will gently steal a story from Evan, our intern.

I heard on the radio that the former mayor of Beckerville has passed away "after a long illness." The former mayor of Beckerville happened to be a petty slimeball named Dean Ryall Cheatworth, who was caught accepting sexual favors in exchange for corrupt activities; to wit, initiating zoning variances to accommodate certain adult-oriented establishments. As mayor of Beckerville, Dean Cheatworth once sold his tie-breaking vote for a two-minute hand job, which ultimately resulted in the grand opening of a nude hot-oil massage parlor next door to a children's day care center. The former mayor of Beckerville would have spent much longer than three weeks in prison had he not been diagnosed with terminal cancer and released on a sympathy parole.

I'm determined that Dean Cheatworth's obituary shall not minimize or overlook his misdeeds, as happens too often at the *Union-Register*. Emma thinks it's callous to provide a full and frank accounting of a dead scoundrel's life. She says it's disrespectful to the grieving kin. I suspect if Emma had been running the show, Richard Nixon's obit would have dealt with Watergate parenthetically, if at all.

Evan doesn't seem upset that I'm poaching the story. "All right, Jack," he says amiably, "but you owe me one." Evan is gangly and cyanotic and fashionably disheveled. He has no intention of becoming a professional journalist after finishing college, but nonetheless I'm fond of him.

"Mr. Cheatworth is one of those thieving schmucks who deserves to be drop-kicked into his grave," I feel bound to explain. "Better for me to do it than you. Emma's likely to make a stink."

Evan nods, saying, "Man, you and Emma!"

Over beers he once predicted she and I would become lovers, based on the "smoldering" intensity of our newsroom arguments. It was such a ludicrous comment that I couldn't bring myself to insult the kid.

Today is different. "Wipe that frat-boy smirk off your face," I snap at him, "unless you want to spend the rest of the summer writing for the Wedding page."

Evan mumbles a bemused apology and slips away. Logging on to the morgue, I retrieve and print out the most comprehensive, unsparing stories about the onetime political kingpin of Beckerville.

After making a few quick phone calls, I begin to write:

Dean R. Cheatworth, the longtime Beckerville mayor driven from office by a sex-and-corruption scandal, passed away Thursday after a two-year battle with cancer. He was 61.

"I don't care what they say, he was good for this town," said Millicent Buchholz, Cheatworth's executive secretary for most of his 14 years at city hall. "Dean made some dumb-ass moves and he paid for them. But we shouldn't forget the decent, honest things he did along the way."

Cheatworth, who served as mayor from 1984 to 1998, is credited with bringing the first food court to the Beckerville Outlet Mall and expanding the town's bicycle-path system by almost three miles.

But two years ago, Cheatworth was convicted of trading his vote on the zoning board for private sessions with prostitutes employed by Miami massage-parlor mogul Victor Rubella. Rubella and three women pleaded guilty in the case, and all testified against Cheatworth at trial.

The jury took only nineteen minutes to convict the mayor, who was suspended from office and slapped with a six-year sentence. He was released early when prison doctors discovered a malignant tumor in his right lung.

Councilman Franklin Potts said Cheatworth felt "real crummy" about bringing disgrace upon the city. "Just last weekend he said, 'Frankie, I know I did wrong, and now it's between me and my Savior.' "

The former mayor had told friends he "found the Lord" during his 22 days behind bars. . . .

Off we go. I knock out fourteen inches by the time Emma emerges from the midmorning editors' meeting. I expect a fuss but she seems distracted. After skimming the story, all she says is: "Let's lose the tumor, Jack. Say they found an 'abnormality' in his lungs."

"Fine by me." I am elated yet suspicious.

In a discouraged tone Emma says: "You're going to love this — Old Man Polk went home from the hospital this morning."

"Figures."

"His doctors say it's miraculous."

"Had me fooled," I admit. "He looked truly awful."

"How was the interview?"

"Pretty interesting, actually." The understatement of the year. Emma would keel over if she knew everything.

"Hey, I've got an idea," she says. "You want to have lunch?"

Thanks to Jay Burns, I feel like someone took a baseball bat to my shins. I hobble to the Sports department, snatch Juan away from his desk and lead him downstairs to the cafeteria. I buy him a bagel and commandeer a table in a corner, where nobody can hear us.

"Couple things," I say. "First, you told Emma about my dead lizard."

"It was a secret? Man, I've been telling everybody."

"This is important — can you remember how the subject came up? Where you were, what you were doing. . . ."

Juan furrows his brow in mock concentration. "The subject of lizards, or the subject of you?"

"This is not funny. You think this is funny? This is my career you're messing with."

"No offense, Jack, but —"

"Don't say it!"

With unnerving precision, Juan slices his bagel into perfect halves. "I'm sorry, Jack. I didn't know I wasn't supposed to mention Colonel Tom. But it's a helluva story, you've got to admit."

"And you've got better ones to tell," I say pointedly, "about yourself. You've got the kind of stories they make movies of, Juan."

His deep brown eyes flicker. "Yeah, well, maybe Emma's not all that fascinated with my life history. Half the time we end up talking about you."

I knew it. The shrew!

"She wants dirt," I explain to Juan. "She's building a case to nail me — see, the annual employee reviews are due soon. . . ."

In Juan's expression I see the obvious but lacerating query, the one he's given up asking: *What more can they do to you, Jack?*

I float my latest theory: "She's trying to get me transferred, I'll bet, to Features or maybe the Business desk. What else did you tell her?"

"Nothing she can use against you. Promise."

"Don't be so sure. She's trickier than she looks."

"No she's not," Juan says.

"Listen to you!"

"A dead-lizard popsicle is not grounds for demotion."

"The offense of moral turpitude, my friend, is open to ruthless interpretation. Don't be so naïve."

"Well, I think you're wrong about Emma."

I practically yowl with derision.

Juan coolly lathers a bagel slice. "Based on my knowledge of women — which is considerably more current than yours, Jack — I think you're mistaken. Emma's not out to destroy you. It's just that you're a problem in her life right now and she's trying to figure you out."

This is too much. How can I argue about women with a guy who's dating (in addition to my editor) a surgeon, a skater and a cheerleader? I lean across the table and whisper: "She asked me to lunch."

"So? Maybe she's trying to make peace."

"No way. It's gotta be a trap," I say. "You've heard of a Trojan horse. This is Trojan pussy."

Juan has the most impeccable manners of any newspaper writer I've ever met. The bagel is gone and not a single crumb is on the table, not a speck of cream cheese on his cheeks.

"Did you know," he says, "that she never took so much as an aspirin until you started working for her? Now it's two Valiums a day, sometimes more."

"She's in the wrong line of work, Juan. I'm trying to show her the way out." The pill-popping business makes me feel guilty; rotten, in fact. "I don't want to do lunch with her because I've got to keep a distance. For her own sake, I've got to stay surly and unapproachable."

Juan smiles skeptically. "Sergeant Tagger's version of tough love?"

"Something like that."

"Naw, you're just scared. Obituary Boy is scared of little ole Emma."

"That's ridiculous."

"Don't worry, Jack, she won't bite," he says drily, "no matter how nicely you ask."

This is getting us nowhere.

"Do me a favor," I say, "don't talk about me anymore when you two are hanging out."

"Okay. But that'll leave us a lot of free time and not much else to do." Juan looks both amused and resigned.

"Oh, come on. You expect me to believe you and Emma still aren't humping like alley cats?"

He shrugs. "Like I said, she's different."

"Gay?"

"Nope."

"Frigid?"

"Don't think so," Juan says.

"Then what?"

"Picky," he says, rising, "or maybe just pre-occupied. Thanks for the bagel, Jack, but now I've got to hustle back to the shop — the Dolphins just signed a running back with no felony record and no drug habit. That's big news."

"What should I do about lunch?"

"Put in a good word for your favorite Cuban," Juan says with a wink. "Tell her I'm hung like Secretariat."

When noontime rolls around, I pretend to be stuck on the phone in order to duck Emma's offer of a ride. I tell her to go on ahead and I'll catch up, thinking I can use the extra time to plot strategy. But my thoughts remain jumbled and I set off with no plan.

The restaurant is Mackey's Grille, not one of the usual newsroom hangouts. I'm surprised to find Emma sipping a glass of white wine. Daringly I order an imported beer. We make agonizing small talk until the waiter shows up — Emma asks for the tuna salad and I decide on a steak, medium rare.

Once we're alone again, Emma says: "I had an unexpected visitor the other day. Race Maggad."

"My hero."

"He came to talk about you, Jack."

"Well, I don't want to talk about him. I want to talk about you, Emma — in particular, your toes."

Carefully she sets her wineglass on the table. A flash of pink appears in her cheeks, but she says nothing.

"That afternoon outside your apartment, I couldn't help but notice your toenails. They were all painted up like bright little orange and red gummy bears. Frankly, it was a revelation," I say. "Made me think I've jumped to some unfair conclusions."

"Jack."

"Yes?"

"Why do you do this?" she asks. There's nothing weak or wounded in her voice; her stare is like a laser.

I've got no good explanation for my nettle-some banter. Nerves, maybe. Unease. Self-consciousness. But about what?

This is why I didn't want to be alone with her. This is what I was afraid of.

"It's a brutal occupation we've chosen, Emma, it takes a terrible toll. Look at me," I tell her. "Once upon a time I was tolerable company. I had my charming moments. I was not immune to empathy. Believe it or not, I could sustain healthy relationships with friends, co-workers, lovers. But not anymore — could you pass the banana nut bread?"

Emma says, "Race Maggad thinks you're a dangerous fellow."

"I would give anything to make that true."

"Yet he wants you to be the one who writes Old Man Polk's obituary. He came by the newsroom to tell me personally, to 'assure' me — his word, Jack — that there's no unspoken corporate directive to keep you off the front page."

"Which you know to be horseshit."

"Totally," Emma nods. "That's why I'm confused. And why I asked you out to lunch."

With relish I explain that MacArthur Polk wants me to do his obituary because he knows it enrages Race Maggad III, whom MacArthur Polk hates almost as much as he hated Race Maggad II.

"Why?" Emma asks.

"Have you looked closely at our newspaper lately? Or any of Maggad-Feist's papers? They're all dumbed-down crapola, fluff and gimmicks and graphics. The old man knows he fucked up his legacy by selling out. He's bitter and spiteful and rich enough to play chicken with these bastards."

"He told you all this?" she says uncomfortably.

"In language unfit for publication," I say. "But here's the glorious part, the real reason young Race Maggad took time off from his precious polo practice to visit you. He's determined to make sure MacArthur Polk gets the obituary he wants. Why? Because young Race wants the old man to sell his Maggad-Feist stock back to the company before he dies, or at least leave those instructions for his estate."

Emma stiffens in her seat. "There's been rumors that somebody outside the family is trying to get control of the chain."

"Bingo."

"Who?"

"A couple of foreign outfits. Polk says Maggad is pissing razor blades."

"So what's the old man want from you?"

"Besides a Page One obit that makes him sound like a cross between Ben Bradlee and St. Francis of Assisi, nothing much," I lie smoothly. "Not a damn thing, really."

"We're being used," she says dispiritedly.

"Me more than you, Emma."

"It's basically just two rich guys screwing with each other."

"Basically, yeah," I say.

A gloom settles upon Emma, affecting her normally flawless posture. She understands she's caught up in a squalid little mess that has nothing to do with the practice of honest journalism. The fact I play a crucial role in resolving the situation only deepens her dismay.

"They don't warn you about this stuff in college," she says.

"Who'd believe it, anyway?"

"Right. Not me." Emma stares emptily at her salad.

"On the bright side," I say, "it might be another five years before Old Man Polk finally kicks the bucket. Both of us could be long gone by then."

She raises her eyes. "What?"

"To bigger and better things." A necessary elaboration.

"But in the meantime, you'll have his obit finished and in the can. Please, Jack?"

"Okay. You win."

Damn, I can't help it. I feel sorry for the woman.

We eat in affable silence. Afterwards we order coffee and Emma calls for the check; lunch is on the newspaper. She asks about the Jimmy Stoma story, and I tell her it's

184

tough sledding though I'm making progress. I know better than to mention my scuffle with Jimmy's keyboard player, but I can't pass up the chance to recount the widow's balcony blow job.

Emma lights up. "So you were right — she killed her husband!"

"Very possible. But I still don't have enough to say so."

"Oh, come on. Obviously she had a motive."

"No, Emma, she had a cock in her mouth. That's not necessarily the same thing. Cleo isn't the type to murder for love; Cleo has a career to manage."

A peppermint candy has glommed to one of my dental crowns, impeding speech. Observing my not-so-suave attempts to dislodge it, Emma stifles a laugh.

I hear myself saying, "This is no good. We can't possibly be friends."

"You're right."

"The planks of this relationship are animus, mistrust and a mutual lack of respect."

"As it should be," Emma says playfully.

Enough of this, I'm thinking.

"How many Valiums have you gobbled today?" I ask.

She is floored.

"You took one before you came to lunch, right?"

"No . . . yeah, I had to," Emma stammers.

"How'd you know?"

I reach across the table and grasp one of her hands. It's impossible to say which of us is more startled.

"You listen," I tell her, "I'm not worth it, and the job's not worth it. We get back to the office, you go straight to the ladies' room and flush mummy's little helpers down the toilet. A drug situation is unacceptable."

"You don't understand, Jack. You can't possibly."

"Take off your shoes. That's an order."

"I will not."

"Emma, I'm counting to three."

"Are you nuts?"

Next thing I know, I'm kneeling under the table and in each hand is one of Emma's taupe pumps. Her bare feet are drawn protectively under her chair, toes curling, but I can see how she's repainted the nails: miniature black-and-white checkerboards!

I pop out grinning from beneath the tablecloth.

"You're going to be fine!" I exclaim.

And Emma slugs me ferociously in the nose.

14

Emma asked me to steer clear of the news-room until the bleeding stopped and the swelling went down. So now I'm at home, avoiding the mirror and noodling on my laptop. I see by the pop-up calendar that I've got eight days in which to avoid dying like Oscar Wilde, penniless and scandalized at age forty-six. Someday I must thank Anne for the warning. My forty-seventh birthday is a week from tomorrow. I have $514 in the bank and a nose the size of an eggplant.

My mother will phone on my birthday, but she'll keep it short. She is fed up with being interrogated about my father, but I can't stop thinking about what she sprung on me the last time — that she'd learned of his death "a long time ago" from a newspaper obituary.

Because nothing turned up in the data search I ran at the newsroom, I'm left to rely on my telephone skills and the kindness of strangers. First, I make a list of cities where my mother has lived in the forty-three years since Jack Sr. walked out. In order: Clearwater, Orlando (where I attended high school), Jacksonville (where my mother met my stepfather), Atlanta, Dallas, Tallahassee and, now, Naples. Unless my mother is fudging about the time frame, my old man's death occurred at least two decades ago. That automatically knocks out the last three cities. Twenty years ago, my mother and stepfather were living in Atlanta, so that's where I begin — with a call to the morgue of the *Journal-Constitution*.

As soon as I identify myself as a brethren journalist, I'm transferred to an efficient-sounding librarian with a honey-buttered Georgia accent. She puts me on hold while she manually searches the paper's old, alphabetized clip files, the stories that predated electronic storage. As I'm waiting, my palms moisten and my heart drums against my sternum and — for one fleeting lucid moment — I consider hanging up. Whether my father croaked at thirty-five or ninety-five shouldn't matter to me; I don't even remember the guy. We had nothing in common except for the name and the blood; any other attachment is illusory, coiled like a blind worm in my imagination.

Yet I don't hang up. When the librarian comes back on the line, she apologetically reports that she cannot find a published obituary for anyone named Jack Tagger, nor any news stories relating to the death of such a person. "It's always possible it was misfiled. I could cross-check the daily obit pages on microfilm," she offers. "Can you guess at the year?"

"Till the cows come home," I say. "Thanks for trying."

I get the same discouraging results from the *Florida Times-Union* in Jacksonville, the *Orlando Sentinel* and the *Clearwater Sun.* No obits, blotter items, no stories, no Jack Tagger in the clips. I wonder if I've overestimated my mother's integrity. Suppose she invented the bit about seeing my old man's obit in a paper. Suppose she contrived to send me off on some winding, futile quest, just to get me off her back.

If so, I went for the bait like a starved carp. Two hours working the phone and zip to show for it. Serves me right.

I dial her number and Dave, my stepfather, picks up. We engage in innocuous chitchat about the tragic state of his golf game until he gets sidetracked, as he often does, on the subject of Tiger Woods. While acknowledging the young man's phenomenal talent, my stepfather fears that Tiger Woods is inspiring thousands upon thousands of minority youngsters to take up golf, and that some of these youngsters will one day gain entry to my stepfather's beloved country club and commence whupping some white Protestant ass.

"I've got nothing against blacks," Dave is saying, "but, Jack, look around. They've already got basketball, they've got football, they've got track. Can't they leave us *something?* Just one damn sport we can win at? Don't read me wrong —"

"Never," I say. Arguing would be futile; Dave is old and dim and stubborn.

"— don't read me wrong, Jack, but what can they possibly enjoy about golf? For Christ's sake, you don't even get to *run* anywhere. It's all walking or riding around in electric carts in the hot sun — can that be fun for them?"

"Is Mom home?" I ask.

"Jack, you know I'm not prejudiced —"

Perish the thought.

"— and, as you're aware, me and your mother give generously to their college fund, that Negro College Fund. We never miss the Lou Rawls telethon."

"Dave?"

"But what concerns me about this Tiger Woods — and God knows he's a gifted athlete — but what troubles me, Jack, is the message that's being sent out to the young people, that golf is all of sudden a game for, you know . . . the *masses.*"

"Dave, is my mother home?"

"She went to the grocery."

"Can I ask you something?"

"Sure, Jack."

"Not to change the subject."

"That's quite okay."

"She ever talk about my old man?"

"Hmmm."

"Because she told me he died," I say. "She said she read about it in some newspaper a long time ago. You wouldn't happen to remember when that was?"

Silence on the other end; rare silence, in Dave's case.

"Even a ballpark guess would be helpful," I say. "I'm just curious, Dave. You can understand."

"Certainly. Him being your natural father and all. It's just . . ."

"What?"

He manufactures a cough. I wish I could say I felt lousy for putting him on the spot, but I don't. Dave sold Amway for a living so it's just about impossible to throw him off stride.

"When your mother and me got married," he says, "we made a pact between ourselves. An unwritten contract, if you will."

"Go on."

"We agreed not to talk about our past . . . what's the word — involvements. Not ever. That includes ex-boyfriends, ex-husbands, ex-girlfriends, ex-wives . . . ex-anybodys. We felt it was water under the bridge that ought to stay over the dam."

"I see."

"We weren't exactly kids when we met, your mom and me. We'd both been around

191

the block a few times. Chased a few rain-
bows."

"Of course, Dave."

"No good ever comes from dredging up
the past," he adds sagely.

"Then the answer would be no, is that
right? She never mentioned my father's
death. Never once."

"Not to me, Jack. A pact is a pact," he
says. "Shall I tell her you called?"

Carla Candilla gets a regular five o'clock
break from the photo counter at the drugstore. We meet at a yogurt shop in the same
strip mall. Heads turn at the sight of her
Vesuvius-inspired dye job, or perhaps it's my
fat purple nose. In a low voice I describe the
scene on Cleo Rio's balcony. Carla begs in
vain for more details, and is slightly disappointed that the object of the widow's affec-
tions wasn't Russell Crowe, Leonardo
DiCaprio or one of the Backstreet Boys,
none of whom matches my description of the
coppery-haired felatee. Carla promises to
snoop around the circuit and report all rumors. She says Cleo's favorite local hangout
is a club called Jizz; down on South Beach,
it's Tetra.

"It's very important," I tell Carla, "for me
to get the boy toy's name."

"Give me the weekend," she says confidently. Then, fishing into her handbag:

"Wanna see something wild?"

"Don't tell me." Previous lectures on the subject of privacy obviously have made no impression.

"Oh, come on, Jack." Carla mischievously fans out the photographs like a deck of cards. One glance is more than enough.

"You can get fired for this," I point out, halfheartedly.

Carla and her minimum-wage cohorts at the drugstore keep watch for raunchy amateur snapshots coming out of the automated developing machine. If the photographs are exceptional, duplicates are surreptitiously made and passed around. Today's glossy sequence features a nude, well-fed couple, a tenor saxophone and a Jack Russell terrier in a porkpie hat. My disapproving grimace impels Carla to say: "Look, if they didn't want anyone to see 'em, why'd they bring the film to the store? Whoever they are, I think they're really diggin' it. I think they're counting on us to peek."

Pushing away the stack of pictures, I promise not to tell Carla's mother.

"Oh come off it, Black Jack. This stuff is real life. Doesn't it make you wonder about the human race?"

"Actually, it makes me depressed. These freaks are having lots more fun than I am."

"Even the dog looks happy," Carla remarks, thumbing through the photos. "By the way, who punched you in the snoot? I'm guessing it was a chick."

"Yup. My boss."

She tosses her head and laughs. "You're the best, Jack."

"Tell me who your mom went to England with."

She says, not too brutally, "You know better than to stagger down that road."

"I'm afraid I don't. That's a gruesome fact."

"Fine, then." Carla returns the purloined terrier portfolio to her purse. "You want the truth or a lie? First, tell me what you can stand."

"A doctor, lawyer, college professor — as long as it's an unpublished college professor."

"Meaning anybody except a writer."

"Basically, yeah," I say.

Carla looks at me compassionately; Anne's eyes again.

She says, "Then I'll have to lie, Jack."

"You're kidding. She went to London with a goddamned *writer?*"

Carla nods.

"Newspaper guy?" I ask, with a shudder.

"Nope."

"Poet? Novelist? Playwright?"

"Novelist," says Carla.

"No shit. Have I heard of him?"

"It's possible."

"Don't tell me his name!"

"Don't worry," Carla says.

"And, for God's sake, don't tell your mother I asked."

"Jack, they're getting married."

Me, I don't flinch. "Can I see those pictures again?"

Carla says, "I've gotta get back to work."

I buy her a mocha-flavored shake and walk her to the drugstore. At the door she pats me on the cheek and says she's sorry about breaking the news. She thought it was something I ought to know, lest I call up Anne and make a fool of myself again.

"How old is this writer guy?" I ask innocently.

"Forty-four."

"Ha!"

" 'Ha!' what?" Carla asks. "What's so bad about forty-four?"

"Never you mind," I say, thinking: Robert Louis Stevenson.

I call home and check the machine: one message from Emma and three from Janet Thrush. As usual, Janet's line rings busy so I drive straight to Beckerville. She answers the door wearing a knit hood with eye slits and a tight-fitting black jumpsuit. A gas mask hangs loosely at her neck, and she's carrying a toy M16.

"So now it's SWAT-Cam," I say.

"Yeah, my pervs got bored with Rita

Meter. Come on in, Jack." Janet peels off the headcloth. "Happened to your nose?"

"Logging mishap," I say. "What's up?"

"You will *not* believe it."

Sitting under the light racks, she tells me she was summoned by a man called Charles Chickle, whose name I know. He's a big-shot lawyer in Silver Beach; not a shyster or a barracuda, either, but legitimate weight. It seems Jimmy Stoma left a clause in his will retaining Mr. Chickle to represent Janet's interests in probate court in the event Jimmy died. Most beneficiaries don't need an attorney, but Jimmy obviously anticipated legal hurdles for his sister.

"He left me a hundred grand," Janet Thrush says excitedly. "You believe that?"

"How much for Cleo?"

"The same."

"Ho-ho. That explains the need for Barrister Chickle."

"But she also gets the boat, the cars, the condo," Janet says.

"And his tapes?"

"You mean the album? He never dreamed he wouldn't live to finish it," Janet says.

"Is it mentioned in the will?"

"Jack, I didn't even think to ask."

As for the house in the Bahamas, Janet says her brother left it to a charity called Sea Urchins, which sponsors marine camps for underprivileged kids. According to Charles

Chickle, it was to Sea Urchins that James Bradley Stomarti left the bulk of his estate, including $405,000 in stocks and annuities, his share of future music royalties, and a $1 million life insurance policy.

"Cleo must be thrilled," I say.

"I guess Jimmy figured she didn't need the dough after her single charted. He figured she was on her way."

I'm on the verge of telling Janet what her songbird sister-in-law was doing yesterday on the balcony of her dead brother's condo when she blurts: "I don't think Cleo killed him."

"What makes you say that?"

"Because she *knew* already, Jack. She knew what she was getting if Jimmy was to pass away. He already told her most of the money was going to Sea Urchins — which is a really cool idea — and he also told her she wasn't getting squat from the insurance. The more I think about it, I just can't believe she'd kill him for a hundred thousand dollars. To me it's a fortune, but to Cleo it's a weekend in Cannes."

She's right about that. A woman like Cleo doesn't get lathered up over anything less than seven figures.

"I'm thinkin' he drowned accidental, Jack, like they told us all along. You always said it was possible."

"It is."

"Even though they screwed up the autopsy."

"And you said you wouldn't believe a word that came out of Cleo's mouth," I remind her. "What if I told you she was having an affair."

Janet shrugs. "What if I told you my brother wasn't exactly Husband-of-the-Year."

The computer on the coffee table bleeps for an incoming call; another cyberwanker. Janet sighs and glances morosely at the toy M16, propped in a corner. I ask if she can think of any other motive for Cleo to have murdered Jimmy, and she says no.

"Would she have done it because she was mad about the will?"

"Then why not just dump his ass?" Janet says. "I'm sure she could've squeezed a lot more than a hundred grand out of a divorce." Another excellent point.

Again the computer bleeps imploringly.

"Aren't you sweating to death in that getup?" I ask her.

"Don't worry, it's comin' off soon enough. This one here" — Janet motions over her shoulder toward the PC — "is Ronnie from Riverside. His deal is boots, panties, bra and assault rifle. He's been hopin' I lose the bra and panties, but he's in for a major letdown. Anyhow, the setup is: I'm in the middle of a DEA raid on a Colombian drug lord's mansion when I suddenly decide to sneak a quick shower, like *that* makes sense. What I don't know is that one of the bad guys — Ronnie, a course — is hidin' in the Jacuzzi, spying on me. This'll drag on for an hour."

"Oh well. Four bucks a minute," I say brightly.

"Only for a few more months," Janet says. "That's how long Mr. Chickle says it's gonna take to get the inheritance."

"If Cleo doesn't contest the will."

"Mr. Chickle thinks she won't. He knows her lawyer."

"And most of the probate judges," I add, "on a first-name basis."

"Jimmy always looked out for me," Janet says tenderly. "Now he's gone and he's still lookin' out for me."

Ronnie from Riverside beeps again.

"Shit." Janet plugs in the light rack and the living room goes white with glare. She tugs the knit hood down over her face and positions the gas mask. This is my cue to leave.

"So, what should we do about the story?" I ask. "You don't have to decide this minute. Sleep on it and we'll talk over the weekend."

Janet's reply is muffled by the hood and the mask, but I can still make out the words. I wish I couldn't.

"What story?" she says.

I'm lying in bed with the lights off, listening to *A Painful Burning Sensation*, the last album recorded by Jimmy and the Slut Puppies. Jimmy's voice sounds huge because at the time he *was* huge, 240-plus pounds of post-rehab voracity. Then he totally changed his life and wound up dying buff, the eternal male dream. Jimmy didn't plan it that way, checking out at thirty-nine, but fans will remember him more fondly for being tanned and fit at the end. Most celebrities would kill to die looking so fine.

> *Baby, you're a fool to count on yours truly,*
> *I'm a self-centered, self-absorbed,*
>   *self-abused boy.*
> *My love goes where it pleases,*
>   *and pleases who gets it,*
> *Don't cry, beg or pray, you'll just*
>   *get me annoyed.*

That's the chorus of a cut called "Slithering Love," and I can visualize Jimmy sneering when he sings "annoyed," dragging the word into three syllables, the way Jagger might. What I enjoy about the Slut Puppies is that most of their songs were base, unpretentious, simple-minded fun. Even the blatantly derivative ones — "Slithering Love" owes everything to "Under My Thumb" — had an appealing, self-deprecatory pose. The more I hear of his records, the more I believe I would have liked Jimmy Stoma as a person.

And I'm still not convinced he drowned

accidentally. Unfortunately, as long as I'm the only one with such doubts I've got nothing to put in the newspaper.

Which leaves me back on the obituary beat, under Emma's leery watch. On Monday I'll begin to write the MacArthur Polk opus, and she should be pleasantly surprised by my enthusiasm. I haven't told her what the old coot has asked me to do, or that I've decided to play along. It no longer matters whether Polk is insane or not; without the Jimmy Stoma story, I'm unglued and adrift. I need something to reach for, a filament of hope. . . .

I must've fallen asleep because the Slut Puppies are no longer singing when I open my eyes. The apartment is dark and quiet except for the sound of someone jiggling the doorknob. Occasionally Juan lets himself in, so I shout his name and command him to go away. Emma probably told him she slugged me, so he's come to appraise my nose and perhaps scold me for the toenail-peeking incident.

"Even a deviate deserves privacy!" I holler, and soon the rattling ceases.

But no departing footfalls are heard on the walkway, so I boost myself to a sitting position and listen hard. I swear I hear breathing other than my own.

I swing my legs out of bed, pad to the doorway and peer around the corner. Immediately I wish I hadn't, because a fist connects solidly with my jawbone. I would gladly fall down except that a second, upward-driving blow has found my rib cage, momentarily suspending me. This is the work of large arcing punches, nothing like Emma's economical left cross. When my head finally hits the floor I squeeze my eyes closed and lay motionless, the cleverest move I've made all day.

The intruder pokes me with a heavy shoe but I don't move. Pain shrieks from every muscle. The man grabs a handful of hair and lifts my head. Next thing I know: blackness and the smell of damp wool. I've been blindfolded.

A ripping noise is followed by a fumbling attempt to tape my wrists behind my back. Terror would be a logical reaction, but for now I concentrate on appearing limp and unconscious. Meanwhile, the intruder roots through the place, yanking out drawers, flinging open cabinets and closets. This shouldn't take long, as my apartment is small and there's hardly anything worth stealing. I find myself feeling smug about having pitched the television off the balcony, thus depriving my visiting dirtbag of at least forty bucks from the corner pawnshop.

But something doesn't add up. I know from covering the police beat that burglars don't usually do fourth-story jobs because it's hard to be stealthy hauling computers, fax machines and home-entertainment components down multiple flights of stairs. Burglars generally prefer first-floor apartments with sliding glass doors. Now, a jewel thief doesn't worry about a building's height because everything he's stealing fits inside a pocket or a pillowcase, but only the most optimistic or uninformed jewel thief would target the one-bedroom flat of a bachelor. I don't even own a matching set of cuff links.

Whoever the intruder is, he definitely needs a refresher course in duct-taping. Two minutes and I've twisted my hands free and undone the blindfold. But now what? I feel like I've been run over by a cement truck, so I'm not especially keen to get up. Besides, the apartment is woefully short of weapons.

On the other hand, I'm extremely curious and more than slightly hacked off. In two days I've been roughed up and punched out more than I have in the last twenty-five years. Plus I can hear the fucker in the bedroom, rummaging through my socks and boxer shorts and books. . . .

Next thing I know, I'm groping down the hallway toward the kitchen. Furtively I tug open the freezer door and reach into the compartment. There, wedged beneath the ice cream bars and a two-pound bag of frozen Gulf shrimp, reposes Colonel Tom. My digging fingers locate the frosted coil of his tail, which makes a suitable handle. With a yank I dislodge the lifeless lizard from his arctic bier, loosing a crashing cascade of ice.

The broad shadow of the panting intruder materializes at the kitchen entrance — I can imagine his puzzlement when he sees me at the refrigerator instead of the telephone. With a growl he steps forward and is immediately halted by a smart blow to the forehead. With its tail curled, the dead monitor lizard is roughly the length of a sawed-off fungo bat, and stout enough to require a firm two-handed swing. I whack the intruder once more and he sinks to his knees.

Slinging both arms around my waist, he tries to pull me down. I take another wild cut but I slip on ice chips. As I fall, the frozen lizard flies from my hand and skids across the floor. Bucking in the intruder's brutish hug, I'm choked by a whiff of cologne that jolts me back to that moment in the elevator with the widow Stomarti's coppery-haired male caller. The overripe scent is unmistakable, though the man in my apartment is shorter and stockier than Cleo Rio's boyfriend. As for hair, the intruder has none — and squirts like a greased egg out of my feeble headlock.

The kitchen is embarrassingly cramped, unsuitable for a life-or-death struggle. We roll around the linoleum like a couple of drunken circus bears until, by blind luck, my left hand comes to rest on the as-yet-unthawed Colonel Tom. I resume whaling at the bald guy with a manic resolve — if he is Cleo's neckless bodyguard, a gun will be close at hand. No sense in holding back.

Groaning, the intruder shields himself with one arm and begins punching robotically with the other; an effective technique, it turns out. A blow catches me flush on the tip of my nose, the same nose earlier tenderized by Emma, and I black out from the pain.

Honestly I didn't expect to wake up. I expected to be shot dead, "execution-style" (as we're fond of saying in the news biz). But I awaken alive and alone, curled in a puddle of blood so bounteous that it cannot be entirely my own. Crimson bootprints mark the intruder's wobbly path from the kitchen to the living room and out the front door.

Gingerly I strip off my sticky clothes and head for the shower; every square inch of me stings or throbs, but at least the bleeding has stopped. Toweling off, I notice a stranger with a misshapen face scowling from the mirror.

One advantage to living the spartan life, it's easy to clean up after a looting. In thirty minutes the place is put back together, and nothing is missing except my laptop. Stored on the hard drive were a couple of canned obits — a railroad tycoon and some retired opera soprano — but that's no big deal; I'd already wired electronic copies to my terminal in the newsroom.

The most unsavory chore is disposing of Colonel Tom, who was soundly pulped in the altercation. Snugly I wrap his cold, scaly form in an old bedsheet and lob it from the balcony. The bundle tumbles into a Dumpster, four stories below, where it lands with a muted *thwock*. Instantly I regret the toss, for there's a sturdy knock on the door and I find myself unarmed and defenseless. The knocking persists, and eventually a flat male voice identifies itself as an authority figure.

Cops!

Neighbors, none of whom have ever shown an interest in my personal affairs, apparently heard the commotion in my kitchen and alerted the police. I open the front door to see not one but two men of similar age and stature, neither in uniform. I'm poised to slam the door when one of them flashes a badge.

"Detective Hill," he says. "And this is Detective Goldman."

Obviously I appear thoroughly puzzled, because Detective Hill adds: "We're from Homicide, Mr. Tagger."

Numbly I step back, my arms falling slack at my sides. Apparently I've killed a man with a frozen lizard.

"It was self-defense!" I protest. "He broke in while I was sleeping. . . ."

The cops exchange perplexed glances. The talker, Hill, asks what in the name of Jesus Christ I'm babbling about.

"The dead guy! The one who busted into my place."

Hill peers over my shoulder, scoping out the tidiness of my modest living quarters. "Mr. Burns broke into this apartment? Tonight?"

"You're damn right he . . . who?"

"John Dillinger Burns," he says. "Otherwise known as Jay."

"No! No, this guy was bald," I blabber, "it wasn't Jay Burns. I *know* Jay Burns. No way."

"Yeah, that woulda been some nifty trick," says Detective Goldman, breaking his silence, "since we just saw Mr. Burns laid out at the county morgue."

"He's been dead since early this morning," Detective Hill adds informatively. "What would you know about that, Mr. Tagger?"

"Not a damn thing." My voice is a dry croak.

"Really?" Hill is holding something inches in front of my eyes, something pinched between his thumb and forefinger. It's a business card from the *Union-Register.* My name is printed on it.

"Burns had this in his pocket," Detective Hill explains, "when his body was found."

"Now, why would that be?" his partner inquires.

"And what happened to your face, Mr. Tagger?" Hill asks.

Me, I don't panic.

"Officers," I say, "I wish to report a burglary."

15

Emma's couch is too short for my legs.

She tugs down the sheet to cover my feet and fits a pillow under my head. She informs me I've suffered a mild concussion, a diagnosis based on the fact I got dizzy, vomited and fainted on her doorstep. She tells me she went to nursing school for two years before switching to journalism, and I say she would have made an outstanding nurse. She appraises my rubescent schnozz guiltily, so I assure her that somebody else punched me harder than she did.

It's one in the morning and Radiohead is playing on Emma's stereo, a neat surprise.

In her wire-rimmed reading glasses she sits cross-legged in an armchair, the calico cat on her lap. She's wearing tennis socklets so I can't scope out her toes. I squeeze my eyelids shut and wish for this murderous headache to abate. In the meantime I'm telling Emma about my scuffle aboard the *Rio Rio* with Jay Burns, who seven hours later was found dead behind a tackle shop on the Pelican Causeway. A bait truck loaded with finger mullet backed up over the ex–Slut Puppy, whose ponytailed gourd had been resting inopportunely beneath the vehicle's right rear wheel. How his head had gotten there was the question that brought detectives Hill and Goldman to my apartment. Hill believed that Jay Burns, being clinically intoxicated, probably passed out in that fateful location. Goldman, however, speculated that an assailant might have clobbered Jay Burns and purposely placed him beneath the truck. The medical examiner offered no insight; so pulverized was the keyboardist's skull that it was impossible to discern if he'd been bludgeoned prior to being run over.

Emma is pleased to hear how I cooperated with the detectives, recounting my visit to the boat (though omitting the substance of my questions, and Jay's tantrum) and providing the precise times of my arrival and departure from the marina. Both Hill and Goldman seemed to buy the idea that I was interviewing Burns for a posthumous newspaper profile of his best friend, the late James Bradley Stomarti.

"Then you're not a suspect," Emma says.

"Try to sound more relieved."

"The guy who broke into your apartment, what do you think he was after?"

"Who knows. My Chagalls?"

"Jack, I'm not the one knocking on doors at midnight."

"Yes, well, you *are* my editor. I felt you should be notified of what happened."

A feeble lie. The fact is, I'm not sure why I came to Emma's apartment. I don't clearly recall driving here. Gazing at the varnished pine beams of her ceiling, I hear myself say: "I had nowhere else to go."

Cat in arms, she leaves the room. Moments later she returns with ice cubes wrapped in a washcloth, which she lays across my eyes and forehead.

"Is that too cold?" she asks.

"Why won't you sleep with Juan? Everybody sleeps with Juan."

"Do *you*?"

"I'm talking about the ladies, Emma. Is it because he's a sportswriter?"

"No, it's because he's your best friend."

"Juan is a gentleman. He never talks about his love life."

"Then how do you know we haven't slept together?"

"I pried it out of him."

"Really," says Emma. "Why?"

I peek from under the washcloth to see if she's miffed.

"You're my boss, he's my friend," I say. "You two get serious and it's bound to affect my pathetic little universe. That's the only reason I cared if you and he were —"

"Having intercourse?"

"What is this, ninth-grade biology?"

"Fucking, then," Emma says pertly. "Is that better?"

I sit up, pressing my knuckles to my ears to keep the brains from leaking out. "Don't worry, I didn't ask Juan for the juicy details. You got any Excedrin?"

Emma brings me three aspirins and a glass of water.

"Lie down. You'll feel better," she says.

Stretching out, I announce: "You should go back to nursing school. You were born for it."

"How about you, Jack? Are you sleeping with anyone these days?"

"Excuse me?" Again I start to rise but from behind I feel Emma's hands lock on my shoulders.

She says, "It's only fair, since you know all about *my* sex life."

"Wrong. I only know you're not sleeping with Juan. And you know I'm not sleeping with Juan, so we're even."

"Don't think so, Tagger."

I like the way Emma laughs, I must admit. I like being in her apartment, as opposed to the emergency room at Charity. I even like the way she's holding me down. . . .

Christ, Jack, snap out of it. Saving Emma will be impossible if I don't soon revert to the irascible prick of her newsroom nightmares. But when she apologizes for socking me in the nose, I tell her I deserved it.

"I'm not a well person," I submit. "I saw those sparkly toenails and was riven with

212

envy. Obviously something inside of you rollicks carefree and fanciful. I've completely forgotten what that's like."

"Doesn't it hurt to talk so much?" Emma asks.

"I can't believe Jay Burns is dead. I can't fucking believe it. Listen, you wanna go for a ride?"

"Jack, it's late. You need to rest."

"Put on some shoes. Hurry up."

The cops had been there first, followed by persons unknown. I show Emma where the yellow crime tape strung around the dock pilings had been broken, then clumsily re-attached. I yank the tape down, roll it into a wad and toss it in a bucket. Then we board the *Rio Rio*.

Whoever sacked the cabin was smart enough to wait until the detectives had come and gone. The place is in shambles now, but it wasn't much neater thirty hours ago when I'd arrived to interview Jay Burns. The porn, pizza cartons and music magazines have been restrewn across the floor and the berths. Add to that mess the unlaundered contents of assorted drawers and cabinets, plus several unappetizing containers from the refrigerator.

Emma and I are poised in the narrow companionway, contemplating a path through the ripening debris. I lead the way, stepping cautiously. Exhilarated, Emma keeps a grip on my arm. The first priority is turning on the air conditioner because the cabin smells like piss, beer and old sneakers.

"What are we looking for?" Emma whispers.

"Something the bad guys didn't find."

I'm guessing it took more than one man to deal with husky Jay Burns. Later, after the boat was searched, the bald intruder was sent to my place on the chance that I'd conned the mystery stash out of Jay, or stolen it outright.

For forty-five minutes Emma and I root through the cabin and turn up nothing but a Baggie of sodden pot, undoubtedly discarded as worthless by the previous searchers. In fact, every hatch, panel and storage bin appears to have been opened and emptied ahead of us. We step back up to the deck and, employing one of Jay's flashlights, check the bait well and the engine compartment. On the console above the wheel is a sprout of loose wires where the bad guys removed some of the Contender's electronics — probably the VHF, depth finder and Loran. This gesture was intended to make it look like a common boatyard burglary, which it most definitely was not. I show Emma the disconnected wires, then flick off the flashlight.

She says, "Now what?"

"Write his obituary, I guess."

"Jack."

"I forgot. He doesn't rate."

Emma says, "If anything, it's a brief for Metro."

Sorry, Jay, but that's how it goes. No space in the newspaper for dead sidemen.

My skull rings like a gong. Carefully I sit down behind the wheel of Jimmy Stoma's boat. I'm wondering what violent chain of events I might have set in motion by surprising Jay Burns and quizzing him about Jimmy's secret sessions. I remember the anxiety in his pig-drunk eyes when he asked me if Billy Preston was still alive, and now I feel like a creep for needling him about outliving Franz Kafka and John Lennon. Maybe he wigged out and did something rash, such as phoning Cleo Rio to warn her I'd been snooping around.

In the shadows, Emma sneezes.

"I'm sorry. I should take you home," I say.

"Sorry for what? This is . . ."

"Fun?"

"Exciting, Jack. I spend all my days stuck in boring meetings, or sitting like a goob in front of a video screen. This is my first crime scene."

"Didn't Juan take you to a Marlins game?"

"Go ahead and make fun. Not everyone . . ."

"What?"

"Never mind." Emma points. "Hey, maybe it's under those scuba tanks."

I aim the flashlight at the deck in front of the transom, where a dozen white dive tanks are arranged in two upright rows, like jumbo milk bottles. The tanks stand undisturbed, indicating the killers weren't interested. They must have believed that whatever they were seeking was concealed indoors.

While Emma holds the light, I move the scuba tanks one by one. The deck beneath and between them is empty. I'm amused to hear Emma mutter, "Damn."

Then we luck out. While hoisting the next-to-the-last tank, I hear something sliding back and forth inside. Flipping the tank on its top, we find the charred weld where the rounded bottom has been cut away, then recapped. It's a crude job, but the marks are well concealed by the way the dive tanks were aligned. Emma opens the door to the companionway and I drag our find into the ransacked cabin. Among the contents of an overturned toolbox Emma locates a small pick and a heavy mallet.

"Turn on the stereo," I tell her. "Loud."

As we're engulfed by Jay's beloved Led Zeppelin, I go to town on the scuba tank. Smiling, Emma cups her hands over her ears. She's having a blast.

Ten minutes of furious hammering breaks the weld. The bottom piece flies off the tank and lands in the galley sink, spinning like a saucer. I reach into the hollow aluminum cylinder and come out with a bubble-wrapped parcel.

"Drugs?" Emma whispers at my shoulder, but I'm thinking: Gun.

As I unwrap the package I notice my fingers are trembling; Emma's breath is coming in shallow bursts. Yet the bubble-wrapped object is neither a lid of grass nor a pistol. At first glance I mistake it for an eight-track cassette, but it's slightly larger and thicker. "Let me take a look," Emma offers. She turns the black plastic box around in her hands. "See that little doohickey? This thing plugs into a computer."

"What could it be?"

"I haven't got a clue," Emma says, "but I know who would."

"Oh no. Not on a Friday night."

"It's now Saturday morning." She points at her watch.

"Three a.m. We can't possibly do this now," I insist.

"Why not?"

"Because." Hell, I tell myself, just get it over with. "Because he'll have company."

"Oh, who cares," Emma says merrily. "Honestly, Jack."

In the car I twist up the volume on the *Stomatose* CD and, in memory of the late Jay Burns, play for Emma one of his collaborations with Jimmy Stoma.

Three days in the sack and my dreams
   came true
But you gotta let me up 'cause I'm all
   black 'n' blue.
Don't take it personal, ooooh, don't pitch
   a fit.
My gums are bleedin' and the motor's quit.
I love you, baby, but I'm all humped out.
I love you, baby, but I'm all humped out.
Aw, I want you, baby, but I'm . . . all . . .
   humped . . . OUT!

"Catchy," Emma says thinly. She remains unconvinced of Jimmy Stoma's genius.

"Could you hear Burns on the piano?"

"Not really, Jack."

"Doing his Little Richard bop."

"Who's Little Richard?" she asks.

"You're breaking my heart."

I'm pulling into the driveway of Juan's house when Emma says, "I've never been here before."

"Then you should be warned: This is where he frequently sleeps with women."

"I'll try not to make a scene," Emma says.

The house is dark. I knock firmly on the door. She stands back, clutching the gadget we found inside the scuba tank.

"Maybe he's not home," I say hopefully.

"His Jeep's in the carport," Emma notes.

I knock again, harder this time. A light appears through a side window and soon we hear voices, plural.

"Juan!" I call out. "Hey, Juan, it's me!"

The door cracks open. "Obituary Boy?"

"Yeah. You decent?"

Juan pokes his head out, blinking fuzzily.

"Hi," Emma says.

"Hi there." Juan reddens. "Look, I —"

Here I leap in with abject apologies and begin to relate the turbulent events of the evening. He cuts me off and waves us in. Emma and I choose an overstuffed sofa and sit side by side, like a couple, while Juan hurries to the bedroom to change. Again voices are heard, but Emma is unflinching. Her expression suggests she approves of Juan's taste in art and furniture. When he returns, in wrinkled blue jeans and a polo shirt, he is accompanied by a stunning black-haired woman whom I recognize as Miriam, the orthopedic surgeon. She now is wearing Juan's robe, making a statement.

"Miriam, you remember Jack," Juan says, nervously smoothing his hair, "and this is Emma, she works at the newspaper, too. She's an editor."

Miriam acts unimpressed but Emma is smooth as silk. The two women exchange cool hellos. Juan looks at me pleadingly and all I can do is wince with remorse.

"We won't stay long," Emma says, and hands the black box to Juan. "We think it attaches to a computer."

He nods. "Sure does. Connects right here, with a cable." Out of courtesy he shows it to Miriam, who also nods. When I sneak a glance at Emma, a smile plays at the corners of her mouth.

"It's an external hard drive," Juan says.

"What does it do?"

"Whatever it's told. Where'd you get this?"

We can't tell him, not with Miriam hovering. She is intently curious about the reason for our visit; only high drama can excuse an interruption at this hour.

"It's a long, messy story," I tell Juan.

Emma pipes up: "Jack's working on an investigation." Words I never dreamed I'd hear her say.

Juan winks at me. I ask him if the hard drive will fit on my computer at work.

"Might," he says, "but it'll probably come up as gibberish on your screen." He explains that the device is like a disembodied brain. "You can't just plug it in anywhere and expect it to zap back to life. You need to figure out how it was programmed before you can find out what's inside."

And what's inside that little box, I'm hoping, is the key to Jimmy Stoma's death.

Emma says to Juan, "Can you give it a try?"

His eyes flick painfully from Emma to Miriam, and then to me. He says, "Um . . . not tonight. How about tomorrow?"

"Tomorrow is fine," I say.

He peers at my lumpy face. "Man, you all right? Looks like you fell down three flights of stairs."

"Two," I say with a crooked smile. "And would you believe I was dead sober."

Miriam, the physician, feels obliged to let us know she isn't fooled by our light bonhomie. "You've been beaten up," she says sternly. "You've been punched in the face."

"Yes, and elsewhere." Suddenly I don't feel so chipper. "Come on, Emma, let's be on our way. These two kids need some shut-eye."

Just as I'm approaching the car, the flagstones in Juan's yard start dodging my feet. Emma orders me into the passenger seat, where I prop my clammy forehead against the window.

"Thanks for driving," I say.

"Welcome."

"You okay?"

"Better than you. Take a nap."

"She's a doctor. Miriam is." For some inexplicable reason — or perhaps as an unfortunate side effect of the concussion — I decide Emma should know that Juan has high standards. He doesn't screw just anybody. "A trained surgeon," I add.

"Well, she's very pretty."

I hear myself saying, "Not as pretty as you."

"Jack, you're so full of shit."

"Fine."

God, do I feel wretched — this is the worst possible time to be alone with Emma. I'm liable to blow everything. When I ask her to turn down the volume on the stereo, she says, "Gladly." It will be her final word on *Stomatose*.

As we pull up to her driveway, she snatches the car keys out of the ignition. "You're in no shape to go home."

"Give 'em here! I'll be all right."

"Don't be a jerk."

So I'm back on her couch, with a sweaty palmful of aspirin and a forehead packed under ice. She's wearing an oversized Pearl Jam T-shirt and padding barefoot around the place, turning off lamps and checking the locks.

"Jack, wouldn't it be something," she's saying, "if they're trying to knock off the band?"

"Who?"

"Well — first Jimmy Stoma dies, and now Jay Burns. What if somebody's killing off the Slut Puppies one by one?"

Emma slips into the bathroom, out of view. I can hear the assiduous brushing of teeth. "Fink a bow id," she gurgles.

"I've heard of careers being murdered," I say, "but never a whole band."

When Emma returns, she smells like a

mint. "Well, who's left?"

"The lead guitarist died a few years ago, so there's really just the two bass players."

"What about a drummer?"

"Jimmy went through a dozen of 'em," I say.

The apartment is dark except for a light on the nightstand in Emma's bedroom.

"Maybe you should talk to them. The bass players," she suggests.

"When — between dead rabbis?"

"Hey, didn't I give you a week to crack the case."

" 'Crack the case'?" All of a sudden I'm Angela Lansbury.

Emma rolls her eyes and heads for the sack. Moments later, her room goes black. I swallow the aspirins dry, and blink exhaustedly. Bedsprings squeak as Emma arranges herself beneath the covers. In the darkness I hear myself saying, "Hey, I never answered your snoopy question."

"What's that?" Emma calls back, testily.

"You asked if I was sleeping with anybody. Well, I'm not."

"I know." She replies so quietly I can barely hear it. "Get some rest, Jack." And I obey. . . .

Later I awake to a rhythm of breathing that's not my own. The ice has been removed from my brow, and my cheeks have been patted dry. Emma is pulling the blanket down to cover my feet.

When I stir, she whispers, "It's just me."

"You missed your calling."

"Close your eyes."

"How old are you, Emma?"

"I'm twenty-seven."

Oh Christ oh Christ oh Christ oh Christ.

"Why do you ask?" she says.

Hendrix Joplin Jones Morrison Cobain — I could scream out their names. But instead all I say is: "Twenty-seven. Wow."

"Wow yourself. It's not as great as you remember."

"Are you kidding? It's beautiful."

"I threw away those Valiums," she says. "After lunch I went back to my desk and tossed them in the garbage, every damn pill."

Silence in the darkness. Has she returned to the bedroom?

"Emma?"

"What?"

Good. She's still here.

"Thanks for taking care of me tonight."

"Thanks for the adventure, Jack." She leans down and kisses me as lightly as a butterfly brushing my lips. Then I'm alone again, tumbling into a fine dreamless sleep.

16

There's nothing wrong with me, not even a mild concussion. That's the word from my doctor, Susan, who is six years younger than I am and works the rookie shift, Saturdays, for a downtown medical group. Susan isn't impressed by my swollen nose, the knots on my jaw or the knuckle-shaped welt on my ribs. However, the tale of how I came by these scrapes and bruises intrigues her, especially the business about the frozen lizard. I feel pressure to be entertaining, knowing she believes my monthly physical examinations are a waste of time. I always insist on the works, of course, including a full spectrum of blood-gas analysis and the ever-popular prostate excursion, upon which Dr. Susan is preparing to embark.

"No offense, Jack," she's saying, "but I'm damn tired of looking up your ass every four weeks. It's totally unnecessary, as the nice folks at your HMO have pointed out."

"Humor me, okay? And don't I always pay cash?"

"There's nothing wrong with you," Susan says again. "You're a completely healthy specimen — physically, at least."

"You married yet?"

"No, but if I was," says Susan, from behind, "I'd keep a three-carat diamond ring on this finger" — the dreaded snap of latex! — "just for you, buddy."

The death of John Dillinger Burns rates two paragraphs on page three of the *Union-Register*'s Metro section. *Police are investigating the circumstances . . . Alcohol and drugs are believed to be involved. . . . Burns, 40, formerly had been the keyboard player for a popular rock band, Jimmy and the Slut Puppies. Ironically, the group's lead singer, Jimmy Stoma, recently died in a diving accident in the Bahamas. . . .*

And that's that. Onward to the Sports page, where Juan has a story about a college basketball star who became a gambling addict by the age of twenty — another superb piece, unsparing and poignant at the same time. What I'd give to have Juan's touch!

"Hey, handsome."

It's Carla Candilla. Her hair is now . . . I want to say turquoise.

"Close enough," she allows. "Sorry I'm late. Is this Pellegrino for me? You're such a sweetheart."

We're meeting at her favorite cafe, Iggy Cheyenne's, which overlooks the beach and the old wooden fishing pier. Seagulls are a menace at lunchtime, but today they're wheeling clear of our table. For this I credit Carla's vivid dye job.

226

She wants to hear all about the break-in at my apartment, enthralled at the thought of me fighting back and drawing blood. I purposely don't mention the handy role of the late Colonel Tom, whom Carla believes to be alive and running free with other lizards.

A bleary-eyed waiter materializes. Carla and I order a calamari appetizer and two Greek salads. Afterwards she sets down her glass, glances around and says: "Well. You're not the only one who had a big Friday night — guess who I saw at Jizz."

"The singing widow!"

"Nope. Her boyfriend."

"You're sure?"

"My sources are primo," Carla says, "but I would've pegged him anyway, on account of the hair. What's up with *that*?"

"I told you it was amazing."

"From behind we all thought it was Mariah Carey. I swear he must do it in a fucking laundry press, that hair."

"What's his name? Who is he?"

I pull out my notebook and fumble for a pen. Carla grins. "Black Jack in action!"

"Did you get his name or not?"

"What do you think? Course I got his name. It's Loréal."

"First name first."

"He doesn't have one," she says.

"Of course he does."

"No, that's his whole name. Loréal."

"Like Sting or Bono —"

"Very good, Jack."

"Except this chowderhead named himself after a shampoo."

"Can you believe it?" Carla squeaks.

"So what does Messr. Loréal do for a living?"

"He's a record producer, is what I heard. Very hot." Carla's watching me scribble in my notebook. "I asked who he's produced and somebody said the Wallflowers but then somebody else said no, it was Beck. I never really got it straight, but everybody says he's hot."

"And they say he's bonking Jimmy's wife?"

"More like she's bonking him."

I drum my pen on the table.

"See, the difference is," Carla says, "like, Cleo's in total charge of the program. She calls, he comes running. The sex is at her convenience, not his. He's the boy toy, just like you said."

I prod Carla for more dope about Loréal and she says he's twenty-nine or thirty, has recently moved here from Los Angeles, drives a motorcycle and, based on firsthand observation, has a fondness for Ecstasy. He tells everyone within earshot that he's producing Cleo's new album.

"I want to meet this guy," I tell Carla.

She beams. "You gonna kick his ass? Jack, I'd pay good money to see you punch somebody."

"What's so funny?"

"I can't picture it, that's all. I just can't!" She pops a batter-fried squid into her mouth. "This dickbrain who busted into your apartment — was he bigger than you? God, what if he had a gun! You ever think a that, Jack?"

"Hook me up with Loréal. But please don't tell your mother you're helping me out."

Carla snaps her fingers. "That reminds me!" She hoists a voluminous crotcheted handbag onto her lap and takes out a thick shiny book. With a flourish she passes it across the table, annoying the waiter who is attempting to deliver our salads.

"What's this?" I ask.

Carla raises an eyebrow. "You heard of him, right?"

"Sure."

The novel is called *The Falconer's Mistress*. On the jacket is a drawing of (naturally) a falcon, wings flared. The bird is perched on the velvet-gloved fist of a woman wearing a sparkling ruby bracelet. Only her bare Corfu-tanned arm is shown. The author of the book, whose name is displayed in raised gold lettering, is Derek Grenoble. His secret-agent novels sell millions.

"Your mother is marrying this person?"

"First I wasn't gonna tell you," Carla says, "but then I figured you'd find out sooner or later. I never read anything the guy wrote but he seems nice enough. Seriously."

I turn the novel over and study the re-
touched face in the photograph. "He looks
like Ann-Margret in an ascot."

"He's British," Carla volunteers. "Or maybe
it's Australian."

"In the first place, that can't possibly be
his real name. 'Derek Grenoble'? No way.
Your mom knows better. Second, he can't
possibly be forty-four."

Carla frowns. "You're taking this worse
than I thought."

"I'm disappointed, that's all." Heartsick is
more like it. And jealous and petulant and
furious at myself for driving Anne away.

"Jack, she's really happy. I'd tell you if she
wasn't."

"Swell. Lady Anne Grenoble — is that
what she'll be calling herself from now on?
When's the big wedding day?"

"Next Saturday."

"You're shitting me."

"Derek's leaving for Ireland to start another project."

"That's my birthday," I say emptily.

"Oh, man. I forgot," Carla says. "How old
now?"

"A hundred and seven."

I open Derek's latest masterpiece to a
random page in the middle. "Listen to this:
'Duquesne turned to the section chief and
eyed him with revulsion, as if he were a
worm in a bright red apple. Incompetence

was one thing, reckless ego another. Kincaid was dead because he'd left her out there too long, much too long, with no way out. That Duquesne could never forgive. From a pocket he drew out Kincaid's empty Walther and placed it on the section chief's desk. Then he spun on his heel and stalked out of the building. By the time he reached the airport, he had decided precisely where to go and whom to kill.' For God's sakes, Carla, tell me he's kidding."

To my horror she puts down her fork and says, "Keep reading, Jack, go on. What happens next?"

No place matches a city newsroom for energy, or ennui. Between big breaking stories are droning, brain-numbing lulls that allow reporters to ponder too deeply their choice of occupation. Burnout is common because of the long hours and the crummy pay and the depressing nature of so much of what we write. As the saying goes, they never send us to the airport when the plane lands safely. Those who bail out of journalism usually beeline for law school, a graduate degree or well-paying gigs in corporate public relations. Personally, I'd rather have my nuts nailed to a poisonwood.

Up until a few years ago, I'd never had any doubts about newspaper work, never thought I'd made the wrong choice. I went into the business not because I was looking to get beat up or training to be a novelist, but because I wanted to be Bob Woodward or Sy Hersh, kicking butt on the front page. Reality slowly set in and I came to understand that I wasn't destined for Washington or New York or even Miami, but still there were good stories; good days when I brought grief and misery and the occasional felony indictment upon lowlifes such as Orrin Van Gelder. I believed the job was important, a public service, and as a bonus it was unfailingly entertaining. Every new story was a fresh education in human guile and gullibility. The headlines made a large splash in a small pond, but the ripples didn't last long. That didn't bother me, either, because usually I was already caught up in something new. It's the best job in the business, chasing crooks in Florida, because the well never runs dry. But then the paper was sold, the news hole shrunk, the staff got downsized, I got pissed off and — when the opportunity presented itself — publicly humiliated our new CEO.

Thus sabotaging my own career.

A brief snapshot of Race Maggad III: rangy and blond, with a smooth plump-looking chin, narrow green eyes and a tan as smooth as peanut butter. His long aquiline nose has a permanent hump where he once whacked himself accidentally with a polo mallet. Twice weekly his fingernails are professionally polished to a porcelain sheen, and the tooth whitener of his preference is imported at no small expense from Marseille. He calls his wife "Casey-Coo" and they own four neutered golden retrievers, in lieu of children. They tend homes in Wellington, Florida; East Hampton, Long Island; and San Diego, California, where Maggad-Feist has its corporate headquarters. The man of the house loves sports cars, particularly those of German pedigree. Recently he turned forty-one, the same age at which Bebe the bottle-nosed dolphin (one of seven who played Flipper on TV) passed away.

Fashion-wise, Race Maggad III aims for a look of relaxed self-importance. Today, for instance, he's wearing crocodile loafers with no socks, khaki trousers and a crisp Oxford with the monogrammed cuffs upturned. To hilarious effect he has knotted the sleeves of a navy tennis sweater around his neck. It is August in Florida.

"Good afternoon, Jack," he says.

"Greetings, Mr. Maggad."

I'm camped at my desk, reading an old *Rolling Stone* interview with Jimmy Stoma that was unearthed for me by young Evan on a mission to the public library.

"Got a minute?" Maggad's tone is one of pained geniality.

"I'm pretty busy, actually."

"Come on. We'll use Abkazion's office."

I scan the newsroom for potential witnesses. It's Saturday afternoon and the place is quiet — Emma's not working, which is just as well.

"So," Maggad begins, settling in behind the managing editor's cluttered desk, "I guess you heard Mr. Polk checked out of the hospital."

"Yes indeed. Another medical miracle."

"How was your visit? How did he seem to you?"

"Feisty and incontinent."

Race Maggad III purses his liver-colored lips. "But mentally how did he seem — alert? Aware of his surroundings?"

"Sharp as a tack. I sorta liked the old bastard."

"Yes, I gather the feeling is mutual. Did he happen to say why he wanted you to be the one to write his obituary?"

It's lame, this fishing expedition of his. What a bumbler.

"Because," I reply, "my unfettered style reminds him of James Joyce."

"Mmmm."

"Or is it Henry Miller?"

I remain the portrait of earnestness, while Maggad gnaws fretfully on the inside of his right cheek. My puffy nose and lumpy jaw have provoked unease and possibly suspicion. He's well on the way to regretting this incursion into the newsroom, where he stands out like the proverbial turd in the punch bowl. He might own the place, but he doesn't belong.

"Jack," he says, "we've never really talked, you know."

"About?"

"About what happened at that shareholders' meeting, I mean. I got your gracious note," he adds, "and I certainly took it to heart."

The apology was written, signed and sent to Race Maggad III without my knowledge. The author was Juan Rodriguez, who was trying to save my position on the investigations team.

"But I've been wanting to sit down like this, privately," says our polo-playing CEO, "to tell you — to *assure* you — that I believe as deeply as you do in thorough, hard-hitting journalism. And I believe it's possible to have great local newspapers that are also profitable newspapers. That's our goal at Maggad-Feist."

Young Race is aiming for annual profits of twenty-five percent, a margin that would be the envy of most heroin pushers.

"Were you ever a reporter?" I know the answer but I ask anyway, to make him squirm.

"No, Jack, I wasn't. I took an M.B.A. at Harvard."

"Ever work in a newsroom?"

"Look, I've been a newspaperman my whole life."

I hear myself cackling like a macaw. "You've been an *owner* of newspapers your whole life, that's hardly the same. Your daddy and your granddaddy were accumulators of newspapers," I say, "just as they were accumulators of waffle houses."

Maggad goes crimson in the ears, for I've touched a sore spot. When Maggad-Feist acquired the *Union-Register*, the press release referred to that part of the company holdings as "a popular chain of family specialty restaurants." One of our business writers, Teddy Bonner, made the mistake of elaborating in a section-front story. Within days a memo came down sternly informing the staff that, when writing about Maggad-Feist, it henceforth was "unnecessary" to mention Wilma's Waffle Dens, or the unfortunate bacterial outbreak that killed nine innocent customers and hospitalized fifty-four others who had dined upon improperly refrigerated breakfast sausages.

"By the way," I say to Race Maggad III, "are any of those pesky wrongful-death cases still kicking around?"

He steeples his long fingers and in a low voice says, "You're trying to get yourself fired, is that it? So you can turn around and sue us for God only knows what. Get your face in the paper, I bet you'd enjoy that."

I hear myself asking what kind of a name Race is. "When you were little, did they call you 'Master Race Maggad'? I bet they did. I bet they engraved it on all your birthday-party invitations."

Glaring hotly, he knifes to his feet. Dark crescents have bloomed in the armpits of his shirt. For a moment I think he's going to lunge across Abkazion's desk to strangle me, and who would blame him.

"Tagger," he hisses through clenched jaws, "what-is-your-goddamn-problem?"

"I suppose I don't like being jerked around. Why don't you just tell me why you're here and then I can tell you to fuck off, and we can both get on with our day."

Taking notice of the sodden half-moons on his Oxford, young Race deftly folds his arms for concealment. "MacArthur Polk's obituary," he proceeds curtly. "I want to read it."

"It's not written yet."

"Bullshit."

"And even if it was —"

"Bullshit. Your editor, Amy, said —"

"Her name is Emma."

"She said she told you to get right on it."

"Indeed she did," I say, "and I will."

"So help me God, Tagger, if you're stone-walling . . ."

I point out that Old Man Polk is not only still alive, but apparently on the rebound. "Whereas other people are dropping dead every day," I add, "significant people who deserve significant obituaries. We are woefully shorthanded, Mr. Maggad, due to severe reductions in our staffing and news resources. I am but one man."

Young Race ignores the dig about his budget slashing. Deep in sour rumination, he fingers the hump on his nose. "I'd like to know what Mr. Polk said at the hospital. Tell me what he asked you to write."

"Oh, I can't possibly do that."

"Why not?"

"Because it's confidential. The *Union-Register* has strict rules against reporters divulging unpublished information."

"Yes, to outsiders," interrupts Race Maggad III. "But I'm not an outsider, Tagger. I sign the paychecks around here."

"No, you sign the paychecks of the people who sign the paychecks. And if you're not an outsider, why does everybody stop and gape whenever you stroll into the building? I know two-headed carnies who don't attract so much attention."

"Have it your way. I'll speak to your editor and we'll get you straightened out, mister, and pronto."

"A solid game plan. And in the meantime, sir" — I whip the notebook out of my pocket — "I need a quote."

Judging by young Race's expression, I might as well have pulled the pin on a live grenade. Reflexively he takes a step backward, knocking over a copper sculpture of an angelfish on Abkazion's credenza.

"A quote for what?" inquires the young tycoon.

"Old Man Polk's obit. It's only fitting," I say. "You're the one who bought his precious newspaper. You're the big cheese."

Maggad re-seats himself. After a pensive pause, he gives the signal that I should prepare to write.

"MacArthur Polk," he begins, "was like a second father to me. He was a teacher, a friend and an inspiration. Mac Polk was the heart and soul of the *Union-Register*, and we are dedicated to keeping his spirit alive every day, on every page of this outstanding newspaper."

A deep, self-satisfied sigh, then: "You get all that, Tagger?"

"Every word." A tidy sentiment from such a vapid yuppie puke, I've got to admit.

"Do me a favor," he says. "Run it by Mr. Polk, would you?"

Again I start to giggle. I can't help it; the guy cracks me up.

"What's the matter now?" he demands.

"You want Mr. Polk to know in advance what you're going to say about him after he's dead."

"That's correct."

I cannot make young Race comprehend why this is so funny, because he doesn't know that *I* know why he's sucking up to the old man. So, let's play it out. . . .

"Mr. Maggad, you needn't worry. I'm sure he'd be very moved by your pre-posthumous tribute."

"Show him the damn quote anyway."

"While he's alert enough to appreciate it."

"Exactly." Race Maggad III checks his wristwatch, which clearly cost more than my car. Now he's up again, striding briskly out of Abkazion's office. I'm hard on his heels. "Tell Amy," he grumbles over his shoulder, "I want a copy of Mac Polk's obituary faxed to me the day you finish it."

"It's *Emma,* and you'll have to kill me first." Young Race and I draw a flurry of glances as we stride past the city desk — it's all he can do to keep from breaking into a trot. When we reach the elevators, he literally punches the Down button. I wait beside him with a companionable air — I'm heading for the cafeteria. I could sure go for a candy bar.

"You don't worry me," snarls the chairman and chief executive officer of Maggad-Feist Publishing Group. "You're a gnat on the radar screen."

"On the windshield, you mean," I say helpfully. "On a radar screen I would be a 'blip.' "

"Fuck you."

It's been mildly interesting, getting to know the dapper young publishing scion. Miserably he pokes again at the elevator button. When the door finally opens, he bolts inside. Quick as a bunny, I join him.

"You know what my career goal is, Master Race?"

"Get away from me."

"My goal is to work at this newspaper long enough to write *your* obituary. Wouldn't that be something?"

17

From the *Rolling Stone* interview with Jimmy
Stoma, dated September 20, 1991:

RS: Are you happy with the way *Stomatose*
    turned out?
JS: *Oh, yeah. The more I listen to it, the
    creamier it gets.*
RS: Some of the cuts sound a lot like the
    Slut Puppies. "All Humped Out," for
    example, blows the doors down —
JS: *Sure, because I had Jay on grand piano
    and Tito on bass. Even though it's a solo
    album I'm not gonna turn my back on the
    band. We still make great fucking music to-
    gether and I'd be a jackass not to take ad-
    vantage of that chemistry on my own
    projects. I just don't want to tour as a
    group anymore. No way.*
RS: Do you have a favorite cut on the new
    album?
JS: *No, I dig 'em all.*
RS: Oh, come on. "Derelict Sea" is a cool
    number, and very different from any-
    thing you did with the Slut Puppies.
JS: (laughing): *Okay, you busted me. That one
    is definitely at the top of the list.*

RS: What inspired you to try the acoustic?

JS: *Hey, I* love *acoustic. Always did. And I love to sing without screamin' at the top of my frigging lungs, but when you're up on-stage with not one but* two *bass guitars, you've gotta howl like a witch.*

RS: Do you plan on writing more songs like that?

JS: *For sure. My next project is a whole folk-rock kind of thing — not all acoustic but thematic, you know, where the pieces weave together into a story. Maybe it'll even be a double album, only this time I'm gonna produce it myself.*

RS: All right, what's your *least* favorite cut on *Stomatose?*

JS: (shaking his head): *Nuh-uh. I ain't fallin' for that.*

RS: Don't wimp out on us now. Even Lennon didn't like every song he wrote.

JS: *The only track that sort of got away from me was "Momma's Marinated Monkfish." A bit too much partying, I'm afraid. The original idea was this real sophisticated, Phil Spector kind of mix. You know, overdub the piss out of the guitars and the keyboards. But somehow it ended up as some ungodly hypermetal . . . head-ache.*

RS: Twelve and a half fun-filled minutes.

JS: *Yeah, and I don't even remember laying down the vocals, I was so bent.*

I'm summoned by Juan to the Sports department, where he hunches like a safecracker over his PC.

"I got that external hard drive hooked up," he says, "but I can't read what's on it. I don't have the software." He taps a finger on the screen. "The best I can come up with is a directory, but take a look."

It's line after line of coded abbreviations, beginning with:

> V7oyst10all
> B17oyst10copy
> BV22oyst7
> LEADoyst.all
> G1deal22
> G2deal22.all
> ALT.Vtitle22 . . .

"Computer lingo?" I ask.

"Nope. Abbreviated file names that were keypunched in by whoever was running the program."

"What kind of files?"

"I don't know, but they're massive," Juan says. "The whole thing is, like, 400-plus megabytes. That's got to be more than text, Jack, to eat up so much memory. I'm guessing there's audio or video on here."

"Where can we get the software?"

Juan looks up ruefully from the screen. "Man, I can't even *identify* the software."

"Oh swell."

"But I know who can."

"Juan, I can't afford a hacker." It will be a miracle if I pay off the Bahamas trip by Christmas.

"He's not a hacker, he's just a whiz kid. And this isn't hacking. Hacking is when you go online —"

"Point is, I can't pay your man anything right now. I'm broke and Emma's got no expense money for the Death page. Her whole budget is basically me."

Juan rocks back and laughs. "The guy I use is twelve years old. Usually I just give him a couple of passes to a ball game."

"Twelve years old."

"Yep. And his room looks like the NASA command center."

"When I was twelve, I could barely change the tire on my bicycle."

"I'll drop the hard drive off with him later," Juan says, "before his bedtime."

"Thanks. And I promise never to disturb you again on a date night."

"*No problema.*" Juan glances around to make sure we can't be overheard. "Was Emma freaked by Miriam being there?"

"How would you like that answered, Mr. Hung-Like-a-Racehorse — the humbling truth, or an ego-inflating fabrication?"

"See, I knew she wasn't interested in me," Juan says. "Tell me, brother. Are you fraternizing horizontally with your editor?"

"Get your mind out of the gutter."

Juan would love to know about the kiss, but I won't be telling him. It's possible I dreamed it, anyway.

"Some goon trashed my apartment and beat me up — I'm guessing he was looking for that hard drive. I figured you'd have an overnight guest, so I crashed at Emma's."

"Emma your sworn enemy." Juan arches his eyebrows.

"She was never the 'enemy,'" I say stiffly. "She's my boss, that's all." Before Juan can press the issue, I tell him about the suspicious death of Jay Burns and our daring search of Jimmy Stoma's boat.

"That's where we found the hard drive."

Juan whistles. "Know what? You should go to the police and tell 'em everything. I'm serious, man. Once people start breaking into your home and pounding on your face, then it's time to quit playing Marlowe."

"First I've got to put it all together."

"Listen, Jack, no story about a dead rock singer is worth getting whacked over."

"Easy for you to say — you're a superstar. What if getting whacked is the only way I can get back on the front page?"

Juan looks stricken. I assure him I'm only kidding.

"Hey, asshole. I'm your friend," he says. "I don't want anything bad to happen."

"Don't worry. I'm damn close to cracking it wide open."

This is the most egregious lie I've told in days. I can't produce a single human being who knows for a fact that Jimmy Stoma was murdered. Assuming he was, I can't figure out a plausible motive, or even cook up a theory that holds together. All I'm doing is kicking over stones to see what crawls out.

"And you'll be pleased to know," I tell Juan, "that Colonel Tom is no longer aslumber in my kitchen. His services were required last night in defense of the homestead."

"Oh no. What the hell'd you do?"

"Used him for a baseball bat, with spectacular results. He's now decomposing in a Dumpster, and could never be fingered for a deadly weapon."

"Jesus," Juan says in a frantic whisper, "don't tell me you killed your burglar!"

"It would be lovely to think so."

"Come on, Jack," he pleads. "This craziness has gone far enough, no?"

"I turn forty-seven in a week. Know what that means?"

Juan waves his hand and turns away, muttering something in Spanish. I'm pretty sure it's not "Happy Birthday."

I drive home and crash for three, maybe four hours — a leaden, dream-free sleep for which I'm grateful. Later I try repeatedly to call Janet Thrush, figuring she might know something about the mysterious computer box hidden on her brother's boat. The phone line rings busy every time; Janet-Cam's Internet fan club, no doubt. I find myself dialing Emma's number and hanging up in a panic before she answers. I fear that by spending the night on her couch I've violated a personal embargo, and there can be no resumption of terms. It weighs gravely that I enjoyed her company probably more than she enjoyed mine, and that the delicate balance of our professional relationship most surely has been tilted to my detriment. That damned kiss, if it indeed occurred, was the clincher. All day long I've been dogged by impure thoughts about Emma, my editor. I suspect I would even make love to her, if the opportunity were cordially presented.

For half an hour I prop myself in a hot shower, and eventually the face in the shaving mirror begins to resemble my own. The message light on the answer machine is flashing when I emerge from the bathroom — Carla Candilla, whispering into her cell phone. She's waiting for me in a booth at Jizz. Get your skinny white ass over here! she says.

So far, Jizz is the only joint on Silver Beach with a red velvet rope and a sullen, T-shirted, steroid-addled doorman. The club's motif combines the exotic ambience of a Costa Rican brothel with the cozy, down-home charm of a methamphetamine lab. By the time I reach Carla's booth, I feel like I'm hacking up bronchial tissue. The first topic of discussion is my wardrobe. "Are those really Dockers?" Carla blurts, horror-struck.

I tell her my boa-skin thong is being oiled at the cleaners. She instructs me to sit down, people are staring. Soon I'm staring, too — at Carla. For a dress she's wearing what appears to be a shrimp net, through which two silver nipple rings are visible. Flustered, I turn away — this is Anne's daughter, for God's sake.

The club is lit with fruity-colored strobes that dice up the cigarette haze like a psychedelic SaladShooter. A Nordic-looking DJ in unlikely rasta garb is in command of the synthesized dance music, thumping as tediously as a cardiac monitor. Everywhere are fashion-conscious couples practicing for the South Beach scene; the guys still look like off-duty valets, and the women still look like cashiers at Blockbuster.

Carla says, "It's Saturday night, Jack. This is how you dress up? That's a fucking golf shirt, if I'm not mistaken."

"Designer casual wear, for your information. Since when do you smoke Silk Cuts?"

"Since my favorite cigar bar went out of business. And I don't inhale, so no lectures, please, daddy dearest." Carla cuts her violet-lined eyes toward a back corner of the club and says, "Check it out."

Cleo Rio and her personal grief counselor, the shimmery-maned Loréal, are jointly embedded in an oversized leather beanbag. They're smoking like a pair of Hallandale bookies, and I'm fairly sure Cleo hasn't spotted me through the smog. She is tastefully attired in a black vinyl jumpsuit complemented by wraparound shades; tonight her pageboy haircut is tinsel blue. Loréal is sporting black stovepipe jeans and a shiny pink shirt with preening flamingos. Out of respect for the dead, he is confining his fondling of the widow Stoma to her left breast.

Other clubbers drift over to the beanbag chair to chat with Cleo; offering condolences, perhaps, or eight-balls of coke. I'm pleased to see no sign of the bald no-neck bodyguard, whom I suspect of being my burglar. Someday, under the proper circumstances, I intend to upbraid him for swiping my laptop.

Carla says, "You believe that shit? Her old man's only been gone, like, a week and already she's out on the circuit with the new boy."

"So much for wallowing in grief. You come alone?"

"I'm meeting some friends." Carla's eyes are locked on Cleo and Loréal. "That's the

250

same stupid getup he was wearing last night, swear to God."

"If Cleo sees me she'll go ballistic. Somehow I need to get Mr. Hotshot Record Producer alone."

"Hang in there," Carla advises. "They didn't arrive together and I bet they won't leave together. That white stretch out front? It's Cleo's. Move over here, Jack, next to me. So it looks like . . . you know."

Uneasily I switch to her side of the booth.

"What's the matter?" she asks.

"Nothing."

"You're so busted. It's the dress, isn't it?"

"Carla, I mean, yeah."

"They're just boobs, Jack."

"But they're *your* boobs," I say. "The boobs of my ex-girlfriend's daughter. You thirsty? *I'm* thirsty."

Smiling, Carla flags down a server. Given the bawdiness of her attire, it's useless for me to remind her that she's too young to buy alcohol. For herself Carla orders a Cosmopolitan and for me a vodka tonic with a twist.

"How'd you know?" I ask.

"Mom told me."

"Wow. She remembered."

"She remembers everything," Carla says.

"Ah, that's right. Fair Lady Grenoble."

"Did you start reading the book yet?"

"You know that dork's real name?"

"Derek's?"

"Yeah, I looked it up: 'Sherman Wilt.' Your mom's about to marry a Sherman — that doesn't alarm you, honey? The man sold RVs before he became a writer."

"No way, Jack, he's from the U.K."

"Well, he moved all the way to Dunedin, Florida, to sell Dream Weaver travel trailers. That's not appalling?"

She rolls her eyes. "Let it go. Drink up."

"His books," I mutter to my vodka, "are fucking unreadable."

"Who's that?" With her cigarette Carla points toward the beanbag corner, where Cleo and Loréal have been joined by a wiry, dark-skinned man with curly long hair and a Pancho Villa mustache.

"That," I say, "is Señor Tito Negraponte, another former Slut Puppy. He was at the funeral."

Cleo and the record producer discreetly disengage, and make space for Tito between them on the beanbag throne. The two men shake hands the old-fashioned way, as if it's the first time they've met.

Carla says, "What did he do with the band?"

"Bass guitar."

"Who's he with now? He looks pretty old and moldy."

"Yeah, he must be all of fifty-two. It's amazing he gets around without a wheelchair."

I'm distracted by two bony models in mini-skirts who are pogo-stomping on the dance floor. They're sucking on baby pacifiers, waving phosphorescent swizzle sticks and flashing their panties at the bartender, or possibly me.

"That's just the kind of chick you need, Jack. Totally." Carla jabs my sore ribs. "Seventeen-year-old X freaks, they'll rock your little world."

"Your mother's the only one who ever did that."

"What?" Carla leans closer. The DJ has ratcheted up the volume to encourage the gregarious dancers.

"I said, your mother's the only one who ever rocked my world. And now she's sleeping with a bad novelist."

Carla shrugs helplessly.

"And marrying the bastard on my birthday." I gulp down the last of my vodka. "The woman who remembers everything."

"Not birthdays," Carla interjects. "She's lousy on those, Jack. You can ask my father. Yo, look who's leaving."

Loréal has risen off the beanbag throne. He air-kisses Cleo, high-fives Tito and makes his way across the floor, dodging the models and heading toward the door.

"Wish me luck," I tell Carla.

She slides off the seat to make way. "Go! Get a move on. I'll keep an eye on the widow and the Mexican geezer."

I peck her cheek and lay out a ten for the drinks, which she promptly shoves back in my palm.

"You got my cell number, right?"

"Listen, Carla, are you really meeting somebody? I feel crummy leaving you here alone."

She finds this uproariously funny. "Don't worry, Daddy, I'll be fine. Now beat it."

I reach the beachfront parking lot just as Loréal is mounting his Harley. By the time I get the Mustang started and wedge myself into the heavy flow on A1A, Cleo's studhunk already has a five-block head start.

Florida's legislature recently passed a law allowing motorcyclists to ride without helmets, a boon for neurosurgeons and morticians. Tonight I benefit as well, for Loréal's lack of a head protector makes him easy to follow even at night, his long hair streaming behind him like a red contrail.

He doesn't go far; a billiards joint called Crabby Pete's. I park my car next to the chopper and wait twenty minutes, enough time for Loréal to get at least two more drinks in his system. Then I grab my notebook and enter the bar.

"What paper'd you say you were from?"
"The *Union-Register*."
"Never heard of it."

"We're the only rag in town."

"To be perfectly honest, I don't have time to read all that much."

This hardly comes as a thunderous shock. Loréal and I have been chatting for an hour and it's my impression he'd need a personal tutor to get through a set of liner notes. Mostly we've been discussing music — specifically, his sizzling career as a record producer. His résumé lengthens with each beer, though he has stumbled once or twice when reciting the various artists who've sought out his genius. My notes reflect a certain recurring confusion, for example, between the Black Crowes and Counting Crows. Young Loréal's credibility has also been dented by boastful references to his clever (though uncredited) studio work for a band he insists on calling "Matchbox Thirty." I've made no effort to correct him because — as any reporter will tell you — there's no finer thrill in our business than interviewing a hapless liar. I've gotten him rolling by telling him that I recognized him from a photo in *Ocean Drive*, and that I need a few quotes for a feature story about Cleo Rio's soon-to-be-released CD.

He says, "She told you I was producing it, right?"

"Actually, she said her husband was the producer."

"For sure, he *was*." Loréal is tracing a tic-tac-toe pattern in the rime on the bartop. "It was a real bummer, what happened to her old man. She came to me all crying and was like, 'I don't know what to do. I need help finishing the record.' "

"I'd gotten the impression they were almost done," I say.

Loréal clicks his teeth and feigns demureness. "Hey, I'm not gonna say anything about Jimmy Stoma, okay? He did a good job, considering it was his first-ever gig on the boards. All I told Cleo was, hey, this record could be even better with a little extra juice. And she's all like, 'Go for it, man. That's what Jimmy would've wanted.' So," he says in a confiding tone, "we're gettin' there. We're real close."

Merrily he watches me jot each golden word. I expect his demeanor would change if I asked about his unconventional way of consoling Jimmy's wife; to wit, placing his pecker between her lips. But I avoid that line of inquiry, tempting as it is, and allow Loréal to imagine himself the portrait of the cool young *auteur*, patiently explaining his craft to the stolid middle-aged journalist. His true roots are revealed, however, by the sound of a thick-soled motorcyle shoe tapping along to a Bob Seger song on the jukebox. I resist the urge to like him for it.

"Maybe you could explain something to me," I say.

"For sure." Loréal has milky girlish skin with a spattering of cinnamon freckles, though I would swear his cheeks have been lightly rouged. He has baptized himself liberally with the same rotten-guava cologne that he wore that day in Cleo's elevator, which explains the bartender's brisk retreat. Every so often Loréal tilts his head so that the glossy mane hangs clear of his shoulders, and gives it a well-practiced shake.

"I thought record companies didn't release a single until the whole album was done. But 'Me' came out months ago," I say. "It seems strange there's still no Cleo Rio CD."

"She's with a small label and they do things different." On this subject Loréal is not so thrilled to see me taking notes. "Plus, the lady's a righteous perfectionist. She wants to take her time and do it her way. But, yeah, there's pressure to get the record wrapped, and we're almost there. Basically it's down to one song."

"Which one is that?"

" 'Shipwrecked Heart.' The title cut."

"The one she sang at the funeral," I say.

"I wasn't there," Loréal says pointedly, "but I heard she did." Two more beers have been delivered, and he snatches at one.

To keep the conversation moving, I ask him if he'd heard about what happened to Jay Burns.

"Yeah, Cleo told me. Unfuckingbelievable,"

he says. "Jay was supposed to play piano on 'Shipwrecked.' "

"Any of the other Slut Puppies working with Cleo?"

"Nope," he replies, between swigs. I'm waiting to see if he mentions meeting Tito Negraponte tonight, but all he says is: "Jimmy had a good band, but Cleo wants her own sound. Definitely."

He stands up, digs into his stovepipes and throws a twenty on the bar. "Listen, I gotta motor. You need anything else, call Cueball Records in L.A. and ask for the publicist. Sherry, I think her name is."

"Thank you, Loréal."

He smiles and sticks out his hand, which is moist from the bottle. "What'd you say your name was?"

"Woodward. Bob Woodward." I spell it for him. He nods blankly. "Good luck with the album," I say.

"For sure, bro."

At that salutation, I'm overtaken by a whimsical urge to mess with his head. "Doesn't all this creep you out?" I ask as we're heading for the door.

"All what?"

"First Jimmy Stoma, now Jay — it's almost like there's a curse on Cleo's record."

Loréal tosses his magnificent hair and laughs. "Shit, man, it's just the music business. People are always dyin'."

18

Nine-fifteen on Sunday morning, Emma calls.

"Hi, there. You awake?"

I can barely hold the phone. My eyelids feel like dried mud. I had only three beers last night so it's not a hangover; I'm just whipped. Pertly my female caller says:

"Everything all right? How's the story going?"

I remember that Emma makes a mean cup of espresso, and it sounds like she's had about seven cups.

"You got any interviews set up for today? I thought maybe you could use some company."

"Sure," I hear myself say as though it's no big deal, Emma playing sidekick. "But first I've got to know: Did you kiss me the other night?"

"Hmmm."

"When I was on the couch."

"Yes, I believe that was me."

I'm too groggy to know whether Emma is being playful or sarcastic. "I need some guidance here," I tell her.

"Regarding the kiss."

"Exactly. How would you describe it?"

"As friendly," she says, unhesitantly.

"Not tender?"

"I don't think so, Jack."

"Because that's how it felt to me."

"You were in pain. Your judgment was clouded." Emma is a tricky one to read over the phone. "Well, what about today?" she sallies on. "You want me to swing by and pick you up?"

"Sounds good. I've got to track down a source of mine in Beckerville." Now I'm even talking like frigging Woodward. It would seem I'm trying to impress her — all I need is a parking garage for the rendezvous.

"Great," she says. "See you in an hour."

You learn a lot about people from the way they drive. Anne, whom I loved anyway, was a rotten driver; inattentive, meandering and, worst of all, slow. Anne behind the wheel made my eighty-three-year-old grandmother look like Richard Petty. But Emma, to my surprise, is a regular speed demon. She's buzzing along the interstate at ninety-two miles per hour, deftly winding through the church-bound traffic, which is light. She says she's wild about her new car.

"Excellent mileage, highway *and* city," she reports, sipping from a plastic bottle of boutique spring water. Like almost everyone else I know these days, Emma travels with her own clear fluids. I should probably do the same, as

I'm entering the stage of life when kidney stones tend to announce themselves. I must have mumbled something along these lines, for Emma is now extolling the wonders of ultrasound bombardment, a technique that successfully atomized a granular constellation in her father's urinary pipes. That's right, her father.

I'm driven to ask how old he is.

"Fifty-one," Emma replies, and I take unwarranted comfort in the four-year gap in our ages.

"He's a reporter, too," she adds.

"Really? Where?"

"Tokyo. For the *International Herald Tribune.*"

I'm surprised Emma has never mentioned this; I had her pegged as the daughter of an academic.

"Are you two close?"

"My best friend," she says, "and a good writer, too. A *really* good writer." She peers dubiously over the rims of her sunglasses. "Didn't run in the family, obviously. That's why I became an editor. Which exit do we get off?"

Emma is wearing snazzy tangerine sandals, but only one of her toenails is painted — with a charm-sized red heart, if I'm not mistaken. What could that mean?

She catches me staring and says, "It's just a scab, Jack. I stubbed my foot on the rocking chair."

My mother has always been a zippy driver, and adept at talking her way out of speeding tickets. When I was a kid she would take me to Marathon every summer, and on the trip down we'd always get stopped once or twice by state troopers. We stayed at a tatty one-story motel on the Gulf, and in the mornings we'd rent a small Whaler and go snorkeling, or fish the mangroves for snappers. I couldn't catch a cold but my mother is a canny, intuitive angler, and more often than not we'd return to the dock with a full cooler. I can't recall why or when we stopped vacationing in the Keys, but it probably had something to do with baseball and girls. These days my mother occasionally goes fishing in the man-made lakes on the golf course in Naples, where she and Dave own their condominium. Once she called to say she'd caught a nine-pound snook on a wooden minnow plug, and offered to FedEx me one of the fillets on dry ice. Dave, she explained, eats strictly red meat.

Yet she loves him still.

"Here's our exit," I inform Emma, who engages the ramp at a gut-puckering velocity.

"Right or left?"

"Left. Guess who showed up in the newsroom yesterday — Race Maggad his own self."

"Again?" Emma's brow furrows attractively.

"We had a conversation that he will likely

recount as unsatisfactory. He demanded an advance peek at the MacArthur Polk obituary —"

"Which you haven't finished."

"Or even started! I told him he couldn't preview it under any circumstances. Rules are rules."

"The CEO of the publishing company — you told him that?"

"Emphatically. Two more lights, Emma, then hang another left."

She's gnawing on her lower lip, a job I would gladly (here I go again!) undertake. "What did he say? Did he mention me?" she presses on.

Once upon a time I wouldn't have hesitated to tell Emma that the chairman of the company had botched her name, but now I don't have the heart. "He'll be speaking to you shortly," I say, "about my impudence and so forth. But he did provide a dandy quote for the story. Old Man Polk would blow out an artery."

"Dammit, Jack," says Emma.

"Oh, come on. You can handle young Race."

"That's not the point. Why do you insist on causing trouble?"

"Because he's a phony, a fop, a money-grubbing yupster twit. And he's murdering this newspaper and twenty-six others, in case you hadn't noticed."

She says, "Look, just 'cause you've given up on your own career —"

"Whoa there, missy."

"— doesn't give you the right to sabotage mine."

Sabotage? A scalding accusation from mild-mannered Emma. Of all my schemes to rescue her from the newsroom, sabotage was never once contemplated.

"You think I want to spend the rest of my days doing this?" she says. "Editing stories about dead scoutmasters and bromeliads?" (Emma is also in charge of our Garden page.)

"How can Maggad blame *you?* He's the one who's too scared to have me canned," I point out. "His lawyers think it would look punitive, after our dustup at the shareholders' meeting. They fear it would generate unwanted notice in the business columns."

"They're afraid you'll sue him," Emma says flatly.

A station wagon hauling a raucous, elementary-school-age soccer squad has stalled in front of us at a traffic signal. That, or the beleaguered parent at the helm has simply bolted from the car. To soothe Emma, I decide to risk a confidence. "What if I told you it won't be long before I'm out of your hair for good. I can't say exactly when, but it's almost a sure thing."

"What in the world are you talking about?"

The station wagon is moving again, Emma accelerating huffily on its bumper. I'm tempted to share the delicious details of MacArthur Polk's offer, but the old loon could easily change his mind — or forget he ever met me — before taking to his deathbed for real. Moreover, I'm not wholly confident that Emma wouldn't spill the beans to young Race Maggad III if the corporate screws were applied.

"Are you job hunting?" she asks me closely.

"Slow down. It's that white house with the blue trim."

"Jack, tell me!"

She wheels into Janet Thrush's driveway, stomps on the brake and whips off her sunglasses. There's nothing for me to do but kiss her, very briefly, on the lips. No retaliatory punch is thrown.

"Come on," I say, stepping out of the car, "let's go commit some journalism."

Janet's banged-up Miata is parked out front but she's not answering my knock. Emma says we ought to bag it and come back later, but I've got a bad feeling — there's a fresh pry mark on the doorjamb. Cautiously I twist the knob, which falls off in my hand.

"What're you doing?" Emma says.

"What does it look like?"

Stepping inside, I break into a sickly sweat. The place has been looted. Half a dozen times I call Janet's name.

"Let's go, Jack." Emma tugs anxiously at my shirt. This isn't as safe as boarding Jimmy Stoma's boat. This time the cops haven't been here ahead of us; only the bad guys.

Janet's makeshift TV studio has been demolished. The tripod racks are down, lightbulbs shattered on the floor. A couch is overturned, the ticking slit open with a knife. Her computer operation — keyboard, monitor, CPU, video camera — is gone.

I expect the rest of the house to be in shambles, but it's not. Emma stays on my heels as we move wordlessly down the hall; at each doorway I pause to gather a breath, in case Janet is lying lifeless on the other side. Oddly, nothing in the kitchen, the bedrooms or the closets appears disturbed. A light is on in a bathroom and cold water runs from a faucet in the sink. I turn it off.

"Maybe she wasn't here when they did this. Maybe she's okay," Emma whispers.

"Let's hope." But I fear that even if Janet Thrush is alive, she's not all right. Her Miata shouldn't be parked in the driveway, and the intruders should have gotten farther than the living room. Something worse than a burglary happened here.

"Jack, we'd better go."

"Wait a second. Let's think this through." We're sitting side by side on the end of

Janet's queen-sized bed. Somewhere in another room a phone is ringing and ringing — Ronnie from Riverside, maybe, or Larry from Fairbanks. Doesn't matter because the computer line is disconnected, and Janet's gone. Emma says, "You know why I think she's okay? Because we haven't found a purse. She must have taken it with her, which means she's probably just fine."

I'm not persuaded. Why would a woman returning to a ransacked house flee with her handbag but leave the car?

Emma follows me out the front door. When we arrived I didn't look closely in Janet's convertible, but now I see why she didn't drive it away. The glove box is ajar, the carpeting over the floorboard is ripped back and both bucket seats have been wrested off their mounts. Whoever broke into the house started first with the Miata.

Which means Janet most likely was at home, inside, when they came through the front door.

"Shit." I kick another dent in the car.

"You think it's the hard drive they were after?" Emma's voice is shaky.

"That'd be my guess."

"You ever had this happen before — a source disappearing like . . . ?"

"No, ma'am." The wise move is to call the cops anonymously from Janet's phone, pretending to be a concerned neighbor, then depart swiftly. There's no point trying to explain our presence here to detectives Hill and Goldman. Emma agrees, not eager to involve herself, or the *Union-Register*, in a possible kidnapping investigation. We're hurrying up the steps toward the house when she suddenly stops, pointing into a flower bed. Carefully I reach through thorny bougainvilleas and pick it up — Janet's toy M16, the prop for her SWAT-Cam costume. I hold it up for Emma's inspection, saying "Don't worry, it's not real."

"Is this hers?"

"Yup."

"What in the world does she use it for?"

"She performs on television," I say, "sort of."

Before we re-enter the house I take out a handkerchief and wipe my prints off the doorknob; likewise the faucet in the bathroom. In the kitchen I Saran-Wrap my right hand before using the wall phone to dial the sheriff's office, Emma pacing in the living room. No sooner have I hung up than I hear her twice cry out my name.

She's rigid when I reach her side. "What is that?" she says hoarsely.

A dark stain on the carpet, recognizable to anybody who has covered a homicide. I hear myself saying, "Oh no."

"Jack?"

I grab Emma's arm and lead her outside

and place her in the passenger seat of the Camry. She assents numbly when I tell her I'll do the driving. I take it real easy down the interstate, checking the rearview every nine seconds like some kind of paranoid coke mule. Emma's clenched left hand, as pink as a baby's, is on my knee.

"Who was she?" she asks finally, in a broken voice.

"Jimmy Stoma's sister."

Standing on the pier watching the horizon bleed away with the last of the sunlight, I'm thinking about the only time I got engaged. Her name was Alicia and she was, I later discovered, mad as a hatter. I met her on a newspaper assignment, a feature story about a beer promotion disguised as a balloon race from St. Augustine to Daytona. Some guy left his boogie board on the beach and I accidentally demolished it with a rental car, distracted at that moment by Alicia in an electric-blue bikini. The guy who owned the boogie board turned out to be her boyfriend, whom she dumped five days later to move in with me. We were both twenty-four. The decision to become engaged was strictly hormonal, which isn't always foolish, but in this case the lust began to ebb long before the diamond ring was paid off. Among Alicia's multiple symptoms were aversions to sleep, employment, punctuality, sobriety and monogamy. On the positive side, she volunteered weekends at an animal shelter.

Soon my apartment filled with ailing mutts that Alicia had saved from euthanasia while secretly consorting with one of the staff veterinarians, who (she later complained) took unfair advantage of her weakness for ketamine and nitrous oxide. Our breakup was a spiteful and messy business, mostly because of the loose dogs, yet I'm amused to recall that I presented myself as heartbroken at the time. Within weeks I was again pursuing waitresses, emergency-room nurses and secretaries, an agreeable social orbit that accepted newspaper reporters without disdain. This carried me along until I met Anne, who worked in a bookstore. During our first conversation she managed to eviscerate Jane Austen with such aplomb that I was smitten on the spot. What she saw in me, I couldn't say.

Anne and I didn't fade out or implode like most of my other relationships. Back and forth we went — together, then apart, then together again — as if caught on a wild spring tide. What finally ended our romance was my crushing demotion to the obituary beat and the morbid preoccupations that came with it. Anne didn't want to hear about people our age dying — whether it was F. Scott Fitzgerald or the friend of mine in Colorado who keeled over while reeling in a ten-inch brook trout. Nor did she care to listen to morose, middle-of-the-night speculations about the demise of my long-gone father, though she was too gentle to interrupt. One morning she simply said goodbye and moved out. That time I knew she wasn't coming back because she took her favorite Nabokov novel, which she'd always "forgotten" before, and a leather-bound volume of sonnets by John Donne (composed at the ripe old age of twenty-five).

Such details make it all the more excruciating to know she has pledged herself to a hack writer of espionage novels. From *The Falconer's Mistress*:

> The woman slipped her hands inside Duquesne's fur-lined overcoat but drew away when she felt the ominous bulge of the holster.
>
> "Now you know who I am," he said, pulling her face close to his. She gazed into his gray eyes with a mixture of dread and excitement. "I'll leave, if you wish," he said.
>
> She shook her head. "It's cold outside," she whispered.
>
> He smiled. "It's Prague, isn't it? It's always cold in Prague." Then he kissed her.

Sweet Christ Almighty, what is there to do but kill him? No jury in the world would convict me. I've bookmarked that page as Exhibit A, and the novel accompanies me now to Anne's house. I believe it will simplify matters for the homicide crew.

Yet the moment Anne answers the door, all thoughts of murdering her fiancé dissolve. She looks fabulous and happy. Carla was right.

Anne invites me inside and, before I can ask, lets on that Derek is at the county library, reading up on Soviet nuclear submarines. "Oh. In Jane's," I say smugly.

"Pardon?"

"Jane's. You can look up any ship in the world in Jane's. A sixth grader could do it."

Anne's sigh is tinged with resignation. "Carla warned me you were taking the news badly. What've you got there?" She nods at Derek's book, which I'm clutching like a hot casserole. "Jack, if you came here to lecture me, you're wasting your time."

"Fine. But his writing is unforgivably wretched. Surely you're aware." This is not my finest hour. Anne would do well to boot me from the premises. Instead she brings me a perfect vodka tonic and tells me to sit down and listen up for once.

"In the first place," she says, "all my favorite novelists are dead, so they're not available to marry. In the second place, Derek is a good guy. He's fun, he's affectionate, he doesn't take life so damn seriously. . . ."

"You've just described a beagle, not a husband," I say. "And, for the record, it's *death* I take seriously. Not life."

"Knock it off, Jack. Please."

"Tell me you didn't meet him at a book signing. Tell me you met him at a Starbucks or a Yanni concert. That I could almost live with."

"He did a reading at our store," Anne says.

"Aloud? He's got balls, I'll say that."

"Enough!"

"You know his real name is not Derek Grenoble? It's —"

"Of course I know."

"And you're telling me you've actually slogged through . . . this?" I hold up *The Falconer's Mistress*.

Anne laughs. "Yes, it's truly awful. But I love him, anyway. Like crazy."

"He isn't forty-four. Did he tell you he was?"

"No," she says, "but I told Carla to tell you that."

"Cute. How old is he then?"

"I don't know and I don't care."

"Well, I know. I looked him up."

"Then keep it to yourself," Anne says sharply. "Didn't you hear anything I said? He makes me feel good. Know what else? He'll be the first to admit he got lucky with those silly spy books. He doesn't pretend to be John le Carré."

"Wise of him," I say.

Anne, who has been pacing, sits down beside me. She's wearing a Stetson University tank top over white jogging shorts. Her legs look astounding, as always, and she smells of jasmine. Taking my hand, she says, "I'm sorry about one thing, hotshot. I completely forgot that Saturday's your birthday. Derek set the wedding date and I said yes and later it hit me. By then it was too late to change the arrangements."

"Right. He's off to Ireland."

"I'm really sorry. I feel lousy about it."

So far, none of this is as devastating as I'd anticipated. Naturally I want to pull Anne to the floor and gnaw off her clothes, but that urge is unlikely to abate in my lifetime. The dolorous tug at my heart, however, seems surprisingly mild and manageable. For this I credit the twin distractions of Emma, hugging my neck when we got to my apartment, and the latest twist to the Jimmy Stoma story. His sister's disappearance is so troubling that it's impossible for me to focus on the task of winning back a lost love.

Yet I take an unmannered gulp of my vodka and give it a shot.

"May I please make a case for myself? I've gotten so much better, Anne, I swear. I don't dwell on all that dark stuff. And forty-six hasn't exactly been a cakewalk, what with JFK and Elvis and, as you so helpfully noted, Oscar Wilde —"

"That was thoughtless of me," she concedes.

"Point is, I've had a pretty strong twelve months, all things considered. And I'm ending on a very positive note, working on a big story — a seriously heavy story that could spring me off obits and turn my career in a whole new direction. Up, hopefully."

Anne gives me the sort of pitiful smile I used to see on the faces of visitors to the animal shelter where Alicia worked; the smile for the doomed mutts who weren't quite cute and cuddly enough to make the cut.

"Your mother called me, Jack. She's concerned."

"Beautiful."

"Don't be angry," says Anne.

"I guess she's only got two things left in the world to worry about — me, and Dave's colon."

"How *is* Dave's colon?"

"Seriously, don't you think I seem better?"

"Yes, honey, for now. But it'll start all over again, like always. The obsessing, the dreams, the midnight monologues. . . ."

She's kind enough not to mention the actuarial charts I once taped to the medicine cabinet.

"I hope I'm wrong," she says, "but I'm afraid it'll kick in like gangbusters on Saturday when you turn forty-seven. This year was Elvis and Kennedy, next year it's bound

275

to be someone else."

My spine turns into an icicle.

"Someone like who?"

Anne shakes her head. "Don't do this, Jack."

"Come on. Who died at forty-seven that I would possibly fixate on?"

Angrily she drops my hand like it was a hot coal. "Here we go again. That goddamn job of yours. . . ."

"You're winging it," I tell her, definitely asking for trouble. "You're blowing smoke. You can't give me one name, can you? Not one."

She grabs the empty vodka glass and steams for the kitchen.

"Anne!"

"Jack Kerouac," she calls over her shoulder.

And I hear myself muttering, "Oh Christ."

19

I couldn't sleep last night so I drove back to Beckerville in a rainstorm at two in the morning. Janet's Miata was filling with water in the driveway and the house was exactly as Emma and I had left it. Incredible: The cops never showed up. I thought about calling 911 again, but decided to hold off.

Now I'm at my desk in the newsroom, looking at a picture of Jack Kerouac on the Internet. He's standing beside a desert highway, his shoulders rounded and hands shoved into his pockets. The biography accompanying the photograph divulges that English was his second language, and that he wrote *On the Road* in three weeks. It's enough to sink me into a funk of disconsolate envy. Reading on, I see that Anne was correct: the man punched out at age forty-seven. I seem to recall that he drank himself into a mortal spiral, and this detail is also confirmed. I will cling to it like a chunk of driftwood for the next twelve months, uplifted by the knowledge that this particular Jack wasn't taken randomly from life; he delivered himself free of it. He wasn't shot by a crazed fan or flattened by a runaway

Winnebago or bitten by a Texas sidewinder. He boozed himself to death, a fate that I'm unlikely to replicate, given my tendency to fall into a snoring coma after three cheap vodkas.

So there.

From across the newsroom I hear a familiar, tubercular hacking: Griffin, the weekend cop reporter, sneaking a smoke. It's unusual to find him working so late.

"Three domestics," he explains in a tone of infinite boredom. "Knife, gun and claw hammer. Two 'graphs each. What the hell're you doing here?"

Griffin favors solitude. He has his own special way of working the phones. On impulse I ask: "Is there anybody worth a shit at the Beckerville substation?"

"Sure." With a pencil he laconically stirs a cup of black coffee. "Sure, I got a sergeant up there on night shifts. He'll talk to me." Translation: He's my source exclusively, so don't bug me for the name.

"You got time to make a call?"

"All depends, Jack."

I'm careful not to tell old Griffin too much. After I'm finished he squints up and says: "What're you working on? I thought you were still stuck on obits."

"Sad but true."

"So who's this 'Evan Richards' I've been reading?"

"Just an intern," I assure him. Griffin is always alarmed by new bylines in the newspaper.

"Ivy League, am I right? Where else do they go for a name like 'Evan'? I'm guessing Columbia or Yale."

"Bingo," I say. Griffin is good. "The kid's helping out Emma while I chase down this story."

"Must be a good one for her to cut you loose."

"I wish I could tell you more but I can't."

Griffin is cool with that; after twenty years on the police beat, he's at ease with secrecy. "So you want to know what happened with this Janet T-H-R-U-S-H. Spelled like the bird, right? You got a date of birth?"

"No, but here's the address. A 911 call was made to the sheriff's office but it doesn't look as if they sent anyone to the house."

"Lazy humps." Griffin plucks the paper bearing Janet's address from my fingers. "I'll get back to you."

Over the next few hours I make four trips to the vending machines and knock out seven paltry inches of background filler for the MacArthur Polk obituary. My brain is working like cold sludge:

Polk learned the newspaper business from his father, Ford, who founded the *Union-Register* as a weekly in 1931. The front-

279

page headline in the debut edition: JELLY-FISH BLOOM CLOSES SILVER BEACH.

As Florida's coastal population exploded, the *Union-Register* broadened its circulation area and its mission. In January 1938 it added a midweek edition during tourist season and by the winter of 1940 the paper was publishing daily. "The Brightest News Under the Sun," proclaimed the motto beneath the masthead.

Ford Polk gave no special treatment to his only son, who started in the newsroom as a telephone clerk and eventually worked his way up to managing editor. When his father retired unexpectedly to breed dwarf minks, MacArthur Polk was given the helm of the *Union-Register*.

That was in 1959, and within a decade he had doubled its readership. His formula for success was simple, Polk later recalled. Serious readers were given plenty of aggressive local reporting; everybody else got color comics.

"We turned the paper into a first-class outfit," Polk said in a candid interview, weeks before his death. "I always believed we should be the conscience of our community."

But in May 1997, conscience and class fell victim to slavering greed when Polk sold the *Union-Register* to the Maggad-Feist Publishing Group for $47 million.

Almost immediately the newspaper took a screaming nosedive into the shitter. . . .

I hear a gasp and spin my chair. It's young Evan Richards, ever the early bird.

"Jack, can you say that in the paper? 'Shitter'?"

"The last intern caught reading over my shoulder is now writing press releases for homeopathic penile enlargers."

Evan tests me with a tentative smile. "Man, you look like you've been at it all night."

"Know who Cleo Rio is?"

"Yeah, the chick that did the 'Me' song."

"Right."

"And flashed her pubes in the video. She's way hot."

"Sorry, Evan, but those were stunt pubes."

"Get out!" he says, goggle-eyed.

"Trust me."

"No way!"

"How'd you like to meet her?" I ask. "Sort of."

"Sweet," Evan says. "You're not kidding? Cleo Rio?"

"In the flesh."

Charles Chickle, Esq., says he was expecting my call — a baffling remark. Did Janet Thrush tell him I was investigating her brother's death? Does he already know something has happened to her?

We're chatting in his law office, which features a Picasso and a stuffed peacock bass on the same wall. Charlie Chickle has thinning silver hair, a ruddy face and sly blue eyes. He's wearing an expensive gray suit, a burgundy silk tie and a University of Florida class ring on one of his chubby fingers. Mounted under Plexiglas on a corner of his desk is an orange and blue football autographed by Steve Spurrier, confirming Chickle as a diehard Gator. That would explain his mystic political connections.

"So," he says, "you saw our friend Mac at Charity."

"Mr. Polk?"

"Of course. How'd he look?"

"Absolutely terrible," I say.

Chickle is amused. "For what it's worth, Jack — may I call you Jack? — in fifteen years I've never seen him look like he would make it through the night. But don't be fooled, he's one tough sonofabitch." The lawyer opens a manila file on the desk. "I've got depositions in an hour. Shall we get right to it?"

"I think there's been a misunderstanding."

"That would've been my reaction, too," says Chickle. "You probably thought he was nuts. That's what I thought, too. But he's not nuts, Jack, he's just vengeful."

Now I get it: Charlie Chickle is also MacArthur Polk's attorney. He doesn't know the

282

latest about Janet Thrush; he thinks I've come to discuss the old man's business proposition.

"Before we —"

"Please." He raises a calming forefinger. "I know you've got questions but I'll answer most all of 'em, you give me a chance."

"I'm listening."

"As you know, Mr. Polk sold the *Union-Register* to Maggad-Feist a few years back. In return he received a considerable heap of company stock and a series of options, which he's purchased during the last six months to add to his holdings. The total held by Mr. Polk comprises roughly ten percent of all outstanding Maggad-Feist shares — a formidable slice of the pie."

The old man had told me eleven percent, not that it matters.

Chickle proceeds: "Last year, two publishing companies independently started buyin' up Maggad-Feist stock, each with an eye toward a takeover. One is a German outfit whose name I can't pronounce and the other is Canadian, Bachman something-or-other. Anyhow, they got Race Maggad scared good and shitless, so he does what? Starts buying back blocks of Maggad-Feist as fast as he can. Meanwhile the price goes up and naturally some investors are sitting on their holdings, waitin' to see if there's a bidding war and so forth. You with me?"

"Yeah. Maggad wants Polk to sell back his shares."

"In the worst way, Jack. Failing that, he wants the old man to put in his will that Maggad-Feist gets first crack at the stock after he dies. Now," Chickle says, glancing up from the file, "Mac Polk wouldn't cross the street to piss on Race Maggad if he was on fire. I don't need to tell you that, do I? The old man is of the belief that Maggad-Feist has plucked his beloved newspaper like a Christmas goose. Some days he won't even look at the front page, on doctor's orders, case he busts a valve."

"You'll forgive me," I say to the lawyer, "if I don't get all choked up. What was Polk thinking when he sold the *Union-Register* to these creeps? All you had to do was look at what they'd done to their other papers."

"Everybody screws up, Jack. I don't think Mr. Polk would mind if I told you he was given certain assurances by the Maggad family — ironclad assurances, or so he believed, about how the newspaper would be operated. Now he feels deceived," Chickle says, "and, as I said, vengeful to the extreme."

"Which is where I come in?"

"That's correct."

"So he wasn't just ranting, that day at the hospital?"

"Oh, I'm sure he was." Chickle nods

fondly. "And I'm equally sure he was sane and sober. He told you about the trust?"

"He did. I said I'd think about it."

"Good answer. It tells me that money isn't what makes you tick." Chickle keeps talking as he leafs intently through more papers. "When Mr. Polk dies, all his shares of Maggad-Feist will automatically be put into a trust. As trustee, your duties would be relatively simple: Keep the stock away from Race Maggad. Throw away his letters. Ignore his phone calls. And when the proxy notices arrive, always vote the opposite of what the Maggad-Feist board recommends. The job description, in a nutshell, is to make Mr. Maggad miserable. Jerk him around at every available opportunity. Does that appeal to you?"

"For a hundred grand a year — he was serious about that, too?"

"Trustees are entitled to a fee, Jack. Some banks would charge much more."

I'm enjoying this conversation, as surreal as it is.

"Why can't his wife be the trustee?"

"Oh, she could," Charlie Chickle replies. "Ellen is a real spitfire. But Mac doesn't want her hassled day and night about selling the stock. He says you, on the other hand, shouldn't mind. He says your opinion of Race Maggad is almost as low as his."

"And I have been chosen because . . . ?"

"Because it will infuriate Mr. Maggad. I'm given to understand that he loathes you."

"Intensely," I say.

"Mac has no children, as you know. That means Ellen will be the ultimate beneficiary of the trust, when and if the stock is sold. What's so funny?"

"I'm trying to imagine the circumstances under which the old man would want me to sell his shares to young Master Race."

"As a matter of fact, the circumstances are quite specific. I could tell you what they are" — Chickle checks his wristwatch — "but that's for another day, when we're farther along."

"Charlie, tell me what you think of all this."

The lawyer rubs a pudgy knuckle across his chin. "Mr. Polk knows my opinion of his little scheme and he's chosen to march ahead. Oh, it's perfectly legal, Jack, if that's your concern. And I'd be lying if I said it hasn't been amusing, drawing up these papers. Probate work isn't usually a laugh riot. Neither is your job, I imagine, writing obituaries all day long."

Chickle intends no insult, but I feel my neck flush.

"You've got a real nice touch," he adds. "You've given a few of my favorite clients a lovely send-off. I'm sure you'll do the same for Mac."

"He may outlive all of us."

"Ha. I doubt it," Chickle says mirthlessly. He rises and I do the same. "It was a pleasure, Jack. Call me when you make up your mind."

"There's one other matter."

He frowns apologetically. "Is it super important? Because I'm really short on time —"

"It's life or death, Charlie. I'm working on a story about Janet Thrush's brother."

The lawyer's face crinkles around the eyes. "What kinda story?"

"Not a happy one. We're looking into the circumstances of his drowning in the Bahamas."

"But your paper said it was an accident."

"Right. And we never, ever make mistakes. Sit down, Charlie." And, by God, he does. "Somebody broke into Janet's house this weekend, somebody who thought she had something of Jimmy's. Now she's missing and —"

"No she's not."

My turn to sit down. "What?"

"She called this morning, Jack. Said some guy she'd been seeing got bombed and busted up her place. She's staying with friends down in Lauderdale or Boca somewhere. Said whatever I do, don't send the inheritance check to her house while she's gone, in case the asshole is still hangin' around." The lawyer chuckles. "I've only told that young woman about a hundred times that her brother's money won't be available for months."

"Did you speak to Janet yourself?"

"One of my secretaries did."

"And they know her voice?"

"Oh, come on."

"Charlie, how many clients do you have — a couple hundred? And your secretaries know each and every voice."

"No, son," he says, "but I've got no reason to suspect it was anyone but Ms. Thrush who phoned my office." The pause is an invitation for me to spit out my theory. I won't.

"Did she leave a phone number?"

"As a matter of fact, no. She told Mary she'll call back," Chickle says. "Now, why don't you tell me what you *think* you know —"

"I can't." The words catch in my throat like a hairball.

And before he sends me on my way, Charlie Chickle says, "Don't let your imagination run off with you, Jack. Sometimes things are exactly what they seem."

Emma wants to go to lunch and she insists on driving. She takes me to a darkly lit Italian joint, where we choose a booth in the back. She looks exhausted and says she, too, didn't sleep all night. Twenty-seven years old — I'm trying not to obsess about that. It's inconsiderate to project one's loony death phobias onto others; I'll have my plate full with Señor Kerouac soon enough.

The restaurant is chilly and Emma is rubbing her hands to warm up. I switch to her side of the booth and put an arm around her, a courtly deed that improves my mood more than hers. She does perk up when I tell her about that phone call to Charles Chickle — like me, she wants to believe it was really Janet. Neither of us mentions the blood on the carpet. Neither of us touches our wine, either.

In a flat voice she says, "You might be right. Maybe I'm not cut out for newspaper work."

"This kind of stuff doesn't happen every day." Still talking about Jimmy's sister.

"What if she's dead, Jack?"

"Then . . . I don't know. We chase it down. We get the damn story."

I'm not fooling Emma one bit. She knows I'm rattled.

"Besides the widow, you have any idea where all this might lead? Why people are dying and disappearing?"

"Give me some time," I say.

"A rock singer who hasn't been heard from in years, an out-of-work piano player —"

It sounds as if she's losing her nerve. I tell her we can't give up now. Especially now.

Emma says, "I just don't want anything

awful to happen to you. I'm sorry but that's the truth."

She locks on with the jade-green eyes. I hear myself saying, "I wonder who'd write my obituary."

"Write it yourself, smart-ass. We'll keep it in the can."

"All right, but I'll need a good quote from you. Being my boss and all."

"Fine," says Emma. " 'Jack Tagger was a deeply disturbed individual —' "

"— 'but a gifted and much-admired reporter. All of us in the newsroom will miss him terribly —' "

"— 'for about five minutes —' " Emma re-interjects.

" 'Especially Emma Cole, since she never got to sleep with him and heard he was absolutely spectacular. . . .' "

"Agghh!" She slaps my arm and pokes me with an elbow and now we're sort of wrestling in the lunch booth, laughing and holding each other loosely. It's nice, bordering on comfortable. Who besides Evan would have imagined — me and my bold plans! The most casual of flirtations and, instead of trying to save Emma, I'm now trying to seduce her. Or hoping to be seduced. In any case, questions of character could be raised.

Emma is saying she phoned her father and told him about the Jimmy Stoma story and

Janet's disappearance. He told her to be careful, told her to stay in the newsroom and leave the hairy stuff to the reporters. She says she got mildly annoyed, and I tell her not to take it the wrong way. If I were her dad, I'd have given the same advice.

"Let's talk about something else," Emma says.

"All right. Now don't get upset, but lately I've been having lascivious thoughts about you. And I mean 'lascivious' in the healthiest and most wholesome sense."

"In other words, you want to have sex," she says. "I haven't made up my mind about that yet. Let's try another subject."

"Fair enough. How about this: I no longer have a frozen lizard in my refrigerator."

"Oh?"

"Ever since the night of my burglary. I used it to clobber the guy."

"You're not serious."

"Oh yes. This was one jumbo lizard, too. I'm hoping it messed him up real good."

Emma says, "What's wrong with a good old-fashioned handgun?"

"Hell, *anybody* can defend themselves with one of those."

Upon returning to the newsroom I find a message on my desk from Griffin, who doesn't believe in e-mail. The coffee-stained note is scrawled in pencil, entirely in capital letters:

COPS DIDN'T GO TO THRUSH HOUSE AFTER 911 BECAUSE SHE'D CALLED THE DAY BEFORE + TOLD THEM NOT TO. SAID IT WAS DRUNK BOYFRIEND WHO TORE UP THE PLACE + IT WAS OVER + SHE DIDN'T WANT TO PRESS CHGS. IF U NEED MORE, LET ME KNOW. G.

When I show the note to Emma, she exclaims: "So she *is* alive!"

I'm not so optimistic. Janet never spoke of having a boyfriend. She mentioned her ex-husband and her pervo Web-crawlers but no particular guy in her life.

"Maybe she's all right," I tell Emma, "or maybe these phone calls are being made by someone pretending to be her."

"Like who?"

"The widow Stomarti springs to mind. Young Evan's going to do some sniffing around."

Emma emits a worried peep. "Evan? *Our* Evan?"

20

The kid's name is Dominic Dominguez but he goes by Dommie. His mother leads us to the inner sanctum.

"G'bye," Dommie calls out, having heard us coming down the hall.

His mother knocks lightly. "It's Juan Rodriguez, honey. He had an appointment, remember?"

"What's he got on?" Dommie inquires from behind the door.

Juan has forewarned me that the kid is quirky and short-fused, so I should lay off the wisecracks.

"A Ralph Lauren shirt," Dommie's mother reports, "a nice pale blue. And no neckwear, sweetheart."

The kid has a healthy phobia about grownups in neckties. My Jack Webb model is at the cleaner's. Juan removed his in the car.

"Come on in," Dommie says.

Before slipping away, his mother touches Juan's sleeve. "Would you mind asking if he's ready for din-din?"

Inside Dommie's room it feels about ninety-seven degrees because of all the electronics. There's a low-grade static hum that sounds like one of those coin-operated bed vibrators. I know next to nothing about computers but clearly Dommie is loaded for bear. Walled in by hardware, he toils intently at one of several PCs, his bony back to the door.

Juan says, "Hey, buddy."

The kid doesn't turn around. "Gimme a minute," he mumbles. "Who's that with you?"

"My friend Jack. The one I told you about on the phone."

"Yo, Jack."

"Hi, Dommie."

The kid's speed-shifting a joystick for a video game: dueling skateboarders, set to the vocal stylings of Anthrax. Juan glances my way and shrugs. There's no place to sit. The bed is littered with open boxes: Dell, Hewlett-Packard, Apple. I'm sweating like a stevedore.

Juan says, "Your mom wanted to know if you'd like some dinner."

"Not now!" The skateboarders on the kid's monitor are battling each other on a half-pipe, twirling and seesawing in midair. "Kill him!" Dommie rasps at the animated characters. "Kill that little bastard, Tony!"

I nudge Juan, whose face registers concern.

"Get outta here! Seriously, dudes!" Dommie screeches, apparently at us.

We retreat into the hallway. "You neglected to mention he was a psychopath," I whisper to Juan.

"He's just a little high-strung."

From inside the kid's bedroom we hear a feral yelp, then a sharp crack that sounds like a gun. I lunge for the doorknob but Juan snags my arm. Moments later Dommie's standing there, cool as ice. Now I can see he's wearing Oakley cutaways, baggy surf shorts and an oversized Ken Griffey Jr. jersey. His black hair is buzzed in wedding-cake layers, and a gold stud glints in one pale nostril. He weighs all of eighty-five pounds. He motions us back into his bedroom, where I notice a chemical tinge in the air. Dommie has shot out the tube of his PC with a Daisy pellet rifle. For now he seems at peace.

He glides his chair over to a working monitor, a raspberry-colored Mac. "Dudes," he says, "it's your lucky day."

Juan smiles hopefully. "You cracked the hard drive?"

"Like an egg. But everything was pass-worded, yo, so it took a while."

"And what was the secret word?"

" 'Detox'!" Dommie chirps. "Now pay attention" — the kid's fingers are flying over the keyboard — "here's a directory of all the files. I'll open one so you can see what it looks like."

The screen brightens with several rows of oscillating waves.

"They're all like that?" I ask.

"What else," says the kid.

"Can't you convert it to text?"

The kid looks at Juan as if to ask: How'd you hook up with this imbecile?

Juan says, "Jack can barely work a car radio. You've got to make things real simple for him, Dommie."

The kid is holding both hands in the air, like a doctor scrubbed for surgery. His fingers haven't quit moving, though, flitting across invisible keys.

"Okay," he says, "in the beginning was Pro Tools. That's software, dudes. High-end software. Lucky I had it, otherwise I couldn't read what's on this drive."

I say, "Dommie, please. Tell me what we're looking at."

The kid reaches for the mouse and guides the arrow to one of the wavy horizontal bands. Then he double-clicks and leans back, pointing to a speaker. "Listen tight," he says.

Thump. Thump-thump. Thump-thump. Pause. *Thump. Thump-thump. Thump-thump.*

"What is it?"

"The file name is DRoyster02," the kid says.

"Yeah, but what *is* it?"

"Dudes, come on. It's music."

Dommie shuts it down and spins around to face us. "This hard drive you brought me, it's all sessions. What they call a master. That gorky-gork I just played for you is the bass drum part for a cut called 'Cindy's Oyster,' somethin' like that. If you want I can pull up the guitar track, harmonica, vocals — it's all there."

"Only one song?" I ask.

The kid chortles. "Try, like, thirty. Some are already mixed down, some are still in pieces. I didn't sit through all of it because it's not my thing. Plus it would take, like, days."

Juan says, "Dommie's into rap —"

"Nuh-ugh, hip-hop," the kid protests.

"He mixes original stuff for some of the club DJs."

"Yeah, that's how come I can afford Pro Tools," Dommie says. "It's radical bad. Sixty-four tracks. No hiss, no wow, no flutter. Plus I've got AutoTune so it's always on key, even if some stone-deaf mother is singing. State of the art, dudes. Everybody's got it."

"Not us," I say.

"State of the art. Wave of the future. Reel-to-reel be dead and gone," the kid zooms on. "This program can run off a Power Book — know what that means? You can mix a whole record on a laptop, yo, and it's cleaner'n twenty-four tracks of tape. Serious, man."

Juan says, "Jack wants to hear everything

on that hard drive. Every single cut."

"Ha, I pity your white ass," says Rapmeister Dommie, twelve going on twenty-nine. It's good that he's wearing sunglasses; I believe I'd rather not see the size of his pupils. He returns to the Mac, closes down Pro Tools and starts diddling with the plug-in board. When he spins around again, the hard drive box is in his hands. He thrusts it at Juan's chest and says, "Hey, they're only eight games out of first."

"Anything's possible, Dommie."

"I really like that rookie shortstop. What a gun, huh?"

"Yeah, and he can actually hit a slider once in a while." From his pocket Juan digs out a couple of tickets to see the Marlins play the Mets. "Hey, buddy, where could Jack listen to all this stuff you found for us?"

"In his car. Duh."

Laughing, the kid stacks a tall pile of CDs on my lap. "I burned these myself, no charge. I'll print out a file directory so you'll sorta know what you're hearing."

"Thank you, Dommie," I say.

"Did my mom say what was for dinner? Better be macaroni and cheese or I'm not leavin' outta this room. It's Tuesday, right?"

"Monday," Juan says.

Something beeps. The kid pulls a pager out of his surfer shorts, glances at the message and snorts. "Douche bag."

"Dommie," I say.

"Kraft macaroni and cheese. Serious, man. Go tell her."

"The music on this hard drive, what kind of — if you had to describe it. . . ."

The kid jeers. "Folk rock. Country rock. Folk country — I dunno whatcha call it. My folks'd probably like it but not me. See, I'm strictly into a street sound."

"Ah, the street."

"Strictly."

Dommie is stashing the pellet rifle under his bed so that his parents won't find it. I can't look at Juan for fear of busting out laughing. I, too, kept a pellet gun beneath my bed when I was twelve. However, I also had a pet snake, an arrowhead collection, a homemade basketball hoop and three shelves full of books in my room. Dommie's universe exists largely inside electronic boxes; his games, his reading, his music. I wonder when he last went out to run around in the sunshine. I wonder if he owns a mitt and a bat, or if all he knows about baseball comes from chat rooms and video games.

Then I remember that my own pellet gun was employed chiefly to raise welts on the broad pimply shoulders of one Buster Walsh, a teenage neighbor who occasionally beat me up at the school bus stop. For revenge I'd climb a mossy old oak at the end of our street and snipe at Buster on his way home from wrestling practice. He'd hop around, bleating and slapping spastically at himself as if he were being dive-bombed by hornets. I'd lie low for a week or two, then nail him again when his guard was down. Plinking him was my entertainment, arguably more fiendish than Dommie's impulsive assault on an inanimate computer component. In other words, I'm not the most reliable authority on who's normal and well adjusted.

"If not macaroni then a cheeseburger," Dommie is instructing Juan. "Medium rare. Go tell her, okay? And if she asks about the bang she heard, tell her it was you or Jack that accidentally broke the PC. Okay?"

"No problem," Juan says.

"Don't worry, she won't do nuthin'."

"Thanks for your help," I tell the kid. "Have fun at the ball game."

"I'm taking a lobster net for foul balls," Dommie says brightly. "If I catch one I'm signing Mike Piazza's name and selling it for big bucks on eBay."

"Thattaboy." I flash him a thumbs-up.

Emma is worried about using Evan, but he's perfect: He looks exactly like a delivery boy, guileless and spacey. After a short strategy session I gave him twenty bucks and dispatched him to Cleo's favorite gourmet deli for subs and pasta. He should be calling from her place within the hour. Meanwhile I studiously listen to the CDs that Dommie made from the mystery hard drive.

Jimmy Stoma's unfinished opus.

The songs are in strands, but I can almost imagine how they're supposed to sound when woven together. For a fan it's strange to come upon a bare guitar track or a detached piano; free-floating background harmonies — I'm betting it's the lovely Ajax and Maria, whom I met at the funeral; or Jimmy himself taking three or four unaccompanied passes at the lyrics. Astoundingly, all those years of shrieking like a banshee with the Slut Puppies didn't shred his vocal cords. He sounds good on these recordings.

At first I wasn't looking forward to sitting through hours of raw cuts, but it's been interesting to hear the songs evolve — and instructive. On an early vocal of "Cindy's Oyster" (filed as V4oyst10), Jimmy began the third verse this way:

> *The girl who saved her pearl for me*
> *Showed it to the world on MTV. . . .*

Obviously a sly dig at his young bride, the former Cynthia Jane Zigler. In a subsequent version Jimmy dropped the caustic pose in favor of a leer:

> *The girl who saved her pearl for me*
> *Keeps it shiny between her knees. . . .*

301

And by the last cut of the song (V7oyst10all), the line had been altered once more:

The girl who saved her pearl for me
Keeps it hidden in a cold black sea. . . .

He was no Robert Zimmerman, but James Bradley Stomarti knew how to have fun with lyrics. It's the only reference to Cleo Rio that I've heard so far on any of the discs. While she might not have liked the song, I doubt she would have been moved to murder Jimmy and then Jay Burns in order to gain possession of the recording.

Yet, as young Loréal so sagely observed, it's the music business. Maybe Cleo is a paranoid, egomaniacal kook. Maybe she couldn't bear the idea of seeing a snarky column item pegging her as the inspiration for "Cindy's Oyster." Or maybe she couldn't stand the thought of her husband getting pop ink at her expense.

These theories rest on several wobbly assumptions: one, that Cleo heard the song; two, that she got the point of the song; three, that she believed Jimmy would actually finish it; and, four, that a legitimate record label would put it out.

Unfortunately, "Cindy's Oyster" is the closest thing to a motive I've found, which is to say that the story of Jimmy Stoma's death is a long way from making the newspaper.

Now the phone is ringing and I snatch at it, expecting Evan on the other end.

"Has he called in yet? Is he okay?" It's Emma, the mother hen.

"Not yet. But I'm sure he's all right."

"Jack, I don't like this. I'm coming over."

"Fine, but don't be shocked if the place is crawling with strumpets and wenches."

"I'm serious. If anything happens to him —"

"Bring whipped cream," I tell her. "And an English saddle."

Like many police departments, our sheriff's office tapes all incoming calls, even those on non-emergency lines. In Florida such tapes are a public record, which means access must be provided upon request to any member of the unwashed citizenry, including news reporters. The quality of such tapes is uniformly awful, and sure enough, Janet's alleged phone call to the Beckerville substation sounded like it came from a Ukrainian coal mine. The voice seemed to belong to a woman, but I couldn't have told you whether it was Janet Thrush, Cleo Rio or Margaret Thatcher. Between fuzz-pops and crackles the voice can be heard saying not to worry about the commotion at her house — her drunken boyfriend wigged out, nobody got hurt and things are under control.

The call came from a pay phone outside a

Denny's in Coral Springs, which makes it worthless as a clue. Of course I'd hoped that the number would trace back to Jimmy's widow, but no such luck. I've been curious about what Cleo's up to, besides dodging my phone calls and blowing her record producer and meeting with her dead husband's ex-bandmates. So I figured what the hell, let's send young Evan to her condo to scope out the domestic situation. The deli bags would get him past the doorman, but then he'd be on his own. Evan said that's cool, he'd know how to play it out. Perhaps I should have let on that Cleo might be a cold-blooded murderess, but there seemed no point in making him more excited than he already was.

Not ten minutes after Emma hangs up, Evan calls from ground zero.

"Yeah, uh, this is Chuck."

We'd worked out a rough script in advance. Evan picked the name "Chuck" because he thought it fit a delivery guy.

"This run to Palmero Towers," he's saying, "you sure it was for 19-G?"

"Hi, Evan. Everything okay?"

"Well, check it again, wouldya," he goes on, " 'cause the lady says she didn't call for no subs."

"Cleo's home?"

"Yeah."

"Excellent. She alone?"

"Nope."

"Here's what you do," I tell him. "Tell her your boss is checking on the order and he'll call you right back. I'll wait about five minutes, that ought to be long enough."

"Absolutely."

"Hang out. Be cool. Don't ask too many questions. But try to remember everything you see and hear."

"Hey, ma'am," I hear Evan saying to Cleo on the other end. "My boss says he'll check on this and call me back. What's the number here?"

"Five-five-five" — Cleo, impatiently in the background — "one-six-two-three. What's the problem — did you tell him we didn't order anything? Is that Lester? Let me talk to him —"

"I'm really sorry, ma'am," Evan says, smoothly cutting her off. Then, to me: "Boss, the number's 555-1623. That's right, apartment 19-G, but it ain't her order."

"You're a natural," I tell him.

Six minutes later I'm dialing Cleo's number.

"Chuck here," Evan answers.

"Still cool?"

"Yep." Keeping his voice low. "She got a long-distance call on another line."

"When she gets off, tell her they screwed up. Tell her the order was supposed to be delivered to 9-G instead."

"But now she wants to keep it."

"What?"

"Yeah, she got a whiff of the meatball sub and it made her hungry. What do I do, man? She gave me a fifty."

"Hell, give her the food."

"Sure?"

"Evan, what would a real deli boy do?"

"Guess you're right."

"And don't forget to ask for an autograph."

"Done," he says.

"Fantastic."

Some things they don't teach in journalism school.

Emma's on her way over, and I'm thinking about the last time I slept with a woman. It was the last Friday in March, five months ago, though it seems longer. Karen from the county morgue. She works for my friend Pete, one of the medical examiners. Lovely Karen Penski; we went out four or five times. She was straw blond and nearly as tall as I am — a serious long-distance runner. Age thirty-six, the same as Marilyn Monroe when she died. Also: Bob Marley. Karen couldn't have cared less. She took no stock in fate, karma or black irony. Every morning she saw death on a slab; to her it was just work product.

We met over the phone when I called the morgue for cause-of-death on a Florida state senator named Billie Hubert, whose obituary I was composing. A famous yellow-dog Democrat, Billie had exited this mortal realm at the same age (seventy) and in the same manner as Nelson Rockefeller, a famous moderate Republican — that is to say, porking a woman who was not his legal spouse. And, like Rockefeller's lover, Billie Hubert's companion hastily had attempted to re-dress him *post mortem*, with comical results. The owner of the motel, not unacquainted with the local vice patrol, offered no theories as to how the dead man in Room 17 had gotten his left shoe on his right foot, and vice versa.

The news story, carrying Griffin's byline, was plenty tawdry enough to make the front page. My chore was the day-after obit, which was to be mildly worded and played solemnly inside the newspaper. The only reporting left was to nail down the medical reason for Senator Billie Hubert's demise, which the autopsy revealed as an aortic aneurism. This fact came from the lovely Karen, who was also kind enough to mention that Billie's right arm bore the explicit scarlet image of a horned vixen riding a pitchfork — a magnificent detail I could not in good conscience omit from the obituary. That, and the squalid setting in which the senator passed on, somewhat diminished his standing with the Christian Coalition, whose members conveyed their disappointment in him (and in the *Union-Register*) via multiple mass e-mailings.

Two days after the obit was published, Karen and I met for drinks. Right away she sized up my problem, and offered to bring me to the morgue for "immersion therapy," which I declined. She said that being among laid-out corpses would help to "demystify" death. I explained that I wasn't troubled by the mystery of it so much as the finality. Nothing to be seen in an autopsy room, short of a spontaneous resurrection, could alleviate my concern about that.

I persuaded myself I was attracted to Karen because of her lanky athletic figure and quick sense of humor, but in truth it was the dark nature of her work that intrigued me — transcribing the narrated observations of Pete and the other dissecting pathologists. I couldn't imagine how she slept at night, her skull buzzing with such gory entries. She insisted the morgue job was the best she'd ever had, owing to the lack of customer complaints. And I must say she was, if not totally carefree, a vivacious and upbeat spirit. Heaven knows she enjoyed sex, which gave us at least one thing in common.

The last time we made love, the aforementioned Friday in March, we first ate dinner at a seafood house on the Jupiter Inlet. I remember nothing of the meal or the conversation, which means the evening must have gone well. Afterwards we took A1A all the way back to my apartment, where the CD deck happened to kick off with *Exile on Main Street*. This elicited a groan of disapproval from Karen, who had already stripped down to a sheer bra and panties. An untimely discussion of musical preferences followed, resulting in my grumpy capitulation. The Stones were replaced with Natalie Merchant, who is splendid unless you're in the mood for "Ventilator Blues," which I was.

Needless to say, the sex was less than transcendental for both of us. I carry a crystal recollection of Karen on top, grinding rather listlessly to some fluttery love ballad while I fumed beneath her, yearning for a backbeat. Her faked orgasm was so unconvincing that I mistook the feeble shudder as a delayed gastric response to the conch fritters, which had been criminally overseasoned. It was a dispiriting end to the relationship, and put lust at a distance for some time.

Now Emma is coming over and I'm pawing through the CD rack in a fevered search for something we both can stand, just in case. Anne's photograph is gone from the refrigerator door and I assume it was I who removed it, not wishing to give Emma the impression that I'm carrying a torch.

The first words I hear upon answering her knock: "Did Evan call yet?"

"He's fine, Emma. Safe and sound."

She ropes me with a fierce hug. You would have thought Evan had turned up alive after forty nights in a Himalayan ice cave. I might be jealous except that I recognize Emma's exuberant relief for what it is: To an ambitious mid-management newspaper editor, the only thing worse than getting one of your reporters killed would be getting one of your interns killed.

"I feel like celebrating," Emma says. She's wearing a pale cotton sundress and sandals. Her toenails, one can't help but observe, are painted canary yellow.

"You like U2?" Poised I am, disc in hand.

"Know what I'd really like to hear? Your man Jimmy Stoma," she says. "I'm dying to know what he was up to when he died."

I show her the stack of CDs from Dommie the Whiz Kid. "About twenty hours' worth. I've barely put a dent in 'em."

"That's all right," Emma tells me. "We've got all night." She smiles playfully and whips something out of her handbag. My desiccated old heart soars.

It's a toothbrush.

21

Something about the first time.

I'm never sure what it means, or how much to believe of what's said. Emma is parsimonious with clues. Meanwhile I hear myself whisper alarming endearments, including at least one spontaneous reference to love (this, while kissing a nipple!). Starved and pitiable I am; a goner.

Meanwhile Emma is as quiet and discreet as a hummingbird. In the shower I nuzzle a soapy earlobe and say: "Will this affect my annual evaluation?"

"Hush. Could you pass the conditioner?"

Later we drag the sheets and pillows off the bed and curl up in the living room, listening to the skeins of Jimmy Stoma's lost album. Within ten minutes Emma is fast asleep, while I slowly drift off to the two-part background vocals of a cut called "Here's the Deal," which is about either marital infidelity or methadone withdrawal — from the chorus it's impossible to tell.

Soon I sink into a dream with a familiar theme, co-starring Janet Thrush. She and I are at the funeral home where we viewed her brother's body, only this time we're staring into an empty velvet-lined coffin. In the dream I'm needling Janet about her belief in reincarnation, and she says there's no harm in keeping an open mind. In my arms is a bucket of fried chicken and I remark that if she's right, we're chowing on somebody's reborn relatives, possibly even my old man. The dream ends with Janet slamming the casket lid on my fingertips.

"Jack!" Emma, shaking me awake. "Someone's trying to break in!"

At the turn of the doorknob I snap upright. Since my burglary I've changed the lock and installed two heavy deadbolts, but my heart still races like a hamster. I bounce to my feet and brace my weight against the door; one hundred and seventy-seven naked pounds of determination. "Go away!" I shout hoarsely. "I've got a shotgun."

"Down, boy."

"Who's there!"

"It's me, Jack. Yer ole buddy."

Heatedly I yank open the door and there's Juan, a margarita glow in his eyes. With a loopy salute he says, "How's it hangin', admiral?" Looking past me, he spots Emma wrapped in a sheet. Before he can turn to flee, I grab an arm and haul him inside. The rustle behind me can only be my comely houseguest, retreating to the bedroom.

Juan topples into a chair. "Man, I'm so sorry."

"Now we're even," I say. "What brings you out at two-thirty in the morning?"

"I've been thinking I should quit the paper."

"You're crazy."

"See, this is why I need to talk."

It occurs to me that a proper host would put on some clothes, but after years of locker-room interviews Juan is oblivious to nudity. He says, "I want to write a book. Actually, I've been at it for about six months."

"That's fantastic."

"No, it isn't, Jack. Not yet." He cocks his head. "Who are you listenin' to?"

"The never-before-released Jimmy Stoma sessions. This is what Dommie pulled off the hard drive."

But Juan didn't come for music, so I reach over and turn it off. Emma emerges in a sundress and sandals. As Juan struggles to rise, spluttering apologies, she very pleasantly tells him to stay put and hush up. Then she tosses me a pair of pants, and heads for the kitchen to make a pot of tea. Her composure is somewhat deflating. I was hoping for a rueful glance or an impatient sigh — something to acknowledge the miserable timing of Juan's interruption. At least then I'd know that tonight amounted to something in Emma's private ledger.

"Is it a sports book?" I ask Juan.

Heavily he shakes his head. "It's about me and my sister. You know — what happened on the boat from Cuba."

"You sure about this?"

"It's a novel, of course. I'm not completely crazy," he says. "I've changed all the names."

"And you ran this by Lizzy?"

Lizzy is Juan's sister, the one who was attacked on the shrimp boat. She now manages an art gallery in Chicago, where she lives with her two children. I met her once, when she came to Florida to stay with Juan during her divorce.

He says, "I can't talk to her, man. We've never said a word about that trip."

"Not in twenty years?"

"What the hell is there to say? I stabbed two guys and threw 'em overboard." Juan blinks into space. "I'd do it again in a heartbeat. Lizzy understands."

He has recurring nightmares about the journey from Mariel harbor; wake-up-screaming, grab-for-the-medicine sort of nightmares. Sometimes he comes by to talk in the dead of night, which is therapeutic for both of us. Emma would understand, but Juan should be the one to tell her. So I'm trying to keep my voice low. . . .

"Look, you can't write a book like this without letting your sister know. That's number one. Number two is don't quit the newspaper — take a leave of absence."

"But I hate my fucking job."

"You *love* your job, Juan. You're just down tonight."

"No, man, I don't wanna come back to the *Union-Register* after I finish this novel. I wanna move to Gibraltar and write poetry."

"Oh, for God's sake."

"In iambic pentameter."

Often I've advised Juan to stay away from the Cuervo. "Emma?" I sing out. Moments later she glides into the living room with three mugs of green tea.

"Juan wants to resign," I inform her.

"No kidding?"

"To do a novel," he pipes up defensively, "and after that, poems."

"The newspaper needs you," Emma counsels.

"Unlike some of us," I add.

"I've probably had too much to drink. Way too much," Juan admits, between slurps of tea.

"What would your novel be about?" Emma asks.

Juan looks mortified until I say, "Baseball."

He flashes me a grateful smile. "That's right. Baseball and sex."

"Well, what more do you need," says Emma.

"How about a spy?" Perhaps I'm feeling inspired by the prose of Derek Grenoble. "Try this: The major leagues are infiltrated by a

315

Cuban espionage agent!"

"A left-hander, obviously," Emma says lightly, "but what position would he play?"

"Middle reliever," I suggest. "Or maybe a closer, so he could fix a big game. Say! What if Fidel was gambling on the Internet, betting his whole cane crop on the World Series?"

Juan rubs his eyelids. "Man, am I wiped."

Emma and I guide him to my bed, tug off his shoes, tuck him in and shut the door. Wordlessly she leads me back to the living room and we make love again, intercoupled on one of my consignment-shop armchairs. This time she murmurs and moans, which I choose to read as expressions of pleasure and possibly fulfillment. An hour later she wakes me to ask if I'm really leaving the newspaper, as I'd hinted on our drive to Janet's house.

"Hush," I say.

"You are, aren't you?" she persists. "Jack, don't do it. Please."

Then she reaches between my legs and grabs me, something no other editor has ever done. As a style of management it proves surprisingly effective, at least in the short term.

Emma and Juan are still asleep when my mother calls at eight in the morning. She says she was planning to drive up from Naples and visit me on my birthday.

"That'd be nice," I tell her.

"Unfortunately, we've got a minor crisis here."

"Nothing life-threatening, I trust."

"At the country club," my mother explains, "a black family has applied for membership and Dave's gone ballistic."

"Dave ought to be ashamed of himself."

"The fellow's name is Palmer. Isn't that ironic for a golfer?" My mother is adorable at times. "The best part, Jack — he's got a five handicap and a teenaged son who can knock a driver three hundred yards. Naturally, Dave's out of his mind. He wrote the nastiest letter to Tiger Woods, of all people, but I ripped it up while he was having his sigmoidoscopy. Dave, that is."

"And you find this an attractive quality in a husband — seething racism?"

"Oh, come on, Jack. He's fairly harmless. It's all hot air."

I ask her what the country-club furor has got to do with my birthday on Saturday, and she says the membership committee is meeting that very afternoon to review the applicants. "If I'm not sitting beside him, Dave's likely to say something he might regret."

"Worse," I say, "there's a chance he'd rally enough support to blackball the black Palmers. Am I right?"

"We've got a few narrow-minded types. Every club does."

317

"So you need to be there to keep Dave muzzled."

"Let's just say he usually defers to me on public occasions. I'm sorry, son, but this one's rather important."

"Don't worry about it. We'll get together some other weekend," I say. "You stay put and hose down your harmless old bigot."

"Did you want anything special for your forty-seventh?"

"Same as last year, Mom — serenity, a cure for receding gums and a new TV set."

"Don't tell me the Motorola went off the balcony, too."

"Also, I'd like to know when and how my father croaked. Please."

"Jack, honest to God" — my mother, clucking in exasperation — "between you and Dave, I'm ready to pull out my hair."

"Look, just tell me where it happened. Which city?"

"Absolutely not."

"Then which state?"

"You think I'm a ninny? You think I don't know what computers can do?"

"How about the time zone? Come on, Mom, give me something. Eastern Standard?"

"I spoke with Anne — I'm sorry, son, but I was worried about you."

"Well, worry about *her*. She's marrying a defrocked RV salesman," I say, "and that's also happening on my birthday."

"She certainly sounded happy, Jack."

"Just for that, I'm sending you one of his cheesy novels. But here's some sunny news: I'll be off of obituaries soon."

"Oh?" My mother warily awaits more information before offering congratulations. I carry the phone into the kitchen in case Emma awakes.

"When will this happen?" my mother asks.

"No date's been set."

"But you'll continue to work at the newspaper."

"Not exactly, but I'll still be involved. It's an unusual set of circumstances."

"Can't you tell me more?"

"In a nutshell, Mom, I'm waiting for a crazy old coot to die."

My mother says, "That's not the least bit funny."

"It is and it isn't. The guy's eighty-eight years old and he's got a helluva plan."

"Yes, I'm sure he does. Jack, have you thought about going back to see Dr. Polson?"

Shortly after Anne moved out, I falsely promised my mother I would consult a shrink. I lifted the name "Polson" from a Montana road map, and awarded my fictitious psychiatrist an array of lofty credentials from Geneva, Hamburg and Bellevue. I pretended to attend two private sessions a month, and in bogus updates I assured my mother that the man was brilliant, and that he regarded my lightning progress as phenomenal.

"I would gladly go back to Dr. Polson," I tell her, "if he wasn't lying in ICU at Broward General."

"What?"

"The details are sketchy, but evidently a deranged patient assaulted him with an industrial garlic press. It's very tragic."

A familiar frostiness creeps into my mother's voice. "I wish you could hear yourself from where I sit. Surely there's someone you can talk to, someone who could help. . . ."

"There *is* someone," I say. "You, Mom. You could tell me what happened to my father."

An inclement pause, then: "Goodbye, Jack."

"Bye, Mom. Good luck with the Dave crisis."

By nine Juan is gone and Emma's soaking in the tub. I'm scrambling eggs while listening to another installment of the Exuma sessions. The title of the current track eludes me, but my concentration has been slipping. Screening the material take-by-take has lost its eavesdropping novelty, and now I'm just slogging along in hopes of lucking into a clue.

Somebody had a reason for stashing the master recording aboard Jimmy's boat, but the more I hear of it, the more baffled I am about why it was worth hiding — or killing people for. Some of the cuts are polished and quite good, some are so-so and a few of them are unendurable. The cold cruel fact remains that the problem isn't the music so much as the market. If indeed Cleo Rio is homicidally driven to acquire her dead husband's recordings, the stupefying question is why. The teenagers who buy the vast bulk of the planet's compact discs weren't yet potty-trained when Jimmy and the Slut Puppies broke up. Assuming a loyal remnant of the band's former audience could be found and fired up, there's slender evidence of an untapped public appetite for a kinder and gentler Jimmy, dead or alive. Once a screamer, always a screamer in the hearts of the fans. Who'd pay money to hear David Lee Roth try to sing like James Taylor?

It's incomprehensible that Cleo could view her dead husband's album as either a potential platinum windfall, or unwanted competition. Sales of a new Jimmy Stoma release would be paltry compared to those that the willowy widow will rack up when her CD comes out, hyped day and night (pubes and all) on MTV.

So, regarding the death of James Bradley Stomarti, I'm still stumped for a motive. And while I've gotten no word from Janet Thrush, I've found myself hoping she was right — that Cleo hadn't any plausible reason to kill Jimmy, so there's no blockbuster story here after all. Because that would mean Janet is most likely alive; that the trashing of her place and the burglary of mine had nothing to do with each other; that it wasn't an impostor who phoned the sheriff's substation and Charles Chickle's law office, but Janet herself. What fantastic news that would be.

I love a juicy murder mystery as much as any reporter does, but the fun quickly goes out of the hunt when innocent persons start turning up dead. Maybe it's because I want to believe Janet's all right that I'm more receptive to the possibility that her brother's drowning was accidental; that Jay Burns's death was unconnected, the randomly squalid result of booze, dope and bad company; and that the concealment of the hard drive aboard the *Rio Rio* doesn't prove anything except that Jimmy Stoma, like many musicians, was obsessed with keeping his project safe from studio rats and pirates. God only knows where Prince hides *his* masters.

Over breakfast I run this scenario past Emma, who says, "But what about all the lies?"

She's perched at the dinette, buttering a piece of wheat toast. Her breakfast attire is a

T-shirt with a parrotfish silk-screened on the front — my only souvenir, besides the credit card receipts, from the Nassau trip. The nape of Emma's neck is still damp from the bath.

"Whenever you were pushing for this story," she says, "you'd remind me how the wife gave out different details about the diving accident. And how she said her husband was producing her new record when his own sister said it wasn't true. And don't forget Burns. You said he lied to you about the recording sessions in the Bahamas."

"He surely did."

It was just Jimmy by himself, the keyboardist had told me; Jimmy picking away on an old Gibson. No side players or singers, he'd said.

"Jack, people don't lie unless they're covering something up." Emma announces this with a world-weary somberness I find endearing.

"Doesn't mean it's a murder," I say. "Doesn't even mean it's a newspaper story." Over the whine of the electric juicer I tell her that people lie to reporters every day for all types of reasons — spite, envy, guilt, self-promotion.

"Even sport, Emma. Some people think lying is fun."

"Yes, I've known a few."

A comment like that should be stepped

around as carefully as a dozing viper. I turn my attention to straining the seeds and pulp out of Emma's orange juice.

"Jack, have you ever been married?"

"Nope."

"But you've thought about it."

"Only when the moon is full."

Emma has put on her wire-rimmed reading glasses to better appraise my responses. She says, "I was married once."

"I didn't know that."

"College sweetheart. It lasted two years, two weeks, two days and two hours. *And* I was twenty-two at the time. Not that I believe in numerology, but it makes you wonder. What happened was so strange. One night I woke up shaky and drenched in sweat, and suddenly I knew I had to leave. So I kissed him goodbye, grabbed Debbie and took off." Debbie is her cat.

Now I'm sitting next to Emma at the table, so close that our arms are touching.

"He was a nice guy," she says. "Smart, good-looking. Great family, too. His name was Paul." She smiles. "I've got a theory. I think Paul and I peaked too soon."

"That's a good one," I say. "It's much better than 'growing apart,' which is my usual excuse. You ever miss him?"

"No, but sometimes I wish I did."

I know what she means.

"Just to feel something," she says.

"Exactly." I figure now is as good a moment as any. "What about last night?"

"You first," Emma says.

"I thought it was wonderful."

"The sex or the cuddling?"

"Both." Her directness has set me back on my heels.

Emma says, "For me, too."

"I was worried, you got so quiet."

"I was busy."

"Yes, you were. So, now what?"

"We tidy ourselves up and go to the office," she says, "and act like nothing ever happened . . ."

"Gotcha," I say glumly.

". . . until next time."

Then Emma takes my face in her hands and kisses me a long time. Her lips slowly widen into a smile, and soon I'm smiling, too. By the end of this kiss we're giggling uncontrollably into each other's mouths, which leads to rambunctious entwining on the kitchen floor. I end up on my back, being scooted in ardent bursts across the cool linoleum. The sledding ends when the crown of my skull thumps the door of the refrigerator, Emma wilting against my chest. Ten minutes later, when we've caught our breath, she lifts her chin and observes that she's late for work. I'm amused to see that she's still wearing her glasses, though they teeter askew on the tip of her nose.

Scampering down the hall, she says, "Jack, I want to be clear about something. I want to make sure you're not bailing out on Jimmy Stoma."

"No way," I call after her. "I'm in this thing till the bitter end."

On the pretense of explaining I slip into the bedroom to watch her get ready. It's an operation I've always found fascinating and enigmatic. "Don't worry about me," I'm saying as Emma shimmies into her sundress, "this is what happens when I hit a wall on a big story. I start second-guessing every damn move I've made."

"You shouldn't, Jack. You've done a great job."

Emma, bless her heart, is too easily impressed. So was I at twenty-seven.

"I'm not giving up yet," I tell her. "I'm going to shake some bushes until something nasty falls out. One bush in particular."

"Speaking of Cleo —" Emma, kneeling to buckle her sandals.

"Young Evan's waiting in the newsroom," I say, "with a full report on his deli run."

"Put some clothes on and let's go."

"That's it? Slam bam?"

Emma points. "There's a slice of orange peel stuck to your butt."

Not exactly a line from a John Donne sonnet, but my spirits rocket nonetheless.

22

Good newspapers don't die easily. After three years in the bone-cold grip of Race Maggad III, the *Union-Register* still shows sparks of fire. This, in spite of being stripped and junk-heaped like a stolen car.

Only two types of journalists choose to stay at a paper that's being gutted by Wall Street whorehoppers. One faction is comprised of editors and reporters whose skills are so marginal that they're lucky to be employed, and they know it. Unencumbered by any sense of duty to the readers, they're pleased to forgo the pursuit of actual news in order to cut expenses and score points with the suits. These fakers are easy to pick out in a bustling city newsroom — they're at their best when arranging and attending pointless meetings, and at their skittish, indecisive worst under the heat of a looming deadline. Stylistically they strive for brevity and froth, shirking from stories that demand depth or deliberation, stories that might rattle a few cages and raise a little hell and ultimately change some poor citizen's life for the better. This breed of editors and reporters is genetically unequipped to cope with that ranting phone call from the mayor, that wrath-of-God letter from the libel lawyer or that reproachful memo from the company bean counters. These are journalists who want peace and quiet and no surprises, thank you. They want their newsroom to be as civil, smooth-humming and friendly as a bank lobby. They're thrilled when the telephones don't ring and their computers tell them they don't have e-mail. The less there is to do, the slimmer the odds of them screwing up. And, like Race Maggad III, they dream of a day when hard news is no longer allowed to interfere with putting out profitable newspapers.

The other journalists who remain at slow-strangling dailies such as the *Union-Register* are those too spiteful or stubborn to quit. Somehow their talent and resourcefulness continue to shine, no matter how desultory or beaten down they might appear. These are the canny, grind-it-out pros — Griffin is a good example — who give our deliquescing little journal what pluck and dash it has left. They have no corporate ambitions, and hold a crusty, subversive loyalty to the notion that newspapers exist to serve and inform, period. They couldn't tell you where the company's stock closed yesterday on the Dow Jones, because they don't care. And they dream of a day when young Race Maggad III is nabbed for insider trading or cheating the IRS or, even better, attaching a transvestite to his cock while cruising the shore of San Diego Bay in one of his classic Porsches. This vanishing species of journalist would eagerly volunteer to write that squalid story or compose its headline, then plaster it on the front page. Once upon a time they were the blood and soul of the newsroom — these prickly, disrespecting, shit-stirring bastards — and their presence was the main reason that bright kids such as Evan Richards lined up for summer internships at the *Union-Register*.

And five years ago most of those kids would have jumped at the chance to return here after college and join the paper at a humiliating salary, just to get in on the action. But after graduating next year, young Evan is heading straightaway to law school, his résumé jazzed by a semester of working journalism once viewed as a baptism by fire, but these days regarded more as an act of exotic self-sacrifice; missionary work. Smart kids like Evan read the *Wall Street Journal*. They know that what's happened to the *Union-Register* is happening to papers all over the country, and that any Jeffersonian ideals about a free and independent press would be flogged out of their callow hides within weeks of taking the job. They know that the people who run most newspapers no longer seek out renegades and wild spirits, but rather climbers and careerists who understand the big corporate picture and appreciate its practical constraints. Kids like Evan know that most papers are no longer bold or ballsy enough to be on the cutting edge of *anything,* and consequently are no damn fun.

When Evan first came to work for Emma, I thought he might be a keeper so I gave him a pep talk. I told him that plenty of reporters start out as rookies on the obituary desk, which is true, and that the talented ones advance quickly to bigger things, including the front page. And I recall Evan looking up at me with such rumpled perplexity that I burst out laughing. Obviously what the kid was aching to ask — had every right to ask — was: "What about *you,* Jack Tagger? Why are you writing obits after twenty years in the business?" And since the answer offered both a laugh and a lesson, I told young Evan the truth. His earnest reply: "Oh wow."

Not wishing to spook him, I hastened to portray myself as an incorrigible hothead who more or less dug his own grave, at which point Evan politely interrupted. He said that while he appreciated my candor and encouragement, he'd never planned to make a career of the newspaper trade. He said that from all he'd been reading, it was clear that dailies were "over." A dying medium, he told me. He had come to the *Union-Register* mainly to "experience" a newsroom, before they were all gone. His second choice was undoubtedly a cattle drive.

So I had no qualms about recruiting young Evan to help on the Jimmy Stoma story. Who wants to spend a whole summer banging out six-inch obits of dead preachers and retired schoolteachers? The kid deserved a taste of adventure, something memorable for his scrapbook. What a gas to be able to tell your college buddies that you helped sort out the mysterious death of a rock star.

And now I'm Evan's hero. He's as high as a kite.

"I almost freaked when she answered the door," he's saying. "I couldn't believe it was really her. And she's like, 'What's going on? I didn't order any subs!' At first I couldn't hardly say a word because she's standing there in a see-through bra. . . ."

"Easy, tiger," I tell him.

We're sitting in the cafeteria, Emma and I sharing one side of a bench table and Evan on the other. I'm taking notes, Emma is sipping coffee and the kid's gobbling a plateful of miniature glazed donuts.

"Who else was there?" I ask him.

"Two guys. The taller one had shiny hair, like, down to his butt. The other one, the baldy, he had one eye and —"

"Whoa, hoss. One eye?"

"He wore a black patch, Jack. It was sorta hard to miss. I asked him what happened and he said he was in a car crash last week."

"Big no-neck guy? Earrings?"

"That's the one," says Evan. "She called him Jerry. The patch was on his right eye, if that makes a difference."

I jot this down not because it's an invaluable detail, but because it makes Evan's day. He got the goon's name right, too; I remember it from the funeral at St. Stephen's.

"His forehead was all lumpy and bruised," Evan says, "like somebody pounded him with a hockey stick."

Emma is giving me a narrow look and I can't help but grin. Now it's official: Cleo Rio's bodyguard was my burglar. And I put out his eye with a dead lizard! Perhaps one day I'll be flooded with remorse.

"What else did you see?" Emma asks Evan.

"Hang on." He reaches into a back pocket and takes out his own notebook. "When I got back to my car I wrote down everything so I wouldn't forget. Let's see — they had Eminem on the CD player. The TV was on, too. Jerry was watching wrestling."

"Half-watching," I quip, avoiding Emma's gaze.

Evan continues skimming his notes, flipping pages. "Cleo was walking around in her bra, like I told you. I figured they were getting dressed to go out. The guy with the mermaid hair was hogging a blow dryer in one of the bathrooms."

"Was anything going on?" Emma asks.

"You mean like fooling around? Not in

front of me," Evan says. "Cleo looked a lot different than on the video. No lipstick and really frail, like a ghost — but still she's way hot."

Emma smiles patiently. I ask the kid if he happened to notice a Toshiba laptop with a Grateful Dead decal, or possibly an Epson CPU in pieces on Cleo's dining room table. He saw nothing of the kind, of course. My stolen portable and Janet's missing computer are probably in a landfill by now, having failed to yield any goodies.

"But the guy with the hair," Evan says, "I did hear him talking to Jerry about a program. He said he was waiting for an upgrade."

"Aren't we all."

"An upgrade for his 'Pro Twos' " — Evan, squinting at his scribbles — "whatever that is."

"Pro Tools. It's a music-mixing program. The guy claims to be a record producer."

"Yeah? What's he done?"

"Exaggerate, mostly."

"Hey, I almost forgot." The kid slaps a takeout menu on the table. Emma and I move closer to examine it. Under the table she gives one of my kneecaps a naughty pinch.

"Cleo's autograph!" Evan exults.

"Nice work."

"Can I have it back when you're done?"

"We'll see." I pocket the deli menu. "How about some more donuts?"

Emma gets up. "I've got a budget meeting upstairs. Jack, we'll talk later." Then, to Evan: "You did a great job."

"Thanks. I just hope I didn't miss anything."

And as soon as Emma is gone, Evan asks why I didn't want her to know the real reason I sent him to the widow's penthouse on Silver Beach.

"Because she'd just get nervous," I say, "and there's no cause for that. So tell me: Where'd you leave it?"

Evan grins. "In the bag with the coleslaw."

"That's beautiful."

"While I was waiting for you to call back," he says, "that's when Cleo decided to keep the food. She got a major jones for that meatball sub. But then she took another phone call and the long-haired guy went off with the blow dryer, and Jerry was icing down his face. So for a couple minutes I'm standing there all alone — that's when I took it out of my jacket and slipped it in the deli bag."

"Quick thinking."

"Then you phoned back and said it was okay to give her the food, which was a major relief since that's where I'd already hidden it," Evan says. "Can I tell you something? She scared me, Jack."

"Cleo?"

"You should've heard her talkin' to Jerry when she got off that other call."

"Was she mad?"

"Mainly just . . . *cold*. Her voice, man, I can't describe it. She's like, 'Do it. Get it done and no goddamn excuses this time.' Cold as ice, Jack. 'All these fuckups, Jerry, I'm over it.' Stuff like that. He's a big sonofabitch, too, and he's like, 'Yes, Ms. Rio. Right away, Ms. Rio.' Like a little kid standing in the principal's office. 'I'm sorry, Ms. Rio. I'll get right on it.' Really creeped me out."

"What were they talking about?" I ask Evan.

"No idea," he says. "But I was shakin' big-time when I handed her the coleslaw. And waiting for that elevator, Jack, I thought I was gonna wet my pants."

"You're a champ, Evan. First-rate job."

"Thanks." He leans closer and drops his voice. "When she was autographing the menu, she rubbed one of her boobs against me. On purpose, Jack, I swear to God!"

"And you're sure you don't want to be a reporter when you grow up?"

Evan's response is muffled by the donut he's cramming into his cheeks. "So, you promised to tell me. What was on that CD?"

"Just music."

"Come on, man. Who?"

"Her husband."

What I gave young Evan for covert delivery to Cleo Rio's apartment was the compact disc containing the first rough cut of "Cindy's Oyster." On the shiny face of the disc I used a red Sharpie to write a time, a date and a phone number.

"Oh wow," says Evan. "Her dead husband's music?"

Lunchtime. Emma's stuck in another meeting, so I take the Mustang and light out for Beckerville. Turning the corner of Janet's street, I feel my palms go clammy on the steering wheel. In my mind I've worked up this visual loop of Janet answering the door in her SWAT-team getup; tugging off her hood and smiling because it's me at the door. . . .

But that's not how it goes.

Janet's Miata is gone from the driveway, and there's no sign of life at the house. The front door has been repaired — new locks, the works — but nobody answers when I knock and ring the buzzer. The blackout shades on the front windows have been lowered to the sills, making it impossible to peek inside. Casually I stroll to the rear of the house. In my cheap necktie and buttoned-down shirt, I could be taken by a glancing neighbor for a city code inspector or possibly a meter reader for the electric company. Here again, my notebook serves as a nifty prop.

The back door is also locked, so I commence a minor felony. I remove two of the jalousie panes and lay them gingerly on the lawn. From my shirt pocket I take a small box cutter, lethally sharp, and slice a gash in the screen. Reaching inside, I twist the knob and lean on the door. The crime is consummated by stepping into Janet's home, which has been tidied up though not reoccupied. Armed with the unsheathed cutter, I hurry to the living room where I intend to excise a swatch of blood-stained carpeting. This will be matched against the blood on a used tampon that I'm praying is still in the bathroom wastebasket, where I saw it two days ago when Emma and I were here.

I'm assuming the worst — that the blood on the carpet belongs to Jimmy Stoma's sister — but it's important to know for certain. My plan for comparing the two samples is to solicit the off-duty services of good old Pete at the Medical Examiner's Office. He began a torrid affair with Karen, his assistant, shortly after she and I called it quits. For some reason Pete is convinced that he was the cause of our breakup. Naturally I've done nothing to disabuse my pathologist friend of this numbskull notion or relieve his misplaced guilt, knowing that someday I'd need a favor.

The carpeting parts like custard under the wicked blade, and I seal a wafer-sized piece in a Baggie. The tampon is retrieved and likewise secured — fortunately, whoever cleaned up Janet's house neglected to haul out the trash. Having completed my b-and-e in less than five minutes, I exit by the back door, pausing only to reset the jalousies. I drive directly to the county morgue, where Karen greets me with that creepy formality reserved for past sex partners. Pete, on the other hand, pumps my hand, gives me a hug and says he'll be happy to work up the blood specimens on the sly. He doesn't even ask where they came from, that's how eager he is to make amends.

"This is your lunch? No wonder you look so skinny." Carla took an early break from the drugstore photo counter to meet me at the yogurt shop.

"I've been busy," I tell her.

"Too busy to call?"

"It's one thing after another with this story."

"Ah ha!" she says. "Black Jack is getting laid again, isn't he?"

How on earth do they know? It's truly baffling.

"No comment," is my mealy reply.

"Well, it's about damn time." Carla stretches across the table and tweaks my nose. "Who's the lucky girl? Tell me everything, Jack. She give head?"

338

"Jesus, Carla!"

"Reason I ask, I'm thinkin' of having my tongue pierced."

"Stop right there." I raise both hands.

"All I want to know is, would it make a difference in the b.j. department? My girlfriend Rae, she says the guys go crazy. She's got a half-carat ruby on a platinum post."

"And that doesn't interfere with her tuba lessons?"

"Come on, Jack, tell me."

"I paid a visit to your mother. How pathetic is *that*."

"Oh, I know. I got the whole story," Carla says.

"And you were right. She's pretty darn happy."

"Told ya."

"Would I be even mildly amused to hear the wedding arrangements?"

"First you've gotta tell me" — Carla pauses to lap up the last smudge of her boysenberry yogurt — "what happened Saturday night with you and Loréal. After you split from the club."

"Not much. I tailed him to some redneck dive and pretended to interview him about Cleo Rio's new album."

"You mean CD," says Carla. "An album is where you keep your photographs, Jack. Speakin' of which, I got some juicy ones if you're up for it. Amateur bondage!"

"No thanks. I turned pro last year."

"So, about Messr. Loréal — tell me more, tell me more. . . ."

"Schmuck city, Carla, I checked him out. All these groups he says he produced, it's bullshit. He's just a studio rat. When Sugar Ray wants a Pellegrino or Snoop Doggy needs an Altoid, this is the guy they send to the mini-mart."

"You're saying he didn't produce the Wallflowers?"

"I'm saying he's lucky to produce a decent fart."

"Then why is Cleo with him?"

"Probably because he comes cheap. He thinks Jimmy's widow is his big break," I say. "So then, regarding the nuptials of Ms. Anne Candilla . . . ?"

"Simple ceremony, Jack. I'm the maid of honor. The best man is Derek's brother Nigel. We're to call him 'Nige.' "

"Will it be at a church or a KOA campground, in honor of the groom's distinguished past?"

"Neither," says Carla. "A private home somewhere down on Miami Beach. Hibiscus Island, I think. My mother has reluctantly agreed to allow bagpipes."

"And the vows?"

"Traditional," she says. "Derek wanted to write his own, but Mom thinks she talked him out of it."

"Thus averting disaster."

"Afterwards the newlyweds are off to Ireland, and then to sunny Prague."

"Ugh-oh."

"Not to wreck your day, Jack, but they're making a miniseries from *The Falconer's Mistress*. Derek's gonna punch up the script."

"It's only fair," I say with level calm.

"Boy, you *must* be getting some. I haven't see you in such a good mood since that big-haired Karen chick was polishing your knob."

"Carla, are you poaching from Emily Dickinson again?"

"You know what I'm talkin' about."

Now I remember what I wanted to ask her. "The other night, did anything happen after I left the club?"

"Yeah. Two Japanese businessmen offered me four hundred bucks for a friction dance. They were incredibly lost."

"No, I meant with Cleo."

"She tried to score some X off me in the ladies' room, but that's about it. Hey, I really gotta get back to work."

"Tell your mom I wish her the best. I mean that, too."

"I know you do." She scoots out of the booth and slings a mailbag-sized purse over her shoulder. "Sure you aren't up for some dirty snapshots? There's this one blond cow, she's got some wrangler tied naked to a barber's chair with a string of Christmas lights."

In a whisper she adds: "The lady who brought in the film, she's a big shot with the Junior League."

"Very tempting," I say to Carla, "but I'll pass."

Naughtily she cocks an eyebrow. "Jack, you old hound. She must be a hottie, this new babe of yours."

" 'Hope is the thing with feathers, that perches in the soul.' "

"Whatever," says Carla, sticking out her tongue.

To avoid working on MacArthur Polk's obituary, I busy myself in the newsroom by scrolling up the many bylines of Emma's father on the *International Herald Tribune*'s database. He is, as she told me, a top-flight reporter. Among other big stories, he covered the fall of Suharto in Indonesia, the bombing of the U.S. Embassy in Nairobi, and the investigation into the automobile crash that killed Princess Diana and her boyfriend. Painfully I realize the disparity between my career arc and that of Emma's father is so vast as to render insignificant the four-year gap in our ages. He's batting cleanup in the big leagues, I'm riding the bench in the minors. Anticipating the withering onset of a depression, I abruptly click off the *Herald Tribune* site and return full bore to Jimmy Stoma patrol.

The obliging archives of the *Palm Beach Post* reveal that the Sea Urchins, the chief beneficiary of Jimmy's estate, is an old and well-regarded charity that sponsors children's marine camps in Key Largo, the Bahamas and the Caribbean. The kids are of elementary-school age, and come from impoverished neighborhoods throughout the United States and Canada. The seven stories on file contain no hint of scandals or misdeeds connected to the program. A recent feature piece about prominent Sea Urchins boosters includes a quote from a "James B. Stomartie" that I assume to be Jimmy, surname misspelled. "Every kid, no matter how poor, deserves a chance to dive into an ocean at least once in his life," he said.

Janet's brother wasn't a complicated man, and his bequest was born of uncomplicated motives. He probably figured that a glimpse of the undersea world would do for those kids what it did for him. Cleo might be fuming about the terms of her husband's will but she'd be an idiot to challenge it now. The headlines alone would annihilate her career (**Pop Star Widow Sues to Claim Kiddie Charity's Loot**). As Janet said, if Cleo wanted Jimmy's money, she'd have been better off divorcing him than killing him. If she did murder him, it surely was over something else.

I hope to learn much more when, at noon

343

sharp the day after tomorrow, the phone should ring in a booth at the end of the Silver Beach fishing pier. Maybe it'll be Cleo calling, maybe somebody in her posse.

Or maybe the phone won't ring at all, and then I'm stuck again. Maybe she never found the "Cindy's Oyster" disc with the phone number. What if she's allergic to coleslaw, and tossed the bag in the garbage?

"Jack."

It's Emma, sneaking up on me like in the old days. Only now, instead of acting officious, she seems rattled and hesitant.

"Do you have a credit card?" she says. "Because I haven't figured out how to get the paper to pay for this yet. But I will, don't worry. I'm waiting to corner Abkazion between the five- and six o'clock news meetings."

"Pay for what?" I ask.

"A plane ticket to Los Angeles. Here, look." She hands me a printout of a short piece from the Associated Press. Before I can begin to read it, Emma blurts: "Tito Negraponte was shot last night."

"No shit," I hear myself saying. "You were right. . . ."

"He's not dead. They've got him listed as serious at Cedars-Sinai. You want to take a crack at an interview?"

I'm dumbstruck. "You mean it? You want me to get on an airplane and go chasing a story, just like a real reporter?"

Emma reaches out lightly to touch my arm, as if she's brushing away a fleck of lint. "You've got to promise you'll be careful."

Already I'm groping in my desk for extra notebooks and pens. "Emma, you were right. You were absolutely right!"

"Sure looks that way."

"Somebody's killing off the Slut Puppies!" Then I clutch her pale startled face and smooch her lustily on the forehead, right there in the newsroom in front of God, the assistant city editors, everybody.

23

By the time I got to L.A. it was ten-thirty at night. Most hospitals are penetrable at any hour, so I was surprised to be turned away by the late-shift lobby crew at Cedars-Sinai. My next stop was the emergency room, but heart-wrenching lies failed to thaw the glacial resolve of a senior trauma nurse who had thrust herself, as demurely as Mario Lemieux, in my path.

At first I figured the problem was me, rusty at double-talk after so long on the sedentary obit beat. Then I remembered this was the Spago of hospitals; every major star of the entertainment industry winds up at Cedars one way or another. Madonna and Mrs. Michael Jackson came here to deliver their babies; Liz Taylor, for brain surgery. This is where they brought Spielberg after his limousine crash, and where Francis Albert Sinatra was pronounced dead of a heart attack at age eighty-two. The place is constantly under siege by tabloid vultures whose subterfuges are elaborate and advanced by fistfuls of cash. No wonder security is tight.

So I retreated to a habitable motel on Wilshire Boulevard near Alvarado Street, and as a light rain fell I dozed off with a can of Sprite in one hand and my portable Sony tuned to the endless Jimmy Stoma sessions. The rhythm guitar track for one of the numbers seemed distantly familiar, which was odd because it was the first cut of the song — "G1title01" — that I'd called up. Yet I found myself humming the tune in the shower this morning, and it played in my skull all the way to Cedars, where I'm now standing in the elevator holding a preposterously large vase of fresh-cut carnations, sunflowers and daisies.

Flowers will get you practically anywhere in a hospital. I've told the front desk I'm taking them to my brother in Room 621. Because my arms were full and I acted like I knew the drill, nobody made me sign in; a plastic pass was clipped to my shirt and here I am, getting off on the sixth floor.

Tito Negraponte was admitted under his own name — this I'd discovered earlier when, pretending to be a florist, I phoned the hospital switchboard. His private room number was disclosed so offhandedly I had to conclude that neither a Grammy Award nor a gunshot wound is enough to elevate a bass player to the A-list at Cedars. I'm feeling optimistic about a one-on-one interview until Tito's door is opened by a cheerless Los Angeles County detective. Even minus the badge on his belt I would have figured him as a cop. Luckily he's on his way out, and I receive only a nod and a cursory glance at my floor pass.

"How is he?" I whisper in the tone of a concerned friend.

"Lucky," says the detective, stepping aside so that I and my flowers may enter the room. Once the door closes I'm alone with the fallen Slut Puppy, who is propped on his side, two pillows lumped beneath his head. Plainly he's not at death's door.

"Now what?" he mutters with a healthy scowl.

Before getting on the plane I'd looked up the news story about Tito's shooting on the *Los Angeles Times* Web site, which gave more details than the short AP item. The attempted murder had occurred inside the musician's Culver City townhouse. A police spokesman was quoted as saying Mr. Negraponte had returned from a trip to Florida and surprised a pair of armed burglars. After a struggle the guitarist was shot twice "in the lower torso" with a semiautomatic machine pistol of a brand favored by street gangs and drug dealers. The article ended with a paragraph about the salad years of the Slut Puppies, and a solemn mention of Jimmy Stoma's recent death "on a scuba-diving expedition in the Bahamas."

"Who sent the flowers?" Tito hoists his head and suspiciously eyes the arrangement. I

348

introduce myself and deposit a business card on his medicine tray.

"You came all the way to California to write how I got capped in the ass? Great." He chuckles in a droopy-lidded way that suggests liberal access to Dilaudid. A tandem IV rig hangs by the bed.

"I saw you at Jimmy's funeral," I tell Tito, "and I was at Jizz the other night when you met his widow."

"You some kinda groupie, or what?"

"I told you what I am. I flew out here because I'm working on a story about how Jimmy died. Jay Burns, too. And now you, almost."

Here's the moment when Tito Negraponte could tell me to get lost — a reasonable response from a man with a .45 caliber hole in each buttock. But instead of kicking me out of his room, Tito invites me to sit. He says, "You think it wasn't an accident, Jimmy dying the way he did?"

"I've had a lousy feeling about it from the beginning. You sure you're up for an interview?"

" 'Up' is definitely the word for it. You shoulda been here before they took away the morphine pump." This time Tito's laugh dissolves into a grimace.

"Let me tell you what's happened so far." And I do, recounting the non-autopsy in Nassau, the balcony scene between Cleo and

Loréal, my interview with Jay Burns, the burglaries of Jimmy's boat and my apartment, Jay's bizarre demise, Janet's disappearance under murky circumstances — and the discovery of Jimmy's hard drive hidden aboard the *Rio Rio*.

By the time I've finished, Tito's eyes are shut and his breathing is heavy. When I step closer to see if he's asleep, he blinks and says, "If this is a joke, it ain't so funny. You're saying they got Janet?"

"I'm not sure. She's gone and it doesn't look pretty."

"Fuckers."

"Tell me what's going on," I say.

"What's the difference? I can't prove nuthin'."

"Let's start with what you gave the cops."

"Can you pour me more water — sorry, what's your name again? More ice, too."

"It's Jack."

He takes the cup and gulps at it wolfishly. Soon the tips of his Pancho Villa mustache are dripping.

"All I tole the cops," he says, "is what I can say for a fact: I walk in the front door and some asshole puts a gun in my ribs while another asshole turns the place upside-fucking-down. Meanwhile the one with the gun keeps saying, 'Where is it? Where is it?'"

"Where is what?" I open my notebook.

"That's what *I* wanted to know. Where's

what? And the asshole says, 'You know damn well *what*.' And after maybe an hour of this shit they tie my hands and put me on my knees. Then the one with the machine gun says he's gonna blow my head off if I don't tell 'em where it is — did I mention they shot my fucking fish? I could use some more water, you mind?"

After the refill, Tito tumbles ahead: "I had a hunnerd-gallon 'quarium full of tropicals. Fact, Jimmy helped me catch a few. I had angelfish and triggerfish and sergeant majors and clown fish — you know anything about tropicals? Oh yeah, I had some cool rock shrimp, too."

Painkillers are one of the miracles of modern medicine, but cogency is not among the documented side effects. I lead Tito back to his account of the home invasion, but not before sitting through a monologue on the mating habits of the orange wrasse.

"The shooting," I remind him. "What happened?"

"Oh. Right. These two bastards scoop all the fish outta my 'quarium and toss 'em on the floor. Then they shoot em! It took like two dozen goddamn rounds, too, 'cause they're floppin' and squirming all over the tiles, plus they're real small. . . ."

"And then they shot you?"

"No, man," Tito says. "First I got up and ran. *Then* they shot me."

"That would explain —"

"How I took two caps in the ass. But I hit the door and kept on runnin'," he says. "These fuckers, on their way out, they stole a DVD and three Rickenbacker 4004s. But I know that ain't why they broke in."

"Do you know who they were?"

"Naw," Tito says, "but here's what: They knew *me*. Called me by name. 'We gonna kill you, Tito,' they kept saying in Spanish — these were Mexicans. Local wets, by the accent. And I believe they did mean to kill me, too, and make it look like a robbery."

"What do you think they were after?"

Tito grunts as he reaches for the call button. "I need another shot. Maybe three. You in a hurry?"

Briskly I step outside as a beetle-browed nurse prepares to re-medicate the wounded musician, cleanse his wounds and change his dressing. A stroll around the floor yields no glimpses of other bedridden celebs, though a detour to the vending machines leads to a casual chat with an orderly who claims once to have swiped a bedpan from beneath Robert Mitchum. "I sold it for seventy-five bucks to a memorabilia shop on Sunset," he says matter-of-factly.

No such market exists, I suspect, for Tito Negraponte's used personal effects. The databases I'd scanned yielded only meager biographical material. He was born in

Guadalajara and as a teenager made his way first to San Diego and then to Los Angeles, where he bounced between rock and Latin jazz in a series of obscure groups. In a 1985 interview, Jimmy Stoma said he recruited Tito after seeing him play drums with a bilingual punk band called Canker. Jimmy tore through drummers like barbiturates, but he liked Tito's furtive smoky presence onstage so he kept him on as a second bass man. "You can never have too much bass," Jimmy explained to the *San Francisco Chronicle*.

Although Tito was the eldest of the original Slut Puppies by ten years, the press clippings indicated he had no trouble keeping pace, socially or pharmaceutically, with the other band members. Three drug arrests and an equal number of paternity suits put his name in the entertainment columns, as did his gloating arrival at the Grammys with the freakishly bosomy wife of the same record-company executive who'd originally rejected "Mouthful of Muscle," the Slut Puppies' breakthrough single. After Jimmy disbanded the band in the late eighties, Tito formed his own group called Montezuma, which opened exactly once for Carlos Santana. A CD featuring a peppy Spanish version of "Hey Joe" was never released.

The most recent mention of Tito Negraponte in print occurred a few years back, when the *Boston Phoenix* asked several heavy-metal guitarists for capsule reviews of the classic rock satire, *This Is Spinal Tap*. Tito said that while he enjoyed the movie, its verisimilitude would have been enhanced "if the bass player had got more pussy."

The article said Tito was keeping busy doing studio work for solo artists. I don't know what he's been up to lately, but this interview should earn him more ink than he's seen in a decade — providing I can steer him through ten minutes of semi-linear thought. Upon returning to the hospital room, I see that the nurse has turned him over to face the window. I drag a chair into his fuzzy vision and sit myself down. Tito is drifting like a feather in the thermals, but I can't sit here and wait for him to float back to earth. This might be my only chance; a relative or girlfriend could show up any moment to chase me off.

Firmly I put a hand on his shoulder. "Remember I told you about the computer hard drive we found on Jimmy's boat?"

His eyelids flutter. "The master."

"Right. That's what everybody's after, isn't it?"

Tito coughs out a laugh. "Not everybody, man. Not MCA or Virgin or Arista. Just the vicious bitch Jimmy was married to," he says. "She thought I had a copy but I don't. I told her but she didn't believe me."

"That was Saturday night at the club."

"Yeah. I hooked up with some Brazilian chick at the funeral, so I hung around Miami for a few days. Then my manager called and said Cleo was tryin' to reach me about a gig, and would I meet her up in Silver Beach." Again Tito's eyelids droop to half-staff. Licking at his gray lips, he adds, "She ain't the quickest fox in the forest, that girl. I didn't play a lick on those Bahamas sessions, man, not one note. I didn't know what the hell she was talkin' about. . . ."

As Tito slides into dreamland, I'm scribbling down his quotes, trying not to lose a single phrase. The fact he was able to say "quickest fox in the forest" is impressive, considering his current dosage levels. The same beetle-browed nurse returns with a plump, fresh IV bag. She frowns at the notebook. I smile innocently, but my remaining time here can now be measured in minutes. As soon as she leaves, I nudge Tito awake. "What does Cleo want with the master? Did she say?"

He snorts groggily. "Stupid twat. She shot the wrong bass player. You believe that?"

"Then who was playing with Jimmy in the Bahamas?"

"That'd be Danny." Meaning Danny Gitt, the former *lead* bass guitarist for the Slut Puppies.

"Where is he now?" I ask.

"On a big jet plane, don't you worry.

Jimmy's wife'll never find him."

"Why didn't you tell this to the cops?"

"That's very funny. Christ, I'm thirsty again."

Dutifully I fetch the plastic pitcher and pour more water for Tito. He levers himself to one elbow and takes a long noisy guzzle. "The cops, they think those two Mexicans came to my place lookin' for dope. If I told 'em they was hired by a pop singer tryin' to rip off her dead husband, well . . ." Tito keels back on the pillows. "They'd never believe it."

I ask him when was the last time he saw Jimmy Stoma. He says four or five months ago.

"Did he talk to you about the solo project?"

"I think he felt weird 'cause he hired Danny instead of me. So all we talked about was fish."

Wincing, Tito repositions himself on the bed. "You wouldn't think it could hurt so much, gettin' popped in the butt cheeks. Fucked me up bad."

He's fading again and I still haven't pried the answer out of him — depressing evidence that my interviewing skills have waned. In the old days somebody loaded on this much hospital-grade narcotics would have been a pushover. By now I'd have had him confessing to the JFK assassination.

"Tito, wake up. Why does Cleo want Jimmy's master recording? I can't figure it out."

"She doesn't want the whole thing," he says irritably. "There's one cut she's hot for, and the rest she couldn't give two shits about."

I assume he's talking about "Cindy's Oyster," but when I try the title on Tito he says it doesn't ring a bell. However, Tito's bell is made of Jell-O at the moment.

"Naw, that ain't the song," he insists. "This is one she wants for her own record. She said Jimmy promised to give it to her, but that ain't what Danny told me. He said it was gonna be on Jimmy's own album. His comeback single, he said."

"Come on, Tito. Try to remember the name of the cut."

"Back off, guy. . . ."

"The long-haired kid at the club with Cleo," I say, "you remember him?"

But Tito is distracted by a stab of pain that causes him to twist around and glower at the door. "Where'd Nurse Wretched go? I believe she shot me up with sugar water."

"Loréal," I press onward, "that's what he calls himself."

"Aw, he's just some junior jerkoff with a Pro Tools setup. His job is to lay Cleo's vocals over Jimmy's guitar, once they lift it off the master. That's my read."

I can't help but notice that Tito has begun to bleat intermittently, like a baby goat. "Think hard," I encourage him. "This is important."

"Know what? This gettin'-shot shit is strictly for the youngbloods. I'm fifty motherfuckin' years old."

"Count your blessings. Steve McQueen checked out at fifty." I am powerless to edit myself.

"That was cigarettes," Tito snaps. "I quit the cigarettes." He curses under his breath. "What's the name of the wife's album again? She told me but I forgot."

"It's going to be called *Shipwrecked Heart*."

He smiles grimly and points a callused finger. "That's it, chico. That's Jimmy's song. The one she wants. The one she sang at the church."

And just like that, bingo, it all adds up.

The guitar part I heard last night sounded familiar for a reason. The widow Stomarti had played it at the funeral, while singing the only verse she knew. . . .

You took me like a storm, tossed me
  out of reach,
Left me like the tide, lost and broken
  on a beach.
Shipwrecked heart, my shipwrecked
  heart . . .

" 'Shipwrecked Heart.' That's it." Tito is

358

pleased with himself for remembering. "One time Jimmy was gonna let me hear the final mix but we went lobsterin' instead. I remember Jay or Danny, they said it was pretty good."

"I'd sing it for you myself but you're in enough pain. Cleo says she and Jimmy wrote that song together."

"What a joke. That girl couldn't write a Christmas card."

This goes immediately into the notebook. Tito watches the transcribing with an amused resignation. "You're gonna put my name in your newspaper?"

"It's very possible."

"Then maybe I should take a long vacation like Danny." He raises himself to look out the window, where the morning sky over Hollywood is pink with sun-tinted smog. "You think they offed Jimmy's sister? I liked her. She was a real decent kid."

"I liked her, too. May I borrow the phone?"

"Be my guest." Tito's curly noggin begins to loll. "I believe I'm fixin' to crash."

It's still early in Florida and Emma's probably in the middle of her workout, but I dial the number anyway because I can't wait. After thirteen days I've finally dug up a motive for the murder of James Bradley Stomarti. It might not have been conspicuous but it was heartbreakingly simple.

His wife killed him for a song.

24

From Cedars I head straight to LAX and catch a flight that should get me home by midnight. Hunkered like a parolee in a window seat, I snap on the Discman and painstakingly tick through the "Shipwrecked Heart" tracks until I locate what sounds like a fully mixed version. It's pretty good, too. I understand why Cleo Rio wants to steal it for herself.

Nothing intricate — just Jimmy playing an acoustic guitar and bits of harmonica. The nimble 12-string bridge is way out of his league, and undoubtedly was contributed by one of his famous pals or a first-rate session player. Ironically, there's no bass track at all, which makes the shooting of poor Tito Negraponte even more insulting.

Above all I'm struck by Jimmy's voice, so stark and subdued that Slut Puppies fans would never guess it was him. A light background harmony comes in on the last two refrains — I'm certain it's Ajax and Maria Bonilla, the singers I met at the funeral.

While the lyrics are a bit top-heavy with similes, the song is still more interesting than most of the formulaic crap on the radio. Over and over I play the piece, and from beginning to end it comes through as one voice — definitely not Cleo's. I'd bet the farm that Jimmy wrote it long before he met her, and that he wrote it for another woman.

You took me like a storm, tossed me out
  of reach,
Left me like the tide, lost and broken
  on a beach.
Shipwrecked heart, my shipwrecked
  heart . . .
Watching for your sails on the horizon.

Years we took the sea, together cold
  and rough.
The weather in our souls, we never
  got enough.
Shipwrecked heart, my shipwrecked
  heart . . .
Dreaming of your sails on the horizon.

The waves won't let me sleep, night whispers
  to the shore.
Stars run behind the clouds, an empty sea
  wants more,
The empty sea wants more.
Shipwrecked heart, my shipwrecked
  heart . . .
Watching for your sails on the horizon.
Watching for your love on the horizon.

Sitting beside me on the plane is a kid of Evan's age, maybe slightly younger. He seems curious about the open spiral notebook and the unmarked CDs stacked on my lap, but he's too shy to speak up. So I take off the headphones and ask his name.

Kyle, he says.

"Mine's Jack Tagger. You like music?"

Kyle is nineteen, it turns out, and attends the University of South Florida on a baseball scholarship. He plays third base and left field, which means he's got an arm. I ask what kind of music he likes, and he says Rage Against the Machine, Korn, stuff like that. "My girlfriend's favorite is PJ Harvey," he adds.

"That's promising. And, Kyle, how might she feel about Ms. Britney Spears?"

He makes a gagging motion with a forefinger.

"You should probably marry that girl," I say.

"Sometimes I think about it."

Kyle hails from Redondo Beach, where the love of his life works in a gym. She drove him to the airport this afternoon and waited at the gate until his flight was called. She's twenty, he adds, opening his wallet to show me a picture. I would have been stupefied if she weren't blond and breathtaking, a statutory requirement for female health-club instructors in Southern California. The name of Kyle's girlfriend is Shawna, and under the circumstances he seems to be holding up well.

"Would you mind doing me a favor?" I say. "Could you listen to a song and tell me what you think."

I hand the headset to Kyle and cue up "Shipwrecked Heart." As the track plays, he gives an approving nod and a thumbs-up. Obviously he thinks I've got a proprietary connection to the recording, some creative or financial stake, because the moment it's over he says, "Hey, that's sweet."

"It's all right if you don't like it. Just tell me the truth."

"But I do. I mean, it's sorta slow but it's . . . I dunno —"

"Pretty?"

"Yeah. Pretty," he says. "Like an old song."

"It was written a while back, but never released."

"Oh," says Kyle. "Is there, like, maybe a faster version?"

"I'm afraid not. Think your girlfriend would go for it?"

"For sure. Who is it, anyway?"

"Ever heard of Jimmy Stoma and the Slut Puppies?"

Young Kyle shakes his head no.

"Well, it's Jimmy solo," I say, "only he's dead now."

"Bummer."

"How about a singer named Cleo Rio? You know who she is?"

"I can't remember what song she does, but I caught the video a few times. My girlfriend calls her Princess Pube."

"What's your girlfriend's last name?"

"Cummings." Kyle knits his brow. "Why are you writing it down?"

"Because if you don't marry her," I tell him, "I intend to fly back here and propose myself. She sounds like a winner, Kyle, and winners won't come along often in this ragged sorry life. And don't think you're something special just because you can hit a hanging curve or turn a hot double play. You're not careful, you'll go home Christmas break and find out young Shawna's engaged to some buck-toothed surfer named Tookie. Now, promise you won't let that happen."

His eyes flick bewilderedly from me to the notebook.

"Don't toy with me, son. I'm a trained journalist."

"All right," he says finally. "I promise."

A disagreement over lane-changing etiquette has resulted in two motorists pulling semiautomatics and inconsiderately shooting each other in the diamond lane of the interstate. The traffic jam is epic, and by the time I reach my apartment in Silver Beach it's one-fifteen in the morning. Emma is asleep behind the wheel of her new Camry in the parking lot. Quietly I wake her and lead her upstairs, where I prop her in a chair, place a cup of decaf in her hand and make her listen to "Shipwrecked Heart."

She says it's good. "But —"

"The answer is yes, she wanted it badly enough to murder him. Remember, Emma, this is supposed to be her big follow-up hit. She's already promised it to the label — a title cut, co-written with her famous ex-rocker husband. But Jimmy says, 'Sorry, darling, this one's mine,' and all of a sudden Cleo sees her Grammy going down the bidet. . . ."

I'm so wired, so stoked by what Tito Negraponte told me, that I'm yammering at Emma like some hyper-caffeinated auctioneer. "Cleo's under incredible heat to put out an album before people forget who she is. That's the record business — blink twice and you're over. There's no ten years down the road, or even five years down the road. Not anymore. Plus, Cleo knows she'd better come up with a new pose, something that makes her look like a sensitive *artiste* instead of just another big-eyed anorexic brat."

"This song's not exactly her style," Emma says. Like every other human under thirty, she has seen the widow's stripteasy performance of "Me" on MTV.

"Cleo's 'Shipwrecked Heart' won't sound

anything like this by the time Loréal gets through with it," I explain. "He'll muck it up with synthesizers and a brainless dance mix, but so what. Cleo doesn't care about the music, she cares about the sell. In her head she's already story-boarding the video."

Emma flinches. "I can see her now. A scantily clad castaway on a long, deserted beach. . . ."

"Bingo. Problem is — and this was painfully obvious at the funeral — she can't do the song until she *learns* the song. And she can't learn the song until she gets her hands on the recording —"

"But that's not the only reason she wants it," Emma cuts in.

"Right. What we found on Jimmy's boat is your basic smoking gun." Even if Cleo got a copy and dubbed her own vocals, she couldn't release it as long as the master is floating around. If Jimmy's original ever surfaced, Cleo would be on the next train to Milli Vanilli-ville. Toast.

Because stealing from your dead spouse is not cool, even in the music industry.

"So now," Emma says, "Cleo's hunting down everyone who might have the hard drive, or know where it is — you, Jay Burns, Jimmy's sister, even this Tito guy. And the other bass player probably would've been next, if he hadn't run."

"That seems to be the scenario."

366

"Question is, how do we get all this in the paper?" Emma is sounding more and more like a serious news editor.

"First, I've got to make sure we're right," I say, "and I'll know that in about twelve hours."

"How?"

"Just you wait."

"Ah. The man of mystery."

"Yes, it drives the babes crazy."

"How about playing that song again," Emma says.

"You need to sleep."

"One more time, Jack. Come on."

So I turn off the lights and Emma makes a place for me in the armchair, and we snuggle there in the faint green glow of the disc player and listen again to "Shipwrecked Heart." Halfway through, Emma grabs the back of my head and kisses me in an arresting manner. This continues as she scissors a bare leg across my lap, adroitly pivots her hips and climbs on top.

Maybe it's the late hour, or maybe it's Jimmy's song. Either way, I owe him.

When a newspaper is purchased by a chain such as Maggad-Feist, the first order of business is to assure worried employees that their jobs are safe, and that no drastic changes are planned. The second order of business is to attack the paper's payroll with a rusty cleaver, and start shoving people out the door.

Because newspaper companies promote the myth that they're more sensitive and socially responsible than the rest of corporate America, elaborate efforts are made to avoid the appearance of a bloodbath. Mass firings are discouraged in favor of strong-armed buyout packages and accelerated attrition. At the *Union-Register*, for instance, our newsroom has sixteen fewer full-time employees today than it had when Race Maggad III got his manicured mitts on the paper. That's nearly a thirty percent cut in the city-desk payroll, and it was achieved mainly by not replacing reporters and editors who left to work elsewhere. Consequently, lots of important news occurs that we cannot possibly keep up with, due to a shortage of warm bodies.

Two years ago we lost a terrific reporter named Sarah Mills to *Time* magazine, which was probably inevitable. Sarah had done outstanding work covering the charmingly crooked municipality of Palm River, and her stories had kept two grand juries occupied for a whole summer. Ultimately three city councilmen were marched off to jail, while the vice mayor fled to Barbados with the comptroller and $4,777.10 in stolen parking-meter receipts.

So we were all disappointed to see Sarah go, though we were glad for her success.

Weeks passed, then months, and still no one was named to fill her job, leading to speculation that the job no longer existed. Sure enough, the reporter who covered Beckerville was asked to "temporarily" pick up the Palm River beat as well. Unfortunately, the city councils of both towns met every Tuesday night and, unable to be in two places at once, our harried correspondent was forced to alternate his attendance.

The politicians in Beckerville and Palm River aren't exceptionally astute, but they soon figured out that every other meeting was pretty much a freebie and composed their venal agendas accordingly. In short order both city councils raised property taxes, hiked garbage fees, rezoned residential neighborhoods to accommodate certain special interests (a tire dump in Beckerville; a warehouse park in Palm River), and then rewarded themselves with hefty pay raises. All of this was timed to occur when our overworked reporter was absent, covering the other town's meeting. He dutifully alerted his editor, who said nothing could be done. Maggad-Feist had imposed a hiring freeze at the *Union-Register*, and Sarah's position was to remain open indefinitely.

Eventually the Beckerville/Palm River reporter got so frazzled that he, too, left the paper. Both his beats were promptly heaped upon the reporter assigned to cover the Silver

Beach city council, which, in a foul stroke of fate, also met on Tuesday nights. For the corrupt politicians in our circulation area, it was a dream come true. While Maggad-Feist was racking up a twenty-three percent profit, the unsuspecting citizens of three communities — loyal *Union-Register* readers whom MacArthur Polk had promised to crusade for — were being semi-regularly reamed and ripped off by their elected representatives, all because the newspaper could no longer afford to show up.

The priorities of young Race Maggad III became clear when out of the blue he announced that the headquarters of Maggad-Feist was moving from Milwaukee to San Diego. A corporate press release said the purpose of relocating was to capitalize on the dynamic, high-tech workforce in California. The truth was more banal: Race Maggad III wanted to live in a climate where he could drive his German sports cars all year round, far from the ravages of Wisconsin winters (the annual salt damage to his Carrera alone was rumored in the five figures). So Maggad-Feist picked up and moved its offices to San Diego at a cost to shareholders of approximately $12 million, or roughly the combined annual salary of two hundred and fifty editors and reporters.

The chain's methodical skeletonizing of its newsrooms affected even Emma's career trajectory. She was hired at the *Union-Register* as a copy editor and swiftly promoted to assistant city editor, with the promise of more big things to come. Then the editor of the Death page unexpectedly dropped dead of a heart attack. This happened while he was on the phone with an irate funeral-home proprietor who was complaining about an ill-worded headline that had appeared above the obituary of a retired USO singer (**Mabel Gertz, 77, Performed Acts for Many GIs**). The stricken editor expired silently and perpendicular, the telephone receiver wedged in the crook of his neck. Nobody noticed until an hour after deadline.

The next morning Emma was summoned to the city editor's cubicle and informed that, as the junior member on the desk, she'd been chosen to "fill in" on the Death page. Thanks to previous staff departures, her new duties would also include the Gardening and Automotive sections of the paper. I think young Emma truly believed the city editor when he told her it was "a golden opportunity." She also believed him when he said it was only a temporary move, and that she'd soon be back on the news desk, editing significant stories. Time passed but Emma didn't make a fuss because she was a trouper, not a troublemaker. That's changing, though, and I'm considering taking some of the credit.

"Abkazion didn't want to pay for your plane ticket," she's telling me, "but I straightened him out."

I'm impressed; Abkazion is a tough customer.

Emma says, "I reminded him what happened at Robbie's going-away party, when he got bombed and pulled me into a broom closet."

Robbie Mickelson was our environmental writer. He left the paper after it was decided the environment was no longer in danger, and his beat was eliminated.

"The broom closet? That's pretty cheesy," I say.

"I nailed him in the testicles with a bottle of Liquid-Plumr. He couldn't have been more contrite."

"You're definitely getting the hang of middle management."

We're eating breakfast at an IHOP, of all places. The sight of Emma demolishing a tower of buttermilk pancakes has left me unaccountably enchanted. Everything she does, in fact, is downright fascinating. The way she folds one corner of the napkin, for example, before dabbing maple syrup from her lips. . . .

"Jack, get a grip," she says.

But it's too late for that. I'm already in the barrel, and the barrel's going over the falls. God help me, I've got a crush on my editor

— the woman whom I vowed to outwit, demoralize and drive out of the newspaper business. My mission has been derailed by raw straightforward lust, and I couldn't be happier.

Emma says, "It's the story, Jack. You're just jazzed about the story."

"Jazzed."

"High," she says.

"I know what it means, and you're wrong. If the story goes bust tomorrow, I'll still —"

"Don't say that. The story's good."

"Emma, what do you think is happening here?"

Pensively she taps her fork on the empty pancake platter. "I wish I weren't your boss," she says.

"And I wish you weren't so elliptical."

"There's no mystery, Jack. I just don't know what to do."

"Here's a modest proposal: We see as much as possible of each other, and screw ourselves delirious at least once a night."

Emma groans. "Obviously you've given this a lot of thought."

"Call me an incurable romantic."

"Try to be serious for a minute."

"Seriously? Let's go to Paris," I say.

She smiles, which is vastly encouraging, but then says: "Jack, you were twenty years old when I was born."

"Nineteen," I shoot back. "What's your

point? And where are you going?"

"To work." She comes around the table and kisses the top of my head, one of those sweet but contemplative pecks that makes you wonder if you've just been dumped.

"How can you leave me here?"

"Finish your sticky bun, old man," Emma says. "You're gonna need your strength." Then she gives me a naughty double wink that knocks me off my pins. Life is pretty good, for the moment.

From the pancake house I drive directly to the county morgue. The contrast in ambience is not especially striking. Upon entering Pete's office I find myself briefly alone with Karen, who gamely engages me in superficial conversation. Our lack of chemistry is so enervating that it's hard to believe we once had a sexual relationship, much less an athletic one. It's remarkable what two uninterested people can do in bed with each other when they set their minds to it. Turns out both Karen and I are doing well, staying busy, looking forward to some cooler weather, etc. We're on the brink of boring each other comatose when I spot Pete at the end of the hall, and excuse myself none too smoothly. He leads me into a lab and closes the door.

"You get my message?" he asks.

"No, I didn't." Sometimes I go for days without checking my voice mail at the newspaper. In my defense, however, the phone doesn't ring all that much. Obituary writers aren't exactly swamped with hot tips.

Pete says, "Well, you were right."

"The samples matched?"

"Yup."

The blood on Janet's carpet was hers. Cursing, I kick my heel into the door half a dozen times. Pete patiently steps back and waits for me to settle down.

"Jack, you know I've got to ask —"

"Please don't."

"I can get in all kinds of trouble," he says. "If this blood is evidence, there's a serious chain-of-custody problem. . . ."

"Throw it away," I tell him.

"Now hold on —"

"Throw it away, Pete. There's plenty more where that came from."

25

After a rough day of kickin' down doors and chasin' after scumbag criminals, all I wanna do is have a cool drink, peel outta this hot gear and get comfortable.

If you wanna get comfy with me, then have your modem call my modem at 900-555-SWAT. Or, if you register now on this site, the first ten minutes of chat time are absolutely free. I accept Visa, MasterCard or Discover. . . .

It took an hour but I've found Janet's Web page, complete with a streaming-video promotion. In it she's wearing night-vision goggles, a lacy black bra, matching panties and military-style boots. In the background I recognize the furniture in her living room. The quality of the video is typically dim and herky-jerky, but the sound of Janet's tomboy voice fills me with unexpected sadness. I click over to her list of FAQs, frequently asked questions, and immediately get a laugh.

Q. Are you really a cop?
A. Yes, I'm a lieutenant with a major South Florida police department.

Q. Have you ever shot anybody?
A. Not fatally.
Q. What's your favorite color?
A. Pearl.

I click back to the host page, activating a brief loop of Janet dancing. It's high-spirited though not especially erotic. Touchingly, the accompaniment is a recording of "Derelict Sea," sung by her late brother.

"Is that porn?" Horny young Evan, peeking over my shoulder.

"Does it look like porn?"

"But she's stripping."

"Not really. It's just a goof."

"Wow, Jack. You know her, like, personally? Check out the freaky shades."

"They're sniper goggles, and don't bother calling."

"What?"

Evan has been busy memorizing Janet's 900 number; I heard him repeat it under his breath. "You're wasting your time," I tell him. "She's not there."

"Come on. What's her name?"

"Forget about it," I said. "She's Jimmy Stoma's sister."

"Oh wow."

"Evan, don't you have some work to do?"

Be sure to check out my live chat schedule for when I'm available, but don't pitch a hissy if some nights I don't answer. You never know when they're gonna call the SWAT team out on a hostage crisis or a drug raid or some other 'mergency.

I do take online appointments — but not from hard-cores and pervs. Remember, being a police officer I got automatic worldwide call tracing. Anybody starts in with that gross sicko talk and I promise there'll be cops at your door before you can hang up the damn phone!

So let's keep our private chats cool and sexy and nice, and I promise you a super good time, every time. . . .

Clicking over to Janet's chat schedule, I notice she's got a regular two-hour block on Thursday mornings. It couldn't hurt to try. Maybe she left a message for her regulars, or possibly she bought a new PC and is back in business somewhere else. On my keyboard I tap in the number of her Web-cam line. On the other end it rings and rings, and keeps on ringing.

Who am I kidding. Janet's gone.

"How do you know this?" Rick Tarkington asks.

"The blood matches. Trust me."

"I don't doubt it, Jack, but how would *you* know? See my point?"

Tarkington is a major-crimes prosecutor for the State Attorney's Office. I'm obligated to admire him because he's a lifer. He could be making a million bucks a year as a private defense lawyer in Miami or Lauderdale, but he can't stomach the thought of representing killers, rapists and nineteen-year-old drug lords. Instead he has a fine old time sending them to prison and sometimes Death Row. Tarkington is an old-fashioned hardhead who believes that certain feloniously bent individuals cannot be rehabilitated, reborn or redeemed. He believes that some are purely evil and others are just hopeless fuckups, but that all of them should be dealt with unambiguously. He also believes that the American penal system functions essentially as a social septic tank, and that nothing more lofty should be expected of it.

"I could probably sell tickets," he's saying, "for the day they put you on the witness stand. 'Mr. Tagger, would you mind telling the court why you broke into the victim's house and stole a tampon?'"

Rick Tarkington is my age but he looks ten years younger. The irony is glaring and nettlesome. Here's a fellow immersed full-time in the ghastliest details of human malefaction, yet he shows no trace of being haunted by cosmic questions or mortal fears. He is cynical to the core, yet happy as a clam.

In the last thirty minutes I've told

Tarkington almost everything about the Jimmy Stoma story, spilling it as breathlessly as I did to Emma. I even brought a small boom box and played "Shipwrecked Heart," which Tarkington said reminded him of early Buffett. I had hoped it would work in my favor that the prosecutor is a rock 'n' roller. On the wall behind his desk is a photo of the Rolling Stones taken backstage at the Orange Bowl. The picture is signed: "To R.T., Thanks for not searching my dressing room. Keith."

"I came here," I say to Tarkington, "because I need direction."

"That you do." He's reclining at a precarious cant, the worn heels of his boots propped on his desk. Tarkington is from Lafayette County, where it's still possible to step in cowshit.

"Jimmy Stoma. I'll be damned," he says, clicking his tongue. "After I saw the obit I went and dug out my old eight-track of *A Painful Burning Sensation*. It kicked butt." Tarkington swings his feet off the desk and hunches forward, looking serious. "But, Jack, I don't know what the hell you expect me to do."

We've been over this twice already, and he's shot holes in every idea I've floated. "There's a woman missing," I say wearily, "and bloodstains in her house. Can we not assume she's hurt and possibly even dead?"

"I need a warrant to search the place, and where's my probable cause? You tell me nobody phoned in a disturbance. Nobody's reported her gone," Tarkington says. "However, if you'd care to sign an affidavit stating you entered the premises and observed what appeared to be a crime scene —"

"You know damn well I can't." That would make me a witness and put me at the center of the story — and then I couldn't be the one to write it. Another reporter would be given the assignment; the newspaper's lawyers would see to that.

"What about Jay Burns?" I ask.

"By all means. The genius who got smushed by the mullet truck." Tarkington raises his arms beseechingly. "He's drunk, stoned and now his head looks like a fucking Domino's deluxe. And you want me to prove it's homicide."

"Look, I know there's problems —"

"Problems? Old buddy, you've already given me enough to pinch you right now for trespass, b-and-e, tampering and obstruction," says Tarkington. "But that's assuming you and I are having this conversation, which we're not."

The Springsteen tickets — I'd almost forgotten. Sometimes it pays to be a shameless suck-up.

"Killer show," Tarkington says, warming at the memory. "Floor seats, fifth-row center. I owe you for life, Jack. But I can't do much with this one. I'm good, buddy, but I'm not a magician."

"And if Jimmy's sister turns up murdered . . . ?"

"I'll be there like a gator on a poodle," he says, "and I'll not hesitate to subpoena your scrawny, white, First Amendment–quoting ass. Now, before you go, play me that song again."

Given the setting, it's a strangely mellow interlude — Tarkington listening with his eyes closed, his chin on his knuckles and his elbows braced on four fat brown file folders: two murders, a DUI manslaughter and the sexual battery of an eleven-year-old child. People think the media is full of bleeding-heart liberals, but most reporters I know root for the Rick Tarkingtons of the world.

"That's nice," he says of Jimmy's singing. "You can tell he was into the island groove."

I switch off the boom box. "So where we at, counselor?"

"Well" — Tarkington, the prideful cracker, pronounces it like "whale" — "we've got an ambitious young widow who may or may not have bumped off her rock-star hubby. What we don't have are human remains to examine, as the decedent has been inconveniently incinerated. However, we do have the corpse — more or less — of a keyboard player with questionable lifestyle habits. We also have assorted sloppy burglaries of a fishing vessel, an obituary writer's apartment and the dwelling of the dead rock singer's sister, who may or may not have been abducted."

"Don't forget Tito Negraponte," I mutter.

"Not for a moment! Our bass player, plugged in the bupkis by a couple of beaners supposedly recruited by the aforementioned ambitious young widow. Unfortunately, we have no suspects, no supporting witnesses and damn little evidence, circumstantial or otherwise. Which brings us to our pretty little love song, the alleged motive behind all this mayhem —"

"Hey, I just figured out what you can do for me."

"Wait, Jack. I'm not finished —"

"Just give me a quote. That's all I want."

Tarkington snorts. "Are you deaf on top of everything else? Let me repeat this: You're not here. I'm not here. We're not having this chat."

"One crummy quote," I nag him. "Not for publication now, but later."

"The only thing I've got to say to you is be very careful, Slick. Don't be a nitwit and get yourself whacked. And that's strictly off the record."

"One quote, Rick, come on. It doesn't have to be substantial, for Christ's sake."

"Oh, there's a load off." Tarkington scowls.

I try dusting off an old standby from my hard-news days. "What if you were to say the state attorney is 'investigating a possible link' between the deaths of Jimmy Stoma and Jay Burns, and the cold-blooded shooting of a third member of the band. You don't have to mention Cleo or the song. Just say you want to find out if somebody's bumping off the Slut Puppies. It's a helluva headline, you've got to admit."

"Except we're not investigating a damn thing."

"Yes, but you *would* investigate — wouldn't you, Rick? — if more evidence turned up. Startling new evidence, as we say."

"Be sure and call me when that happens. Then you'll get your precious quote."

My predicament, which I'd rather not explain to Tarkington, is that I'll need more than a string of baroque incidents to sell the Jimmy Stoma story to our managing editor. Abkazion might be a Slut Puppies fan, but he's also a hardass when it comes to the front page. He'll want to see a quote from somebody in law enforcement saying they smell a rat. Tarkington would be ideal. Unfortunately, he's a hardass, too.

"Are you telling me," I plod on, "it's all coincidence, everything that's happened since Jimmy died?"

"Hell, I don't believe much in coincidence," he replies matter-of-factly. "I think you're probably onto something."

"And the blood's not enough to make you pick up the phone? His own sister's blood?"

Tarkington glares as if I've just spit up on his boots. "What blood, you fucking bone-head? The sample you *stole* when you broke into the lady's house? Jesus W. Christ."

"Rick, I needed to know for sure. That's why I did it."

"And I need a warrant, old buddy. You find me some PC and I'll find a judge and then we'll go cut us a piece of that rug, nice and legal." He stands up, stretches his arms. Throws in a yawn, in case I'm not taking the hint. "Jack, don't get bummed. You've got quite a story here. . . ."

"But what?"

"A helluva story, as you say. But you're not done yet. It's still missing the pretty ribbon and the bow." Tarkington nods toward his stack of files. "Now you'll excuse me, I've got a couple widows of my own to interview. They aren't nearly as chipper as yours."

"Okay, but first give me your impression — in a word, Rick — of everything you've heard so far."

"Intriguing," he says.

That's good, but it's not what I'm looking for. Abkazion will demand something stronger.

"How about 'suspicious'?" I venture.

"Yeah, all right. It's suspicious."

"*Highly* suspicious, would you say?"

"I would say goodbye now, Mr. Tagger. And if my name appears in the paper this week under your byline, it'd better be because I've croaked in some newsworthy way."

That's what I mean about Rick. I couldn't even joke about something like that. As soon as the office door closes, I take out my notebook and jot the following:

Asst. State Atty. R. Tarkington says he's preparing to investigate circumstances of J. Stoma death and disappearance of Stoma's sister. "Highly suspicious," says the veteran prosecutor.

Forgive me, Woodward, for I have sinned.

The pier at Silver Beach is not a big draw at high noon on a hot August day. I arrive half an hour early and, from the safety of my car, I scope the place thoroughly with binoculars. Team Cleo has had two days to run the phone number I wrote on the compact disc, an easy job for any private investigator.

But I don't see any egregious lurkers, anyone who looks as if they don't belong. There are a couple of shirtless teenagers drinking beer and snagging pilchards; a row of retirees in folding chairs, dozing under hats the size of garbage-can lids; a smoochy young Hispanic couple sharing a single fishing rod, taking turns reeling in baby snappers; a trio of weekday regulars, leathery and windblown, laden with bait buckets and bristling with heavy tackle.

After yanking off my necktie and loosening my shirt at the collar, I set off at a breezy amble for the phone booth at the end of the pier. Each step puts me that much farther from a clean escape, but it's not as if I haven't got a backup plan — should one-eyed Jerry burst out of a trash bin and start shooting, I'll simply dive over the rail and swim away like a dolphin.

Pretty darn clever. Always be halfway prepared, that's my motto.

And naturally some old guy is tying up the damn phone. I check my watch — twelve minutes until noon. I hope Cleo doesn't give up because the line rings busy once or twice.

Assuming she tries to call.

I sit down on a worn wooden bench and notice too late that it doubles as a bait table, leaving the seat of my pants covered with ladyfish scales and gummy snippets of rotting shrimp. I am one smooth operator.

The man at the phone booth hangs up and waves to me. "It's all yours, son."

A cheery little fellow topping out at maybe five-two, he's got small wet eyes and fluffy gray hair and a pink pointy face with sparse white whiskers. He looks like a 120-pound opossum.

"Thanks, I'm waiting for a call," I tell him. "Shouldn't be long."

He says his name is Ike and he was talking to his bookie in North Miami. "Don't ever bet on a horse named after a blonde," he advises ruefully.

Ike is fishing three spinning rods. He reels in one and rebaits with a dead pilchard plucked from a five-gallon bucket. "I caught a twenty-three-pound red drum standing at this very spot," he says, "on August 14, 1979. That's my personal best. What's your name, son?"

"Jack."

"Strange place to take a phone call, this pier."

"It's going to be a strange phone call."

"You look familiar. Then again, everybody looks familiar when you reach ninety-two." He laughs, flashing a mouthful of shiny dentures. "Either that, or *nobody* looks familiar."

I whistle. "Ninety-two. That's fabulous."

"When I get to ninety-three," he says, "I'll have lived longer than Deng Xiaoping."

"That's right."

"And Miss Claudette Colbert, too." Ike's button-sized eyes are twinkling.

"And Greer Garson!" I exclaim.

"And Alger Hiss!"

"Hey, you're good."

"Well, I been at it a long damn time," the opossum man says.

This is too much. I can't help but laugh.

"Just look at you!" I say.

"It's this healthy salt air. And the fishing, too." Ike rears back and casts the silvery minnow over the rail. "But that's not all," he says. "What I did, son, early on I made up my mind not to die of anything but old age. Stopped smoking because I was afraid of the cancer. Swore off booze because I was scared of driving my car into a tree. Gave up hunting because I was scared of blowing my own head off. Quit chasing trim because I was afraid of being murdered by a jealous husband. Shaved the odds, is what I set out to do. Missed out on a ton of fun, but that's all right. All my friends are planted in the ground and here I am!"

"Where'd you start out?" I ask him.

"At *The Oregonian*. After that, three years at the *Post-Intelligencer* in Seattle." He pauses to put on a faded long-billed boat cap with a cotton flap in the back. After nearly a century under the ozone, Ike's still worrying about sun damage. "Then the *Beacon-Journal* in Akron, briefly at the *Trib* in Chicago, and a bunch of rags that aren't around anymore."

Phenomenal. He's probably the world's oldest living ex–obituary writer. I ask him what else he covered.

"You name it. Cops, courts, politics." Ike shrugs. "But obits is what stayed with me. Funny, isn't it, how it gets a grip? That was the first beat I had out of college and the last beat I had before retiring. Twenty-seven years ago that was. . . ."

The opossum man has noticed a subtle twitch at the tip of one of his rods. He reels up the slack and sets the hook so zestfully that he nearly loses his balance. With bony kneecaps braced against the rail, he hauls in a husky mutton snapper, quickly thrown on ice.

"Don't get me wrong, Jack," he says. "I was a fairly decent writer but not in your league."

His delivery is downright rabbinical, otherwise I'd swear he's blowing smoke. "How'd you know who I was?"

"I read the *Union-Register* faithfully every morning," he declares. "Also I had my eyes peeled, because some young lady phoned here about twenty minutes ago asking for you by name."

"That's impossible."

"She'll be calling back any second, I expect," Ike says.

Suddenly the sun is blinding and the heat is suffocating and I'm breathing nothing but dead-fish stink. Frantically I scan the pier to make sure no one's coming, while Ike is saying he'd be honored to loan me his Norwegian fillet knife, which he assures me is sharp enough to penetrate dinosaur hide. The sensible microfraction of my brain issues the signal to run like hell, but the reckless re-mainder says I should stay and ascertain how Cleo Rio already figured out that I'm respon-sible for the disc in the deli bag.

And they could be anywhere, the widow's boys, watching and waiting — on the beach, in a boat, even in a small plane.

Yes, this was quite the crafty plan of mine.

"Ike, you might want to try your luck someplace else."

"Hell, I'm not budging." He chuckles as he cranks in another fish. "I've had three heart attacks, son. I lost half my stomach, fourteen feet of intestines and even my trusty old prostate to one nasty thing or another. Plus I've been through two divorces, both in com-munity-property states, so there's not much on God's green earth that scares me any-more. These are rough customers?"

"You could say that."

"Just tell me it's not over dope."

"This isn't about drugs, Ike. It's about a newspaper story."

The old opossum man beams. "Good for you, Jack Tagger."

Then the phone rings.

Here's how I messed up. I assumed Cleo would panic the moment she discovered the compact disc in the deli bag — or at least after she listened to it. I figured she'd be too rattled to bother snooping after the phony delivery boy, our intrepid Evan.

But I underestimated the little barracuda. She must have called up the restaurant manager to find out if there'd been a pickup order for meatball subs with a side of slaw. From there it would have been easy to match the bogus delivery to my phone order. Lots of takeout joints use caller-ID logs, which work just dandy on most non-published numbers. That's likely how the deli man got my name, which he provided to Jimmy Stoma's wife as blithely as he would to any booty-flashing celebrity customer.

Big mistake on my part. Major fuckage. Tomorrow I'm calling the phone company and springing for the trace-blocking option.

For now, there's nothing to do but strap on an attitude and act like I'm having a ball. I wait until the fourth ring before lifting the receiver.

"Is this Cindy?" I say sweetly. "Of oyster fame?"

The desired effect is achieved — a long pause, broken by edgy breathing, on the other end of the line.

Finally: "Fuck you, Tagger."

"How's widowhood treating you, Mrs. Stomarti? Is it all you hoped it would be?"

"What a flaming asshole you are. I don't even know why we're talking."

"I'll tell you why. Because, A, you're dying to find out how I got a copy of that track.

And, B, you want to know if I've figured out what really happened to your husband."

Not much return fire from Cleo's end. The static leads me to think she's on a cellular.

"Listen closely," I tell her. "I know you don't give a shit about 'Cindy's Oyster' but there's another song you've been searching all over creation for. I've got that one, too. Your title cut."

"Oh, I'm so sure."

Snideness is such an unattractive quality in the bereaved. Now I'm thinking I ought to sing the song, just to give the needle to Cleo. So I do the verse that has the nice line about night whispering to the shore — Ike, gutting a fish, sways appreciatively — and for good measure I finish big with:

Shipwrecked heart, my shipwrecked
   heart . . .
Watching for your sails on the horizon.

Not a peep from Cleo's end.

"I'd sound a whole lot better with a band," I tell her. "By the way, if you're charting the chords on the refrain, it's C, G, A-minor, A-minor seven, then back to G —"

"You bas-tard!" she explodes in the strangled cadence of a nine-year-old brat.

I suppose I should be more sensitive. "Cleo, I'm just trying to help. You missed that minor seven when you did the song at Jimmy's funeral."

Three years of lessons and I'm spouting off like I'm frigging Segovia. I've played barely a lick since college, though I've still got my old Yamaha and a fairly reliable ear.

"Hey, Tagger? You're done." Impressively, Cleo Rio has composed herself. I get a sense of what young Evan experienced that night in the condo — her voice has turned glacial. She says, "You're fucking done. I'm not wasting another minute on you."

Lord, who can blame her.

A man comes on the line.

"We got your girlfriend," he says.

"She's not my girlfriend, but she'd better be alive."

"She is."

"Can this be Jerry?" I say. "Bodyguard to the stars?"

"Be at Jizz tonight. Main room. Ten sharp."

Exactly what I'd hoped for: They're offering to trade Janet for Jimmy Stoma's song.

"Ten sharp, dickhead. Bring the package."

Package? This is what comes from watching reruns of *Hawaii Five-O*.

"Oh," I say. "You must mean the master recording that belongs to the estate of the late James Bradley Stomarti?"

"Ten o'clock. Come alone." Jerry doesn't seem eager to get to know me over the phone.

"How's that empty eye socket, big fella?"

Boy, when I get rolling I just can't shut it down. It used to drive my mother nuts; Anne, too.

"Jerry, you listening? I want my laptop back, you worthless simian fuck."

"I shoulda" — more heavy interference, like they're driving past an airport radar tower — "when I had the chance."

"Put her on the phone," I tell him.

"No, dickhead. She don't wanna talk anymore."

"Not Cleo. Your guest."

"She ain't here," Jerry informs me.

"That's convenient."

"She's alive, okay? Just like I told you."

"I'd love to take your word for it, Jer, but that would require me having an IQ no higher than my shoe size. So I won't be making another move until I hear the lady's voice."

Out of the corner of my eye I spy the eavesdropping opossum man, loping nimbly away. From the end of the phone line comes a muffled rustling — Jerry, covering the receiver while he and Jimmy's widow debate strategy. Then: "Okay. The girl, she'll call you at three-thirty. Gimme a number."

"It's 555-2169."

"Where the hell's that?"

"Brad and Jennifer's place. We play rummy every Thursday," I say. "It's my office phone, you ass-scratching baboon."

Jerry unleashes a string of bilious epithets. It's possible I've offended him. In the background, the former Cynthia Jane Zigler is yowling like a bobcat caught in a belt sander.

"They should make a movie about you two," I tell Jerry. "Whitney Houston could play Cleo. For you I'm thinking either Kevin Costner or RuPaul."

"Blow me," he responds, then hangs up.

Instantly I feel drained and fuzzy-headed. Frightened, too, mostly for Janet. I rest on the bait bench, drying my sweaty palms on my trousers. Ninety-two-year-old Ike is chasing a larcenous pelican down the length of the pier. He's my new hero. Buying a fresh set of teeth at the dawn of one's tenth decade — talk about a positive outlook! He returns triumphant from the pursuit, brandishing a slimy handful of mushed pilchards. He alights next to me, saying, "Jack, that was the ballsiest half of an interview I ever heard."

"Sorry. I got caught up in the moment."

"Don't be sorry, it was priceless. All my years in the business, I could've never gotten away with something like that."

Putting an arm around his spindly shoulders, I hear myself say, "What makes you think I'll get away with it?"

26

A cardinal rule of the business is that reporters should never become part of the story. I'm hopelessly up to my nuts in this one. And while I'm dying to tell Emma about the telephone call from Cleo, I know she'd want me to call the cops.

But here's what would happen: Hill and Goldman or some equally unsmooth detectives would show up at Jizz to confront Jimmy's widow. Indignantly she would deny drowning her husband or snuffing Jay Burns or kidnapping her sister-in-law. She'd claim to have no interest in obtaining the master copy of Jimmy's recording sessions, and insist she didn't even know it was missing. And she'd say that meeting at the nightclub was my idea, and she had no idea what we were to discuss. The detectives would bluff, badger and ask a series of uninformed questions before calling it a night. Tomorrow Cleo would quietly start shopping for a songwriter to hammer out a new version of "Shipwrecked Heart," Janet Thrush would never be seen again and I'd have no story for the newspaper.

On the other hand, it won't be my story

anyway if I meet with Cleo and things get ugly. Griffin, the crime reporter, would be writing about me, possibly followed by young Evan, which is no less than I deserve: an obituary penned by a college intern. At least the kid would get a front-page byline, which might be enough to change his mind about law school.

Dying is not in my plans, though it would certainly elevate my profile at the *Union-Register*. American journalists are rarely slain in pursuit of a story, so the paper would trumpet my heroic demise with moonwalk-type headlines. Abkazion, smelling a Pulitzer, would unleash a squad of all-stars to unravel the crime. Emma, stoically overcoming her grief, would volunteer to edit the project. . . .

I wouldn't be so worried if Cleo Rio were smart, because a smart criminal would never bother to kill a reporter. It's easier, and infinitely more effective, to discredit them. Killing one only brings out an infestation of others, banging on doors, asking impertinent questions. In fact, dying in the line of duty is one of the few ways for an obscure middle-aged obituary writer to make a splash, the last thing Cleo should want. Tonight I'll explain to her the downside of murdering me, in case she and Jerry haven't thought that far ahead.

In the meantime, I'll tell Emma that I

spoke to Jimmy's widow but she admitted nothing, which is true. I'll also tell her that the blood samples we took from Janet's house matched up, and that I shared our information with a state prosecutor who found it "highly suspicious." I will *not* tell her of my plan to trade Jimmy's music for the release of his sister, as I haven't yet figured out how to pull that off. The less anyone at the paper knows about tonight's summit, the better for me.

No sign of Emma when I arrive at the newsroom, but young Evan is eagerly waiting. He crowds my desk, whispering, "Well? Did it work?"

"Like a charm. She called at noon sharp."

"How cool is that! I guess she found the CD."

"Unfortunately, she also figured out who it came from."

Evan blanches. "It wasn't me, Jack! Swear to God."

"My fault. The deli guys probably went back and got the phone number off the original order."

"So what'd Cleo have to say?"

"Nothing that a howler monkey on acid couldn't understand. Evan, let's not mention our infiltration scheme to anybody, okay?"

"Why? Did I do something wrong?"

"No, buddy, you were perfect. But Abkazion's got a thing about reporters 'misrepresenting' themselves."

Evan's face goes gray. "You mean like pretending to be a delivery man."

"You're new here. You didn't know any better."

"But you *asked* me to do it!" he splutters. "You trying to get me in trouble?"

"No, I'm trying to save a woman's life. Sometimes rules need to be twisted, Evan. This can't possibly come as a shock, given your choice of a future career."

"But Emma knew!"

"Don't blame Emma — lately she's been under my ambrosial spell. Is she still at lunch, our fearless leader?"

"Haven't seen her all day. You sure I'm not in trouble?"

"For God's sake, you're an intern. Newspapers don't *fire* interns," I assure him. "Worst that could happen, they'll move you to the Food and Fine Dining section. You'll spend the rest of the summer fact-checking matzo ball recipes." I pause while Evan shudders. "Just the same, I don't see why anyone except you, me and Emma needs to know about the deli caper."

Evan agrees wholeheartedly as he backpedals toward his desk. I wish I felt worse about using him, but at least the kid had some fun. A nubile MTV starlet rubbed an unfettered breast against his flesh — how many pre-law majors can make that claim?

Time crawls toward three-thirty. My eyes tick between the phone on my desk and the clock on the newsroom wall. Two o'clock. Two-twenty. Two forty-three.

Ridiculous. Emma must be stuck in a meeting.

Now I remember: It's Thursday, and Thursdays are a marathon day for meetings at the *Union-Register*. Emma has come to hate them, which is a positive sign. All good editors hate meetings because they steal precious hours from the hectic task of putting out a paper. It's the very same reason bad editors love meetings; some Thursdays they can make it through an entire news cycle without having to make an independent decision or interact with an actual reporter.

Looking around the place now, I see a few stiffs and climbers but also plenty of authentic talent; as good as Emma could be if she ignores my advice and sticks with the business. Nobody with a living brain cell goes into the newspaper business for the money. They're in it because digging up the truth is interesting and consequential work, and for sheer entertainment it beats the hell out of humping product for GE or Microsoft. Done well, journalism brings to light chicanery, oppression and injustice, though such concerns seldom weigh heavily on those who own the newspapers. Race Maggad III, for instance, believes hard-hitting stories are fine as long as they don't encroach upon valuable advertising space or, worse, affront an advertiser.

It's pleasing to report that since Maggad-Feist acquired the *Union-Register*, circulation has declined commensurately with each swing of the budget ax. This trend suggests newspaper readers expect some genuine news along with their coupons and crosswords. Young Race Maggad will tolerate losing readers only as long as profits rise, which he achieves by the aforementioned paring of the budget, shrinking of the staff and cold-blooded gouging of local retailers. Eventually, however, Wall Street will take note of the sliding circulation numbers and react in a manner that could jeopardize young Race Maggad's blond and breezy lifestyle. His trepidation over this prospect has leached into the management ranks of all the company's newspapers, including ours. The result has been the urgent convening of even more newsroom meetings, one of which undoubtedly imprisons Emma at this moment.

Quarter past three on Thursday afternoon.

Phone rings. Eddie Bell from the Bellmark Funeral Home.

"Jack, you been out sick, or what? I miss your stuff in the paper lately. That Evan kid, he's okay but —"

"I can't talk now, Eddie. I'm waiting on a call."

"This'll just take a sec. I got one cries out for your golden touch, Jack. I'm so glad you're not sick, God forbid," he says. "Remember a few years back, widow lady shot some dirtbag that was breaking into her condo? Eighty-four years old, she popped him like five times point-blank. Pow! Blew his gourd off."

"Yeah, I remember, Eddie. Let me call you back —"

"Made all the networks. Maury Povich, too." One thing about Eddie Bell, he loves the hype. "Lady name of Audrey Feiffer?"

"How could I forget."

The burglar had gotten stuck sneaking into Mrs. Feiffer's kitchen through the kitty door. She thought he was the neighbor's chow, trying to get at her Siamese, and emptied her late husband's revolver into him. Then she fixed herself a cup of chicken broth and lay down for a nap.

"Well, she finally passed on," Eddie says. "Natural causes, God bless her. We happen to be handling the arrangements —"

"Evan'll do a nice job on the story."

"Wait, wait! The best part, she asked to be buried with her NRA patches — the ones they sent her after she wasted that guy." Eddie is breathless. "She was so proud, she stitched 'em to the front of her favorite housedress. By hand!"

"Patches," I say.

"Plus an autographed picture of Charlton Heston — she wanted that in the casket, too. Come on, Jack. This one cries out for your touch, no?"

"I'll have Evan call you."

Two beats after I hang up, the phone rings again.

"Jack?"

It's Emma. What lousy timing.

"Where are you?" I ask. "I can't talk now — Janet's supposed to call on this line any second."

"I don't think so," she says dully.

"What does *that* mean?"

"This is your phone call, Jack. The one you're waiting for."

I'm telling myself no, it can't be.

But in a chilling monotone she says: "Do whatever they tell you. Please." Then the line goes dead.

"Emma?" a tremulous voice repeats. My own.

"Emma!" My hand is shaking as I hang up the receiver. Almost instantly the phone rings again, and I jump like a mouse.

"Hello." It feels like I'm shouting though I can barely hear myself. I seem to have forgotten how to inhale.

"So, dickhead." It's Jerry on the other end, gloating. "What d'you think now?"

"I think maybe we can work something out."

404

"Okay then. Be there tonight."

"Not so fast." I've lost my relish for smart-ass banter, so this won't be easy. "Let me speak to the boss."

"She ain't available."

"Jer, please don't make me hurt you again."

"I shoulda killed you when I had the chance."

"Yeah, and I should've bought Amazon at fifteen and a quarter."

Cleo's bodyguard hangs up. I turn to see the approach of Rhineman, our eternally queasy Metro editor.

"I was looking for Emma," he says. "The diversity committee meets at four."

This is a group that convenes regularly to suggest ways for the *Union-Register* to become more ethnically diverse. To date, its only useful recommendation is that the paper shouldn't employ so many white people.

Rhineman asks me to remind Emma about the meeting. "Four o'clock in the executive conference room."

She's not here, I tell him. She called in sick.

I entrusted the thing to Carla, who entrusted it to a young woman known on the club circuit as Thurma, a breeder and keeper of exotic wildlife. It was from Thurma's private collection that Carla had procured my Savannah monitor, the late Colonel Tom.

Thurma lives in the piney glades on the western edge of the county, and in my agitated condition I'm pleased to let Carla do the driving. She is mercifully casual with her questions, even though she knows there's a shitstorm in the works. Today her hair is the color of watermelon, arranged in whimsical cornrows.

"Mom called last night, half out of her skull. Derek's written a poem to read at the reception Saturday. It's three frigging pages!" Carla reports delightedly. "He's having it printed up special and handed out to all the guests — hey, Black Jack? Wake up. This is for your benefit, pal."

"Sorry. Go on."

"Guess what it's called, Derek's matrimonial poem."

"Got to be an ode to something," I say absently. "Ode to a princess. Ode to a maiden. . . ."

Carla crows, banging her hands on the steering wheel. "You are *good!* It's 'Ode to a Brown-Eyed Goddess.' I swear to Christ, if he goes through with this, the wedding's gonna be a pukefest."

"Hey, your mom's happy. That's all that counts."

"Don't go soft on me now, you gnarly old fart."

"Carla, I need a favor."

"What else."

406

"Something happens to me" — I've got my notebook open, trying to scribble Rick Tarkington's name and number — "if something happens to me, you call this guy. Tell him I went to meet the merry widow tonight at Jizz."

"Hey! I'll go with you and we can flirt disgracefully."

"Like hell." I tear the page from the notebook and slip it into her handbag. "Also, please tell him there's a woman who's been abducted. Her name is Emma Cole and she works for the paper. She's only twenty-seven."

"Oh God, Jack. What did you do?"

"Outsmarted myself. How much farther?"

Thurma and her creatures dwell in a double-wide trailer enclosed by a tall chain-link fence. The name on the mailbox says "Bernice Mackle." Chained to a pine tree in front of the trailer is a coyote, of all things, pacing irritably in the shade.

Thurma is out running errands but she taped a note to the front door: "Cage #7. Slow and easy."

Carla digs the door key out of a flower pot and we enter warily. I don't know where Thurma eats or sleeps, the trailer is stacked with so many glass terrariums. Each contains one or more formidable reptiles. Thurma has accommodatingly unlocked the lid to number 7, which is home to the largest Eastern diamondback I've ever seen, its head the size of my fist. The rattler is coiled upon an anvil-shaped rock. Next to the rock is a water dish, and propped next to the water dish sits a familiar black box, once the secret pride and joy of James Bradley Stomarti.

"I told her to stash it in a safe place," Carla explains.

The snake is oblivious and somewhat lethargic, a condition attributable to a bunny-sized lump in one of its coils.

"Now what?" I ask Carla.

She points to a pair of barbecue tongs. "Slow and easy, remember."

"How much do you adore me?"

"Not that much, Jack."

"Honestly, my reflexes aren't what they used to be."

"Come on. It's practically in a coma," Carla says.

Carefully I lift the plastic lid off the tank.

"You want, I'll try and distract him." Carla presses her nose against the glass but jumps back when the rattler halfheartedly flicks its tongue.

"Screw *that*," she says.

Wielding the barbecue tongs, I take aim at the hard drive. Twice I panic and yank my arm away before getting a solid grip. On the third try I snatch hold of the box but, while lifting it, I see the snake's skin ripple and its nose turn slightly toward me. Then comes the rattle, which is unlike any other sound in nature. Brilliantly I pull my hand from the tank just as the beast strikes, fangs ticking harmlessly against the glass. Carla squeals as the tongs and the hard drive clatter to the floor.

Somewhere, Jimmy Stoma must be laughing his ass off.

If I'd checked my voice mail like a real reporter I would have known that Janet Thrush was neither dead nor being held captive by her sister-in-law. She'd left three messages, starting with: "Hi, Jack. It's Janet. Something super weird happened and I had to get outta Dodge for a while. I'm staying with some girls down in Broward. Call me, soon as you get a chance. It's, uh, 954-555-6609." The number connected to a service, where I left word for Ms. Thrush to phone me at home as soon as possible.

But when I returned from Dommie's house, the tape on my answer machine was empty. So I'm sitting here, in the same faded old armchair where Emma and I made love, waiting for calls and plotting the big rescue. The most ambitious version of my plan is to save Emma, get Cleo busted, break open the Jimmy Stoma story and sail onto the front page of the *Union-Register* for the first time in 987 days.

But I would gladly settle for saving Emma, period.

Nothing momentous will take place at the club; of that I'm sure. They'll want the exchange to go down somewhere else, someplace quiet and remote. They might not even agree to do it tonight. I've tried to convince myself that all Cleo cares about is Jimmy's song, and that once I give it up she'll free Emma. Except that Emma is now a major problem because she can nail Cleo — or at least Jerry — for abduction and assorted other felonies. So can I. Thus a case could be made for eliminating both of us. It would be moronic, true, but the prisons of Florida aren't overflowing with Mensa candidates.

Here's something: When I told Carla I had a heavy meeting with some unpleasant characters, she offered to loan me a pistol.

And I took it. Guns scare the daylights out of me, but dying scares me more. So on my kitchen counter now sits a loaded Lady Colt .38, which supposedly is more petite and purse-friendly than the macho-oriented model. That's fine by me; I've got my dainty side. Also on the counter are two external hard drive units — Jimmy's original, and an identical copy made this afternoon by Juan's whiz-kid pal in exchange for twenty dollars' worth of Upper Deck baseball cards.

Juan is the person I most need to consult, but he's over in Tampa covering a Devil Rays game. He's the one fellow I know who is intimate with the primal impulse; he could tell me what it's like to make that decision and then live with it. My plan doesn't include killing anybody but I believe I might do it for Emma; that and more. Once the realization sinks in, I feel oddly liberated and energized. Emma's alive, and I'll do whatever it takes to get her back. No other option exists, so why fret?

When I asked Carla Candilla why she owned a pistol, she said, "Get real, Jack — hot single chick, living alone. Hul-lo?"

"Does your mother know?"

"That's who gave it to me."

"No way," I said.

"Seriously. She's got one, too."

"Anne packs a rod? *Our* Anne?"

Carla said, "She never told you because she didn't want you to freak. No big deal."

The things I didn't know.

I arrive at the club at quarter past ten. Cleo Rio suspects I'm wearing a wire so, in a scene worthy of a Derek Grenoble potboiler, Jerry leads me to the men's room and roughly pats me down. Fortunately, I've left Lady Colt under the front seat of the Mustang.

In the coziness of the toilet stall I remark upon the stylishness of Jerry's black velvet eye patch. "That cologne, though, smells like fermented pig piss. Why does she make you wear it?"

"Shut the fuck up," he says, slugging me in the ribs.

When my respiration stabilizes, we return to the table. Loréal has arrived, hair aglimmering, to complete the motley foursome. Cleo is sporting white leather pants and a matching vest with nothing but skin beneath it. Tonight her pageboy is magenta while her eyelids and lips are done in cobalt. The look clashes badly with her Tortola-caliber tan.

Drinks are ordered and small talk is commenced, mostly by Loréal. He has been creatively inspired by something "funky" he heard on a No Doubt CD, and is confident he can replicate the effect on Cleo's record. She nods impassively and lights another cigarette. No screwdrivers for the widow tonight; it's black coffee. Loréal and I are tending Budweisers, while one-eyed Jerry sticks with Diet Coke. For a goon he's quite the sober professional.

As soon as the Nordic Rastafarian DJ takes a break, I invite Loréal to shut up so I can talk business with Cleo. She seems amused by my rude treatment of her boyfriend — clearly she'll be dumping this joker as soon as the album is finished. I expect she's already gotten stingy with the blow jobs.

"Here's the situation, Mrs. Stomarti," I begin. "You want Jimmy's song. I want my friend back."

"It's not just Jimmy's song. We did it together."

"Save that crap for the media tour. I listened to the tracks myself. Your husband wrote that number a long time ago, probably for another girl."

Cleo takes a hard drag. Her hand is steady. Eyeing me, she says, "Tagger, you got a death wish?"

I feel the hairs prickle on the back of my neck. "It's a good song," I say, "wherever it came from."

"A damn good song," Cleo says with a chuckle.

"And we'll make it even better," Loréal chimes in. "Time we're done, it won't sound anything like Jimmy's."

The widow and I ignore him. To her I say: "When I get Emma, you get the computer drive with all the music."

"Don't forget the discs you made."

"Them, too. Absolutely."

Jerry, sipping his soda, gives a scornful grunt. Turning to him, I can't resist saying: "You know what I belted you with, that night you busted into my apartment? A frozen lizard."

Reflexively Jerry touches a knuckle to his patch.

"That's right, tough guy. Your eye was put out by a one-hundred-and-seventy-seven-pound weakling armed only with a dead reptile. It's something to tell your grandchildren, when they ask how it happened."

Loréal says, "That's not funny, dude."

Jerry angrily states that I'm full of shit.

"Cleo, you should've been there," I say. "Your man saw all that blood on the floor and figured I was dead, so he ran away. But I wasn't dead."

"Unfortunately not," she says. "But you're gettin' closer by the minute, Tagger."

Her tone is not entirely unconvincing, but I laugh it off. "Is that supposed to be a threat? For God's sake, you're twenty-three years old!"

"Twenty-four," she says, "and my coffee's cold. So, how we gonna do the trade?"

I hear myself warning her to watch her step. "If you harm Emma or me, prepare for an eternal rain of shit. Lots of people know what I've been working on, and they'll come inquiring. And then they'll come back again and again."

Here I lay it on thick, dropping the names of detectives Hill and Goldman and of course Tarkington, the prosecutor. "By the way," I tell Cleo, "he was a big fan of your husband's."

She appears unmoved. "How can I, like, trust you to keep quiet?" she demands. "About the song, I mean."

"No, you mean about *everything*." Here comes the hairy part. "Look, I know you killed Jimmy, but I'll never prove it because the autopsy was a joke and the body's been cremated. Jay Burns was cool with the program because you promised he could play on 'Shipwrecked,' and who doesn't want to be on a hit record? But then I showed up at the boat, Jay went jiggy and you guys decided he wasn't all that terrific a piano player. The cops are ready to believe he got drunk and dozed off under that mullet truck. I seriously doubt it but, again, where's the proof?"

I shrug. Cleo yawns like a lioness and bites into an ice cube. Loréal starts to say something but wisely changes his mind. Jerry, meanwhile, folds his cable-sized arms across his chest. I think he picked this up from a Mr. Clean commercial.

"Now, let's talk about Tito Negraponte," I say. "Poor Tito wasn't lying when he told you he didn't know anything about 'Shipwrecked Heart.' He had nothing to do with the Exuma sessions. Jimmy didn't use him."

Cleo levels a moist glare at Loréal, who looks as if he wants to crawl under the ashtray.

"That's correct, darling," I inform the widow. "You tried to murder the wrong bass player. I'm guessing the Mexican gentlemen who took the job were recruited by Jerry here. Old prison chums, am I right, Jer? You look as if you spent some time in the yards."

The bodyguard's lips curl into a pale smile.

415

I wink obnoxiously and plow ahead:

"I'm also guessing that the two fellows who visited Tito are no longer with us, meaning the shooting can't be traced to anyone at this table. Which leaves me with what? A song."

"*The* song," says Cleo, whose sphynx-like composure is unnerving.

"Yes, the song you claim was a conjugal effort. I know the truth, but the only people who can back me up won't do it. Danny Gitt, the singers, the other studio players — they figure you'll sue 'em if they say anything, and who needs the hassle. Long as they got paid for the sessions, they'll stay quiet."

We are interrupted by an autograph seeker, a gothed-out Ecstasy twerp with a silver safety pin in each nostril.

"You rule, girl," she says to Cleo, who brusquely signs the cocktail napkin as "Cindy Zigler," her given name. Puzzled but grateful, the young fan departs.

"Getting back to the song," I say to Cleo, "maybe you just want to swipe the lyrics, or maybe you want Loréal to loop some of Jimmy's vocals, too — sort of a duet with the dead. That'll get some crossover air play. And I can't wait to see the pop-up video."

"Why the fuck should *you* care?"

"I was a fan, that's why. But as long as I get Emma back, I don't give a damn what you do with Jimmy's song. It'll never be as good as the one he did, but that's show business."

Cleo says, "You're forgettin' one thing. His sister."

"What about her?"

"She don't like me."

"So what? She doesn't know about all this." The secret of big-league bullshitting is to keep it coming.

Loréal says, "I bet she knows about the Exuma sessions."

"No doubt." Cleo scowls and crunches another ice cube.

"She doesn't know anything about this song," I say firmly. "Jimmy never told Janet — I asked her myself." Another hefty lie. I've got no idea if he ever played "Shipwrecked Heart" for his sister. The crucial thing is to convince Cleo that Janet poses no threat.

"She seems perfectly thrilled," I add, "to be getting a hundred grand from the estate."

Cleo laughs acidly. "Her and the goddamn Sea Urchins." She turns to Jerry. "Whaddya think? You said he wanted money."

Jerry says, "He will. Don't worry."

Guys like this, they make it too easy. "That's right, Jerry. The first time I saw you in that snazzy bomber jacket and those Beatle boots, I told myself: I'm gonna squeeze a couple million bucks out of that chrome-domed, noodle-dicked troglodyte."

Now, getting in Cleo's face, I really crank up the charm. "And no offense, Mrs.

Stomarti, but if you were sitting here having drinks with Clive Davis, I might be impressed enough to hit you up for a few bucks. Unfortunately, you're here with a dork who's named himself after a fucking hair product, and couldn't get into the Grammys with an AK-47."

A plum blush rises in young Loréal's cheeks, and he huffily challenges me to fisticuffs in the nearest alley. The rest of us stare at him pitilessly.

"Someday you might be a star," I say to Cleo, "but so far you've had exactly one hit single for a rinky-dink label. Whatever money you made is already spent on dope and wardrobe. Beyond the fact you're not worth blackmailing, it's significant to note that I've got nothing to blackmail you *with*. I can't write a story alleging you stole your husband's song without somebody else saying so. The paper wouldn't print it — please tell me you're not too fried to understand."

The widow paws absently at her bangs. She seems cordially immune to insult. "Suppose you burn another copy of Jimmy's solo version — that'd queer things up for me, it ever got out on the Net. What's to stop you from shakin' me down six months from now? Or a year?"

"Nothing," I say, "except an intense distaste for clichés."

Cleo puffs her cheeks and snorts. "Bottom

line, all you want is the chick?"

"Correct."

"What's her name again?"

"Emma. And I want my portable computer, too." I grab one of Jerry's earlobe hoops and pull his grimacing mug close to mine. "The laptop doesn't belong to me, Jer. It belongs to the Maggad-Feist Publishing Group, a publicly held company that is fiercely accountable to its shareholders."

Loréal says, "Jesus, knock it off. We'll buy you a brand-fucking-new Powerbook."

Now the DJ has returned to the podium, and I feel the mother of all headaches taking hold. I release the bodyguard's ear and lean my face across the table into a cloud of Cleo's cigarette smoke. "Let's get this over with."

"I gotta pee." And off she goes.

"So, when can we do it?" I ask Jerry.

"Not tonight," he says. "That's for damn sure."

"Then when?"

He cuffs me sharply on the side of the head and says, "We'll call you tomorrow, asswipe."

"Yeah, we'll be in touch," says Loréal.

As I rise from the table the speakers in the rafters start pounding — a hideous house-mix version of "MacArthur Park."

"You two should cut loose," I advise Cleo's boys. "Don't wait for something slow and romantic. Just let it happen."

27

Knock-knock. Emma opened the door. They snatched her.

Smooth and easy, it appears. The apartment is unlocked. Her purse is on the bed; on the kitchen table, car keys and a cold cup of espresso. For breakfast she had toast and a bowl of Special K.

Two in the morning, this isn't the best place to be. If I stay much longer I'll put a fist through the wall. Emma is gone and it's my fault.

But somebody's got to feed the cat, which cries and turns figure eights on the tile. I lift her into my arms, saying, "It's all right, Debbie. She'll be home soon."

Staring at the damn telephone, just like in the old days.

I remember once waiting seven hours for a source of mine to call — Walter Dubb, the bus-fleet supplier who was helping me nail Commissioner Orrin Van Gelder for bribery.

Walter's wife had gotten on his ass about making waves, so he was experiencing a crisis of faith. And so was I, because without Walter's cooperation the feds had no case and I

420

had no story. The day before the dinner at which Orrin Van Gelder was to be arrested by the undercover FBI man, Walter went deer hunting and failed to return in time for evening mass. His wife called up to rant. She said he must've got depressed and killed himself, and it was all because of me. She said he should've paid off the commissioner and kept his damn fool mouth shut.

Seized with dread, I sat glued to my desk from four that afternoon until eleven at night. My bladder was the size of Arkansas by the time Walter Dubb finally called. He'd killed a buck and skinned it out and then the pickup broke down in the woods and then a bear showed up and made off with the deer meat before Walter could get his rifle out of the rack — this was the tale he laid upon Mrs. Dubb, anyway. Whatever really happened that evening had put Walter in a highly contented frame of mind, and that's all that mattered to me. I whooped and danced all the way to the john.

Tonight I missed another call from Janet Thrush. She phoned the apartment while I was with Cleo and crew at Jizz.

"Meet me Sunday morning at the donut shop," she said in her message. "Try to be there 'round ten-thirty, okay?"

When I called back, the service answered so I hung up and put "Shipwrecked Heart" on the disc player. I tuned my old acoustic guitar and now I'm working through the chords of the song. The opening line of verse starts with a D, but then Jimmy changes keys and I believe the second line begins with an F-major seven, followed by a C, E-minor and an F. This is catchy but it's not exactly Derek and the Dominos. If a klutz like me can play it, so can Cleo. She can also sing the melody in that fashionably wounded way that sells jillions of records for young female artists.

This is how I'm guessing it started. They were hanging out at the house in the islands, Jimmy and his bride. She probably walked into the studio and caught just enough of the track to know it was better than anything she had in the can. She asked her husband to play it again and he probably said no, it's not ready. Then she batted her eyes and stroked his neck and asked if he'd give her the song and he said sorry, babe, this one's mine. Time went by and Cleo's label was hounding her and she kept nagging Jimmy for the cut. She probably flirted and teased and begged and cried and threw a hissy, but he wouldn't budge. And when it became plain to Cleo that her husband was keeping "Shipwrecked Heart" for himself, she decided to kill him.

And what little she remembered of the song, she sang at his funeral.

Touching.

I messed around with the guitar until an hour before dawn. Then I packed what I thought I'd need, drove to the paper and promptly fell asleep on the floor by my desk. The janitors worked around me, and the phone didn't ring. Now it's nine o'clock and the staff trickles into the newsroom. Abkazion is one of the first to arrive. Somewhere between the elevator and his office door, he spies me and alters course as silkily as a hawk.

"Jack," he says pleasantly, "you look like shit on a Popsicle stick."

Abkazion is one of those editors who prefers to see his reporters rumpled and raw-eyed. It means they're either working too hard or playing too hard — either way, he approves.

"It's this damn story," I say.

"Yeah, Emma told me. How's it going?"

"Ask me in twenty-four hours." I'm tempted to chum him up with my inflated Rick Tarkington quote, but that would require more energy than I can muster. Selling a story to the front page is hard work.

"How was Los Angeles?"

"Productive," I say. "Thanks for the green light."

"Thank Emma. She said you were hot on the trail."

Abkazion isn't tall but he has broad muscular shoulders and carries himself like the collegiate wrestler he once was. He is new to the *Union-Register* but already has endeared himself to the troops by disregarding several penny-pinching directives from corporate headquarters. He is the newspaper's fourth managing editor in six years and, like the others, Abkazion took the job because he thought he could staunch the bleeding. Soon enough he'll learn that he is working for vampires; vampires with stock options.

"That'd be a helluva twist," he's saying, "if it turns out Jimmy Stoma got snuffed by his old lady. You ever see 'em in concert — the Slut Puppies?"

"No, I never did."

"Lord, he was a wild man onstage," says Abkazion, "and he sure got the girls gooey. Know which song I really liked? 'Basket Case.' I think it was on *Reptiles and Amphibians*."

"Actually, it's from *Floating Hospice*," I say.

"You sure? 'Bipolar mama in leather and lace'?"

"That's the one."

"You're the expert." Abkazion smiles. "I hope this story works out for you, Jack."

It's a kind thing to say. He knows my history here.

"When will Emma be in?"

"I'm not sure," I tell him. "I think she called in sick again."

I log on my PC and find the site for the *International Herald Tribune*. Her father's name is David Cole. His most recent byline appeared three days ago. The dateline was Bhuj, India, where he has been sent to cover a horrific earthquake. I'm sure David Cole's editor knows the hotel number where he can be reached, in the awful event I need to call and tell him his daughter is lost.

Laying my cheek on the mouse pad, I doze off.

The dream is one of my regulars. I open the door and a bare-chested man greets me; a man my age. He's tall, and his sandy hair is shot lightly with gray at the temples.

He grins and says, "Hullo, Jack Jr."

And I say, "Dad, this isn't funny."

His face hasn't changed from the photograph my mother kept; the three of us on Clearwater Beach, me in a baby stroller. He looks like his son around the eyes, this man. The chin, too.

"You thought I was dead but I'm not," he announces impishly.

In the dream, here's what I do next: I grab him by his suntanned shoulders and heave him up against a wall. He looks solid but he's as light as a child.

"What happened to you? What happened?" I'm yelling into his face.

"Nothing," he bubbles. "I'm fit as a fiddle."

"How old are you?"

"Same age as you are," says my smiling father. Then he wriggles free and runs away. I chase after him and we end up on a golf course, of all places, tearing up and down the fairways. In the dream my old man is fleet and cagey afoot.

But I always catch him on the fringe of the thirteenth green, tackling him from behind. I lie there in the soft dewy grass for the longest time, pinning him while I catch my breath.

And when I finally roll my father over, he's not smiling the way he did in my mother's snapshot. He's stone dead.

In the dream I start shaking him like a movie-prop dummy, this fellow who looks too much like me; throttling him not out of grief but in a fever of exasperation.

"You're not funny!" I scream at the whitening face. "Now wake up and tell me how long ago you died!"

That's the way it always ends, me shaking the ghost of my father so ferociously that his teeth fall out of his skull like stars from a black hole.

After a dozen or so nights like that, who could blame Anne for bolting?

I wake up to face Juan and Evan, staring as they would at a five-car pileup.

"Long night?" says Juan.

"You're supposed to be in Tampa."

"Got your message. I woke up early and drove back."

"Evan," I say, "would you excuse us?"

The kid nods disappointedly and mopes toward his desk. What am I now, the entertainment committee?

Juan has brought a bag of breakfast from the cafeteria. He drags an extra chair to my desk and sets out bagels, croissants and orange juice.

"Congratulations," I tell him. "I saw where you got your leave of absence." It was posted on the bulletin board.

"Yeah. Starting Monday."

"I'm proud of you, man. Aren't you juiced about the book?"

He shrugs. "My sister's not so thrilled."

"I'm sorry. That's rough."

"She understands, though. Least she says so."

"You'll do a terrific job," I tell him. "Lizzy will be proud of you when she reads it."

I dive for the phone: Eddie Bell again, calling to flog the Audrey Feiffer obit. Quickly I transfer him to Evan's line and replace the receiver.

Juan says, "Tell me what's happened with your story, Jack."

"It ate me alive, that's what happened. They've grabbed Emma."

At first Juan doesn't say anything. He sets

his half-eaten bagel on the desk and looks around, making certain we're not being overheard. Then he takes a drink of juice before calmly asking, "Who's got her, Jack?"

"The widow and her boys."

"What do they want?"

"A song." I tell him the title. "It was on the hard drive we took to Dommie's."

"So, give 'em the damn thing," Juan says.

"I fully intend to. The problem is —"

"They might kill you anyway. You and Emma both."

"Bingo. So I've borrowed a gun."

Juan looks alarmed. "Jesus. Why don't you go to the police?"

"Because they'd never find Emma alive," I say. "This is not your textbook kidnapping, this is *Fargo* squared. These dipshits are making it up as they go along."

Somberly he eyes the silent telephone. "When are they supposed to call?"

"Any time," I say. "You know what numbskulls they are? They think I want money, in addition to Emma's return. They don't seem to grasp the concept of ransom — that it's the kidnappers who customarily make the demand. See what I'm dealing with?"

Juan leans back, staring into the distance. "What kind of gun?"

"Lady Colt. And don't laugh."

"Jack, you ever fired a pistol?"

"Once or twice. Okay, just once." It was on

a police range. I plugged a paper-silhouette felon in the thigh, then wrote a humorous twelve-inch feature story about it.

Juan gets up stiffly. "Man, I need to think about this. Call me as soon as you get the word."

"You'll be the first."

Leaning closer, he says, "Where do you think they're keeping her? What's your best guess?"

"I've got no idea, brother. Not a clue."

"Mierda."

"Just tell me how you did it," I whisper, "that night on the boat from Cuba. Was it reflex? Or did you plan it all out? I need guidance here."

"I'll tell you what I remember, Jack. I remember it seemed easy at the time." Then he squeezes my shoulder and says, "The bad stuff comes later."

Half past noon, the phone finally rings again.

"Tagger?"

"Jerry, you old rascal. What's up?"

"Party's at eight-thirty," he says.

"Tonight?"

"You're gonna need a boat and a GPS and a spotlight."

"You're nuts," I say.

"And bug spray, too. Better get your ass in gear."

"Where?" I'm scrambling to take down everything he says, word for word.

"The big lake."

"Not Okeechobee. You've got to be joking."

"What's your fucking problem, Tagger?"

"For starters, it's about forty miles long and thirty miles wide."

"Yeah, that's how come we're meeting in the middle. To make sure you ain't bringin' company."

"Jerry, you watch entirely too much TV."

"Write this down, fuckface." He reads me some numbers and instructions for navigating the lake, departing from a marina in Clewiston. I tell him I don't know how to work a GPS.

"Then it's gonna be a long night," he says.

Lake Okeechobee — what unbelievable morons.

"I don't suppose you checked the weather station. What if the boat sinks and the 'package' gets ruined? Ever thought of that, Jer?"

"Then maybe *our* boat sinks, too. Get the picture?"

He's a lost cause. Time for a different strategy. "Tell Mrs. Stomarti there's a better way to do this. A smarter way."

"She don't care. She won't even be there."

Showing uncharacteristic good sense, I'm thinking.

Hurriedly Jerry adds, "Anyway, I don't

know who you're talkin' about. I never heard a that person."

"Golly, you're too slick for me!"

"Eight-thirty," he says again. "Be sure and come alone."

"Where do I get a boat at night?"

"Steal one, you dumbass. That's what I'm doing."

I'm halfway to the elevator when Abkazion intercepts me. The gravity in his voice makes me think he's found out about Emma. That would be a large complication.

"Where you headed, Jack?"

"I've got to meet with a source."

"Better postpone it."

I follow him to his office, the same room where I bonded so warmly with Race Maggad III. Abkazion, however, is a different species of animal. He has no poses or pretensions; he fits comfortably in the newsroom, and his word is usually final. If he knows — and how he would, I can't imagine — that Emma has been kidnapped, it will be damn near impossible to make him back off.

The assertion that I alone can devise her safe return would strike Abkazion as preposterous. Yet that's the pitch I'm preparing to make when he says something startling:

"MacArthur Polk died this morning."

"No way."

431

"At home," Abkazion says.

"For real?"

"Oh yes."

"How? In his sleep?" I ask pointlessly.

"More or less. You ready to rock and roll?"

The irony, ruinous as it may be, is exquisite.

"I can't do the obit," I inform the managing editor of the *Union-Register*.

"What're you talking about?"

"I can't miss this meeting today. The source says it's now or never."

Abkazion peers at me as if he's examining for factory defects. "This would be a front-page story, Jack. Your first front-page story in about a thousand years."

"Yes, I'm painfully aware."

"Then you're also aware," he says, "there's a high level of corporate interest in Mr. Polk receiving a first-rate obituary. Not that I'm happy about the meddling but, hey, we learn to pick our battles."

I tell him I'm sorry. "This really sucks, I know."

"For reasons I don't pretend to understand, Mr. Maggad himself has been calling in advance of this story. He is emphatic, Jack, that you should be the one to write it."

"So he told me."

"Which makes it all the more baffling," Abkazion says, the cords of his neck going taut, "as to why you're refusing such an important assignment."

"I told you why."

It's Emma, I want to tell him. I've got to save Emma.

"For Christ's sake, talk to this source of yours. Explain the situation. Tell him to meet you tomorrow instead."

"That's impossible," I say.

"This is for that Slut Puppy story, right? The man's been dead two weeks and your source can't wait one more lousy day to spill his guts? Who is it?" Abkazion is shouting like a hypertensive Little League coach. "What's so goddamn important?"

But I can't tell him. Not about Emma or Cleo, or even about the song. Certainly I can't tell him about Maggad's covert quest to obtain MacArthur Polk's stock holdings, or about my perverse deathbed deal with the old buzzard.

Charles Chickle, Esq., was unequivocal: The trust agreement is contingent on my writing Polk's obituary. By dumping the story, I'm surrendering not just a hundred grand in estate fees but the opportunity of a lifetime — a chance to coerce Race Maggad III into reviving the *Union-Register.*

Abkazion might be pissed off, but I'm the one who's sick at heart.

"I've gotta go," I tell him.

"You're serious, aren't you?"

433

"Tell Mr. Maggad . . . know what? Tell him I threatened to dismember you with needle-nosed pliers. Tell him I went delirious and started quoting from Milton. 'Avenge, O Lord, thy slaughtered saints, whose bones lie scattered on Alpine mountains cold. . . .'"

"Jack," Abkazion says, "I'm late for the one o'clock."

"Of course."

"You've been waiting for a chance to dig yourself out of this hole. Now take it."

"Yes, chief," I say, exiting with a crisp salute.

It's all here on my desk — the stack of printouts of old stories, the notes from my hospital interview with Polk, the tepid background paragraphs I banged out a few days ago, even the fatuously reverential quote from Race Maggad III.

When I present this armful to Evan, he rolls back his chair and looks up at me guardedly.

"Congratulations, champ," I say. "You're going to be the star of the front page tomorrow."

"I'm sure."

He's a sharp kid. He'll do fine with the story.

"Have a blast," I tell him. "Write your balls off."

"What is this stuff?"

"Listen, the boss'll be asking for me. Tell him I vanished in a blur."

"Jack, wait a minute. Hey, Jack!"

But I'm already gone.

28

The drive to Lake Okeechobee takes about three hours. Emma likes Sting, so I brought along *Synchronicity* for the ride home. For now, though, Juan and I are sticking with the Stones. He's stretched out in the backseat, skimming the instructions for the hand-held GPS we bought at a sporting-goods outlet in Fort Pierce. Included in the purchase were a Q-beam spotlight, a waterproof tote, a yellow plastic tarpaulin, a bait bucket and two cheap spinning rods. I will be posing as a fisherman.

When Juan insisted on coming along, I didn't argue. If events take an unpromising turn, levelheaded assistance will be welcome. Also: *cojones* of steel. We're proceeding on the assumption that Jerry will have somebody in place, watching, when we arrive at the lake. Juan is keeping low, out of sight. Along the way he has confided that he broke off his relationship with Miriam, the beautiful orthopedic surgeon. "The others, too," he said, meaning the figure skater and the halftime dancer for the basketball team. "I've got to buckle down. I've got to focus on the book."

"You're confused," I told him. "It's prizefighters who give up sex. Not writers."

"The sex is the least of it," he said, most seriously.

Clewiston is on the southern rim of the lake, in the heart of sugarcane country. The land is as flat as plywood. As instructed, we seek out a garishly appointed facility called Ernie Bo Tump's Bass Camp. Ernie Bo is an internationally famous conqueror of largemouth bass. He has his own syndicated television program, and a product-endorsement package that would be the envy of an NBA all-star. Ernie Bo's fish camp, however, has fallen on tough times. Farms and cattle ranches have dumped so much shit-fouled runoff into the lake that miles of prime bass habitat have been transformed into impenetrable cattail bogs. The decline in sportfishing commerce has been exacerbated by water levels so treacherously low as to discourage navigation by high-speed fanatics with 175-horsepower outboards — Ernie Bo's bread-and-butter clientele.

This glum tale is related by a young dock hand named Tucker, with whom I am negotiating the rental of a bare fourteen-foot johnboat. While Tucker is gladdened by the sight of a paying customer, he's concerned that I'm launching so late in the afternoon. He advises that the craft must be returned no later than one hour after sunset. I hope he doesn't intend to wait.

"Dusk is when they bite the best!" I say, which is what my mother always told me.

"There's thunder boomers out to the west. We sure as hell need the rain," Tucker says, "but you better keep an eye out. The lightning gets hairy, this time a year."

"Thanks, I'll be careful. How much?"

"Fifty bucks, plus the deposit." He snatches my credit card. "You need some shiners?"

I ask him to scoop me a dozen. "Did anybody else head out of here this afternoon? I was supposed to meet a couple of friends who were driving over from the west coast."

"Naw, you're it," says Tucker. "Maybe they put in at Moore Haven instead."

"Maybe so."

So far I haven't spotted anyone at the marina who is behaving like a lookout, but I'll take no chances. I stow Jimmy Stoma's hard drive, the compact discs and the Lady Colt in the waterproof tote before loading it with the rest of the gear on the johnboat. The engine is a Merc 25, which barks to life after a few yanks on the cord. With one hand on the tiller, I putter innocently from the docks, heading out toward the big water. If someone is watching, he will report to Cleo's bodyguard that I am en route to the rendezvous, and that I'm alone.

Juan is waiting at a pre-arranged location a half mile away, by a drainage culvert below the levee. He slips into the bow and conceals

438

himself beneath the yellow tarp. Without a breeze the August heat is strangling; the lake steams like a vast tub of gumbo. It's not so bad after I goose the throttle and the boat planes off, creating its own breeze. Soon no other fishermen are in sight. Juan partially emerges from under the tarpaulin and intently begins working the keypad of the GPS, talking to satellites high in space. Flawlessly they divulge our latitude, longitude, ground speed and direction, as well as our lengthening distance from the marina. The only drawback of this astounding technology is that it enables virtually any knucklehead to blunder into the deepest wilderness, with little or no chance of getting lost. So much for natural selection.

Jerry's directions have put us on a course of almost due north, with deviations around flats and grass islets. Using the satellite readouts, I am to fix my speed at precisely twenty-two miles an hour. After passing Observation Island, I'm supposed to run for forty-five minutes, then shut the engine down and wait. Only one-eyed Jerry and the amazing GPS will know where we are.

Young Tucker was correct about the weather. A colossal thunderhead blooms over the lake's western shore, cooling the air but robbing us of a sunset. Later the wind kicks up and a fresh chop spanks rhythmically against the aluminum hull. Juan's gaze is locked apprehensively on the purple-rimmed clouds spilling our way. I'm trying to push Emma out of my mind, trying not to imagine her on a boat out here with Cleo's brutish bodyguard.

The first misting rush of rain is cold on the skin, and I envision Emma soaked and shivering and afraid. A spear of lightning flickers and I'm counting one thousand, two thousand and so on, until the thunder breaks. This, too, I learned from my mother. Four beats, four miles — that's the distance to the face of the storm.

My mother has a reckless lack of respect for weather. If the fish are biting, she refuses to budge. I recall one scary morning, hauling in lane snappers on a patch reef off Duck Key, when a squall rumbled across from the Gulf. The rain arrived in sheets and the waves started pitching the boat, and I begged my mother to let me free the anchor so we could make a run for shore. She told me to quit griping and start bailing. "Be quiet about it, too," she said. "Don't you spook my fish." What a character. I think of her whenever I'm out on the water; those summer trips together. If she were here now, instead of golfing with Dave in Naples, she'd probably tell me to stop the boat so she could cast a bait into the lily pads. To hell with the storm, Jack.

And actually I'd be delighted to stop the

damn boat if I wasn't worried that it would put us off schedule. Jerry is holding Emma somewhere out here, and he's waiting for me. But Sweet Holy Jesus, lightning is starting to crash around us and the air smells burnt, hissing between thunderclaps. Juan has withdrawn, turtle-style, beneath the plastic tarpaulin. Now and then a hand snakes out to signal for a slight adjustment of course. The raindrops feel like needles on my cheeks — it's impossible to see more than forty feet beyond the bow.

But I can't slow down. Every so often I swerve sharply to avoid a snake or a big gator. The lake is so low, the critters have moved out to the middle. That fucking Jerry, he's going to get an earful if I make it through this storm alive.

A bolt strikes so close to the boat that Juan lets out a yell. Instinctively I slide to my knees, hunkering between the bench seats while keeping a grip on the tiller. Now we're running blind, and it's only moments before we plow into something — either a log or an alligator. The boat jolts and the lower unit kicks out of the water, the propeller spitting duckweed and muck. I twist back on the throttle to kill the motor.

Rocking in the sudden silence, Juan peers doubtfully at me from beneath the tarp. Tiny rain bubbles sparkle in his eyelashes.

"Iceberg," I say.

"You gotta take it easy, Jack. I'm not kidding."

A ding in the skeg is the only visible damage to the engine, which re-starts on the first pull. There's about three inches of rainwater in the boat, so Juan dumps the shiners and employs the bait bucket as a bailer. Meanwhile I check the tote bag to make sure that Jimmy's music and Carla's gun are still dry. Then, working quickly, I attach the wires of the portable spotlight to the posts of the twelve-volt battery mounted in the stern.

Juan reports that the GPS still works splendidly and that the mishap has cost us only seven minutes, which can be made up with extra speed. Darkness is rolling in but the worst of the weather has passed. We take a northbound heading and set off again in a muggy drizzle. The time is five past eight. As the storm leaves the lake, clouds high to the east pulse with bright jagged veins of orange and blue. The bursts are so regular I can steer by the light. Thirty-one minutes later, Juan's hand shoots from under the tarp and makes a slashing motion.

We're there.

No sooner do I turn off the engine than the mosquitoes find us. They are famished and unbashful. "That's what we forgot — the damn bug juice," the lump in the tarpaulin mutters.

Five minutes pass. Then five more. I begin

to sweep the spotlight back and forth through the blackness. Insects scatter and minnows skip away from the stabbing glare. I count six different pairs of gator eyes, glowing like hot rubies in the marsh grass.

"Where the hell are they?"

"Relax," says the voice under the tarp.

"I bet we got lost in that storm."

"The hell we did," says Juan.

"Then I bet *they* got lost."

So I switch off the spotlight and wait. It doesn't take long to become frantic about Emma. Jerry's had another brainstorm, I'm sure. He's not clever enough to let the meeting pass without trying something outlandish. This is a problem with many criminals; this is why we need jails.

In anticipation of trouble, Juan and I have talked through possible scenarios, devising a fitting response for each. Yet now, drifting in a darkness without horizons, all our slick ideas seem puny or improbable. There's no way to know what Jerry will do, but I doubt he intends to behave. Every time he stares in the mirror he's reminded of what I did, and it is impossible to believe he won't try to settle up.

"I hear something," Juan says.

"Me, too."

It sounds like a small plane, flying low to dodge the weather.

"Try the spotlight, Jack. Maybe they're looking for you."

I paint a slow high arc with the Q-beam, flashing it on and off repeatedly. As the engine noise grows louder, I'm thinking Juan's right — Jerry probably sent up a spotter to pin my location.

From the bow: "You see it yet?"

"Maybe they went into some clouds."

"I'm not moving," Juan announces, "in case they've got infrared."

Flying without lights is not unheard of in South Florida, but it's still ballsy. The boys in Customs are quite proud of their fancy radars. And something else seems wrong: Whatever is buzzing toward us is every decibel as loud as an airplane, but not nearly as fast. A plane would have passed over us by now.

I point the spotlight in the direction of the approaching din but it turns out I'm aiming high. A more powerful beam shoots back at the johnboat and I spin away, to save my eyes. The onrushing roar is now so intense that I put down the spotlight and press my knuckles to my ears. Suddenly the engine changes pitch, and trails off to nothing with a *thwocka-thwocka-thwock*.

Now I know what we're dealing with: Cleo's bodyguard has swiped an airboat.

The light plays back and forth across our little fishing craft, lingering on the yellow tarpaulin a moment too long for my ragged nerves. I snatch up my own light and aim for the guy's face. He ducks, but not before I catch a telltale glint of an earring and a flash of bare pate.

"Knock it off, dickhead," the shadow barks.

"Jerry, my brother, you're late."

Simultaneously we kill the spotlights. The distinctive L-shaped profile of the airboat becomes visible against a pinkish swath of low sky — the faraway glow of West Palm Beach. I see Jerry's burly silhouette on the driver's platform in front of the big propeller. In the bow are two other figures; one is standing and one is seated, cloaked in a hood.

"Where's the package?" Jerry shouts at me.

"Not yet, you silly man!"

The standing figure prods the hooded figure, who says, "Jack, it's me."

I feel like a mule just kicked me in the gut.

"It's me, Emma." She sounds doped and exhausted.

"How are you doing, princess," I hear myself calling in a strained voice. "It's gonna be all right."

I'm shaking so badly it must be rocking Juan in the front of the boat. If I tried to stand up now I'd keel sideways into the lake. "How do you want to do this?" I ask Jerry.

"Right here. Bring your boat over."

Boy oh boy.

The tall figure in the front of the airboat is loosening the hood on Emma's head. I feel for the starter cord on the Mercury and I pull on it once, twice, three times.

That figures — the fucker won't start. Its moist wheezing reminds me of the late Mac-Arthur Polk.

"Hurry it up," Jerry snaps.

Easy, Jack. Don't panic. Try the choke — but let's not flood it, okay?

"What's the problem, dickhead?" Jerry zaps me with his spotlight. He thinks I'm stalling.

Twice more I yank on the cord before the outboard chugs to life. I put it in gear and idle toward the kidnappers. What else is there to do?

"You look very cool in that contraption, Jerry. Have you driven one of those things before?"

"Shut up, Tagger."

"If you ever get canned by Cleo, maybe you could get a job on the Seminole reservation. Nature tours!"

"Eat me," says Jerry. Descending from the driver's seat, he keeps the spotlight trained on my chest. I guess he wants to make sure I'm not reaching for another frozen lizard.

Pointing my own Q-beam at the bow of the airboat, I see that Emma's hood is a burlap feed sack. She slumps round-shouldered and unmoving. The man guarding her is none other than Loréal. His eyeglasses are bug-splattered and his lustrous waist-length mane is pulled back in a drenched and unglamorous ponytail — the life of a big-time record producer! Under any other circumstances he'd have me in stitches. His distressed expression suggests he'd rather be anywhere else on the planet but here. Obviously Jerry has given him a preview of what lies ahead.

Easing up to the airboat, I put down my light, slip the outboard into neutral and move to the bow. I'm careful not to step on Juan, who remains motionless under the yellow tarpaulin. When I reach beneath it, a large plastic cartridge is pressed firmly into my hand — Jimmy Stoma's unfinished creation.

Jerry's spotlight is scorching the back of my neck, and I know he's looming over me, a gun in his other hand. The glare is so hot that I can't look up.

"Give it here," he says.

"Not until you hand down the lady."

The spotlight's beam jiggles as he shifts positions. I've already decided to knock him into the water if he tries to board the johnboat. The light clicks off, and as my eyes adjust, I can see Loréal leading Emma by the arm; leading her to me. This I can scarcely believe.

Yet now I'm helping her into the johnboat, gently squeezing her arm and whispering that everything's going to turn out fine. In the cloud-glow I see the black stripe of Jerry's eye patch encircling his naked skull. The spotlight bobs restlessly in his left hand, which means the gun is in the other. I expect he'll shoot us the moment he gets his mitts on Jimmy's music.

"Now give it here!" he says.

I pick up the computer box and dangle it above the water on the opposite side of the boat, so that Jerry can't grab at it. "If this baby gets wet, it's all over," I say. "The unit is ruined and the song's lost forever." With such morons it's impossible to belabor the obvious.

"Tagger, what the fuck're you doin'?"

"Your gun, Jer. Throw it as far as you can."

"Yeah, right."

"Listen, Cyclops, I'm counting to five. If I don't hear your *pistola* hit the water, the package will. Then you can go home and explain to Mrs. Stomarti what happened to her hit single. Explain how you're a tough guy, and tough guys can't part with their guns. I'm sure she'll understand."

Jerry raises his right arm. It's not so dark that I can't make out the shape of the barrel, aimed more or less at my beak. Soiling myself would not be an inappropriate reaction.

Yet I continue to brandish the prized hard drive over the water. "One," I hear myself saying. "Two . . . three. . . ."

"Shit, Jerry, do what he says!" Finally Loréal has something to contribute. "If he drops the damn thing, we lose all the tracks

448

and then we're screwed. I'm fucking serious."

"Listen to the man, Jer. He's a pro."

The bodyguard emits a crude slur on my ancestry, then he rears back and heaves the gun. From the sound of the splash, it was a big one.

He says, "Okay, now gimme the fucking package."

I'm a man of my word. "Here, Jerry. Catch."

I toss the plastic box at his squat silhouette. The hard drive bounces off his chest and falls to the deck of the airboat. While he and Loréal clamber to retrieve it, I shove off.

Stepping to the stern of the skiff, I twist the throttle wide open.

"Jack?"

"It's okay, Emma. Everything's fine."

I reach for the hood and tug it off. She looks haggard and dazed. Smiling numbly, she clutches at my hand. Juan peeks out from beneath the tarpaulin. "We cool?"

"Not quite." A mild understatement.

We'll never outrun that airboat if they come after us, which is a distinct possibility. Jerry didn't even ask for the CDs that we burned from Jimmy's master. It would be calamitous for Cleo if they turned up on some radio station at the same time her album came out. She made a point of telling me to bring those discs tonight, so that she could destroy them. I'd have been pleased to hand them over, too, but that sonofabitch Jerry never said a word.

Which means he either forgot, or he doesn't intend to let us get off this lake alive.

Juan crawls back to take the tiller and to deliver Carla's gun, which he'd held cocked for the duration of the rendezvous. That was one of our contingency plans — in the event of an especially violent double cross, Juan was to burst from beneath the tarp and plug Cleo's bodyguard in the brain. It wasn't a particularly original idea, but we were looking to keep things simple.

Delicately I slip the Lady Colt into my waistband, the challenge being not to shoot myself. I move forward to sit beside Emma, who is wobbly and shuddering. I wrap one arm around her and with the other I point the Q-beam at twelve o'clock, so that Juan is able to see where we're heading. In his fist the GPS screen glows a cozy green, and the unanimous hope is that it will guide us back to Ernie Bo Tump's marina.

For all the neurotic ruminating I do about death, I never before felt the ice-cold breath of the beast. In all my life I cannot recall a singular moment I thought would be my last. Even when no-neck Jerry was whaling on me in the apartment, I was more angry than scared, which doesn't say much for my survival instinct. Tonight a large-caliber handgun was pointed at my nostrils, and my response was cinematic defiance. Whether that was brave or merely idiotic, it plainly reveals a new, more flexible attitude toward the concept of dying. Emma has no frame of reference, but Anne might call it a breakthrough.

In any case, I'm not off the hook. None of us are.

"Jack, look! Look!" Juan points ahead. Emma stiffens in my embrace. Streaking off our port side is another white light — the airboat, angling on a course to intercept us. Instantly I kill the Q-beam and start fumbling for the gun. I tell Juan not to slow down, no matter what.

Jerry the goon is wilier than I thought. He circled far around us to get downwind, so that we couldn't hear him coming until it was too late to hide. And he's not going to leave us full of bullet holes, which would arouse suspicion. Instead he intends to run us down, making it appear as if we accidentally wrecked the johnboat. Jerry figures that even if the cops wonder about the mess, nobody will put it all together.

The lake was dark, they must've hit something. . . .

Their spotlight slashes back and forth as Cleo's boys feverishly try to find us again. We're all crouched low, Juan panting and Emma's fingers digging into my leg. We're holding to a steady speed, a daring strategy

451

in inky darkness. If we strike another log, the chase is over.

"Shit," I hear Juan say. "Jack! They're . . ."

His warning is smothered by the rising roar. I twist around to see the airboat skimming up our wake, not more than fifty yards behind us. Loréal is braced in the bow, manning the spotlight. The beam is fixed on the back of Juan's head, radiating an unwanted halo. In the glare I can't see Jerry on the driver's perch, but he most certainly can see us.

The gap shrinks with a sickening inevitability — powered by a cropduster-sized aviation engine, the airboat is nearly twice as fast as our dinky outboard. It's also twice as wide and probably three times as heavy. At fifty miles an hour it will flatten us like a lily pad. Either we'll die on impact or go down screaming.

In any event, we will be long past caring by the time the gators get around to us.

Juan thumps my arm and gestures disgustedly at our motor. The prop is picking up weeds and we're slowing steadily. Jerry has taken dead aim at our flimsy transom.

"Grab Emma," Juan tells me, "and jump."

"Oh, I don't think so."

"Jack, please!" Emma says. It's the same tone she uses in the newsroom when I'm being impossible.

"Everybody get down!" I hear myself

452

yelling, though I'm standing as straight as a fence post. Carla's gun is gripped with both hands and my arms are extended, the way the cops showed me that day at the firing range. I'm squinting because Loréal is blasting the spotlight in my face. The airboat bears down with a rising backbeat of heavy pistons, like an oncoming locomotive. At roughly one hundred feet I start pulling the trigger, the pistol jumping in my hands. The odds of me actually hitting these pricks with a .38 slug are slender indeed, but Loréal appears to have taken due notice of the muzzle flashes. A yelp of alarm goes up from both men in the airboat, and the spotlight beam wavers madly. A heated downshifting can be heard, then a sibilant rush of air.

Unfortunately, we're no longer moving. The outboard has quit. As I throw myself upon Emma, Juan jumps off the stern.

The next sound isn't the expected crunch of impact but rather a long turbulent splash, followed by the thumping, fading grind of the aircraft engine. A gargled cry arises before silence reclaims the darkness.

In a whisper I ask Emma if she's all right.

"Yes, but I'm very thirsty, Jack. Thirsty and tired." Her voice is somnolent and hollow, from another galaxy. They must have drugged her with a goddamn horse tranquilizer. Hastily I make a bedding of the yellow tarp and lay her down on the deck. Meanwhile Juan has jetted out of the water like an otter. Wordlessly he cleans the duckweed off the outboard's lower unit while I re-attach the Q-beam cables to the battery.

The crashed airboat is easy to find. Bow skyward, it rests in a dense bank of cattails. The gunshots evidently spooked Jerry into cutting the rudders sharply, a maneuver for which flat-bottomed watercraft traveling at high speeds are not favorably designed. Also working against him was the lack of one eye, which undoubtedly affected his depth perception as he struggled to control the boat. It spun violently before tipping backward at a radical cant, its stern embedding in the mud.

I'm guessing Jerry got bucked off when the airboat began to whirl. He was probably sitting on his ass in the cattails, gaping in dull wonderment as the boat upended and wallowed back on him, the blade still very much a blur. His head should be landing in Pahokee any time now.

Loréal went next, though not as instantly. His fall appears to have been stopped by the frame of the driver's seat, but his silken ponytail slipped unluckily through the mesh of the engine cage. The propeller must have snagged it and continued to rotate, dragging his face in a brutally concentric pattern across the metal grid, until the scalp ripped loose. It now hangs like a soggy red pennant from one tip of the blade.

What this looks like is a dreadful accident. Two joyriders in a stolen airboat.

The lake was dark, they must've hit something. . . .

Emma is breathing softly — in the sudden quiet she has fallen asleep. I hear Juan slap at a mosquito. I hang over the gunwale and vomit as discreetly as possible.

"It's getting late," Juan says.

"Maybe I hit 'em with a shot."

"Right, Jack. And maybe one day hamsters will sing opera."

"That bad, huh."

"Yeah, but it sure did the trick."

Not far from Jerry's body, my spotlight snares the flash of an object submerged on the muddy lake bottom: a black plastic box, slightly larger than an eight-track cassette.

Jimmy Stoma's widow will be mighty disappointed.

29

Emma and I lounge in bed until nearly noon. Juan calls to check on us.

"That was a bad scene out there." He sounds tired though unshaken. "Those guys got what they deserved, Jack."

"The case could be made. But what a godawful mess."

"So, from now on you'll be sleeping with the lights on. Welcome to the club," he says. "How is Emma? That's the most important thing."

"Emma is strong."

In fact, she has insisted on preparing a lumberjack's breakfast — an omelette, flapjacks, sausages, grapefruit and toast. I hang up the phone in time to dart out of her path as she twirls through the kitchen wearing nothing but my Jaguars jersey and mint-green toenail polish.

Bravely she relates the details of her abduction. Jerry and Loréal were staking out my place the night I returned from Los Angeles, then tailed Emma home from the pancake house the next morning. She thinks they got in through the front door, which she'd left unlocked after letting in the cat. The men waited as she dressed for work, then tossed the burlap hood over her head as she came out of the bedroom. She was dosed with sleeping pills, bundled in the trunk of a car and driven to an unknown location — based on a whiff of bathroom cleanser, Emma believes it was a cheap motel. There she was kept for thirty hours until they doped her again, took her to the lake and placed her aboard the airboat. She never saw the faces of her captors, and never once heard them mention Cleo Rio by name.

So, as anticipated, it will be impossible to pin the kidnapping on Jimmy's widow. After what happened last night, the crime is destined to remain unreported anyway. Mrs. Stomarti will get away with everything, except her dead husband's song.

I can live with that. We got Emma back.

While the omelette is frying, she ambushes me with a boisterous hug. "You are hereby forbidden from touching a loaded firearm ever again," she teases.

"I told you how much I hated those damn things."

"From what I remember, you were very gallant last night."

"Lucky I didn't shoot off my own fingers."

"You still saved our lives. Think about it, Jack."

I haven't told Emma what happened to Jerry and Loréal. She was in dreamland when

Juan and I went to find them.

"The men who kidnapped you died in the airboat crash."

After a troubled pause, Emma asks: "You're sure?"

"You've heard of blunt trauma? This was the opposite."

"Should we call the police?"

"And tell them what — the dead guys tried to kill us to cover up the theft of a pop song? The cops would roll us both in bubble wrap and ship us to the psycho wing at Charity."

Breakfast turns into a quiet affair. Emma isn't angry; she's engrossed. It's no small weight to bear, the experience of a soul-rattling event that may never be acknowledged.

Yet that's how it must be. There was no abduction. No meeting on the lake. No lethal chase.

Emma says, "But what if somebody figures out —"

"Never. It was an accident. The weather was lousy, the sky was dark."

"I understand, Jack."

The *Union-Register* sits in a lawn wrapper on the counter; I haven't got the appetite to peek at the front page. Emma opens it and spies the headline. "What! Why didn't you tell me?"

"I was waiting until the drugs wore off."

Excitedly she slips on her reading glasses and spreads the paper over the table, across the breakfast platters. "That figures — Old Man Polk finally dies and I'm not there to edit the story."

"Read it aloud," I say.

She gives me a peckish look. "Well, aren't you something."

"Please?"

So she reads to me:

The man who shaped and guided the *Union-Register* for nearly four decades passed away Friday after a long illness. MacArthur Polk was 88.

A community icon and fervid philanthropist, Polk died at his Silver Beach home with his wife Ellen at his side. Friends said the couple was playing Chinese checkers when he collapsed.

Though he had been in failing health for some time, Polk remained engaged and outspoken, never losing his passion for the newspaper he inherited from his father.

In an interview last week at Charity Hospital, he said, "There's no greater privilege than publishing a daily newspaper, and no greater responsibility than delivering the truth, even when it ain't so pretty."

Emma glances up. "He really say that?"

"Word for word. Did young Maggad's quote make it on the front?"

"If it didn't, somebody's out of a job." Emma continues:

Headstrong and visionary, Polk transformed the *Union-Register* from a folksy, small-town journal to a dynamic, award-winning newspaper with an increasingly urban circulation of 82,500 weekdays and nearly 91,000 on Sundays.

"We turned it into a first-class outfit," he said. "The conscience of the community."

The only son of the *Union-Register*'s founder, Ford Polk, the kid known as Mac started in the newsroom fresh out of college as a telephone clerk, working his way up the ladder to managing editor.

When his father retired unexpectedly in 1959 to open a dwarf mink farm, Polk took over as publisher. His firm-handed stewardship of the paper continued until 1997, when he sold it to the Maggad-Feist Publishing Group for a reported $47 million.

"MacArthur Polk was like a second father to me," said Race Maggad III, the chairman and chief executive officer of Maggad-Feist. "He was a teacher, a friend and an inspiration."

This is too much for Emma, who blurts:

"What a hypocritical little prick!"

The old man would be hopping mad, that's for sure.

"Otherwise I think he'd have liked the story," she says. "You did a nice job, Jack, considering all the distractions."

"What are you talking about?" The piece isn't badly done, but plainly it is not my style. "Fervid philanthropist"? Give me a break.

"What I mean," says Emma, "is that it must've been hard to sit down and write this yesterday, waiting for Cleo's goons to call."

"But I didn't write it, Emma. Look at the byline."

"I *am* looking at the byline."

Lunging forward, I grab the story out of her hands.

Outrageous. That craven sonofabitch Abkazion crumpled like the bumper on a Tijuana taxi. He stuck my name on top of Old Man Polk's obituary!

"Evan wrote this," I protest, waving the newspaper at Emma, "while Juan and I were driving to the lake."

"I don't get it."

"Simple. Maggad ordered me assigned to the obit. Abkazion was scared to piss him off so he put my name on it, thus screwing a decent hardworking kid out of a byline."

"Pretty shitty," Emma concedes.

I turn to the jump page and skim the re-

461

mainder of the obituary. There, below the last paragraph, is an italicized credit line: *Staff intern Evan Richards contributed to this story.*

I feel rotten and helpless. So does Emma. "You want me to read the rest of it?" she asks halfheartedly.

"Not aloud. No."

Another illustrious milestone in the career of Jack Tagger Jr. Finally I get back on the front page, and I didn't even write the damn story.

Soon I'll be getting that phone call from Charles Chickle offering the cushy trustee gig, yet even the prospect of being paid to torment Race Maggad III fails to cheer me. What happened to Evan sucks; I hate seeing any reporter get shafted.

Emma tries to help by reminding me that the kid cobbled the old man's obit from my notes, clips and interviews. "It was mostly a rewrite job," she says. "The bulk of the work was yours."

"Nice try." I reach for the phone. "Has our Evan got a listed number?"

He answers on the third ring, which is encouraging. I've known interns who would have already hung themselves in despair.

"Hi, Jack," he says quietly.

I launch a virulently indignant diatribe against shifty spineless editors, which Evan spoils by informing me that he is not the aggrieved party. He didn't write the MacArthur Polk obituary, either.

"I choked, man," he confesses. "Abkazion bailed me out. He grabbed all your notes, sat down at the city desk and banged the whole story out with, like, twenty minutes to deadline."

"I see."

Evan can't stop apologizing, and he's wearing on my nerves like a whining Chihuahua. "Once you told me the obit was for the front page," he says, "my brain locked up big-time. I'm really sorry, Jack."

"Don't be. It was wrong for me to dump it on you like that."

"What do you think Emma's gonna do?"

"To you? Nothing," I say. "I'm the one who's in trouble."

"Really?" the kid says anxiously.

"Oh, she's an animal sometimes. It's scary."

Emma peers curiously over the top of the newspaper. "Who's an animal?"

"See you Monday," I say to Evan, and hang up smiling.

We're back in bed when the telephone rings. Emma's head is resting on my chest and I'm not moving, period.

The answer machine picks up. The call is from Carla Candilla, her voice hushed and urgent.

"Derek really did it! 'Ode to a Brown-Eyed

463

Goddess' — Jack, it was so fucking lame."

She's calling on her cellular from Anne's wedding, which I'd come tantalizingly close to forgetting.

"It took him half an hour to read," Carla says, "meantime I had to pee like a racehorse. I wrote down a couple lines 'cause I knew you could use a laugh."

Emma stirs against me. "Jack, who's that on the phone?"

"The daughter of an old friend. She's the one who loaned me the gun." The gun now resting somewhere in Lake Okeechobee, where I tossed it.

"Dig this," Carla is saying on the machine. " 'My heart melts anew each time your brown eyes light on me. Passion sings in my breast like the soaring sparrow's harmony.' "

"Ouch," says Emma.

"And that's a best-selling writer," I feel duty-bound to report. But at least he wrote her a poem, which is more than I ever did.

"Can you believe it — birds in his breast!" When Carla's giggle fades, her tone turns more serious. "Anyhow, Mom looks awesome and the champagne is killer, so I guess I'll survive. The real reason I called, I want to make sure you got home okay from your big adventure last night, whatever it was. And I hope your friend's okay, too. Someday I'll get you drunk and make you tell me about it. Oh, one more thing: Happy Birthday, Black Jack."

Oh Jesus, that's right.

Emma raises her head. "Today's your birthday? Why didn't you say something?"

"Slipped my mind." Incredible but true.

Emma snaps her fingers. "How old again?"

"Forty-seven."

So long, Mr. Presley. Hello, Mr. Kerouac. I suppose this will never end, until I do.

Emma springs out of bed. "Get up, you old fart. We're going shopping."

That was the most time I'd spent in a mall in ten years. Emma was buoyant and sassy; she likes birthdays. She bought me the new Neil Young CD, two pairs of stonewashed jeans and a bottle of cologne that she says is "the bomb." Then she wanted to treat me to a movie, and she wouldn't take no for an answer. It was an action remake of the TV series *Petticoat Junction*, starring Drew Barrymore, Charlize Theron and Catherine Zeta-Jones, three beautiful sisters who live at a rural railroad depot. In the old television show, the girls had weekly comic encounters with cranky relatives and colorful characters who came and went on the train. In the movie version, however, all three sisters are working undercover for the Mossad. For me, the plot never quite came together.

A small FedEx box is sitting by the door when Emma and I return to the apartment. My mother's birthday present: a first edition of Zane Grey's *Riders of the Purple Sage*. Where she found it I can't imagine, but what a beauty! I've got a shelf devoted to books my mother has given me on birthdays. Tucked into the pages of the Zane Grey novel is a card, and also a long brown envelope. For some reason I open the envelope first.

Inside is a photocopy of my father's obituary.

Ever since my mother revealed that she'd seen it, I've been imagining what the article said. Not everybody's death gets written up by a newspaper, so it was intriguing to think that, after ditching Mom and me, Jack Tagger Sr. had done something in life to merit notice of his passing. Perhaps he'd become a beloved saxophone teacher, a crusading social worker or a feisty small-town politician. Maybe he'd invented something new and amazing, some nifty gizmo now taken for granted by the entire human race, including his estranged namesake — the electric nose-hair trimmer, for example, or Styrofoam peanuts.

I've also pondered the unappealing prospect that my father earned an obituary not because of anything good he'd done, but because of some newsworthy fuckup, scandal or felony. Bruno Hauptmann got quite a boisterous send-off in the media, though I doubt his family made a scrapbook of the clippings.

I myself have written obits of local scoundrels that elicited sighs of relief if not cheers from our readers. Communities usually are pleased to be rid of bad eggs, and I've been bracing for the possibility that my father was one.

Yet it turns out he was neither a miscreant nor a pillar of the establishment. He was merely a character, small and harmless to the planet.

His obituary is from the *Key West Citizen*, and is dated March 12, 1973. That explains why it didn't turn up in a computerized library search — many newspapers didn't switch to electronic filing until the late seventies or early eighties. My telephone chase was fruitless because my mother never lived in Key West, so I'd had no reason to call the paper there.

The headline says:

Local Performer Dies in Tree Mishap

Emma, watching me from the opposite armchair, says, "What's the matter?"

It's the oddest sensation to read about my own father's death yet to hold no living memory of the man. I feel slightly guilty for not feeling sad, though truly I didn't know him. One lousy snapshot was all I had to go on.

"Read it to me, Jack."

"That's very funny."

"I mean it. Fair is fair," she says.

What the hell. I clear my throat and begin:

A popular Key West street entertainer died early Monday morning in an accident near Mallory Square.

Jack Tagger, known locally as "Juggling Jack," was killed when he fell out of a tree, police said. He was pronounced dead at the scene.

Tagger had been out walking with friends when he spotted a raccoon perched in the top of an old avocado tree on Whitehead Street. According to witnesses, he shouted, "I saw her first!" and began scrambling up the trunk.

A limb broke under Tagger's weight, and he plummeted headlong about thirty feet to the pavement.

The accident occurred at 2:30 a.m. Police said there is a possibility alcohol was involved.

Emma thinks I'm making this up.

The bad news is, my old man was a drunken goofball. The good news is, apparently I've got show business in my veins.

I continue reading:

Tagger was a familiar figure during the nightly sunset celebration along the Old

Town waterfront. He boasted that he could juggle anything and, to the delight of tourists, he tried. He tossed wine bottles, flaming tiki torches, conch shells, cactus plants and even live animals.

Last year, he debuted a new act in which he juggled four talking cockatoos. The birds had been taught to recite well-known passages from Shakespeare, Chekhov and Tennessee Williams, a home-town favorite.

Williams himself quipped, "Jack's damn cockatoos do a better job with 'Streetcar' than half the actors I've seen."

Emma says, "All right, stop. That's enough."

"No, please. Let me finish."

"This is your dad? Really?"

"It was."

The obituary is accompanied by a black-and-white photograph of my father juggling lobster buoys on a pier. He's wearing a wide-brimmed straw hat and rectangular black sunglasses, but the smile is unmistakable; the same smile from my dreams.

Onward:

Little is known about Tagger's life before he arrived in Key West about three years ago. Like many of the island's vagabond street performers, he did odd jobs by day while honing his evening act for the crowds at Mallory Square.

"He was a fun-loving cat. He made me laugh," said Samuel "Snake Throat" Procter, a local sword-swallower who once crewed with Tagger on a lobster boat.

Police records show Tagger had been arrested here twice for marijuana possession, and once for driving a moped while intoxicated.

Funeral arrangements are incomplete at this time. A short sunset ceremony honoring the juggler will be held at the Mallory Square docks on Wednesday. He was 46 at the time of his death.

Forty-six at the time of his death.
Damn, that was a close one.
"Are you all right?" Emma asks.
I hand her the newspaper article, then I open my mother's birthday card. Inside it, she gaily wrote:

Happy 47th, Jack! (See? You made it!)
Love, Mom.

30

I found a newsstand that sells the *Palm Beach Post*, and I'm reading it at the counter of the donut shop. The story about the airboat accident is in the local section, with an aerial photograph of the craft upturned in the lake. One of the dead men remains unidentified while the other is known to be Frederick Joseph Moulter, a sound engineer formerly of Santa Monica, California. The self-styled Loréal. His age is reported as twenty-nine, the same as Hank Williams when he died. I'm guessing Cleo's bodyguard eventually will be identified from fingerprints; a mug shot would be of no use.

At random moments my mind flashes back to that gothic image of Cleo's boys, Jerry sitting headless in the reeds and Loréal no less dead, scalped and gaping. Juan says we're not meant to forget such things — it's the price of surviving.

According to the news story, the crashed airboat was stolen from a deer camp near Palmdale. A game warden is quoted speculating that the men were probably out hunting for alligators when they got caught in rough weather and wiped out at high speed. A loaded .22 caliber pistol — a favorite of gator poachers — was found in a jacket worn by young Freddie Moulter. That sneaky little shit!

The *Post* says the police are continuing to investigate the two deaths, but foul play is not suspected. The absence of .38 caliber holes confirms my ineptitude with the Lady Colt.

"Hello, stranger!"

It's Janet Thrush. I give her a squeeze as I lead her to a booth in the corner. "You had me scared to death," I whisper.

"Doofus." She laughs. "All you had to do was check your messages." She's wearing a lime-colored halter, a flowered bikini bottom and feathered earrings made from salmon streamers. Her nose is sunburned and her ash-blond hair has been dyed auburn.

"Wanna hear what happened?"

"Oh heck, why not."

"This was, like, Friday a week. The afternoon you and me talked about Jimmy's last will and testament. Anyways, that night I was gettin' ready for work — hey, can I have a croissant or a muffin? Coffee would be good, too."

I snag a waitress so that Janet can order.

"Anyways, I'm gettin' dressed for work —"

"For Janet-Cam."

"Right. I'm in the bathroom puttin' on the SWAT gear when all hell breaks loose. The front door busts open and then there's voices, men's voices, and they're trashin' out my place big-time. I don't know whether to jump out the window or hide."

"Did they know you were home?"

"I don't think it mattered, Jack. I don't think they cared," she says. "So I'm locked in the john, scared shitless — pardon my French — when I hear the TV lights go crashin' down. I swear to God, I just lost it. I mean I really wigged . . . those damn lights cost me a week's pay. So I pull on the black hood and go busting out with my nine-dollar plastic rifle. 'Police! Police! You're all under arrest!' And the two guys, they freak. I don't know what they were expectin' but they took one look at me in that SWAT getup and they hauled ass."

"Did you recognize them?" I ask.

The croissants arrive and Janet pauses to gobble one. "Never saw 'em before in my life. One guy was bald and had a pirate patch over one eye. The other was tall and freckly."

"Long hair?"

"Down to his butt. I first saw him, I thought he was a chick. He was messin' with my computer — that's another thing, Jack, these assholes ripped off my PC. I got no idea why."

"I'll tell you in a minute."

"Anyway, they ran off like their balls were on fire."

473

"And then . . . ?"

Janet calls another time-out for a blueberry muffin. Afterwards she says, "They garbaged my car, so a friend came and got me. I've been down in Lauderdale ever since, just chillin'."

"Was it you who called the sheriff's office and told them not to check the house?"

She nods guiltily. "I remembered I had a bag of buds under the mattress. I knew the cops'd find it and I wasn't up for a hassle, so I gave 'em a story — 'My boyfriend raised some hell but everything's okay now so please don't send a squad car.' "

"Well, it worked."

"Remember I told you about the Convent-Cam setup, the girls who dress up like nuns? That's who I've been stayin' with. To be honest, Jack, I been scared to go home."

"You want to know what scared me? The blood on the carpet, Janet. What the hell happened?"

"I stepped on a broken lightbulb, that's what." She swings a long leg up on the breakfast table and kicks off her sandal, revealing a large dirty bandage on the sole of her foot. "When they broke my kliegs, the glass went all over the place. I bled like a hippo."

A waitress carrying a coffeepot is poised beside our table, staring uneasily at the grungy gauze.

"Stitches?" I inquire politely.

"Seven," Janet reports. "No biggie."

"The big bald goon was Cleo's bodyguard. The long-haired one was her so-called record producer."

Janet hoots. "That little bimbo has a bodyguard!" She pulls her leg off the table. "Why'd they bust into my place? What'd they want?"

"Your brother's music." I signal for the waitress to deliver the check. "Jimmy's final album."

"No way!" Janet sits forward, smoldering. "No way. That is *not* happening."

"Don't worry. They're both dead."

"If only."

I slide the *Post* across the table and point to the headline next to the picture: **Airboat Theft Ends in Fatal Crash**. Her eyes widen.

"Come on," I say. "Let's go for a drive."

Certain details of the story need not be disclosed. For instance, there's no reason for Janet to know that Emma was kidnapped, or that I was shooting a gun at Jerry and Loréal when they swamped.

But I'm telling her enough to paint the picture.

"What they wanted was the master recording of everything Jimmy wrote in the islands. We found it hidden on the boat after

Jay Burns was killed."

"Jay was in on this?"

"At least the pirating of the tracks, yeah. Maybe more."

"His 'best friend,' " Janet says acidly. "I'm so over these people. But why'd they kill him?"

"He got spooked."

"And what's with this 'accident'?" She taps two fingers on the newspaper photo.

"I told Cleo Rio I had the master. We set up a trade. The guys on the airboat were coming to get it when they wrecked."

"A trade for what?"

"Something personal. Something they stole from me."

We're cruising in the Mustang because a busy donut shop isn't the best place to be chit-chatting about murder.

Janet says, "I can't believe they shot Tito. Holy shit."

"They thought he had a copy of the hard drive. That's the computer box where your brother stored the album tracks. They figured you had one, too. That's why they broke into your house."

"This is nuts. Totally."

"It's Cleo," I say.

"But why would she care about Jimmy's stuff? She's the one with the dumbass hit song." Janet gazes out the window, shaking her head. "Crazed," she mutters.

I ask her if she sat in on any of the Exuma sessions. "Did your brother ever play any of the songs for you?"

"Long time ago," she says. "He wrote it for some girl, she dumped him for one of the Ramones."

"What was the name of the track?"

"God, lemme think. Jimmy only had a few lines written. Mostly he just hummed and played along on the guitar."

"Would you know it if you heard it again?"

"I dunno. I remember it was a really nice song, but we're talkin' like three years ago. Maybe longer."

I insert the disc of "Shipwrecked Heart" into the stereo and twist up the volume. Janet hunches intently toward the speakers. After about eight bars she says, "Pull the car over!"

This requires some slick navigating, as we are boxed in the center lane on the inter-state.

"Jack, come on!" She's beating the dash-board with both fists.

Flashing my headlights, I shoot through a Fiat-sized gap between two eighteen-wheelers. Snaking a course toward the shoulder of the highway, I'm greeted by upraised digits from a corpulent biker and a swarthy businessman in a Lincoln. As I brake to a halt, Janet be-gins stabbing at the buttons on the stereo console.

"Play it again! I want to hear it again," she demands tearfully. "Where's the damn Replay thingie?"

"Calm down. Deep breaths."

I re-cue the disc and take her hands in mine. Once more we listen to her brother's song, Janet protesting, "But isn't that the name of Cleo's album — 'Shipwrecked Heart'? How can that be?"

"Is this the one Jimmy played for you?"

"Yeah, Jack, it's the same song. He didn't have a title yet, but now I remember what he called it."

"Tell me."

" 'Kate, You Bitch.' "

Gershwin, eat your heart out.

"That was the name of the chick who dumped him," Janet explains. She shakes a finger at the speaker: "Listen right here, where he's singin', 'Shipwrecked heart, my shipwrecked heart'? When Jimmy did it for me, it was, 'Kate, you bitch. You skanky bitch.' "

"I believe I like the new lyrics better."

"Come on, Jack. He wasn't finished yet."

Fair enough. A Paul McCartney tune called "Scrambled Eggs" eventually became "Yesterday," the most widely covered song in music history. While it's the same syllabic hop from "Kate, You Bitch" to "Shipwrecked Heart," I somehow doubt the genealogy of Jimmy's composition is destined for pop lore.

In any case, the number's over and Janet is getting weepy again.

"It turned out so pretty," she says.

"Remember when you couldn't think of a reason Cleo would kill your brother? This is why she did it. She needed a hit song and this is the one she wanted."

"And Jimmy wouldn't give it up."

"Bingo." I ease the Mustang back into traffic. "But here's the pisser: I can't prove a damn thing. Except for Cleo, everyone who knows the truth is dead — Jay Burns, the two imbeciles on the airboat. Tito's alive but he can't offer much. Hell, he didn't even play on the sessions."

"So there's nothing to give the cops," she says gloomily.

"I'm afraid not."

"And nothing to put in your newspaper."

Tragically, that is true.

We're driving back toward the donut shop. Janet has slipped behind sunglasses to hide the redness in her eyes. Miles ago she turned off the stereo. I ask her what she's thinking.

"I was just wonderin' how Cleo did it."

"We'll probably never know."

"But if you had to guess — I mean, you've wrote about stuff like this before, right? Murders and all."

The truth is, I've been thinking a lot about the same question. "She probably drugged him. Slipped him something before he went in the water, to knock him out."

The centerpiece of my theory is the fish chowder.

After I first interviewed Cleo, she must have realized her story wasn't seamless. That's why she embellished it for the *New York Times*, saying Jimmy had gotten sick from the chowder and she'd begged him to stay in the boat. Clearly she was trying to cover herself in case somebody demanded a legitimate autopsy. She wanted it to appear as if she'd tried to prevent her husband from making the dive, and would thus be an unlikely suspect in his death. Once the cremation was complete, the widow Stomarti never again mentioned bad fish, or her phony premonition.

Almost inaudibly, Janet says, "I hope it wasn't too painful. Whatever happened."

"I hope not, too."

In front of the donut shop, she points out a sporty Mercedes convertible. "Raquel loaned it to me while the Miata's in the shop. She's one of the nuns." Janet laughs self-consciously. "You know what I mean — one of the strippers posing as nuns. But they've been so nice, honestly, Jack."

"Ask them to say a rosary for me." I lean across the seat and kiss her on the cheek.

She says, "Can I please hear the song one more time? He sounds so damn good, doesn't he?"

"He'll sound even better in that sixty-thousand-dollar nunmobile."

I pop the disc out of the dash and place it in Janet's palm. Then I reach into the backseat for the bag containing the extra copy of the hard drive. "This is everything he wrote for the album," I tell Jimmy's sister. "It's yours."

"What about Cleo?"

"Starting today, Cleo's looking for a different sound. That's my prediction."

Janet lifts the sunglasses off her nose and studies the plastic computer box from all angles, as if it were a puzzle cube. Her shoulders are shaking when she looks back at me.

"Jack, I still can't believe he's really gone."

And I can't believe his wife is getting away with it.

"I'm so sorry, Janet." I couldn't be any sorrier.

She sniffs away the tears and gathers herself. Propping the car door open with one knee, she says, "Look, I need to show you something. I want you to follow me."

"I'm meeting a friend in about ten minutes."

"Then bring her along."

"But —"

"No excuses," says Janet Thrush, with SWAT-team authority.

At age forty-six my father got drunk and

fell out of a tree and died. It was a pathetic finale, and I'll have the rest of my days to picture it happening. I am now forty-seven, grateful and relieved and joyous to have spent more time on this earth than the man responsible for my being here. This might sound appalling but it's honest. For me to have loved or hated my old man was impossible, but it wouldn't have mattered either way. Black irony is known to be indifferent. I would have been pleased to see him make it to his nineties, juggling dentures and pacemakers for the tourists at the Mallory docks. I am pleased, however, not to have followed in his woozy footsteps by punching out at the absurd age of forty-six. If there is (as my mother alludes) a fuckup gene running through his side of the family, I will proceed as if it's recessive. I intend not to get plastered and chase feral wildlife through avocado trees. I intend not to die idiotically, but to live a long reasonable life.

Perhaps even with Emma.

Jimmy's sister has led us across the causeway to Breezy Palms, a small cemetery. There aren't many large cemeteries in Florida; coastal real estate is much too valuable. Many of the folks who die here get airfreighted north for burial — someone back home was considerate enough to save them a plot.

"What's up?" Emma wonders as we pass

through the gates of Breezy Palms.

"I wish I knew."

I picked her up in front of the gym. She's worried that sneakers and sweats are inappropriate for the solemn venue.

"Wait'll you see Janet," I say.

The introduction is made in a shaded cupola overlooking a sloping field of gravestones. No natural hills are found in this part of the state, but one has been created here by dredging out a limestone rockpit. The rockpit is now called the Pond of the Sacred Souls.

Janet stuffs a wad of gum in one cheek. "I know this must seem really weird. Thanks for coming."

"Emma's my editor."

"You mean, like, your boss?"

"That's right. The iron fist."

"So you know about everything," Janet says to her. "What happened to my brother, and so forth? The stuff Jack told me, that's all true?"

"It is," Emma says, boss-like.

"But you can't do a story in the paper?"

"We need evidence, just like the police."

"Or we need the police to say they've *got* evidence," I add.

Janet frowns, nervously tapping one foot.

"Jack, I don't wanna break down again. I'm not a damn crybaby."

"It's nothing to be ashamed of." I go to

pieces every time I see *Old Yeller*.

To Emma she says: "Can I ask you something? You believe in reincarnation?"

Emma looks to me for an assist, but on this subject I'm useless. After a moment's contemplation, she says, "I believe anything's possible."

"Me, too." Janet steps closer. "Look, this is dead serious. You gotta look me in the eye and tell me for a fact Cleo Rio murdered my brother. How sure are you guys?"

"Ninety-nine percent," I say.

"Ninety-eight," says Emma.

"That'll do, I guess." Janet pops her bubble gum. "C'mon. This way."

Sandals flopping, she stalks down the hillside through the winding rows of graves. We follow; Emma going first, swigging from a plastic bottle of spring water.

Surprisingly, I make no effort to avert my eyes from the markers or the telltale numbers etched thereon — the date of the dearly departed's birth, and the date of the dearly departed's . . . departure.

If the years should add up to forty-seven, so what.

Happy Birthday to me.

It hammers everybody in different ways, at different times. Seventeen days after Jimmy Stoma's death, the awful reality has overtaken his sister. Janet is kneeling on a patch of fresh sod in front of a gleaming new head-stone.

Emma seems puzzled but it's beginning to make sense to me. Jimmy's gone, every mortal trace of him, and there's no place where Janet can mourn.

She says, "You remember him, Jack? Such a sweet little man."

"Of course."

The name on the headstone belongs to Eugene Marvin Brandt, the medical-supplies salesman who was laid out smartly in his favorite golf duds, spikes and all. "My Gene," his wife had called him.

At the time I'd thought it was flaky of Janet Thrush to crash the viewing at the funeral home. And undeniably I was creeped out when she asked me to join her at the side of the old man's open casket.

Looking back, though, the scene doesn't seem quite so twisted. Soon her brother would be ashes, and Janet knew she'd be grieving over thin air. She wanted a special place to go, a surrogate gravesite, so she adopted Eugene Marvin Brandt. I believe I understand.

Or maybe not.

"Aw, Jack, I've done something terrible!"

She breaks down in seismic sobs. Emma takes her by the shoulders.

"The worst . . . thing . . . I ever . . . did . . . in my whole . . . damn life!" Janet stammers wrackingly.

"It's all right," Emma says.

"Oh no, it's not. Oh no."

I stoop beside her. "Tell me what's the matter."

"I feel so bad for Gertie."

"Who's that?" Emma asks gently.

I nod toward the headstone. "Mrs. Brandt," I whisper.

Emma leans closer to Janet. "You're both hurting, you and Gertie. You've both lost someone dear."

"You don't understand. Jack?" Janet turns to me, her cheeks shining with tears. "Jack, I did a really bad thing."

Now I'm puzzled, too. Jimmy's sister gets up off the grass, discreetly tugging the wedgie crease out of her bikini bottoms.

"I saw this thing about reincarnation, it was on the Psychic Network," she's saying, "about how some people think it doesn't work so good without the actual body in a grave. And the more I thought about it, I wanted Jimmy to have a chance, you know? At least a chance to come back as a dolphin or a flying fish. Whatever he's supposed to be."

"Janet, what are you saying?" I feel Emma's fingers tighten on my elbow.

"See, Cleo *knew*. She knew Jimmy wanted to be cremated."

"Convenient for her, as it turned out."

"Jack, I love my brother and I respect his wishes, but I wasn't ready. Cleo was pushing so hard to get the cremation over and done, I just knew somethin' wasn't right. Plus I wasn't ready to say goodbye." Janet's hands are fluttering, like she's tossing a Caesar salad. "And Cleo, she didn't give a damn how I felt. She wouldn't even return my phone calls."

Mildly Emma says, "So what did you do?"

"Something real bad." Janet takes a deep breath, shuddering as she exhales. Sadly she glances over her shoulder at the headstone of Eugene Marvin Brandt.

"I switched the burn tags," she says.

"You did what?"

"That day at the funeral home, when you almost fainted and we went outside for some air? Well, afterwards I went back to put the Doors album in Jimmy's coffin — that's when I switched the burn tags. After Gene's service was over they moved him to the back room, right next to Jimmy. I had it all planned out. Isn't that terrible?"

It is terrible. I want to hug her, it's so terrible. I want to go waltzing through the tombstones, Emma on one arm and Janet on the other.

"Jack, what's a burn tag?" Emma asks.

"It's what the funeral home attaches to coffins that are going into the crematorium."

"Ugh-oh."

487

Janet says, "I'm in deep shit, huh?"

Collectively we turn to stare at the name on the gravestone. We are shoulder to shoulder under the high August sun, and our shadows look like three pigeons on a wire. The back of my shirt is damp, and the lenses of Janet's sunglasses have fogged from the heat. Only Emma looks cool. I am holding her hand; no, *squeezing* her hand.

"Now, let's be clear on this." It's a struggle to keep the glee out of my voice. "Eugene Marvin Brandt, God rest his soul, isn't really buried in this plot."

"Nope," Janet Thrush admits dolefully.

"So this would be your brother" — I motion with what I hope is somber reserve — "lying here beneath us. James Bradley Stomarti."

"Yup," says Janet. "It's been over two weeks, I figure that's enough time."

"For?"

"Him to get reincarnated, safe and sound."

Emma says, "But is it enough time for *you?* Are you ready to let go?"

Jimmy's sister nods. "Yeah. I am. After what you guys told me about Cleo, I'm more than ready." She blows a peach-sized bubble and pops it with a glittery fingernail. "I feel so bad. Poor Gertie's gonna have a cow."

Emma is holding up like granite — must be that nursing-school training. "What would you like us to do?" she asks Jimmy's sister.

"Help me nail that pube-flashing tramp for murder. Then put it in your newspaper." Janet mutes an angry sniffle. "Jack, you told me before but I forget — who is it I'm supposed to call?"

"For an autopsy?"

"What else." She manages a laugh. "My brother's famous for his encores."

Epilogue

Jimmy Stoma's anaconda tattoo got ruined by my friend Pete, the pathologist. This was almost a year ago, after the grave of Eugene Marvin Brandt was opened up with a judge's order and a two-ton backhoe. In the hole was Jimmy's coffin, just as his sister had promised.

Over the frothing objections of Cleo Rio's attorneys, an official autopsy was ordered. The elaborate Y-shaped incision did a job on Jimmy's snake-humping temptress. "A thing of beauty," Pete later told me, ruefully. "I felt like I was taking a machete to a Monet." Dutifully he went spelunking through Jimmy's body cavities, gathering sashimi-style tidbits for the lab. The liver is where he struck the mother lode: Benadryl, a common over-the-counter cold and allergy remedy. Two capsules put the average adult into a deep sleep. Cleo wasn't taking any chances. She emptied no less than twenty caps into Jimmy's grouper chowder, enough to zonk a buffalo. Then she called him up to the deck for lunch. Afterwards he strapped on his dive tank and jumped off the boat. Pete said he probably passed out within twenty minutes, a cataleptic slumber that left him drifting in the currents across the sandy bottom.

The Benadryl capsules had been purchased — with a roll of Sweet Tarts and a bottle of platinum hair bleach — at a drugstore in Silver Beach, two blocks from Jimmy and Cleo's condo. At first she claimed somebody had forged her signature on the credit card receipt. Her tune changed after the prosecutor, Rick Tarkington, offered to produce a handwriting expert and the sample of a recent signature on a deli menu. The singer had autographed it to a fan known only as "Chuck," posing as a delivery boy.

To my surprise, Cleo called me one night before she got indicted. She was hanging out alone at Jizz. For giggles — and a witness — I took Carla Candilla.

The widow was half in the bag when we arrived. Gone was the silky pop-star glow. Her pageboy had been weed-whacked into some sort of unisex mop, and her face looked blotched and gaunt. Under the strobes her neglected tan took on a sickly greenish hue. It's no day at the spa, being the target of a murder investigation.

We followed her to one of the club's private rooms, where Cleo bummed a Silk Cut cigarette off Carla and said, "My lawyers'd shit a brick if they knew I was here."

"Why? Are you going to confess?" Eagerly I slapped my notebook on the table.

Cleo wrinkled her nose and leaned closer. "What's that you got on?"

"Your favorite cologne."

It was called "Timberlake." Carla and I spent an hour sniffing samples at the men's counter in Burdines until we found the right one.

"All your fellas wear it," I said to Cleo. "Loréal. Jerry the gorilla. You even doused it on Jimmy in his casket."

"I like what I like," she said, "but on you it would gag a maggot."

Carla hooted. I deserved no less.

Listing slightly to starboard, Cleo said, "I gotta know, Tagger. Was it really you who did this to me? All by your lonesome?"

"Don't be ridiculous. I'm just a tired old obituary writer."

"As if," she snorted.

Here Carla cut in: "Cleo, honey, your sleeve's in the salsa."

"Shit. This is a Versace."

The bartender sent a club soda, and Cleo went to work scrubbing on the stain. I asked if it was true that the record label had canceled her contract. She said so what, it was a chickenshit outfit anyway. "After the trial I'm getting an incredibly sweet deal. My new manager's talking mega."

"Awesome," I said, which seemed to please her. "Hey, have you found a new producer yet?"

Cleo's response was to pulverize an ice cube with her molars.

"Or a new bodyguard?"

"That's not funny, man. When this is over," she said, "I'm gonna sue your newspaper for about twenty million bucks."

"When this is over, Cindy Zigler, you'll be in prison."

"Yeah, right."

Carla couldn't help but notice the wane of bonhomie. "Cleo, before we say goodbye, I gotta ask — in the video, was that you or a body double?"

The widow perked up. "It was all me. Every curly little hair."

Her arrest was bannered on the front page: **Singer Charged in Death of Rock-Star Husband**. That was the headline. Here was the byline:

By Jack Tagger
Staff Writer

For the first time in four years I sent a clipping to my mother. I also saved a copy for Anne, at her request. She and Derek were in Italy where he was researching a new spy novel, *The Bishop's Chambermaid*. Anne mentioned it, with a gently appropriate joke, in a postcard.

The truth behind James Bradley Stomarti's death received heavy play in the celebrity press as well as the music trades. By the time the trial started, Jimmy and the Slut Puppies were hot all over again. The record company repackaged *Floating Hospice* and *A Painful Burning Sensation* as a double album, spiced with previously unreleased bonus tracks. In only three weeks, a digital re-mix of the "Basket Case" single drew sixty-two thousand downloads off the band's interactive Web site. A new video, starring Kate Hudson as the bipolar mama, features never-before-seen concert footage of the Slut Puppies, including Jimmy's lewd spoof of Pat Robertson.

The group is making money again. Miraculously, some of it has found its way to Jimmy's estate, and many deserving little urchins will be trundling off to sea camps next summer.

Cleo Rio's trial lasted three weeks. Danny Gitt flew in from the Seychelles to testify about a heated argument he'd heard between Jimmy and his wife in the studio, an argument about a song. Tito Negraponte arrived from California with his pockets full of Percocets, so Rick Tarkington wisely elected not to depose him. He didn't need to. Janet Thrush proved to be a devastating witness, shredding Cleo's contention that she and her husband had collaborated on "Shipwrecked Heart."

I'd anticipated that Cleo's defense team

might try to drag me into the case, but they must have figured out it would backfire. Their client already had plenty to explain without adding the criminal antics of Jerry and Loréal. It was no surprise that the widow Stomarti declined to take the stand in her own defense. Her lawyers gamely presented the theory that Jimmy had accidentally overdosed himself before the fatal dive. Their star witness was a retired ophthalmologist who claimed it was not impossible for a far-sighted person to have grievously misread the label on a Benadryl package.

The jury was out less than three hours. Cleo got convicted, and the judge gave her twenty-to-life. On the day of sentencing, the number 9 rock single on the *Billboard* charts was "Cindy's Oyster," recorded by Jimmy Stoma.

"Shipwrecked Heart" was number 5.

And Janet Thrush was moving from her modest house in Beckerville to a three-bedroom waterfront apartment on Silver Beach. From there she will manage her dead brother's career, and a charitable foundation established in his name. The tracks from the Exuma sessions were purchased for $1.6 million by Capitol Records, and the full *Shipwrecked Heart* CD is due for release in six weeks. A company press release said there's enough material for two more compilations.

Before signing the deal, Janet had called

from Los Angeles to ask my advice.

"Well, what would Jimmy have done?" I said.

"Grabbed the money," she replied. "What the hell am I thinking?"

Janet never told another soul that she'd switched the tags on the coffins. The court order to open the grave emanated from a confidential tip to Rick Tarkington's office. I was the only journalist to report that Jimmy Stoma's favorite Doors album was found with his body. Ultimately, the mistaken cremation of Eugene Marvin Brandt was pinned on Ellis, the thieving funeral director, who proclaimed his innocence even as he quietly settled out of court with Gertie Brandt for a sum rumored to be in the six figures. It might have been less had Ellis not pried the custom golf spikes off Gene's dead feet, and had he not been wearing them the day the process server found him on a public driving range in Port Malabar.

The investigation, indictment and prosecution of Cleo Rio generated thirteen front-page articles in the *Union-Register*, all of them written by me. Race Maggad III was said to be enraged by the reappearance of my byline, but Abkazion refused to delete it, or to yank me off the story. Usually such adherence to principle would cost a managing editor his job, but those days might be over.

On the morning Cleo was convicted, I walked into the newsroom and asked Emma to fire me. She said no. Immediately I took her into a broom closet on the third floor, removed her panties and made love to her.

"You're cruising for trouble," she warned.

After lunch I did it again.

"Now you've gone too far. You've made me miss the one o'clock," Emma declaimed after we'd caught our breaths. "You're fired, Jack."

"Thanks. I'll see you tonight."

Charles Chickle, Esq., had the trust documents ready to sign when I arrived. Race Maggad III was stewing outside, so Charlie and I took our sweet time. I commended him on prolonging the probate of MacArthur Polk's estate until the Stoma story ran its course. Then we talked bass fishing and Gator football.

Finally, Charlie said, "You ready?" He'd already spent an hour with Maggad, tenderizing him.

"Bring in the sulky young mandrill," I instructed.

Presently a secretary escorted the chairman of the Maggad-Feist Publishing Group into the lawyer's office, and barrister Chickle excused himself.

"Master Race, sit down!" I bubbled.

He wore a peerless wool suit but otherwise he looked terrible, drawn and sleepless, with scrotal bags under his anxious green eyes. Even his hair refused to shine.

"Good afternoon, Jack," he said tautly.

"You never told me how you liked the old man's obit."

"Didn't I? I thought it was fine."

"I'll pass along your compliments to the writer."

Maggad scowled. "But I thought *you* wrote it."

"At my right hand was a college intern named Evan Richards. Bright kid, too. He's not coming back to the *Union-Register* because he noticed that you've run it into the shitter."

I reminded young Race that it had been several months since we'd last spoken, and that significant events had occurred in the interim. Maggad-Feist lost a costly antitrust suit in upstate Washington, and had been forced to sell two profitable radio stations. The price of company stock spiraled from 40½ to 22¼, a five-year low. Two competing media conglomerates — one German, one Canadian — had initiated hostile attempts to take over the chain.

And MacArthur Polk, one of the largest individual shareholders, had passed away.

"Tell me something I don't already know," Maggad grumbled.

"How about this, hoss? As of tomorrow, you'll no longer be paying my salary."

"Whoopee-do. Where's the champagne." Young Race was in a tough spot, so I let him blow off steam. "Newspapers are in the business of making money, Tagger, so don't be so naïve and self-righteous. Journalism can't exist without making a profit."

"Well, you damn sure can't have *good* journalism when you're milking the cow for twenty-five percent. We might as well be working for the Gambinos," I said. "By the way, how are the Porsches enjoying that dreamy Southern California climate? No more slush in *your* tailpipes, I'll bet!"

For a moment it appeared that Maggad was sucking his own cheeks down his throat. I'd touched a raw nerve with that California jab — *Forbes* had recently done a snarky article about the obscene cost of relocating Maggad-Feist's headquarters to sunny San Diego. Shareholders were seething.

Stonily he said to me, "We publish twenty-seven very good papers. They win awards."

"In spite of you, yes, they do."

The Race Maggads of the industry have a standard gospel to rationalize their pillaging. It goes like this: American newspapers are steadily losing both readers and advertisers to cable TV and the Internet. This fatal slide can be reversed only with a radical recasting of our role in the community. We need to be more receptive and responsive, less cynical and confrontational. We need to be more sensitive to our institutions, especially to our advertisers. We can no longer afford to shield our news and editorial operations from the pressures and demands that steer the business side of publishing. We're all in this together! In these difficult times we need to do more with less — less space in which to print the news, fewer reporters with which to cover it, and a much smaller budget with which to pursue it. Yet even as we do more with less, we must never forget our solemn pledge to our readers, blah, blah, blah. . . .

It's an appalling geyser of shit and nobody with half a brain believes a word, not when polo-playing CEOs can confidently talk of twenty-five percent annual profits. Like most publishing tycoons, Race Maggad III is oblivious to his own vulgarity. On the positive side, he has (unlike the Hearsts and Pulitzers of their day) no hidden political agenda to peddle, no private vendettas to promote on the pages of his newspapers. Maggad cares about one thing only.

"What, you want me to grovel?" he said. "You know we need to repurchase Mr. Polk's shares, and you know why. Try to put aside your petty personal bitterness, Tagger. Think of all your friends and colleagues whose jobs would be jeopardized if one of these hostile entities gained control of our company."

"You're implying things would get worse in the newsroom? How's that possible? Are you suggesting these people have less interest in decent journalism than you do?"

Maggad desperately longed to kick out my front teeth, but the task at hand required civility. Lord, I'd have loved to see his expression when Charlie Chickle broke the news that Old Man Polk had put his Maggad-Feist stock holdings in a trust. A trust to be managed by me — the same wise-ass who'd insulted Maggad in front of his investors, the same impertinent prick whose career he had conspired to destroy.

"The irony is delicious, isn't it, Race?"

"Fuck irony. How much do you want for the stock?"

"Mr. Polk left very specific instructions," I said.

Maggad steepled his manicured fingers. "We're flexible, up to a point."

"Flexible won't cut it," I told him. "You need to be whorishly compliant, prompt and unquestioning. The price of the shares is simple market value, averaged during the preceding thirty days."

"That's doable," Race III allowed coolly.

"But before the stock changes hands" — here was the kill shot — "Maggad-Feist must divest itself of the *Union-Register.*"

My natty visitor went rigid. "Horseshit," he snapped.

"Aw, don't look so blue."

"No deal. No way."

"Fine," I said. "The more you stall and fart around, the richer I get. Did Mr. Chickle happen to mention what they're paying me to bust your balls?"

"Sell the *Union-Register*?"

"Yes, but not just to anybody."

Maggad gripped the arms of his chair as if he was about to eject himself from an F16. The trunk of his neck turned florid, pulsing like a fire hose.

"Who?" he asked. "Sell it to who?"

"To *whom*." I was unable to conceal my disappointment with his grammar. "Really, Race."

"To whom," he sneered. "Tell me, goddammit."

"Ellen Polk. The old man's wife."

"The nurse?"

"The heiress," I said.

"Christ Almighty. This was your idea, wasn't it, Tagger?"

I didn't deny it, which was tacky of me. The old man himself dreamed up the scheme. But Maggad looked so wretched and beaten that I couldn't bring myself to set the record straight.

"For how much?" he asked.

"A straight-up trade. She gets the newspaper, you get Mr. Polk's stock."

"That's asinine." He was doing the math in his head. "The Dow is in the toilet right now, so the *Union-Register* must be worth ten, twelve times the value of the old man's shares. Easily."

"As you wish, Master Race. Tomorrow I'll be lunching with the Canadians."

"Jesus, hold on."

"By the way, that's a gorgeous suit," I told him, "but it's eighty-four fucking degrees outside. And you were born for khakis, my friend."

In the end, Race Maggad III chose to give up one newspaper so that he might keep twenty-six others, God help them. The deal was signed one week before young Race's favorite polo pony attacked him in the stall, stomping on his cranium. With therapy he seems to be recovering steadily, though doctors doubt he'll ever drive a five-speed transmission again.

Last month, Ellen Polk became the first woman publisher of the *Union-Register*. The first thing she did was expand the news hole by twenty-five percent. The second thing she did was order Abkazion to fill the empty desks in the newsroom. Today separate reporters are assigned to Palm River, Beckerville and Silver Beach, blanket coverage which has compelled the politicians there to quit running their council meetings as weekly bazaars.

Under Mrs. Polk, even the Death page has been restored to its former glory, with two full-length obituaries running daily. Emma is no longer in charge of that section. As a reward for supervising the Jimmy Stoma stories, she was promoted to "deputy" assistant city editor. I asked if that meant she had to wear a silver star on her chest, and she told me to get out of the bathroom so she could finish drying her hair. She refuses to leave the newspaper business, and she refuses to leave me. I'm the luckiest nutcase I know.

After the airboat adventure Emma skated without incident through the remainder of her twenty-eighth year. Last Saturday was her birthday, and we drove to Naples for dinner with my mother, my stepfather, Dave, and the Palmers, whom Dave now extols as blue-chip additions to his country club. This racially enlightened attitude has evolved only since Mr. Palmer's son taught Dave how to fade a three-wood off the fairway.

As we cleared the table I cornered my mother in the kitchen and asked her how she came to receive Jack Sr.'s obituary. She told me that his older brother, a lawyer in Orlando, had mailed it to her. "He's the one I should've married. The attorney," my mother remarked, only half jokingly.

Included in the envelope was a check for $250 to cover a pair of small pearl earrings that my father had swiped on his way out the door, and later hocked. After his death, the pawn ticket (and a Fodor's tour guide to Amsterdam) was found in a shoe box beneath his bed in a Key West rooming house.

"What do you make of that?" I asked my mother.

"He was a flake job. Case closed," she said. "Listen, Jack, I'm quite fond of your new girlfriend. Please don't scare her off, like you did with Anne. Keep the morbid stuff to yourself, okay?"

"I'll try, Mom."

Emma and I spent last evening on the couch trading manuscript chapters of Juan Rodriguez's novel about his voyage from Cuba to Key West. It is heart-stopping but also humbling; Juan is gifted beyond my most improbable aspirations. A serious New York publishing house is launching his book in the fall, and I anticipate it will bring him wealth and acclaim. I only hope it will bring him sleep. He's dedicating the novel to his sister.

Today Emma and I have come to the Silver Beach pier for lunch, as we often do. One windy morning a few months ago, Janet Thrush joined us. She kicked off her flip-flops and clambered up on the rail and poured her brother's sworling ashes into the Atlantic. "Bye, Jimmy," she sang out, heaving the empty urn into the water. At that instant, I swear, a dolphin came up and rolled in the surf — just once. We never saw it again.

I keep bringing Emma here because I want her to meet Ike, the ancient obituary writer, yet he hasn't reappeared since the day we first spoke. I'm beginning to think I dreamt him up. Emma wonders, too, though she's too kind to say so. Even if it means I'm still wacked, I'd prefer to know that I imagined Ike than to learn he has died.

As always, Emma and I choose the bench near the phone at the end of the pier, the same phone on which she called me after being kidnapped. Once I mentioned that to her, and all she said was: "Those creeps."

Today the Atlantic is flat and glassy, the perfect mirror of a cloudless periwinkle sky. Kids are out of school so the pier bustles; above, a circus of swooping gulls and terns. Emma and I shield our pasta salads, in case of bombardment. Squinting against the fierce summer sun, I search for Ike's fluffy gray head among the anglers lined along the rails.

"Maybe he went back north until the weather cools off," Emma suggests.

"Maybe."

"Or he's laid up in the hospital. Have you called Charity?"

"Not yet." I don't even know the man's last name.

We're distracted by a lumpish, hirsute tourist in a sweat-stained tank top. He has reeled in a small barracuda, which flops frenetically on the wooden planks. The tourist has his heart set on supper, for he's endeavoring to stomp on the fish before it flips back into the sea. He seems unheedful of the ample dentition of barracudas, impressive even in juvenile specimens. Within minutes the man's pallid ankles are striped crimson, and in retreat he can be heard moaning like a branded calf.

Emma walks over and, with the toe of a conservative navy blue pump, carefully nudges the wriggling fish off the pier. Rejoining me on the bench, she says, "It's that time again."

"No, I'm begging you."

Every day she asks: "When are you coming back to the paper?"

Abkazion has offered me a slot on the new investigations team, but the time isn't right. I'm still having night sweats about what happened on Lake Okeechobee. These I don't mention to Emma, because she's had some unsettling dreams of her own.

"Jack, you should take the job. You worked hard for it."

"Maybe that's the problem. As Jimmy Stoma would say, I'm all humped out."

"And, as Emma Cole would say, I'm going to hurt you now." She thumps the side of my head. "Come back to work, dammit. I miss you."

"She's right. What's your problem, Tagger?" a scratchy voice demands at my back.

I spin around and there's Ike, a sly smile on his whiskered possum face. He is carrying an orange bait bucket, a small cooler and his three spinning rods. He looks fit and frisky.

"Where've you been?" I ask.

"Battling an unmannered polyp," he replies cheerily, "but fear not. I prevailed."

"Ike, this is my friend, Emma."

He sets down the fishing gear and takes her hand. "You are most lovely, Emma. I'm dazzled to meet you."

The old hound!

"You had a birthday, didn't you?" I ask him.

"Number ninety-three," he reports proudly.

"Incredible," Emma says.

"Not really. I planned it this way. All those years, writing all those hundreds of obituaries — well, pretty lady, I paid attention. I learned a few tricks."

Emma is taken with the old guy, as I knew she would be. After arranging his clutter of fishing tackle, he methodically rigs a bait and casts it over the rail.

"Sunscreen." He cocks his head our way. "Both of you should be basting in the stuff. Forty years from now you'll thank me."

Ike's rod begins to bend, and he gallantly passes it to Emma. She cranks up a nice snapper, which he guts and tosses on ice.

"Fish is the healthiest food in the world. Cemeteries are full of people who didn't eat enough fish."

"Ike," says Emma, "please tell Jack why he

should come back to the newspaper."

He wipes the blade of his fillet knife on a leg of his trousers. "Number one, you're not cut out for a regular job."

No argument there.

"Number two, you still get a bang out of the news." His crooked fingers are working a large sharp hook into a bloodless chunk of mullet. "And number three, you can make things happen, writing for a paper," he says. "Make a difference in the world. That's a damn fact."

Emma lightly claps her hands. "Well done!"

What the opossum man says is true. "But if I came back," I say, "I wouldn't be writing obituaries."

"That's all right. It was a helluva piece you did about that wild young gal killing off her husband," says Ike. "It wouldn't surprise me if you got an award. I'm serious, Jack."

He rears back with the rod and arcs the fresh bait toward the water. The heavy lead sinker makes a faraway plop. Emma motions that it's time for us to go. Now that she's a *deputy* editor, she cannot miss the one o'clock meeting. Some things haven't changed at the *Union-Register.*

"Ike, it was an honor meeting you."

"The honor was mine. Come angle with me anytime." He flashes his handsome store-bought teeth. Then, turning to me: "When

509

will I see your byline again, Jack Tagger?"

"Sooner or later." I shake his hand, mullet slime and all. "You're a piece of work, Ike."

He leans close and drops his voice. "When's the last time you had a checkup? I mean the works."

"Last year." With Emma's support, I've been able to break myself of those compulsive monthly treks to Dr. Susan.

"Next time you go, be sure and have 'em check the plumbing," Ike advises. "They stick a camera up your ass, but it's no worse than your average divorce."

"I'll keep that in mind."

"Live a long time, Jack. Remember, it's all diet and attitude."

Emma and I are halfway down the pier when we hear a hoarse cry. Ike has hooked up to a huge tarpon, which is exploding in silvery somersaults across the water. I can see the old man slammed fast against the wooden rail, struggling to keep a grip on the U-bent spinning rod. A few of the other anglers are gathering to watch, but no one seems to be helping. Wispy Ike is easily outweighed by the thrashing hulk on the end of his line. This isn't my sport, but I remember enough from fishing with my mother to know what might happen if the drag on the old man's reel freezes.

"It looks like he's in trouble," Emma says.

I'm already running.

And I'm already thinking, God forgive me, of his obituary. Undoubtedly Hemingway would be invoked. Then some dim acquaintance of the opossum man would be quoted as saying he died doing what he loved best, which is what — gagging on seawater?

Still, being dragged off a pier by a magnificent fish wouldn't be the silliest way to die, not by far. It's not nearly as pointless, for instance, as getting shitfaced drunk and tumbling out of a tree while attempting to romance a raccoon.

And I suppose the mythical aspects of being drowned by a silvery beast of the sea might appeal to a fellow who spent most of his life writing about the mostly ordinary deaths of others. Still, I can't stand back and watch it happen. Ike's had a grand ninety-three years, but I don't believe he's done. I don't believe he's ready to check out.

So I push my way through the gawkers to find the old man doubled over the rail. Of course he won't do the sensible thing and let go of the damn fishing rod; neither would my mother, in the same preposterous fix. The tarpon has run out all of Ike's line, so he has stubbornly wrapped the last loop in the fist of his right hand, which is seeping blood. Meanwhile he teeters like a human seesaw on the weathered railing, his head and shoulders extended above the water and his spindly legs waving in the air.

My view is of the bait-encrusted soles of his deck shoes. I feel a hand in the small of my back, pushing me forward. It's Emma.

Grabbing Ike by the belt loops, I haul him back onto the pier. In the distance the tarpon jumps once more, shaking its bucket-sized mouth. The line goes slack in the old man's doll-like fingers.

"I'll be damned," he says breathlessly. "That was something!"

The other anglers clap amusedly, murmuring among themselves as they drift away. Emma, the would-be nurse, is inspecting the bloody slice on Ike's wrinkled palm.

He's laughing so hard, his button-sized eyes are brimming. "Can you imagine the headline?" he says. "Can you, Jack?"

Basket Case

by Jimmy Stoma and Warren Zevon

My baby is a basket case
A bipolar mama in leather and lace
Face like an angel — she's a perfect waste
My baby is a basket case

Dracula's daughter, Calamity Jane
Smoke on the water, water on the brain
Pretty as a picture — and totally crazed
My baby is a basket case

She's gonna make a madman outta me
She's gonna make a madman outta me

She's manic-depressive and schizoid, too
The friskiest psycho that I ever knew
We're paranoid lovers lost in space
My baby is a basket case

My baby's gonna celebrate
I'm bein' dragged through the nuthouse gates
Got my straitjacket on, and I'm takin'
*   her place*
My baby is a basket case

She finally made a madman outta me
She finally made a madman outta me
My baby made a madman outta me
She finally made a madman outta me. . . .

About the Author

Carl Hiaasen has been a journalist at the *Miami Herald* for twenty-five years. He is the author of eight previous novels, including *Tourist Season*, *Skin Tight*, *Lucky You* and *Sick Puppy*. He and his family live in the Florida Keys.

We hope you have enjoyed this Large Print book. Other Thorndike Press or Chivers Press Large Print books are available at your library or directly from the publishers.

For more information about current and up-coming titles, please call or write, without obligation, to:

Publisher
Thorndike Press
295 Kennedy Memorial Drive
Waterville, ME   04901
Tel. (800) 223-1244
Tel. (800) 223-6121

OR

Chivers Press Limited
Windsor Bridge Road
Bath BA2 3AX
England
Tel. (0225) 335336

All our Large Print titles are designed for easy reading, and all our books are made to last.